THE
ONE
WHO
loves
YOU

OTHER TITLES BY PIPPA GRANT

For the most up-to-date booklist,
visit Pippa's website at www.pippagrant.com.

The Girl Band Series

Mister McHottie
Stud in the Stacks
Rockaway Bride
The Hero and the Hacktivist

The Thrusters Hockey Series

The Pilot and the Puck-Up
Royally Pucked
Beauty and the Beefcake
Charming as Puck
I Pucking Love You
Hot Heir (Royally Pucked spin-off)

The Bro Code Series

Flirting with the Frenemy
America's Geekheart
Liar, Liar, Hearts on Fire
The Hot Mess and the Heartthrob
Master Baker (Bro Code spin-off)

Copper Valley Fireballs Series

THE ONE WHO *loves* YOU

PIPPA GRANT

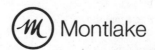
Montlake

Published by Montlake, Seattle

www.apub.com

Amazon, the Amazon logo, and Montlake are trademarks of Amazon.com, Inc., or its affiliates.

ISBN-13: 9781542037655
ISBN-10: 1542037654

Cover design by Caroline Teagle Johnson

Printed in the United States of America

THE ONE WHO *loves* YOU

Chapter 1

Phoebe Lightly, aka a Woman Who Should Probably Hang Up That Phone

There are three rules to being a Lightly, the first of which is *Do not make Gigi wait.*

The other two?

Inconsequential if you break the Gigi rule.

"Antoinette. Call Oscar at La Fleur, and order the Luxe Stella orchid arrangement to be delivered to my grandmother tomorrow," I instruct my personal assistant as my driver pulls to a stop in front of Gigi's Upper East Side town house two minutes and eighteen seconds past the time when I could've had a tolerable evening. "No, make that tonight."

"The standard arrangement, Ms. Lightly?" Antoinette asks through my earbud.

"Upgrade to the Baccarat crystal vase, and add a box of Vendetté truffles. The wasabi-ginger truffles. She likes them on fire. Like her soul."

"Yes, Ms. Lightly. Oh, and Mr. Barrington has called six times since you left the office. He's requesting his grandfather's Rolex back."

"Perhaps Mr. Barrington should ask his other girlfriend if she's seen it."

"I suggested that, Ms. Lightly. He was insistent he'd given it to you."

"How unfortunate for his memory. If he calls back again, tell him I've misplaced six months of my life with a philandering rectal cavity, and ask if he might help me get those back in return. Mention I'm acquainted with his *other* lover's husband, too, and I'd be more than happy to direct the press to the juicier part of our breakup story." I disconnect the call and step out into the midspring evening, which would be lovely were it not for the invisible cloud of sulfur and ash swirling about the steps to the arched double door of Gigi's brownstone. I take two steps, pause, and turn back to my driver, who's still holding the door. "Philippe—"

"Byron, ma'am."

Why can I *never* get that right? "Yes, yes. Don't you have a daughter with a birthday coming up?"

"I'm single and relatively certain I have no children, ma'am."

I channel Gigi and lift a delicate eyebrow.

He clears his throat. "But I'm sure one day I'll have a daughter with a birthday coming up, ma'am."

"Excellent. You can give her this." I slip a Rolex watch from my Hermès handbag into the pocket of his uniform coat, smile the trademark Lightly smile, and turn to glide up the steps to face my punishment for being tardy.

Gigi's butler swings the door open before I knock, and he wordlessly helps me out of my coat, taking my gloves and clutch as well. "Second-floor dining room, Ms. Lightly," he murmurs. "Shall I escort you?"

"No, thank you, Niles." It *is* Niles, isn't it? He's average height, white, shoulders a bit droopy for a butler, gray hair balding. He doesn't look familiar. Does he? Gigi goes through butlers like my sister, Tavi, goes through B-listers, so I rarely pay attention. "No need for both of us to be incinerated on the spot."

I steel myself while I take the curved staircase to the second-floor gallery one step at a time, picturing myself arriving on time rather than three minutes and forty-six seconds late, shoulders back, head high, refusing to reach up and verify that my hair is still smooth, my diamond earrings are still in place, and the clasp on my pearls isn't showing.

Never show fear.

Own the room.

And if you arc *late to meet Gigi, have a damn good excuse.*

"Gigi, you look fabulous," I say as I breeze into the dark-wood-paneled dining room off the gallery. She's already seated at the head of the Italian marble table, her short white hair and white silk Saint Laurent button-down giving off Jane Fonda vibes, if Jane Fonda were more of an angry old white lady. Her crystal water goblet is full, her bordeaux glass half-empty, and her Limoges soup bowl steaming.

Bordeaux means she's in a mood.

Already-served soup means I would've been better off lighting my own hair on fire instead of waiting for her to do it for me.

She gives *me* the Lightly eyebrow. "You're late."

Show no fear. Show no fear. "There was a safety issue with paper towel production at the Knoxville plant."

"If I wasn't called, it wasn't an issue."

"You weren't called because I took care of it." I smile as I take my place at the foot of the table, with eight empty velvet-backed chairs on either side and a crystal chandelier hanging from the fresco ceiling between us.

My ancestors snort in derision from their spots in their paintings along the wall. They, too, are unimpressed with my show of confidence.

"I *was* called about the tabloids," she murmurs over her wineglass.

"I'm taking care of that."

3

"With subtle digs about the size of his anatomy in the *Post*? Phoebe, dear, is that truly your best? You should take lessons from Octavia. She told the *Post* that her last boyfriend was off to find himself after realizing what eating meat did to his anatomy. If you're going to insult a man, insult him in a way that puts the blame squarely on him instead of his genetics."

"I was misquoted." Lightly rule number two: *Don't make excuses.* I'm on a roll. "The Sandovals are hosting their annual masquerade tomorrow, and I heard the Bancroft sisters didn't get an invitation. They'll crash, and everyone will forget that I'm being painted as 'the other woman' and that I dared insult Fletcher Barrington's manhood in public. Did I tell you I requested a transfer at work into the environmental-sustainability department for experience broadening?"

She dips her spoon into her soup and sniffs. "I heard from your father."

Translation: *I'm well aware you were afraid to tell me yourself that you were turned down for a transfer into the skin-care division's global marketing department when the paper-goods division failed to meet production expectations last quarter, hence why you were summoned tonight.*

For a woman whose position on the board of directors for the world's largest consumer goods manufacturing company is ceremonial only, she still has pull, and she still hears all.

At least, when it comes to the portion of the company she inherited from her own father-in-law.

No surprise.

Gigi is the reason the Remington family is no longer involved in any of the operations of Remington Lightly.

Not that much of our family is left in the family business either. It's Gigi on the board of directors, my father in the legal department—also a ceremonial role at this point, as I understand it, and I'm surprised to hear he knew anything about what I've been up to—and me working my way up through the management chain. My mother, brother, and sister have pursued other interests, though all of us together hold the largest minority share of stock in the company.

Held in trust funds controlled by Gigi, but unlike my siblings, I work for what I earn.

But it's not about the paycheck.

It's about the fact that I'm on track to be the next Lightly to sit at the helm of the company my ancestors founded, which hasn't been done since my great-grandfather retired.

I want that top-floor office. The Manhattan-skyline view. The role my family heritage has bred me for. The destiny I was born to fulfill.

I, Phoebe Sabrina Lightly, will be the first Lightly in three generations—and the first woman—to rule as chief executive officer of Remington Lightly.

I want it all, and when I have it all, I'll get the other thing I've always wanted—my grandmother's unconditional seal of approval.

I take a glass of bordeaux from Gigi's personal assistant. "A good leader understands the challenges faced in every department, and environmental issues aren't going away. We can't stay at the forefront of consumer goods if we don't—"

"Yes, yes, save the whales, bamboo is the future, talking points, buzzwords, et cetera. Did you hear that Alexander Bentley is back from his Italian sabbatical?"

This is dinner with Gigi.

Work hard. No, harder. Care about something. No, something else. Your roots are showing. Marc Jacobs doesn't suit you, Phoebe. You would've gotten the promotion if you'd worn your McQueen. The eligible bachelor I picked for you last quarter is no longer worthy of a Lightly, but have no fear—I've found another. No, I'm not yet ready to speak about the real reason I've called you here. I need to torture you with a litany of your other disappointments first.

We've made it through soup, salad, and her dissertation on why Spanx has ruined the younger generation's self-control when my phone buzzes inside my blazer.

I ignore it, because I don't have a death wish.

Gigi's chef enters the dining room with two Limoges plates covered with silver cloches. He sets the first before her and unveils it with a flourish. "Kobe filet mignon with peppercorn brandy sauce on a bed of mesclun, with shaved brussels sprouts and flash-fried shallots on the side, madam."

"Thank you, Arlo, that will be all." Gigi manages to murmur softly yet still speak distinctly enough to be heard across the room.

"Yes, madam."

My phone buzzes again as Arlo delivers my plate and quietly slips out the side door toward the elevator to the kitchen. Gigi dismisses her personal assistant with the subtlest flutter of her eyelashes, and then we're alone.

Just me, Gigi, the elephant without a name—there is *always* an elephant, the question is merely which one—and my persistently vibrating cell phone.

"Are you watching more of that reality television, Phoebe?" Gigi asks while she slices a delicate piece of meat.

"No, Gigi. I don't have time for television." I am 100 percent bingeing *Lola's Tiny House* before bed this week. Lola Minelli and I went to the same college-prep school, and even knowing everything's staged, I *cannot* believe she's actually forcing herself into that tiny house, even if it's only for filming.

My shoe collection won't fit into that house.

No idea how Lola's ego is managing.

And no, I don't want to talk about the reality show that my sister talked me into for one season in college either.

I pretend that time in my life doesn't exist.

Gigi eyeballs me like she knows my life outside the office and social commitments is ruled by my streaming services. "I don't understand anyone's need for that rubbish when you can have *actual* scandal and gossip in real life."

"Gigi, not everyone can live in New York. Some people lead honestly boring lives."

My phone stops vibrating.

But I've barely sliced my own filet before it vibrates again.

And now I'm getting another Gigi eyeball. "Would you either answer that or turn it off?"

I slip it out of my pocket, fully intending to shut it off, except *Tavi* is calling me.

My sister hasn't called me in months. And she's now called three times in a row. "Excuse me, Gigi. It's the office. If production in Knoxville is being held up by the picketers . . ."

She makes her displeased noise. There *are* actual picketers in Knoxville—being handled by someone three levels below me, but still there—so I have a verifiable reason to slip away. And while I don't talk to my sister often, I will 100 percent take a call with her over whatever it is Gigi is planning on dropping on me next.

I'm already doomed.

At this point, it can't get much worse. Maybe if I stall, she'll be struck with a rare bout of amnesia and forget all my sins. "Hello, this is Phoebe."

"Phoebe, love," the deep baritone of Fletcher Barrington, ex-boyfriend currently at the top of my shit list, replies in my ear, "you've been avoiding my calls."

I pull the phone away and glance at the caller ID, confirming that my phone does, in fact, think Tavi is on the other end. "What did you do with my sister's phone?" I hiss.

"Darling, never underestimate an heir to a telecommunications empire."

It takes a second for me to catch up, which is a bad sign. "You spoofed her number so I'd answer."

"Desperate times, desperate measures."

"I have nothing—"

"I heard a rumor your grandmother's rewriting her will. Give me back my grandfather's watch, and I'll tell you what I know."

How convenient that he'd have a rumor about my grandmother when he wants something from me. "I don't have your grandfather's watch."

"I'm serious, Phoebe. Give it back, or I will make your life hell."

"You overestimate your importance in my life. Enjoy your time pretending to be the hero here. Everyone falls from grace sooner or later."

"You think you're low now? Your real fall is coming sooner than you know, darling."

"I'm shaking in my Louboutins, Fletcher. *Shaking.*"

"And what happens when Grammykins hears the true reason you were passed over for the international marketing position?"

My veins fill with glaciers, and my clammy palms betray the outward calm I'm suddenly struggling to hang on to. "Goodbye, Fletcher. Might want to hit the gym. You're going to need your right fist in shape to keep you warm at night *very* soon. And if you don't want the world descending on your busboy lover, you'll *back off.* Two can play this game, and you know I will."

I hang up on him.

I'd tell myself the lie that there's no way he knows the inner workings and secrets of the executive-level drama at Remington Lightly, except I also know better than to underestimate an enemy.

Especially an enemy working at a family corporation with its own drama.

I need to go on the offensive. I sink onto the velvet couch in the gallery outside Gigi's dining room, perfectly positioned for her to sit and gaze at her favorite painting—a lone woman leaning on a cane and surrounded by beasts pawing at the ground, an impressionist-style piece of art that she had commissioned not long after Gawgaw passed—and I fire off a text to my assistant.

Antoinette—I need the doormat files first thing in the morning. We're going to war.

How *dare* he threaten to blackmail me?

Who does he think he is?

You'd think he'd know who *I* am by now.

You're letting your grandmother eat by herself. That's who you are.

I snap upright again, smooth down my skirt, check my lipstick and earrings as I pass a gilded mirror on the way back into the dining room, and stroll back inside as though I've just hung up.

I've already angered the beast enough. "Honestly, Gigi, some people can't do anything themselves. An employee was threatening to—Gigi?"

She's not in her chair.

But—*oh God*—"*Gigi!*"

Her wineglass is upended. Plate skewed. And her Jimmy Choos–clad feet are visible on the floor beside her chair.

I dash up the length of the table, tripping on the carpet runner, until she comes into view.

Her face is mottled purple, her mouth gaping open, eyelids shut, hands resting on her neck. "Oh my God, Gigi, are you choking? Did you have a heart attack? Gigi? *Gigi!*"

I shake her.

She doesn't open her eyelids.

"*Help!*" I scream. "*Help!*"

I'm suddenly shoved aside while Niles leans in to give her mouth-to-mouth. It's slow motion and all too fast at the same time.

Gigi's larger than life. She drives me crazy. She's demanding and catty and shrewd.

She's everything I want to be when I'm a seventy-year-old billionaire widow.

And her butler is hefting her limp body off the floor, fisting his hands under her breastbone, and pumping her.

"That's not how you do CPR!" I scream.

The last syllable is still hanging on the air when a chunk of Kobe beef comes flying out of Gigi's mouth, hits my collarbone, and falls down between the lapels of my suit jacket, landing in my cleavage and dropping into my bra.

Niles drops her again and bends over her mouth, and a lifetime that lasts mere seconds later, Gigi gasps on the floor.

I'm sobbing.

I didn't know I knew how to sob, but I'm sobbing as I drop to my knees and grab her hand. *"Gigi."*

She has blue eyes.

How did I never pay attention before to the fact that she has blue eyes?

She does. She has blue eyes, and they're staring at me in horror. "Phoebe," she croaks, "I think I just went to hell."

Chapter 2

Teague Miller, aka a Man Who Has No Intention of Letting Anything about His Life Change

One month later . . .

Largemouth bass aren't biting today.

At least, not on Deer Drop Lake.

Now, over on the bank?

Largemouth something might be biting there, where the newest wannabe citizens of Tickled Pink, Wisconsin, are gathered to watch my ex-wife negotiate with me on their behalf.

"You're really not going to row over there and answer one simple question?" Shiloh asks. She's in the town's party pontoon, holding it steady six feet or so from my fishing boat as we rock here out in the middle of the lake, discussing a situation I don't see any need to discuss. Her brown hair's in its normal bob, and her white skin's getting its usual summer sprinkling of freckles across her nose. No doubt she'll be fussing over sunscreen for all of us as soon as she notices.

I shake my head. "Don't trust rich people."

"Teague. They're here because they want to become better people, and they just saw the school. I wouldn't live in that school. *You* wouldn't live in that school. Maybe try to meet them halfway?"

I lift the brim of my fishing hat and pin her with a stare that didn't work when we were married, hasn't worked in the decade and a half since we got divorced, and probably won't work now, but does that stop me from using it?

No, it doesn't. "Know an angle when I see one. They're working an angle. That Lightly lady's here because she thinks re-creating a forty-year-old movie about heaven on earth will magically morph her into the type of person who can go to heaven for real. Won't last. Not once the mosquitoes start biting and she realizes we don't stock foie gras in the Pick-n-Shop. So I won't help the cause of keeping them here."

"You realize that having a family who's always in the tabloids staying in Tickled Pink might be just the boost we need to get tourism back up, don't you?"

I give her another hard stare. Don't need nosy-ass rich people and tourists invading our little slice of heaven. We get by just fine without all the tourists. You ask me, it's been nice that the crazies quit coming around trying to drink from the Fountain of Everlasting Eternity, which got torn down six years ago, by the way, since movie set props aren't built to last forever.

Fewer people telling us we're going to hell for preaching the wrong way to get into heaven.

Get by even better without all the tabloids.

Shiloh crosses her arms and gives me the same look that led to me keeping a herd of goats on my land.

I hate that look.

Especially since she was right about the goats.

"Didn't say I won't talk to the old lady's family," I tell Shiloh. "Just said I won't row over there to do it. They want to talk, they can come to me."

Her lips stay flat, but something flickers in her eyes, and I know I've got her.

"What's that the old lady said she wanted?" I know what she said. She repeated herself sixty-five times while we were signing the paperwork for her to hand over a wad of cash to the town in exchange for buying the disaster of an old high school building. "Ah, right. You just said it yourself. The whole damn family wants to be better people. Maybe learning to row a boat would be a good start."

"You are truly awful."

"I'm truly right, and you're welcome. How many other ex-husbands do you have who can milk thirty goats, go sit out on a lake, catch fish, sell falling-down old eyesores for cash, *and* do your mama proud by sticking up for what this town's really about, all in less time than it takes one of those people over onshore to fix her makeup for the day?"

And there's the lip twitch.

She's amused, and she knows I'm right.

"If they crash their boat into yours and you all sink in the lake and I can only rescue one person, I'm not saving you, for the record," Shiloh says. "I'll probably save Tavi's dog, actually. Pebbles is adorable, even if the rest of them . . . need work. Not that I have time for any of you today. I'm late for a meeting with the high school principal."

I lift the brim of my hat again to look at her. Talking to your kid's principal falls under the jurisdiction of *things you do with your ex-wife*.

Happily, for the record. We tend to get along well, except for when she's telling me to accept a family of no-good socialites moving to town. "You need backup?"

"Not unless you want to help plan the back-to-school carnival."

"It's barely June, Shiloh. Haven't even had this year's end-of-school fish boil."

"And yet we're still behind." She flashes the smile that hooked me sixteen years ago, the same one her mama used to hook a generation of superfans for *Pink Gold*, the movie that temporarily put Tickled Pink on the map decades before I moved here. "You know, I could just give one of them your phone number."

"Don't make me chuck my phone in this lake."

"If you were going to chuck your phone in the lake, you would've done it the sixth time I called you from shore. But you win, Teague. You win. I'll tell them to borrow a boat and come out and negotiate with you in person. Be nice. We need the tourism, or we'll all be getting jobs over in Deer Drop." She fires the engine back up on the pontoon, backs it away, and heads to shore.

I reel in my line and cast again while the wake of her departure rocks my little boat.

Consider popping a beer. Acknowledge *she* won't need to go to Deer Drop for a job, since she's on her way to being the fire chief at the station here in Tickled Pink. Wonder if these clouds will actually give us rain. Scratch myself. Reel in and cast out again.

Cut a glance at the shore, where a very animated blonde who's probably a natural brunette is using that pink power dress-suit thing she's wearing to emphasize every point she's apparently trying to make.

Can't hear what they're saying—not with the earplugs I just popped in—but I get the gist by the body language.

No way is Miss Priss rowing herself out here to tell me what for.

And no doubt my ex-wife is telling her I won't talk about what's gotten her all upset unless one of them does.

Probably also that I'm all set with everything I need to sleep out here for days, so there's no sense in waiting me out either.

She wouldn't be wrong.

So I lower my brim back over my face, settle deeper into the easy chair I fixed into my boat for more comfy fishing, and go back to casting out, looking for a big score.

But only for a minute.

Can't help feeling a little curious.

I shift my head enough to peer out from under my brim without lifting my fishing hat, and *hot damn*.

Color me almost impressed.

Miss Priss is trying to get into a boat.

Dylan Wright's eighteen-foot outboard motorboat, to be precise. He's not fishing today, number one because it's a Thursday, number two because he's working a big job out in Deer Drop, and number three because even if it were a Saturday or Sunday, his plumbing business would probably be getting calls for emergencies.

Clogged toilets don't respect the weekends.

And Miss Priss doesn't respect fishing boats.

You can tell by the way she's still wearing those spiky heels with the red soles and that tight skirt while she's trying to climb in. Looks like a tall pink penguin trying to lift a leg.

Ain't gonna go far that way.

Not that any of the other boats lined up onshore are better options for her. They'd all have the same problem.

Namely that they're boats, and she's a big-city socialite.

I twitch my lips back into submission and cough instead of snickering, because that's the polite thing to do.

And I don't laugh when her shriek echoes across the water, cutting through my foamies so that even I can hear her.

No, sirree.

I don't laugh.

It would be rude to laugh at a lady finding her feet stuck in lake mud for the first time in her life.

So I assume.

If she'd encountered a lake before, odds are good she would've learned what to wear around it.

Or maybe I'm dead wrong, and this is how she always approaches boats and lakes. Maybe they bend to her will.

What do I know?

She finally figures it out, turning her back to the boat, lifting her hips, and sitting on the edge to slide in.

I shake my head. Lucky she's only in a foot of water there by the shore, or that thing would be rolling over.

But you know what's really getting to me right now?

It's not that the princess is getting into the boat.

It's that there are four other people who aren't Tickled Pinkers standing around watching her do it.

The two women lurking safely on the shore are in fancy clothes, too, and I know without a doubt that the one in pants is wearing fancy pants. You can tell because she's topped her getup with a boa.

A *boa*. And a gold one at that.

Women don't wear sweatpants and *boas*.

Even I know that much about fashion.

The heavier of the two men in their group is in a suit, but the other's in jeans and a flannel shirt.

Lot like my flannel shirt, matter of fact.

He could've helped.

He could've been the designated spokesperson to come tell me why I'm an awful human being—and yeah, given what I did before these five rich white fools got here, selling their grandma the most god-awful piece of real estate in all of the Northwoods, there's no doubt in my mind that's what's about to happen—but Mr. Flannel's letting the blonde do all the dirty work.

Probably means the flannel's just for show.

Exactly like the old lady.

Something tugs on my line.

Hot damn. Got a live one. I wrangle and wrestle it in, eventually pulling up a five-inch crappie.

"Got some fight in you for a little guy," I tell him.

His mouth gapes, and his eye stares at me.

"Go on, then. Go warn the rest of 'em that I'm coming for them too." I toss him back in the lake and reset my lure.

And then I make the mistake of looking at the blonde again.

She's floating this way and that, trying to use one oar to make progress on getting out here to me, but she's mostly just going in circles, banging the wooden oar on the side of the metal boat.

I pop one foamie out.

No wonder I only hooked a five-incher. She's making enough racket to scare the fish three lakes over.

"There's a motor, Phoebe," the older guy calls from the shore. "Try turning on the motor!"

"Don't turn on the motor," I mutter.

If she turns on that motor, we'll be picking her body parts out of the evergreens on the Deer Drop side of the lake until it freezes over, assuming she makes it that far without falling out and drowning first.

She drops an oar, which falls into the lake, and then she twists to peer at the outboard motor.

Dammit.

I grunt to myself, put my fishing pole away, and rip the cord on my own motor.

She got in the lake.

Close enough to a compromise.

I'll meet her halfway, tell her no to whatever demands she's about to make, escort her off my lake, and offer to escort her out of my town when I'm done fishing for the day.

But when I motor up next to her, she peers down at me from the higher seat in Dylan's boat like she's the queen of bloody England. Her hair's coming out of its fancy twist. Her pink power suit is splattered with dirty water. I know she's coated in lake mud up to her calves, which are probably tucked under her like she's trying to sit in a fishing boat like a duchess. Yet those sparking green eyes, that long nose, and those red lips are all working together to make me believe peons truly do bow before her.

Rich people make me twitchy.

"Are you Mr. Miller?" she asks with that *you will answer me, because I say so* tone that comes with never being denied a thing in her life.

I glance around the lake.

It's Thursday. Means only Willie Wayne Jorgensen's out here too. At least, this week. Next week, school's out, and we'll get a few more of us.

I nod to her instead of suggesting she go ask Willie Wayne if he's Mr. Miller first. He's a white guy in his late thirties, like me, so odds are good I could confuse her for a while if I wanted to. But then I'd have to take more time away from fishing. "What my driver's license says."

She leans over and extends a hand, then jerks it back and grabs the side of her seat when it rocks. "I'm Phoebe Lightly. I need to discuss the property you sold to my grandmother yesterday."

"All sales are final." I tip my hat. "Have a nice day, Ms. Lightly."

"There is an animal carcass in the hallway."

I nod. "Bats in the theater too. But those are live."

"Charming as it may be on the outside—" She pauses, and I swear she's mentally choking on her own words.

I would be.

The old Tickled Pink high school isn't charming inside *or* out. The three-story neoclassical block building with its arched windows and stamped concrete door marker, first built back in the 1920s and updated not enough back when *Pink Gold* hit big, has been closed for about ten years now. When we realized how much it would cost to update the building to code, we formed an unholy alliance with Deer Drop and agreed it would be more efficient to jointly build a new high school to service both of our communities. The only things the old high school's been good for since are target practice for shooting out windows, growing grass and weeds on the football field behind it for my goats to eat in the summer, and housing wild animals looking to get out of the rain, snow, and sometimes even sunshine year-round.

Until Estelle Lightly marched into town three days ago, declared she needed a place big enough for her and her son's family to live together while they soak up the vibes here to learn to be genuine, good people who won't go to hell when they die, and agreed that she was willing to sell her soul, no matter the price.

Then the old high school became a profitable moneymaking venture for Tickled Pink—and exactly the kind of property that the old lady won't last in for three whole hours.

Not even if they last long enough to get it cleaned, which is far from what it'll take to make the building truly livable.

Like I said.

All sales are final.

"Charming as it may be on the outside," Phoebe Lightly repeats, "it is uninhabitable on the inside. I'll need to see the inspection reports, and I also intend to discuss your real estate license with the county commissioner."

I jerk a thumb at Willie Wayne, who does a lot more than fishing too. At least, when he has to. "County commissioner's right over there, and your grammy didn't ask for an inspection. Bought it as is and paid cash. She already talked to Willie Wayne about having that beaver carcass taxidermized and set up in the cafeteria as a reminder of those who came before and made the ultimate sacrifice."

She blinks one slow blink. "How . . . big . . . are beavers?"

I hold my hands about a beaver's length apart.

Her lips purse out in an O. She reaches up to fiddle with her diamond earring, then yanks her hand back to her lap. "Mr. Miller, we found an animal carcass *this big*." She stretches her arms wide. *"Does that sound like a beaver to you?"*

I scratch my beard. "Reckon you'll find a few more once you look in all the classrooms."

"And we're back to *that building is not inhabitable.*"

"Ms. Lightly, you'll have to discuss that with your grandmother. Sure she won't mind if you pack on up and head back to New York. Lady like you must have better things to do than improving your own soul in a little country town."

Her face doesn't change. Her green eyes don't narrow. Her lips don't tighten. Her spine doesn't stiffen.

But something shifts in her.

I can *feel* it, and that connection sets me on edge.

Whatever she's about to try next, it won't be good.

"Mr. Miller, my grandmother is recovering from a traumatic experience, and she is not well. I'm sure you don't want the legal headaches that my family are prepared to set at your doorstep if you don't rescind the sale of that building *today.*"

"Ms. Lightly, your grandmother passed a Breathalyzer test, which she took voluntarily, she knew what day it was, she could recite the Gettysburg Address and her favorite Robert Frost poem, and she was as lucid as my last dream about flapping my arms and flying over the top of that half-done Ferris wheel at the edge of the town square. She was also clear as crystal that she wanted that school building as the first project on the path to turning herself and all of you into better people. I don't know what kind of skeletons you have in your four-story fancy-schmancy Manhattan closet that made her think you're not a good person, but that's between you, your grandmother, and your own conscience. Prefer that you leave me out of it."

She's holding her hands in her lap so tightly her knuckles are turning white. "I'll be happy to leave you out of it, Mr. Miller, as soon as you return her money and rescind this sale. I don't think you realize who you're dealing with here, and I promise you, you do *not* want to find out."

She should be irritating the snot out of me, but there's something shining out of Phoebe Lightly that I can't help but recognize.

It's that feeling of being trapped.

And that's what she is.

She's trapped here.

She's a wounded animal, lashing out at anything she sees as a danger, and I, the man who won't help her by giving her grandmother her money back and unselling that high school, am a danger.

Do I want her to stay?

No.

But am I refunding her money?

Hell no. That'll go a long way toward shoring up the town's budget for a few new roads around here, not to mention fixing up the bridge Deer Drop keeps insisting is our responsibility, even though the county commissioner's drawings clearly say it's theirs and they're not hurting for money the way we are.

They say the county commissioner's biased.

Might be, but nobody from Deer Drop ran against him last time, so they can zip it.

Plus, the bridge still has to get fixed, whether or not the Lightly family stays long enough to move into the old high school.

I jerk my chin toward the four people still standing on the shore. With everything Estelle Lightly said since Shiloh found her trying to break into the shut-down land that was supposed to be an amusement park based on *Pink Gold*, I've got a pretty good feeling they're the rest of the clan. "How'd you get picked to be the one to come out and negotiate with me?"

"Are you suggesting one of the men should've done it?"

"Gender's got nothing to do with it. Just wondering if you're supposed to be the most charming of the bunch or the scariest of the bunch."

Her eye twitches.

Feels like a victory to get an honest reaction out of a socialite.

"All right, Mr. Miller." She glares down her nose at me and pulls herself to her feet like she's ready to walk away from this and leave me the one about to suffer the consequences. "If we can't—*aaaah!*"

Yeah, that boat's wobbling.

And she's not ready for it.

You can tell because she's flinging her arms out wildly to the side while Dylan's boat rocks this way and that, tipping harder every time she overcorrects her balance, until one Ms. Phoebe Lightly tumbles headfirst and lands with a mighty splash in Deer Drop Lake.

She sputters to the lake surface. *"My Louboutins!"*

I toss her the orange life ring that I store in my boat to keep the game warden happy.

So much for catching anything else today.

Anything other than a fancy city lady who should've stayed onshore.

"Thing about fishing boats, Ms. Lightly, is that they can't fight physics either. One more thing money can't buy. I won't give your granny her money back, but you're welcome to leave anytime. And since I'm feeling generous, I'll even do you one better. Say the word, and I'll help make sure no one else in your family wants to stay here either."

Chapter 3

Phoebe

Gigi did *not*, in fact, go to hell when she choked on her filet mignon.

How do I know?

Because the place she described as she was getting checked over in the hospital sounded nothing at all like Tickled Pink, Wisconsin.

Her hell?

Fire. Brimstone. Terrifying evil laughter. Screams. Demons.

Tickled Pink?

No cell service to check my work email. No car. No Prada store for self-therapy. No dry cleaner to take care of the McQueen suit that went into the lake with me yesterday. Not that I'd trust them with my McQueen. The grocery store down the way has a massive sign advertising 80 percent lean ground beef on sale, accompanied by a picture of a grated beef pile that resembles brains more than it resembles any pictures in that meat subscription box I got my assistant after I overheard her complaining that there was no good sausage left in Manhattan.

Don't tell me I'm not a giver.

Also, I was nearly attacked by a crow when I left the motel this morning, which Gigi insists we're moving out of today after a hard day's work of "cleaning our new home," which she also insists we're all living in, together, for the next *year*, just like Whitney Anastasia moved into a run-down former post office when she came to Tickled Pink for her moral transformation in the movie *Pink Gold*.

Except, as Gigi wisely pointed out, the six of us won't fit in a closed-down post office.

Nor was there one available.

So we get the condemned school building.

I can't believe she's actually made me prefer the 1980s green-and-orange decor of the motel. She's still there, sitting in the lobby, drinking their burnt generic brew, because "people who want to go to heaven have to make sacrifices."

She can have her sacrifices.

I'm having decent coffee.

Or at least better coffee.

And thank Oprah "I'm supporting the local economy by getting my coffee at the café on the square" worked. Although given the way it smells vaguely like cheese, I'm no longer convinced this coffee will be better.

Also? There's a sign about getting a discount on quarterly oil changes at the auto shop on the back half of the building if you sign up for the coffee-and-a-lube-job subscription combo.

When I say *what the hell?* I truly mean that in all senses of the question.

Still, I step smartly across the cracked tile floor and stop at the large bakery case stuffed with lumpy muffins, crooked donuts, and cakes missing their polish. Is that cake *actually* finished, or is someone coming in later to smooth the edges and add a proper garnish?

Do people actually eat it like that?

Would it look better if all the lights overhead were working properly and not buzzing?

Hold that question. I need coffee first.

"Large caramel macchiato, but make the three squirts of vanilla sugar-free, and I want my nonfat milk frothed to one hundred fifty-five degrees exactly, stirred *six* times with a wooden spoon, not metal, with a sprinkle of Ceylon cinnamon on top," I tell the barista when she bustles through swinging green saloon doors from what I assume is the kitchen but could very well be the mechanic's shop. She's a dark-haired woman with light-brown skin in a pink shirt with *Café Nirvana* stitched on her left breast, and her lips are twisting and twitching while she gives me a quick once-over. I ignore her scrutiny and point to the only thing in the case that doesn't look like sugar and butter formed an alliance to plot visual and arterial carnage. "A sprinkle. Not a dash, not a shake, but a sprinkle. And three of those sous vide egg white bites."

She lifts an untamed eyebrow at me. "We got regular and decaf, and those are Ridhi's famous oatcakes. Have a seat. She'll be out to take your order in a minute."

I blink at the woman. "Who is Ridhi, and why do I care?"

"Ridhi's the one who'll spit in your food if she hears you saying that." She leans across the bakery display cabinet. "Is it true Teague's using a new body spray that smells like lemon-meringue pie? You're the only one who got close to him before he smelled like fish again yesterday."

"That's disgusting, Aunt Anya," a kid at a nearby booth says. She's white, with brown hair hanging down to her shoulders, a white crop top with black stencil drawings of faces all over it, a sprinkle of freckles over her nose, and rainbow flag earrings dangling from her ears. She's maybe twelve, maybe nineteen. I don't know. I don't know kids. I do know that I sincerely hope she takes lessons in brow maintenance from someone *other* than Aunt Anya.

Maybe I'll tell her.

That could be my good deed for the day. People who are going to heaven do good deeds.

I know, because Whitney Anastasia did dozens in *Pink Gold*, which I've watched with Gigi approximately seven thousand times now.

But again—good deeds can also wait until *after* coffee.

"I'm not staying," I inform the barista. "I just want my caramel macchiato and to get out of here."

The kid snorts with laughter.

It sounds similar to the snort *Teague* made yesterday while hauling my soggy ass back to shore, when I informed him that a Lightly can do anything, even while dripping in disgusting lake water.

"Isn't he a lovely professional?" Gigi said when he pulled me to shore. "His name is Teague. Rhymes with *league*. He gets extra credit for knowing to take my first offer on that school building."

I'm clearly still triggered by snorts and mention of the fishing lumberjack.

And Anya's clearly unsure about my macchiato. "Sweetie, we're not Starbucks."

I can't tell if she's sympathetic to my plight or if she thinks I'm an idiot. Neither are good options in my world.

I open my mouth to suggest she might do a little more business if she *were* more like Starbucks, but before I can utter a word, the bells tinkle on the door, and Aunt Anya gasps. "Oh my stars, it's Tavi Lightly." She bustles out from behind the counter and grabs my baby sister's hand and pumps it. "Hi. Oh my stars. Hi. I'm Anya. That's my niece, Bridget. Stepniece, but full niece in my heart. Naturally. Hi. I'm Anya. Oh, I said that, didn't I? We *love* you. That picture on Instagram of you in Tuscany at sunset with your silhouette and the colors and the—"

"Aunt Anya, it was doctored." You can *hear* Bridget rolling her eyes. I want to buy *her* a caramel macchiato for the eye roll. "Still a fab piece of art. Duh. But it wasn't raw. Not like that totally swag video on TikTok."

Tavi lifts her Tiffany sunglasses and pushes them up to rest on her Hermès headband. She's several inches shorter than me, with adorable round cheeks, a widow's peak in her caramel-brown hair that works on her, since *everything* works on Tavi, and curves that she keeps in check with religious workouts and the most insane no-sugar, no-meat, no-dairy, no-flavor diet I've ever heard of. She's currently in workout clothes that probably cost more than this entire coffee shop, and despite the early hour, she's smiling like her motel room didn't have a lumpy bed, weak water pressure in the shower, and an odor of fish urine hanging in the air.

I hate her on principle, because if I were as jet lagged as she should be—until three days ago, she was somewhere in Europe or Asia—I'd be walking around looking like the love child of Medusa and Frankenstein.

"Ten points to Bridget," she says. "It was filtered, but the colors make you so happy, don't they?"

Bridget smiles back.

Anya smiles too.

Tavi keeps smiling.

And all these smiles in hell make my shoulders twitch.

"Coffee?" I prompt Anya.

"Oh, that's a great idea, Phoebe." Tavi shifts her Margot Lightly tote slash dog purse to her other shoulder—yes, Mom has her own shoe-and-purse line, and yes, Tavi shills it shamelessly across social media, which is her "day job"—then crosses deeper into the coffee shop and leans in for air-kisses with me. She turns back to Anya, pulling things out of her bag as she does, working around Pebbles, her teacup Yorkie, who's sniffing the air from her spot inside the purse like she, too, can smell cheese in this shop and wants to know where it's coming from. "May I please have a large caramel macchiato with these beans, fresh ground, and here's my favorite vegan, sugar-free caramel sauce (three squirts, please) and also my oat milk—exactly two ounces, please, and I would *adore* it frothed as close as you can get it to one hundred forty-five degrees. Could you please add a sprinkle of cinnamon on top? Do you have cinnamon? Here. Here are a few organic Saigon cinnamon sticks. They're *heavenly* when fresh grated. Do you have a superfine grater, or do you need to borrow mine?"

Anya blinks twice, looks at me, then back at Tavi as my sister hands her everything she needs to make an organic, vegan, fair-trade, kissed-by-angels macchiato. "You bet, sugar. Let me run a quick Google, and I'll get that out to you in three shakes."

Bridget snickers while I glare at my little sister.

"What?" Tavi asks me. She whips out a diamond-crusted compact and flips it open while her furry-faced mini dog gazes at her as though she can do no wrong. "Is my lipstick crooked? Did I forget to put mascara on both eyes?"

"You look fabu, Tavi." Bridget slides out of the booth and hands my sister a piece of paper. "Not that you have far to go or much competition. If you stick around, maybe you can show me how you do that thing with your lipstick? I can't make it work right."

"You bet, sweetie. And oh my God, look at your hair. It's totes gorge."

The teenager squeals. "Really?"

"I mean, *duh*. Look at those waves." Tavi beams, the heavens open up and serenade us with old-school Britney Spears, the oatcakes magically morph into sous vide egg white bites, and I remind myself that I'm too old to pull her hair just because she's prettier and more of a people person than I am.

I'm a businesswoman with a very important job that I'm currently unable to do because I couldn't connect to the motel's Wi-Fi and my phone is still not getting a signal.

I don't have to pretend to be everyone's best friend.

Nor do I have the energy for false fronts. Not when there's so much work to be done if I'm ever going to fulfill my destiny of being the first Lightly to run Remington Lightly since it went public, and the first female CEO to boot.

While Tavi's entire life is built on looking good on social media so that she can keep getting free stuff to shill and so that Mom can sell a few more Margot Lightly bags and shoes, mine is built on actually putting in the hard work to do the important things, like ruling the whole damn world.

There's a reason we don't talk much beyond air-kisses at fundraisers and galas that we both coincidentally end up attending.

"Can we, like, hook up later?" Bridget asks Tavi. "That would be so swag to do each other's hair. But I have this thing that I have to get to. School. Like, *why*, you know?"

My sister flashes her influencer smile while the teenager backs to the door. "Of *course*. We'll do lunch and hair and pedis. Such a drag to have to learn *all the things*, right?"

"Have a good day at school, Bridge," Anya calls.

"That's impossible, Aunt Anya," Bridget calls back. "I have a *geometry* final. On the *last day* of the year. *Ugh.*"

The door closes behind the kid, Anya slips back behind those swinging doors to what I'm still hoping is the kitchen, and Tavi's smile falls away. She grabs my arm and drags me to a booth, which she makes me sit in without wiping it down first. "Oh my God, what are we actually doing here?" she hisses with a covert glance at the doorway behind the bakery case, like she's making sure Anya isn't spying on us.

As if she's not most likely preoccupied with googling how to make a drink for Tavi that she wouldn't make for me, considering Tavi brought *her own beans.*

Does that put her ahead or behind on the All the Lightlys Go to Heaven scoreboard?

I don't know.

"Getting vastly different experiences in getting coffee?" I hiss back dryly.

"I meant *in this town.*"

Do not twitch, Phoebe. Do not twitch. Do not twitch.

Tavi missed all the family drama with Gigi choking because she was flitting around the world getting pictures of various products for her socials while I was holding Gigi's hand and watching that infernal movie over and over again this past month.

"We're becoming better people." Look at that. I almost kept my sarcasm in check.

"Yes, but *why here?* Did you see that sign by the register? Who puts a lube shop at the back of a café? And what's that massive plant monster across the way at the edge of the square?"

For the record, if I'd had my caffeine, I would've caught on to why she's asking *much* faster. "*Oh my God*, you didn't watch the movie, did you?"

"What movie?"

"*What movie?* Are you serious? Have you not read the six thousand text messages on that family text thread about Gigi's plans for us? Or looked around at the signs *everywhere* in this town? Or even googled this place?"

"Phoebe, I was in some very undeveloped places doing some very important work, and I have zero cell signal right now too. I'm lucky I got the SOS at all that we all had to be here to support Gigi in her emotional struggles, and I'm not exactly at the top of my game after my travel schedule this week. Could you maybe wait until after coffee to chew me out?"

I grit my teeth. While Tavi usually annoys me—*very important work*, my ass—we need to become hard-core allies, *fast*, so we can get out of here. "*Pink Gold*," I whisper. "The movie. *Pink Gold.*"

Her eyes bug out. "That's a *movie?* I thought all of her texts were about investing in some new jewelry store."

"It's about a fancy white rich lady trying to get into heaven to see her kid after a literal train wreck." And I have seen it so many times, thanks to Gigi, that I *dream* in *Pink Gold*.

Tavi stares at me expectantly.

How does she manage to look adorable like that while still clearly confused and slow on the uptake?

How is that fair?

I heave a sigh. "It was filmed here. The town itself is basically the star of the show. The actual town. Just like it is, except Hollywood-ified forty years ago. This woman, Whitney, gets lost here on her way to a business trip not long after her only kid dies in this freak train accident, realizes Tickled Pink is where the gates to heaven are, and goes on this journey to being a better person so she can earn her ticket to pass through and see that her kid is happy in heaven. In the end you find out she was dead all along and Tickled Pink was some kind of purgatory. But she's reunited with her kid, everyone cries, blah blah, emotions, blah blah, and Gigi thinks *this town* and *that movie* are her blueprint to all of us becoming better people."

And now Tavi's staring at me like I'm speaking gibberish and probably need to see a professional as much as Gigi does.

Fabulous.

Exactly what I need today.

But it does beg the question—"What does Gigi have on you? Why did *you* agree to this?"

"Phoebe. I can't *not* be here when the tabloids are reporting that my grandmother is on the verge of the kind of nervous breakdown that could wipe out seventy years' worth of building her image and legacy. Do you know what that would look like for my brand if I wasn't here for family in her time of need?"

I momentarily feel better. At least I'm here out of true guilt that Gigi almost choked and died while I was fighting with an ex-boyfriend I never actually *liked*, not because I'm afraid not being here will ruin my vegan fitness social media brand or make my trust fund mysteriously dry up so that I have to find a real job to support myself.

But as I smirk at the table, I notice the paper Bridget handed Tavi, which she's set on the table while she slips Pebbles a dog treat. "The *Tickled Pink Papers*? What is—*what is that?*"

It's a gossip sheet.

It's a small-town gossip sheet with a giant picture of me climbing out of the lake, mascara dripping, my Alexander McQueen peplum jacket and pencil skirt ruined, my feet bare and missing the Louboutins that I will never see again, my hair a federal disaster zone.

I don't bother reading the article. Instead, I pull out my phone and dictate a text to my assistant. "Antoinette. Find whoever prints the *Tickled Pink Papers* and burn their house down."

Tavi frowns at me. "We are not burning houses down."

"You're right." I lift my phone and dictate again. "Antoinette, correction. Find someone we can pay to burn their house down."

"*Phoebe.* If Gigi hears you say that—"

I shudder.

She's right. Yesterday afternoon, after we checked into the motel and Tavi disappeared because of a headache, Gigi laid out for us exactly what's in our future.

I've been placed on administrative leave from Remington Lightly for "family issues." Mom and Dad came along for their own reasons. Tavi too. And Carter—well, that's obvious.

Gigi must've cut my brother off financially, considering money is the only thing he cares about when it comes to the family. He says he's a rock star, but as far as I can tell, he's actually a mooch. One song that barely cracked the top forty does not a rock star make.

And we're all supposed to work together for *an entire year* so that we can learn, as a family, using that god-awful film *Pink Gold* as a guide, to be better people and save our souls from eternal damnation.

Starting today.

When we begin the task of cleaning up our new home.

Which we're moving into.

Today.

"How are we supposed to treat classrooms like bedrooms?" I whisper to my sister.

This is possibly the first thing we've seen eye to eye on in twenty-nine years.

"I don't know, but I'm claiming the chemistry room."

"You *cheated*! You looked and made sure it didn't have any dead animals in it, didn't you?"

"No, Phoebe. I asked some local last night if it was set up with those gas thingies, and when she said they're still attached but she doesn't know if they work, I decided one of us needs to make sure Carter doesn't take that room, or he'll try to turn on all the gas thingies and either asphyxiate all of us, or he'll burn down the whole school. I watched those recycled eighties public service warning videos in grade school about doing chemistry without a teacher, and I know he did too. He knows how to burn the school down. We all do."

I tilt my head at her. "And that would be a *bad* thing?"

"Phoebe."

My phone dings with a notification before I can lie to her and tell her I was kidding.

Text failed. No service.

I grimace.

I can't do my job while on administrative leave if I can't get freaking cell service, and I can't work my way up to CEO of Remington Lightly if I can't do my job while on administrative leave, and I also can't tell Fletcher to go to hell with his blackmail threats if I can't see his latest threats, and if he thinks I'm ignoring him, Oprah only knows what he'll do.

My life in New York might already be over.

And that has my chest tightening worse than it did when I lost my Louboutins to the Lake of Doom.

Tavi lifts Pebbles and cuddles her, giving me the same look Mom always does when I talk about taking the shortcut and sleeping my way to the top. "Don't make that face. You'll get wrinkles. You'll be making that face enough anyway if Gigi's in charge of determining when we've all become better people. Gag me with a solid silver spoon."

Wow.

I think I've actually missed my sister.

I glance at the kitchen again to make sure Anya's still occupied and not listening in on us. "Why is Mom here?"

Tavi makes a face that'll give *her* wrinkles.

"Seriously," I whisper. "I know Gigi has to be threatening to tell the world about Dad's latest mistress to keep *him* here, and we all know Carter's being threatened with being cut off from his trust fund, but why did Mom come?"

Mom, aka Margot Lightly, was born in Iowa, moved to New York to be a Broadway actress, and was waiting tables and getting rejected for role after role when Dad, aka Michael Lightly, aka the original version of my lazy rock-star-wannabe brother, fell in love with her and swooped her away to his fancy Upper East Side life. I came along a year later, and Mom's been trying different side businesses ever since.

Her luxury-accessories line has lasted longer than anything except for her tarot-card addiction. While it doesn't make her the kind of money being a Lightly makes her, Gigi couldn't prevent her from getting a massive settlement if she finally decided to divorce Dad.

The truth's ugly sometimes.

Tavi shrugs. "Maybe she's here because she loves Gigi?"

Anya bustles out from the kitchen as I'm giving my sister the *no, that's not it* look.

"Here you go, Tavi," Anya says. "One vegan, sugar-free caramel macchiato with steamed oat milk. Did you want me to go get you some broccoli? We don't have any beets or a juicer, but I could *totally* dash to the store to get you some broccoli."

I do *not* want to know what's all over Tavi's feed that's making people offer her beets and broccoli at eight in the morning.

Nor do I want to know just how wrong that macchiato is when Tavi almost spits it back up as soon as she sips.

Not that Anya will notice.

You have to watch just right to catch Tavi's true feelings, and they're revealed in the pause / mini grimace / eye twitch before she visibly swallows and beams up her biggest fake smile, which is brighter than the spotlights at a Levi Wilson concert in Madison Square Garden.

"Yum. Perfect. Just the right hot." She beams at Anya. "And that's so sweet of you to offer broccoli! But this will be plenty. Thank you. Actually, I do have one question I would *love* to ask you."

"Oh, *anything*." Anya shifts in place like she doesn't know what to do with her hands. Or her legs. Or her whole body. "I know everything there is to know about Tickled Pink. Happy to help."

"Do you have Wi-Fi? I would simply *adore* the password, since I haven't been able to check my socials since we got here."

Anya freezes.

Hard freezes. Like, you can see both her shoulder devils arguing with each other and also her heart going stone-cold still in panic.

Tavi and I lock eyes.

Gigi *didn't*.

Except she did.

She told everyone in town to not let us have access to the Wi-Fi.

Probably until we earn it.

"Did, um, you still want a macchiato too, Ms. Lightly?" Anya says to me.

I shake my head, and not because I saw the telltale signs that my sister will be feeding her drink to the nearest houseplant, and I'd rather have caffeine withdrawal than drink sludge.

Mind made up.

I know how this game works, and I don't care if I'm not in Manhattan anymore. I will play this game until it's dead, or until I am.

"No, thank you. I just remembered I have somewhere I need to be."

Chapter 4

Phoebe

Teague Miller is a very hard person to find.

As if that will stop me.

Navigating the uneven sidewalks and cobblestone streets in a pair of Jimmy Choos won't either.

But my moment of hesitation comes when I realize the address I've been given is a field of goats surrounded by mile-high Christmas trees, undecorated and in their native land.

"Hello?" I call.

A resounding *"Are you kidding me?"* echoes over a field of bleating goats behind a fence and tells me I'm in the right place, though there's not a house in sight.

Does he live in a hole in the ground? This part was *not* in that damn movie that Gigi wants to re-create in order to find her soul. "Mr. Miller? Hello?"

"How may I be of assistance, Ms. Lightly?"

Is he in a tree? Is he seriously *climbing trees*?

The flannel and the beard made him look like a fishing lumberjack yesterday, but I did *not* expect to find him actually sitting in a tree.

"Where *are* you?"

"Almost exactly where I want to be."

"Which is?"

"In my home."

I am so confused. I lower my sunglasses and peer through the goats. "Where *is* your home?"

"Right where I'm at."

"I had a professor who liked to talk in riddles once. He's now unemployed and living in Greenland."

"Must've been before your grandmother's great awakening."

"Where are you?"

"In my home. But not alone, since you're here now. Hence, exactly where I do and don't want to be."

The man would be funny if he weren't irritating. "Mr. Miller, I have a proposal for you, and I would very much like to present it without yelling across a herd of goats."

Herd? Flock? Uprising? What *do* you call a group of goats?

A large wooden crate on a rope drops from the sky near one of the trees at the back of the goat field, and *oh my word.*

There's a *house* in the trees. An actual tree house. It blends in. I missed it the first time.

My gaze drifts upward, over the shimmer of glass, brown wood, more glass, more wood—it's not merely a tree house. It's a several-story tiny town house on stilts built into his forest.

Lola Minelli would die ten thousand deaths on her reality show if someone put her tiny house up in a tree.

I wonder if I can reach the producers to suggest they try it?

"If you can get up here, we can discuss your proposal," he calls from somewhere in the heights, drawing my attention back to the crate.

It's not a crate.

It's—it's—it's a crude elevator system.

"Leave any food outside the gate, or the goats will eat you. I have an appointment with a largemouth bass in twenty minutes, and I'm not waiting for your highbrow little ass to get over yourself if you're serious about a proposal."

I pick my way through a row of prickly weeds and grasses along the fence until I find a gate with a rusty latch.

I miss New York. Concrete. Coffee. Cell signals. Private manicurists. Trustworthy sushi. Silk sheets. Spas. Staff. Strangers who mind their own business.

Making deals with devils of my choosing, instead of the devils I'm stuck with.

The latch gives way after six tugs, and the entire herd of goats swarms me.

I shriek—which is *not* something I do in my regular life, despite the number of times I've done it since I got here—and hug a fence post while goat after goat races past me, their furry bodies brushing my Chanel skirt while I try to climb the fence so they can't trample my Jimmy Choos.

"What are you doing?" Teague yells.

"I'm coming to see you!" I yell back.

"You let my goats out!"

"I did not! I opened the gate, and they let themselves out!"

Three slowpoke goats lift their heads from inside the gate. One bleats at me.

All three go back to eating.

I take that to mean *it's safe to come in now*, so I let go of the fence and carefully lower myself to the stubbly green ground. Grass and weeds poke up through a layer of last year's dead plants on the uneven terrain, and since there's no sidewalk, I pick my way across the field in my heels while the goats ignore me.

Dress for the life you want to have apparently won't last long here.

Not if I don't want to keep ruining $3,000 shoes, which keep sinking into the earth in unexpected places. And let's not talk about the rest of my wardrobe.

"Leave the damn gate open so the goats can come back when they get bored," Teague orders.

"Yes, Your Holy Majesty," I mutter.

"And don't call me that, or my offer's off the table."

"I *muttered*," I yell at him.

"You're predictable."

I'm getting closer to his voice, picking my way around mud pits and piles of things that I do *not* want to step in. "You don't know me well enough for me to be predictable."

"I know your type. That's enough."

The crate's sitting crooked, like it landed on a rock. I peer inside it.

"There's a gate that you *can* open on that thing. Lock it when you get in so you don't fall out and break your neck on the way up. Or don't. Your choice."

I spot the gate in question on one side of the big wooden box. "We can negotiate from here."

"I don't negotiate with people who can't pull their own weight."

I peer up.

He's leaning over a deck, bare arms dangling over the edge, one hand holding a mug, his eyes hidden behind sunglasses, hair hidden under that ridiculous hat, mouth hidden by his beard, so it's impossible to judge if he's proud of himself for making an awful joke or if he doesn't realize his double meaning.

From what I know of Teague Miller so far, I'll assume he's aware he made a joke but also that he assumes I'm too haughty and highbrow to recognize that fact.

As if I didn't already severely dislike the man. "You want us gone, so I don't need to negotiate with you at all. *You* have more to lose here."

"Maybe I changed my mind. Maybe someone convinced me that it'll be another profitable venture for the town to leak pictures of you doing things like walking through goat shit and falling out of boats to a few tabloids back in New York. From where I stand, Ms. Lightly, you're the one with a greater incentive to leave."

I eyeball the crate again.

It's hooked up on all four corners to a center pulley above the middle of the crate, and unlike the gate on the fence, the gate on this wooden box has a latch that's not rusted.

He thinks I can't figure this out and get up there?

He thinks I'm too *precious*? Too *pampered*? Too *spoiled*?

The man has no idea who he's dealing with.

So I climb into that crate, and you're damn right I figure it out. *Without* asking him where the button is.

I might be a rich city girl, but I'm not stupid enough to think he'll make this easy on me. "If I fall to my death," I say between grunts as I yank on the rope to lift the whole thing off the ground, finding it's easier to move than I thought it would be but still not *easy*, "my family will sue you to the ends of this earth."

He smirks over his coffee mug. "You assume they care that much."

I twitch. *Good morning, nerve. Get your sensitive ass back behind your gold-plated armor.*

And then I slap my arm, where it feels like someone just stuck a needle into my skin. I pull my hand back, and— *"Eew!"*

"Ah, mosquito season," Teague says.

I grimace and wipe the carnage on his rope while my makeshift elevator sways in the breeze. I'm two feet up.

I think I have twenty to go. "That was *not* a mosquito. It was—it was—it was a *vampire bat*."

"Was too a mosquito," he replies. "And that was a little one. Wait until July. They get as big as your fist then."

"Mr. Miller, you've already sold me on leaving this hellhole. I'd like to discuss you channeling your energy to convince my grandmother."

"Right here whenever you feel like joining me."

The bastard truly is going to make me get all the way up into his tree house, yanking on a rope to tug up this makeshift elevator six inches at a time.

Also, I have no idea how to make this crate lower me back to the ground, as there's some safety mechanism to prevent it from falling when I let go of the rope.

It does appear he has me at a disadvantage and out of other options.

"For the record, Mr. Miller, I'm not doing this because I like you."

"Right back at you, Ms. Lightly."

There's a hint of a southern drawl in his speech that intrigues me.

In a know-thy-enemy way. Nothing more.

And by the time I reach the first level of his tree house, he is very much my enemy.

I've sweated through my blouse. I'm sporting six more bug bites on skin I can't reach, and I have an itch on my ass that I refuse to scratch in public, as I *am* a Lightly, and I'm in danger of being late to Gigi's family meeting if this negotiation doesn't go well.

She'll probably make me scrub toilets or chase the bats out of the theater myself.

Her brush with death hasn't changed the rules. They're simply now under the guise of *I'm doing this to make you a better person.*

I manage to get myself out of the basket and onto the solid platform, and then I make the mistake of looking at Teague Miller.

He's moved so he's now leaning against the railing on the deck, shirtless, with a coffee mug declaring him the world's best tree hugger. And where he should be pudgy with a lazy man's posture and have a birthmark in an unfortunate shape or a tattoo with his mother's name misspelled across his chest, instead, his shoulders are broad, his pecs and biceps are chiseled in a manner that suggests he built this tree house by hand, he has a manly thatch of dark chest hair threaded here and there with errant silver strands over his tanned skin, all of it narrowing down his abdomen to point below the belt of his jeans, and he clearly isn't experiencing any natural slouch for spending his days reclining in a *cushioned chair* on his fishing boat.

I subtly sniff, inhale the most delicious coffee scent to tease my nose in what feels like a lifetime, curse Anya at the coffee shop, then curse Teague too.

He crosses one ankle over the other and gives me the same once-over I'm giving him. "You look different dry—no, wait . . ."

"Fuck off, Miller."

"Elevator's behind you if you'd rather not bask in my presence."

"I *don't* want to bask in your presence, but until my grandmother is convinced this is a terrible idea and lets us all go back to our real lives, I don't appear to have many options."

He sips his coffee.

It doesn't escape my attention that I haven't been invited inside, beyond the ridiculously adorable red door to wherever his magical coffeepot is. Nor has he offered me a cup. And I swear I detect a hint of vanilla lingering in the air too.

I lift the Gigi brow.

He snorts into his cup, coughs like he's choking on his coffee, and sets the mug aside to wipe his beard. "Does that look actually work for you?"

"Let's get to the point, Mr. Miller. You want us to leave. I want us to leave. I've considered your point that we're free to leave without requiring that you allow us to return the school building in exchange for a refund, and I agree to your terms. However, my grandmother does not. She needs extra convincing."

He sips his coffee again.

He also continues to neglect to offer me a mug of it.

I order myself to keep my coffee lust in check, but it smells *so* damn good, and I haven't had a decent cup in two days, and I don't think I'm succeeding.

I want his coffee.

I *covet* his coffee.

I would drink it straight out of the pot right now. Hell, I'd drink it out of a hollow log at this point.

"Ask you a question?" he says in that soft drawl, snapping my attention back from my desperation for a decent cup of joe.

"We *are* negotiating, Mr. Miller. I expect questions."

"Why don't you just pack up your fancy matching luggage and haul your curvy ass back to New York without your grandmother?"

Forget the Chanel skirt. I should've worn actual plated armor. "My grandmother sits on the board of directors for Remington Lightly, where I'm the executive assistant director for the vice president of production for the paper-goods division, and where I intend to one day run the whole damn company, same as my great-grandfather did before me. She's convinced the board and the CEO that I need a year of administrative leave in order to continue my career advancement properly. In other words, I don't currently have a job to go back to."

"So quit and find a different job."

"I don't want a different job."

"Because you couldn't be a low-level manager with a big fancy title just because of your name at another job?"

I square my shoulders.

He smirks behind his coffee mug—or so I assume, given the way his beard is twitching—and I realize he's baiting me.

The man doesn't want to help me convince my grandmother this is a terrible idea.

He wants to pick us off one by one. "Do you enjoy being disagreeable, Mr. Miller, or do you honestly think so much of yourself that you believe you, *by yourself*, can take on Estelle Lightly and convince her to leave after you've gotten rid of the rest of us?"

He tilts his head. "Yes."

Wonderful. No cell signal. Bloodthirsty mosquitoes. Six of his goats will probably take up residence in the school that Gigi is insisting we'll be cleaning ourselves, and the only person in this godforsaken town who might be able to help me is an uncooperative royal ass.

"Then maybe I'll decide I *want* to stay."

He chuckles, and a shiver dashes across my skin, making my breasts tighten and something catch in my throat.

How can a man so irritating also be so *manly*?

I don't like beefcakes. I prefer my men slender, blond, and academic. We *look* right together.

Yet here I am, my subconscious wondering what it would be like to have Teague Miller at my mercy in the bedroom if that's where our negotiations need to go next.

Less than twenty-four hours after I first set foot in this town, it's breaking me.

I don't like breaking. "Mr. Miller, you *are* aware that with two phone calls, I could have half the paparazzi in New York crawling through your little town and digging up dirt on each and every one of your friends here, aren't you?"

His beard and sunglasses leave me at a distinct disadvantage for reading his reaction to my threat, but his biceps and pecs tighten.

And that makes my thighs clench.

Dammit.

I remind myself I get turned on by a good fight and not by muscles, but I don't think I believe myself.

He takes another sip. "If you really think they'd want to cover Willie Wayne's broken garden fence and the way my goats will be spending all day eating his lettuce shoots, or Ridhi's fight with Deer Drop Floyd over him stealing her family's coconut-pudding recipe, then be my guest. Call away. If you can find cell service to make that call, that is. Got a notion they'd be far more interested in you falling into more lakes, though. And probably digging into how your sister's handling motel living and what your brother's doing without easy access to weed and groupies. Love your family that much, do you? Or is it the trust fund you like?"

So he's doing his homework. This could be good or bad. "I make my own money, Mr. Miller."

"In a job at the family company. Yep. Self-made woman, all right."

"*Some* of us have a heritage we're proud of and working hard to live up to, and for the record, we don't control enough of the company for things to just be handed to me. Do you want us gone or not?"

"Dunno, Ms. Lightly. World might be a better place if you learn to be a better person."

"I'm a *very* good person. I donate to charity. I give my assistant a Tiffany's gift card every year on what I think is her birthday. I make my own mortgage payments, and I compliment even the ugliest babies on the street." Okay, that's a stretch. I don't like babies. I don't understand babies, and the idea of being responsible for a human being that can't speak and randomly projects vomit *Exorcist*-style terrifies me. But if I liked babies, I would compliment even the ugliest babies.

His lips twitch behind that lumberjack beard. "Ten-thousand-dollar-a-plate charity dinners where most of the funding goes to keeping the board of directors traveling to the Hamptons in the name of getting token donations from their garden-club members?"

That's entirely too close to home. "Someone's been streaming too much *Gossip Girl.*"

"Why are you here, Ms. Lightly? You seem bloodthirsty enough to handle this all on your own."

"If we were in New York, I'd have this done in an afternoon. But I'm in this godforsaken town, where I don't know every tool at my disposal. Tools like *making Gigi fall into a lake*. I'm fully aware of my shortcomings, and after yesterday, I'm positive it's a far better use of my time to contract out the plotting to someone who already has an innate sense of what will horrify my entire family the most." I slap another mosquito trying to make breakfast out of me to emphasize my point. "I'll leave this town willingly the minute my grandmother releases me from this ridiculous forced leave of absence. You don't have to convince me to go, Mr. Miller. I'm willing to work with you, on two conditions. One, we agree falling in the lake is the worst I'll have to do, and that's already done. And two, you don't harm a single hair on my grandmother's head. Make her life unpleasant? Yes. Harm her? No. Are we agreed?"

And coffee.

I very much should insist he provide me with coffee.

Mostly because I'm about to leap at him to steal the cup he's sipping from again while he supposedly contemplates my proposal, but I also know the minute I add the coffee to the list, he'll use my desires against me.

I cross my arms and tap my fingers over my bicep when he doesn't answer right away. "I have what's sure to be an unpleasant family meeting to get to, Mr. Miller. I repeat: Are we agreed?"

His lips purse to one side, and then he gives a short nod. "Mostly."

"Mostly?"

"Would look weird if you're the only person in your family not being subjected to the best Tickled Pink can bring."

I'm twitching. *Again.* The man has brought out the twitch in me. "I get warning if I'm to be humiliated."

He hides his mouth behind his coffee mug again. "I'll do my best, Ms. Lightly."

The first item on my to-do list once Gigi releases us for the day is *Find a new partner in crime*. But for now, I stick a hand out. "Then we have a deal."

His long fingers wrap all the way around and swallow my hand, hot and smooth, sending another shiver racing up my arm, over my shoulder, and down my chest.

I've made a deal with the devil.

Thank Oprah it's not the first time, or I might be in trouble.

Chapter 5

Teague

Phoebe Lightly might be a pain in the ass, but she's not afraid to get her hands dirty. I'll give her that.

She made it up into my tree house, and she didn't even ask me to pull her up.

I respect that.

Didn't expect it out of her. She might be made of sterner stuff than I was inclined to give her credit for.

She still needs to leave, but maybe she's only 80 percent princess.

And I'm looking forward to tormenting the hell out of that 80 percent.

First step?

Sneaking into the light booth in the theater at the school to watch the Lightly family's first meeting go down, even though I'd rather be fishing. And I'm not alone.

"Anybody pulling hair yet?" I murmur to Ridhi Denning, Shiloh's wife, as I join her at the glass. The six members of the Lightly family are spread out in the theater chairs. From what I hear, odds are just as good that they're not sitting as a cohesive unit because they can't stand each other as that it's because most of the plush seats in the theater are broken, are stained, or otherwise have issues and it's hard to find two in a row that work right.

"Not yet. Estelle barely got three sentences out about how she was clearly the inspiration for *Pink Gold*, despite it being filmed forty years before she choked on her dinner, before Carter Lightly yawned and scratched himself and asked if there was a CliffsNotes version for the test."

"Fucking upper-crusters."

"So long as they keep dropping money, they can stay."

"No, they can't."

"The world won't end if Tickled Pink welcomes a few more tourists, Teague. It's *good for us*."

"Normal tourists, yes. National attention? No."

She tightens her mouth in a grim line, and it's not because I'm being a ridiculous dick.

Not entirely.

She shifts her gaze back to Shiloh, who's sitting with the family, and I don't know why. "Day by day, okay? Let's take the good while we have it and battle the bad if we have to."

It's the same philosophy that's gotten us through being our own version of normal as three parents taking care of Bridget for the past thirteen years. I can't argue without being a bigger dick than I've already been today.

Tomorrow's a new chance to be a dick, though. And it's not really "being a dick" when I'm trying to do my best for my family.

Shiloh and Ridhi got married when Bridge was two, a while after Shiloh and I got divorced, and yes, I truly do like seeing my ex-wife happy, because that makes my kid happy.

Or at least, not unnecessarily unhappy.

The idea of Bridget being subjected to the same scrutiny Shiloh got while growing up as the closeted bisexual kid of a Hollywood star?

Seeing things written about herself in newspapers that made her question who she was and her own self-worth?

And knowing that Shiloh's far from the only person to have ever had her life interrupted by publicity like that?

That does not make me happy.

I take a glance at the ceiling, which appears free of bats today, then look down at Shiloh, too, seated in the front-right-corner row of the theater, which fits maybe two hundred people. It's small. Intimate. And the acoustics are top notch.

"As I was saying," Estelle says with a glare at Carter as she stands center stage in dress pants, heels, a custom-fit blouse that probably cost more than my annual electric bill, and enough bling around her neck and hanging from her ears to make a pharaoh jealous, "since Whitney Anastasia in *Pink Gold* and I have so very much in common—"

"Didn't she stumble into Tickled Pink while on a road trip after losing a child?" the older gentleman of the family interrupts. Michael, Shiloh told me his name was. The father of the younger generation, son of the devil on the stage. Don't know anything about him.

Don't want to.

I've met enough of his kids to judge him. And yeah, Phoebe is the only one I've truly met, and she's enough.

Estelle's glare could solve global warming. "I *have* lost a child."

"George Lightly isn't dead," Ridhi whispers to me. "He's in prison for tax fraud."

I grunt. Not much else to say about that.

"*Gave up* on your child," Michael throws back. "And you didn't order *his* kids to come here, when they're much worse. How's that helping your soul?"

Estelle does that thing with her eyebrow that Phoebe tried to do to me not an hour ago. "God doesn't believe in lost causes, dear, and that cause is *clearly* lost. Take this for the opportunity it is for *you*."

"Do we have to watch that awful movie again?" the middle-aged woman asks. Phoebe's mother, I presume, since no one else appears to be the right age. She's sitting nearest the back of the theater, and we can see her trying to connect to the internet on her phone.

"Once we get this place cleaned up and a new projector installed in here, yes," Estelle replies. "In the meantime, I've invited Shiloh Denning to share a few words with us. Her mother was Ella Denning, executive producer and star of *Pink Gold*. Welcome, Shiloh."

Estelle turns and does a rich-lady clap in my ex-wife's direction, glaring at the rest of her family until they all start clapping delicately too.

Shiloh shoots a look at us in the booth. Lights are out in here, so she can't see us, but she undoubtedly knows we're here. Question isn't *if* we're here. Question is how many of us there are.

She turns a smile that looks like her own mother's to the Lightly family. "We're so glad to have you here in Tickled Pink. We were founded as a logging town in the 1840s, and our biggest claim to fame, as I'm sure Estelle has mentioned, is that my mother was born here, which is why *Pink Gold* was filmed here as well. She worked closely with the scriptwriters to make sure Tickled Pink was captured accurately, and we had a run when I was little when tourists would—"

Carter Lightly yawns loudly.

Estelle Lightly uses her eyeballs to grind him into a paste. "Pay attention. You need this most."

"Nobody cares about some prehistoric movie," he replies.

Shiloh smiles brightly at him. "We figured that out quickly when the postpremiere crowds died away and left us with a Ferris wheel that we couldn't afford to finish instead of visitors sticking around to turn us into the next Hershey, Pennsylvania, or Wamego, Kansas. You know, home of *The Wizard of Oz*? And that's an excellent example of how you never know exactly what life will throw at you. My mother used to say all the time—"

"That Tickled Pink is the path to heaven," Estelle interrupts.

"'Tickled Pink can show you the path to heaven,'" Willie Wayne corrects softly on Ridhi's other side. "Can't even get the quote right."

Can't see Shiloh's nostrils flaring, but I'd bet they are. She doesn't have a lot of patience for tourists who don't respect the spirit of Tickled Pink, either, even if she's more open to having them back to help the local economy. "Actually, I was going to quote another of her favorite sayings. 'It's not what life gives you but what you give back.'"

Estelle nods. "Life's thrown me for a loop, and I intend to loop the hell out of that life. Quite literally. Starting with improving each and every one of you, whom I've clearly failed."

"Is she planning on making them play on our snowshoe baseball team as part of their journey?" I murmur to Ridhi.

She turns a horrified stare on me. "There isn't a snowball's chance in hell that we're letting those prissy socialites mess up our record. We want to win."

"Against Deer Drop, yeah. The other teams? Standing room only, you and Anya would sell out of cream puffs and cupcakes, and we might make enough in side bets about who'll face-plant first to do the roads *and* the bridge."

"Plus we'd get to see them play snowshoe baseball," Willie Wayne agrees.

"And how do you plan on getting Estelle Lightly's buy-in on that?" Ridhi asks. "Whitney Anastasia didn't play snowshoe baseball in *Pink Gold*."

For the first time since Phoebe Lightly tried that eyebrow thing on me, I'm grinning again. "Pretty sure if flattery doesn't work, telling her we're shorthanded and also in need of a manager will."

"Shiloh's right. You're awful."

Willie Wayne grins at me. "Awful, maybe, but not wrong."

"And how are you going to explain to Bridget that you're replacing her?" Ridhi asks.

"She's fifteen. She has lots of years to play manager."

Estelle's spelling out her family's transgressions while Shiloh keeps shooting more and more desperate looks our way.

Her mother might've worked in Hollywood for a while, but she was one of the most honest, kind, and *real* people I've ever met. She walked away from her career when the tabloids started attacking Shiloh, and to her dying day, she insisted her only regret was not doing it sooner.

Margot Lightly lifts a hand. "Could we please get on with the torture? You can't finish what you don't start. Also, I work best with a mimosa."

Octavia—Tavi, according to Bridget—has done nothing but take selfies of herself and her dog this entire time. Carter, Estelle's only grandson, is still slouching like the one-hit wonder Bridget tells me he is. "His stage name is Carter Hardly," she mentioned with an eye roll last night. "He was trying for a play on Lightly and has no idea how stupidly ironic his name is."

"No mimosas until you've improved your soul," Estelle tells Margot.

"My soul is just fine."

"You blackmailed Berta Svendali into picking a god-awful spokes-person for her perfume line."

"That was for her own good. If she'd used a better spokesperson, that horrid scent would've been all over Manhattan, and her reputation would've been ruined."

"That was for *Tavi's* good, since it launched her reputation as an influencer. And yours. And don't get me started on you stealing Magnus Ricardo's shoe design."

"Back off, Mother," Michael Lightly says. So apparently he *does* stick up for his wife. Didn't see that coming. "We all know where we got all our worst qualities from. How about you fix *you* first and then see how much that fixes the rest of us?"

"Oh, shall we talk about your indiscretions?" Estelle replies. "Or about your lack of a record of doing real work for the family company? I should take your last twenty years' worth of pay out of your trust fund."

"This is better than that last episode of *Lola's Tiny House*," Willie Wayne whispers.

"Gigi, we have our dysfunctions, but we still love each other, and *that* has to count for, like, *so much* when it comes to staying out of hell." Tavi pauses long enough in snapping selfies to lift her dog and make it talk for her. "There's nothing I'd change about our family."

"Except for us to be related to other people," Carter mutters.

"Other people with trust funds?" Phoebe asks him. "Or were you planning to get an actual job?"

"Family game night," Estelle says. "Yes, we'll add that to the list. We need to experience this family-game-night thing. 'The family that games together dances through the heavenly gates together.'"

"'The family that *came* together,'" Willie Wayne mutters. "And it's 'danced in joy together,' and it's about found family, not biological family. She's ruining the movie."

"She's also bringing a crap ton of cash into Tickled Pink," Ridhi says.

Money money money. I shove a frustrated hand over my hair. "If this is just about the money—"

"Shove it, Teague." Ridhi pins me with the same look she gave me when Shiloh told me to get goats. "It's not about a onetime cash infusion. You know what an increase in tourism, even a small increase, could do for us? You can quit fighting off all those cookie-cutter subdivision developers trying to creep in from Deer Drop. Could probably even stop showing houses in Deer Drop and sell a few here instead. Get a bigger herd of goats. Imani and Dante could fix up the Pearly Gates Inn. Patrice could run the spa full-time again. We'll finally be able to afford to tear down that damn Ferris wheel."

My nose twitches.

Once I got over the shock of Shiloh telling me she was pregnant, the first thing I wanted to do was finish that Ferris wheel so I could take my kid on a ride.

Now, Bridget's fifteen, and an old fifteen at that—she was born thirty-two, swear she was—and the Ferris wheel can't be "finished."

What's there is too rusty under too many layers of wild overgrowth. It needs to be rebuilt.

"I hate to interrupt," Shiloh says below, cutting through another argument that's broken out amid the Lightly family, "but Estelle, having been on several renovation projects myself, I can safely say—"

Tavi lifts the dog and makes it talk for her again. "Excuse me, but we're not *actually* cleaning up this school building, are we?"

"Yes, Octavia, we are 'getting our hands dirty,'" Estelle says. "'One cannot get clean without first getting dirty.'"

Willie Wayne groans. *"That is not the quote."*

"We most certainly *are not*." Margot rises from her seat and grabs her handbag. "Estelle, I have a fashion empire to run. I'm a good person. I donate *hundreds* of clutches and slingbacks to charity every year—"

"Mismatches and factory rejects," Estelle interrupts. "And you don't donate them. You have Octavia give them away as a marketing sham."

"—*and* I personally funded a pet shelter—"

"That was a dog mill, dear, and you used *my* money to run it."

"—and I also serve food at a community food bank *every* Christmas."

"You attend a gala at the Bergamot Club every year with your personal assistant standing in at the food bank." She crosses her arms over her chest, lifting her chin and frowning at her entire family. "Community service is next to godliness. It's time we engage with the masses and grace the lowly with our commitment to them."

"It's not actually *community* service if we're doing it for our own good," Phoebe says. "How does it benefit the community for us to sleep in a building free of dead birds and rodents? If we really wanted to be better people, we'd live like paupers and see how much we like it. Whitney Anastasia lived in a *small* building."

"Because when we've become better people and departed this quaint little slice of heaven, I'm donating the building back to the community to be used as the Estelle Lightly Memorial Exhibit. You could say I'm making an improvement over the original screenplay."

Carter makes a grumbling noise, finishing with an explosion noise and a sweep of his hands.

"Carter's right," Michael says. "You'd do the community a greater service if you tore it down."

None of them agree with Phoebe's suggestion that they should live like paupers.

Suspect she probably knew that wouldn't fly.

Tavi pauses in her selfies to point her phone at her brother. "I saw a building like this when I was in Ireland having a girls' weekend with Alessandra Garofano, except it was actually a castle, and there was ivy growing all up the sides, and it was bigger, and there wasn't concrete stamped with gender restrictions above the outside entryways, and there were staff to bring me grilled tomatoes in bed. And then make my bed. And provide turndown service. And book our spa services for us. There's potential. Probably. Maybe."

"Who's Alessandra Garofano?" Willie Wayne whispers to Ridhi.

"Some TikTok star living off a trust fund," Ridhi whispers back. "Bridget's obsessed."

I lift a brow. "*Bridget* is obsessed? Just Bridget?"

She shushes me.

"We are *not* tearing down the future site of the Estelle Lightly Memorial Exhibit," Estelle announces. "Rather, we'll be participating in this community as though we live in a village. Just like Whitney Anastasia did when she learned to buy baked goods from her neighbor to take to other people's houses for family dinners."

"She learned to bake herself." Willie Wayne snorts. "I can't listen to this anymore."

"Um, excuse me?" Tavi lifts a hand. Her dog barks at the same time. "Shh, Pebbles, Mommy's talking. Yes. Excuse me, Gigi. I lived in a Malawian village for three months once."

Willie Wayne pauses on his way out the door, like he knows things are about to get good again.

"You lived in a five-star hotel a day's drive from a Malawian village," Carter says.

"*But I went there.* And it was hard, Carter. You have *no idea* what a five-star hotel is like in Malawi. It's not like the Plaza. And *they didn't have air-conditioning in the village.*"

"We don't have air-conditioning here either," Estelle says dryly. "And if you would *please* let me finish, I was *going* to say that the lowly citizens of this small town have agreed to demonstrate how community works by helping us clean out the larger messes inside the building. Not that any of them have anything better to do, but one can only assume they won't actually enjoy it either. We're helping *them* get to heaven as well."

Carter sits straighter and eyeballs Shiloh. "We get to be management and boss you around."

"No, you get to get your hands dirty," she replies.

He jerks his chin at her. "I'll get *you* dirty."

"I might be bisexual, but I do have taste, and I don't like to throw up in my mouth this early in the morning. Also, I'm married."

"Oh, *snap*," Ridhi says.

Willie Wayne makes a silent tick mark in the air.

My gaze drifts to Phoebe. She's frowning, arms crossed, still in the same outfit she wore to pull herself up Bridget's elevator, and she's staring at Estelle like she's waiting for the catch. "You're allowing us to have help?"

"Yes, Phoebe."

"And that doesn't break your principles or stray too far from the plot?"

Estelle claps her hands in what I'd call glee on any other woman. On her, it's mildly terrifying. "Our *help* is the management. They get to tell *us* what to do. And at the end of the day . . ." She pauses, making sure her whole family is watching. "At the end of the day, our helpers will give us *report cards*."

"Estelle, is that honestly necessary?" Margot says.

"There's even a spot on the report cards for marking down how many bribes you each offered someone else to do your work for you. Bribery will earn you attic duties, my darlings, and undoubtedly a straight trip to hell if you happen to ingest poisoned food while we're in this backwoods town. Don't do it."

Phoebe's frown is growing. "Are you working too?"

"Of the two of us, dear, I do believe I'm far more acquainted with the consequences of not doing the hard work."

Phoebe's cheeks flush.

"Oh, snap, again," Ridhi whispers.

"Yep," Willie Wayne says. "Way better than *Lola's Tiny House*."

"Shiloh, please call the townsfolk," Estelle says. "It's time to pair up and rid the hallways and classrooms of those animal carcasses and live rodents."

"Tell me Abe's coming in," I say to Ridhi.

Willie Wayne snorts. "Already came through while Estelle wasn't looking. You think any of us are dumb enough to give her a reason to sue the town for rat bites when she realizes this was a bad idea? He got the bats rehomed too. Family don't have any clue how easy they're gonna actually have it."

"Relatively speaking." Ridhi's smirking.

And now I'm catching on. "How many deer carcasses did you pull out of the woods and plant in here before their tour yesterday?"

"Only the one."

"Had it checked for disease first," Willie Wayne adds.

"Don't make that face, Teague." Ridhi wrinkles her nose at me. "If they were gonna wimp out, we wanted them to wimp out on the first day before we got our hopes up."

Willie Wayne rocks on his heels in glee. "Think of it like an initiation."

"Rite of passage," Ridhi agrees with a nod.

"A first-class welcome."

"A test of what they're made of."

"They stick it out and live here, yeah, I'll have mad respect for that."

"I have fifty bucks on Carter bailing first, though." Ridhi grins. "He got drunk at Ladyfingers last night and told everyone this town has no vibe for his creativity."

I'd bet every dime I have that Carter Lightly will be the last to bail, no matter how much I want Ridhi to be right, because he seems like the one that needs his trust fund the most.

Unless I can find a reason to encourage him to go first.

"Friends?" Shiloh calls. "Come on out. It's time."

"For Tickled Pink," Ridhi says, lifting an invisible champagne flute.

I clink with my own imaginary flute. "Let's do this."

She's completely unaware that my "this" is making sure Estelle Lightly leaves with her family as soon as humanly possible, but that's okay.

In the meantime, we're getting a cleaner school and a *small* amount of attention.

I can handle this.

So long as they leave *soon*.

Chapter 6

Phoebe

I get stuck with Carter and some local named Ridhi for cleanup duty, and we're assigned the locker rooms.

The locker rooms.

Gigi points me down the dank hallway outside the theater. "It's one floor down and to your right. Best give it your all, Phoebe. Whoever gets highest marks on their chores today gets first choice of bedrooms."

Don't talk back. Don't talk back. Don't—screw it. What more can she *actually* do to me? "What is this, *The Lightly Family Reality Show*? Are the cameras coming next?"

"The landfill for reality television trash is already overflowing, dear, and we're trying to be more ecologically sound. Step two in being a better person. Less trash, more value. Did you miss the part of the movie where Whitney Anastasia learned to recycle? Of course you did. Blink and you miss it, which is what you *should've* said to the *Post* if you were going to insist on insulting Mr. Barrington's member. Ridhi will get you a gas mask and rubber gloves."

There's irony in that statement—rubber gloves aren't recyclable, and I have my doubts about the gas mask, too—but I know better than to point it out.

Especially since this Ridhi person is kissing my grandmother's ass. "My pleasure, Mrs. Lightly."

"Thank you, Ridhi."

Ridhi.

Ridhi.

I know that name.

Why do I know that name?

Ridhi looks me up and down. She's a little shorter than me, with brown skin, hair tucked back in a bun, lines at the corners of her eyes that I'd guess put her five to ten years older than I am, and lips twitching in what I sincerely hope is not amusement. "Thrift shop two blocks over might have some plain old Levis, and the Pink Box is running a sale on *Pink Gold* T-shirts. I won't mark you down if you take fifteen minutes to change and get back. Assuming you found yourself some coffee and can operate like a functional human being now?"

Ridhi.

From the café. The one who'll spit in my food.

Wonderful.

"I like pink boxes," Carter says with a brow wiggle.

I refrain from gagging but just barely. "I did *not* miss you."

Now Ridhi's actually smiling.

Bad omen.

I try smiling back. "Ridhi. You work with Anna at the Europa Café."

"My sister, *Anya*, at Café *Nirvana*."

Dammit. "Right. Bernadette's your niece?"

"*Bridget* is my *stepdaughter*."

Carter snorts and tosses his shaggy hair. "Nice, *Phenelope*."

"Shut up, *Hardly*." Truly *did not* miss him while he was on his tour.

And that's a tour of the world to get supposed inspiration, *not* an actual concert tour.

Ridhi seems amused by us. At least she's not hiding it like Teague Miller, who had best be plotting ways to show Gigi the worst that Tickled Pink has to offer, or I'll have to show him the worst of what Manhattan transplanted to Tickled Pink has to offer.

"What'd you do to irritate your grandmother?" she asks. "Locker room has to be the worst of all the areas in the school to clean."

"Phoebe tried to let her die when she choked," Carter offers.

"As opposed to trying to suck the life out of her by being the worst kind of leech," I reply. "*You* got locker room duty too."

"Fighting on the job . . . ," Ridhi murmurs as she lifts her clipboard. *Dammit.*

"Fifteen minutes?" I say to her.

She looks me up and down again. "Fifteen minutes."

"I'll see you in the locker room."

Hello, my name is Phoebe Lightly, and I've never met a challenge I wouldn't take or obliterate in my own way.

I'm three minutes late getting back to the locker room, but I have a very good reason.

And that reason is the bakery bag and to-go mug in my hand. I smile the smile my mother taught me before my first beauty pageant when I was four, before Tavi took over as pageant queen of the family, as I approach Ridhi in the locker room. "Oatcakes and hot—*oh my God*, what is that *smell?*"

I truly am gagging now as I clap a hand over my mouth, still dangling the bakery bag, which is suddenly the worst idea *ever*.

Who could eat anything here?

Ridhi hands me a face mask and rubber gloves. "That's the smell of eighty years' worth of pubescent boys doing what pubescent boys do in locker rooms. Wait until we get it wet and really dig in."

Carter's nowhere in sight, though there are a few more people with terrible fashion taste standing between the lockers and the shower area now.

Locals, undoubtedly. More people whose names I'll screw up.

Teague is not among them, and it bothers me. I'd like to know where he is.

I'm not entirely certain he won't stab me in the back and try to chase *me* out of town before the rest of the family.

"Locker area or showers?" Ridhi asks me.

"Locker area. I volunteer to clean out the lockers." I cannot believe those words are tumbling out of my mouth, but they are.

Would I rather I'd already found a way to convince Gigi that this entire idea is ridiculous?

Yes.

But I haven't, so for now, I'll play her game.

I'll play her game so well she'll have no choice but to admit I've passed my good-person test with flying colors and release me to go back to my real life.

Preferably as soon as possible.

And that's why I'm opening locker after locker along the far wall, tossing out petrified gym socks and copies of *Playboy* magazine and notes about which teachers these teenage perverts wanted to bang while townsfolk whose names I've already forgotten check the wiring and start shopping lists with things like *fluorescent bulbs* and *boards for the broken windows* and *radon and carbon monoxide test kits*.

Carter's still missing.

We still have to clean the showers, because they're apparently the *only* showers in the building.

Group showers.

In the locker room.

"Can you please add shower curtains and separators to that shopping list?" I call to Selma or Terri Lou or whoever that is.

"We'll put it on the list to run past your grandmother," Ridhi replies.

I huff to myself as an odd *wwoooooooooo-oooo* floats through the air, followed by a muttered *damn kids ain't got no respect for a clean floor.*

No one else seems to notice.

It happens again—the *woo*, this one followed with *yeah, yeah, get the mop*, and I pause and tilt my head, trying to identify the source.

"Back to work, Ms. Lightly."

"Where's Carter?"

"Girls' locker room. He annoyed me. It's worse."

"It's *worse*? The girls' locker room is *worse*?"

"School had to shut down unexpectedly a week early the year we closed this building for good, and it meant the kids weren't allowed back in to do a final clean-out of the lockers. Nobody ever got around to it, matter of fact. He's hip deep in tampons and boy band posters."

I stop and study her more closely. Is it—do I—do I actually want to *hug* her?

And cackle with her?

I think I do.

But before my lips can fully spread in a smile, it happens once more.

The weird, unidentifiable, ghostly noise.

But this time, it's an *aaaarrrrrrgggghhhhh.*

Moment over, and I'm struggling not to roll my eyes.

Don't make that face, dear. It makes you look so plebeian.

Thanks, Gigi.

"Very funny, Carter," I yell toward the air duct that seems to be the source of the noise.

"That's not your brother," Steve or Harry or Bob, or whoever is following after me with disinfectant spray, says. "That's Floyd."

"Floyd?"

"Tickled Pink Floyd," Anna-Selma-whoever replies solemnly. "Not Deer Drop Floyd."

"Deer Drop Floyd stole Ridhi's family's coconut-pudding recipe," Steve-Harry-Bob tells me. "Tickled Pink Floyd was the janitor here back in the day. Still sticks around, you know?"

My eyeball is not twitching.

It's not.

I'm not moving into a haunted school with my entire family, who are all self-absorbed trust fund babies who don't understand the value of hard work, and I'm not living in a place without cell service and tailors and massage therapists and personal chefs, and this will not last the full year.

It can't.

It seriously *cannot*.

I fling open the next locker, and an army of small, furry, rabid, miniature gray pandas hisses and spills out.

I scream.

Steve-Harry-Bob screams.

"Are you kidding me?" Ridhi mutters. She digs her phone out of her pocket, dials a number, and while I dive behind her, cowering while the other locals grab brooms and try to corral the raccoons, she starts talking. "Abe? Locker room. Missed a couple. Yeah, looks like Big Bertha wasn't ready to let the kits brave the great outdoors."

"Big Bertha?" I gasp.

More locals start poking their heads in, including one Mr. Teague Miller.

"It was just Big Bertha," Steve-Harry-Bob calls to them. "Sorry for the scream. Didn't recognize her. Plus, Phoebe screamed first. Didn't want her to feel lonely."

"Ah." Teague nods. "Big Bertha. Makes sense."

"You named a raccoon Big Bertha?" I'm shrieking. I'm shrieking, and I can't stop, and—*"Oh my God, your phone works?"*

Ridhi hangs up, shoves her phone back in her pocket, and makes a *duh* face at me. "We *do* have electricity up here in the backwoods."

"But—but—I can't get a signal."

"Lightning took out the cell tower last month. We're all on Wi-Fi."

"There's Wi-Fi?"

She smirks. "Yes, Miss Priss. Tickled Pink has town-wide Wi-Fi."

"I'll give you ten thousand dollars if you give me the password."

"Your grandmother's offered to donate a million dollars to seed a town scholarship fund if we don't."

That ruthless, two-faced harpy.

Big Bertha hisses at me, and I squeal and dash for the door.

I quit.

I quit. That's it.

I can't do this.

I can't— *"Oof."*

I can't get out of this godforsaken building.

There's a giant wall of a man in my way.

A giant wall of a man who *does* smell a little like lemon-meringue pie, which has never been more appealing to me in my life, and *that* pisses me off on a new level.

"Just can't resist me, can you, Ms. Lightly?" Teague Miller says in that subtle drawl.

I momentarily consider sticking a spiked heel down on his shoe before I remember I tossed them in a bag that I left in the front hall, along with my sweat-stained Chanel skirt, after I stripped and changed in the café's restroom when I stopped to get Ridhi the worthless peace offering.

Peace offering.

Bribe.

Whatever.

"Where's my grandmother?" I ask.

"Right here, Phoebe." Gigi turns the corner and steps into the short hallway outside the locker room, all of it lit with sunshine streaming through dirty windows and illuminating more plumes of dust than I have ever seen in my entire life, and I once witnessed a dust storm in the Sahara. "Coming for you, actually. I have a separate assignment just for you. Come, come. We can talk in the library."

Teague's still holding my arm, keeping me steady after I barreled into him.

He smirks down at me, and this time, I get the full effect of his bright hazel eyes too. "Good luck, Ms. Lightly. And remember—that which doesn't kill us makes for a great story later for our enemies."

Chapter 7

Teague

There's nothing like fresh-grilled walleye under the stars on a warm night in late spring, but tonight, my evening ritual is lacking.

Probably because there's a woman picking her way through my goat field.

Again.

"Mr. Miller?" Phoebe Lightly hisses.

I crack the top on a False Hope pale ale and pretend I don't hear her. Walleye's getting cold, and if I'm not eating with Bridget, I like to eat in peace.

"Mr. Miller?"

Nope. Don't hear her.

"Mr. Miller, I *will* climb this tree if you don't answer me."

Dammit. She probably would.

"And here I was thinking I wouldn't get a show with my dinner."

She heaves a heavy sigh, and for the first time since Estelle Lightly showed up in my town announcing her intentions to bring her family of socialite miscreants here to make them into "good people," I feel a twinge of something I didn't expect.

Actual sympathy for a spoiled rich woman.

Is it possible for a sigh to sound exhausted?

How is she still upright? Last I saw, she was scrubbing the boys' locker room shower with a vengeance while muttering to herself.

"Mr. Miller, I've battled through a field of goats and mosquitoes to get here, and I would *very* much like if you would send down the elevator." She punctuates her sentence with a slapping noise.

Undoubtedly another mosquito.

Best thing about my house?

Mosquitoes don't come as high as my lowest deck. They like it closer to the ground.

Heights are nature's mosquito repellent.

"Goats are only back no thanks to you," I point out. "Took me an hour to find the last three. Better not have let them out again."

"Perhaps you could allow a woman to acclimate to your hell jungle before insisting she know how to handle feral animals. And all of your goats are here. I climbed the damn fence so I wouldn't let a single one out. Happy now?"

There's nothing feral about my goats. The mosquitoes, yes. Goats, no.

Phoebe Lightly?

Yeah, she's probably hiding a feral side.

Not tonight, though.

Tonight, she's coming back to see me when by all rights she should be passed out dead on her floor after all the work she did at the school today.

Fine.

I'm curious if she's on drugs or if she's truly that stubborn.

Or superhuman.

I drop my feet off the balcony, set aside my fish, flip on the lone outdoor light, and take the steps down two floors to send her Bridget's elevator. "Don't make me regret this."

"I already regret it enough for both of us."

There's the distinct sound of skin slapping skin again, then the clink of the elevator latch shutting, followed by a grunt.

I pinch my eyes shut and heave a sigh of my own. "Hold tight."

Four quick yanks on the pulley system later, there's Phoebe Lightly, arms braced, legs braced, eyes wide as the elevator sways at the first deck level. She's in filthy jeans and a stained *Pink Gold* T-shirt, her hair falling out of a ponytail, and the makeup she started the day with is completely gone. Or maybe the soft yellow glow of my night lighting makes her look like she's not wearing makeup. "Do you just leave this thing on the ground when you go places during the day?"

"No." I smirk. "I use the stairs."

She silently mouths my words back to me, brow furrowed, until it sinks in. *"There are steps?"*

My goats all answer with bleats of *Shut up, lady, it's bedtime.*

And I find a real smile for the socialite lady boss, which I hide by turning back to the stairwell taking me up to my dining balcony.

Of course she didn't notice the steps.

They're across the bridge to the smaller tree house that Bridget uses when she wants a quiet place to do her homework, and where I usually leave my fishing gear so it doesn't stink up my main house.

Helps that the natural camouflage works well out here. Hides my garage and goat barn too. "What brings you by to disturb my dinner tonight?"

"It's doomed. Gigi's not giving this up. She didn't even flinch at the raccoons. We passed a rat on the street in the city once, and she practically called in the National Guard, but today, she just stood there laughing at your raccoons. No, not just standing there and laughing. She *took pictures*. And then she *made a meme* with the pictures. She thought *Be as happy as a raccoon in a gym locker* was a meme-worthy phrase, and now she's talking about having it printed and framed outside every classroom in the school and making *Big Bertha* our family

71

mascot." She hustles along after me with nary a whimper, but I do catch a subtle grunt or two when she turns at the first landing.

"Huh. Probably should've tried to catch a wild one instead of Big Bertha to put in there then. Thought the kits would be a nice touch."

"You planted them there on purpose?"

Every time she shrieks, my goats bleat back, and this time, a few bats take off too. An owl or two call in to check on us too.

"It's just Phoebe," I call back in answer to the *whoo, whoo*s.

"Oh my God, are we a reverse Cinderella? Do you keep mice in here too? Where's your evil stepfather and stepbrothers?"

That almost makes me twitch. "Tavi's come to Tickled Pink to save me, has she? The princess to my Cinderfella?"

"Yes, she's going to take pictures of you and post them all over social media until your horrific existence in this ridiculous Peter Pan tree house is saved by the kindness of strangers donating to build you a real house."

Despite the sarcasm dripping from her words, every muscle in my body tenses and my balls threaten to shrink back into my body. I turn the final corner on the outer stairwell and make myself take a deep breath before I answer. "She's claiming us publicly? She's posting pictures from Tickled Pink?"

"I have no idea. It's not on brand, so probably not. Plus, do you know what you need to post pictures on the internet? *You need access to the internet.* Can I borrow your Wi-Fi? I swear I'm only up to a minimal amount of bad."

"She needs waivers or something to use images of all of us." I kill the lights again, sink into my chair, prop my feet up like I'm not suddenly sweating, ignore her request for my Wi-Fi, and grab my fish, which is rapidly cooling.

Phoebe audibly sniffs. "Oh my God, that smells amazing. We had to have veggie burgers for dinner from that bar, and I don't think they knew how to make veggie burgers, or else Tavi's vegan diet has completely killed her taste buds, because she actually called them delicious, and she ate them without a bun since the bun *had sugar* in it."

Dammit. I need to hear that her sister won't post pictures of all of us little unimportant people all over her Tikstagram or whatever it is.

But I can't push the issue with Phoebe without clueing her in to the fact that I have more reasons for not wanting her family here than that they're annoying. Give her a chicken leg, she'll take the whole damn farm.

I flake off a bite of fish, already plotting the best way to scare the shit out of Tavi Lightly first thing in the morning over what I'll do if she posts a single picture of anyone here without permission. "Tastes good too. Talk. What do you want?"

She slumps into the chair, pitches forward, and drops her head between her knees.

I think.

Hard to see more than just her outline with things this dark.

"Even if we convince her to leave here, I won't get my job back."

"Ah. You've realized *your* existence is futile and need someone to confirm it for you."

"Very funny."

I take another bite of fish and gaze out at the night sky, visible through the threaded branches of the red pines around my house. "So quit. You have an education. You have experience. You clearly have a solid work ethic, much as it pains me to admit it. You can find a new job."

She mutters something to the floor.

"I don't speak sullen teenager, Phoebe. You're going to have to enunciate."

I expect to feel a glare when she straightens and leans back in my deck chair.

Instead, she tips her head back like she's planning on falling asleep right there. "Remington Lightly is part of my heritage. It's who I am. I've known since before I could walk that one day, I'd be the first woman in my family to follow in my great-grandfather's footsteps and run the entire company. Actually, the next Lightly after him to run the company, period."

"But is that what you want?"

"Yes. Clearly."

"Or are you afraid of what would happen if you didn't have family money to fall back on?"

"*This is what I want*, Teague. And this isn't about me. Not fully. It's also about giving you back your town without my family upending everything so you can milk your goats and catch your fish and do whatever else it is you do on a normal day when you're not selling condemned real estate or planting raccoons in lockers to scare the ever-loving hell out of me."

Is she arguing in her sleep? The outline of her chest is rising and falling steadily under the baggy T-shirt that she was still wearing when I pulled her up into the tree house.

"Scaring the hell out of you was a nice bonus," I agree. "Can't wait until tomorrow when you find out what I planted in the old chemistry lab."

"In other words, you've planted a stink bomb somewhere that is *not* the chemistry lab, so I should volunteer there for my next cleaning shift."

"Stink bombs are old school. What I have planned is much better."

I have nothing planned.

The high school itself is torture enough, and it really will be good for the community to have it fixed up.

Despite Estelle's stipulation that when she donates it back to the town, it forever becomes known as the Estelle Lightly Heritage Museum for Good.

Spent all day embellishing what she wanted to call it.

Lady clearly still needs a few lessons in humility herself.

"Did you attend high school in that building?" Phoebe asks.

"Nope."

"Why not?"

"I went away to *Peter Pan* boarding school."

She makes a noise that I'd call amused on any other woman.

Maybe she *is* amused. Maybe she has a sense of humor, and she's finally worn down enough to show it.

But admitting that would be akin to admitting there's something to like about her, and I can't have that.

I like my life here. It's quiet. Predictable. Safe. Bridget's here. Shiloh and Ridhi are family, too, even if it's supposed to be weird to be friends with my ex-wife and her spouse. Hell, the whole town is family.

That's the part I like best about *Pink Gold*.

The part where Whitney finds a true family that's not blood or money but *real*.

That's what I want to keep.

Rich people coming here and finding their souls? That *only* happens in the movies.

In real life, they come with snooty superficiality, judgment, and an unhealthy emphasis on the importance of their money. Bridget's already making more of a fuss about her hair and makeup, "in case Tavi wants to do selfies or whatever."

Next she'll be basing her self-worth on unachievable goals and unrealistic expectations set by people who are more adept at looking fabulous and put together than they're good at doing what actually matters.

Not to mention the stress that'll come if the paparazzi start poking their heads around here to watch the Lightly Train Wreck Show.

But sparring with Phoebe the past two days has been fun. Unexpectedly fun.

Not saying I'll miss her when I chase her and her family the hell out of my town, but I won't argue with taking the joy where I can while my life is temporarily disrupted.

Finding there's more to Phoebe Lightly than I thought there was?

It's a weird kind of joy. Like discovering that rock you've had in your shoe all day is actually your kid's lost favorite bead.

Sucks, but it's not as bad as it could be.

Phoebe could be completely intolerable instead of just *mostly* intolerable.

"You ever sleep under the stars?" I ask her.

"I fell asleep on the beach in the Hamptons once."

Of course.

She sighs again. "But security woke me up and made me go inside, so no, I have never slept under the stars a full night. And why would it even matter? You can't *see* the stars when you're sleeping. Your eyes are closed."

I peer through the trees again at the dark night sky dotted with billions of diamonds, then glance at my companion, who's either not looking or completely unimpressed.

Her loss.

She sighs once more, and I swear I can see her sinking deeper into the padded deck chair. One leg flops to the side. Her breath gets deeper.

It's like she's not sighing but slipping into a reluctant slumber.

And then she talks. Again. Is she physically incapable of turning herself off? "What sort of deal would I have to make with you to get the community Wi-Fi password so that I can make sure nothing's burning down back at work?"

"Depends. You asking for you, because you want to feel important, or are you asking because you left an actual problem without anyone trained to handle it while you're gone, and real people are in danger if you don't do something?"

She flops her head to the side so that her face is aimed in my direction. "Do you know what I like about you, Teague? I like that you think to ask that question. It's not about what my grandmother has ordered everyone else in the town to do. It's about the best outcome for all involved."

"Everyone else turned you down and I'm your last option, hm?"

"But no one else asked if there was an actual emergency. You're a very good person, Teague Miller. And I appreciate that."

I stifle a grin. She's good at this game, I'll give her that. "Know what happened to the last person who showered me with false flattery?"

"It is *not* false flattery. If I were lying, I'd tell you that you could be our next model for Remington Lightly's beard oil. Our Kangapoo-brand body-care line is expanding. Shh. Top secret. Also? If I'd been in charge when they launched Kangapoo, it would've been called something *entirely* different. I will never understand the people who buy a name like that, but enough of them do that management refuses to consider changing it, despite my best efforts. First thing I'm changing when I'm running the company."

"Aren't you supposed to be having family game night somewhere? Murdering one of your siblings over their refusal to give change in ones when you owe them rent in Monopoly?"

"Gigi's having a private meeting with my father, so the rest of us were dismissed. The Monopoly massacre has been postponed for another night. What do you mean, 'refusing to give change in ones'? Is that a thing? Does it help you win? If I had access to Wi-Fi, I could learn the rules and help my brother or sister utilize the loopholes to their best advantage so they could win instead of me."

"You realize it does no good to work hard to earn good-person points all day if you're going to lie about why you want internet access the minute your grandmother turns her back."

"My ex-boyfriend was attempting to blackmail me the last time we talked. If I don't reply to his threats, there's a very high chance he'll come hunt me down in person, and if you think *I'm* brutal, wait until you meet him."

I take my last bite of fish and shift my gaze to peer at her in the dark.

I don't know what's true and what's not with her. Her ex-boyfriend isn't my problem.

But there's a primitive beast stirring to life inside me.

Overprotective instincts for wanting to keep my family safe from the kind of ex-boyfriend Phoebe Lightly comes with.

Yep.

That's all it is.

No way I want to protect Phoebe herself. She can clearly handle anything life throws at her. She doesn't need a warrior leaping to her defense, no matter how human and breakable she seems tonight, both physically and emotionally.

It's a trap, I tell myself.

She's playing weak to appeal to my chivalrous side, which she assumes exists because I wear flannel, talk back to her, and have a beard.

There's no way Phoebe Lightly is weak in anything beyond possibly morals.

But I still ask. "Blackmailing you with what?"

She flops her head against the back of the chair so she's staring up at my overhang again. "Upper East Side life is eat or be eaten. Survival of the fittest. I like to survive. That doesn't make me a bad person. It makes me an achiever, playing within the rules of my own universe."

"Blackmailing you *with what?*"

"Oh, wow." She pulls herself straight. "You really can see the stars from here."

Discussing anything with her is hopeless. She won't tell me a damn thing she doesn't want me to know. So I nod to the stars. "Yeah. You can see the whole actual universe. Not just the Upper East Side."

She doesn't answer.

I set my plate aside and cut a glance at her profile again. She's sinking back into the seat, but slowly, like she's testing the view, seeing how far she can sit back before the overhang blocks the best of the night sky.

Like she's never seen stars before and wants to keep staring, but she's also bone tired.

Hell, I'm bone tired, and I didn't do half of what she did today.

Despite my initial impressions of her, she really does know how to do the hard work.

"Doesn't look like that on the beach in the Hamptons?" I ask her. "Or did you never actually look up?"

"Shh. Don't ruin it."

Now that, we can agree on.

I lean back myself, kick my feet up again, and let my eyes wander over the night sky.

Could go up to the roof.

Got a telescope up there. Straight view up all the way to the heavens. No overhang or scraggly red pine branches blocking nature's canvas.

But that would require moving.

And leaving Phoebe alone.

She's not bad company when she's keeping her mouth shut.

But more, I don't want her snooping in my house.

The minutes stretch on, and eventually, I realize she's not gazing in wonder at the stars anymore.

Nope.

Phoebe Lightly, headstrong, arrogant, out-of-place, take-no-prisoners boss lady, is snoring softly in my deck chair.

I stare at her in the darkness. I can only make out her profile, but I still stare.

She's pretty in her own way. I'll give her that. Probably has a gym membership to keep her naturally slender body in its original shape. Doesn't need the YouTube videos on makeup that Bridget's always watching to know how to put her face on. Has drive. A person can't *not* have drive and survive a place like Manhattan.

Yeah, she's right. I've watched enough *Gossip Girl*—two episodes, for the record—to know that.

But the thing that keeps giving me pause?

She made me promise not to hurt her grandmother.

Take Estelle Lightly's money and name away, and she'd be a public nuisance.

Or possibly that schoolteacher everyone was terrified of in sixth grade.

But there was a raw threat in Phoebe's *do not hurt my grandmother* this morning.

She cares. She cares about someone other than herself. And isn't that the first step in being a good person? Who would Phoebe Lightly be if you took *her* money and name away?

Hell.

There I go.

I'm doing it.

I'm starting to believe in the damn movie, too, all because someone new turned up in town, lost but unafraid of the work to get through it.

"You know better," I mutter to myself.

She doesn't stir.

So I do what anyone who's a good person would do in my situation, and I let her be. Even if I don't want her here. Even if everything she stands for is everything I've avoided my entire adult life.

She's still a person. She worked hard.

She's earned her peace.

For tonight, anyway.

Chapter 8

Phoebe

Teague Miller is a mystery.

Mr. Grumpy Lumberjack covered me with a wool blanket and let me sleep on his tree house deck under the stars, and now he's providing me with the best cup of coffee to hit my lips in my entire life.

Not that he's aware he's providing me with coffee.

I'm helping myself, since I don't know where he is. The door into his secret lair was unlocked, and this level just happens to have a working kitchen with a coffeepot that I figured out all on my own.

If he didn't want me in his private areas, he would've locked the door to keep my cranky bones and stiff muscles from getting inside so easily.

Actually, there might not be a lock on the door. I wonder if that's because the lower levels lock? Something tells me it's not because he doesn't care about his privacy.

As soon as the caffeine makes its way through my system, I'm investigating the hell out of this little house in the trees.

Eat your heart out, Lola Minelli.

This tiny house is actually charming.

In addition to the galley kitchen with the life-giving coffee maker, there's a small dining nook and an alcove with a desk on this level. The floor is warm under my bare feet—I had to ditch the *Pink Gold* shoes I grabbed at the Pink Box because they were rubbing my Achilles tendon wrong and leaving a blister—and there's also an open hatch with a ladder leaning down to the floor below, along with another hatch and ladder across the room leading to another story above.

Eventually I'll get there, but right now, I'm utterly fascinated by the wall of pictures over the dining room table set for two.

There's one of Teague holding a baby wrapped in blue in a hospital. Another of Teague with a little boy on his shoulders at an aquarium. Teague and Sherry—no, *Shiloh*—swinging a slightly older little boy between them with elephants in the background, like they're at a zoo. The little boy by himself in a formal picture, wearing a blue graduation cap with *Kindergarten Bound!* scrawled across his gown, his brown hair thick and peeking out from under the cap.

The little boy with his hair to his shoulders, laughing over a bowl of ice cream.

The same face, a little older still, wearing a flowery dress and Easter bonnet and a larger smile than should fit on his face.

Until that little face morphs into the same face that was smirking at me and fawning over Tavi and sassing her aunt Anya at the café yesterday morning.

"What are you doing?"

Oh, good. Cranky Teague has reentered the building. I start to gesture to his wall with my coffee mug—this one a custom mug printed with Bridget's smiling face over bubbly letters spelling out *I heart my dad*, which was one more surprise about Teague Miller this morning before I processed the wall of photos here—but I glance over my shoulder, find half-naked Teague glowering at me with all those pecs and biceps and abs tight and ready for battle, and I slosh hot coffee all over my hand as my eyes try to drink in the sight of him all at once. He's like

Lumberjack Thor, and I like it way more than I should. "*Ow!* Dammit. Ow. Hi. Good morning. I'm snooping. There's coffee for you, by the way. I made a full pot."

I lick at my hand, sucking the life juice off instead of wasting it by finding a towel, while he stands there radiating so much anger that he can't seem to find his voice.

Do I *really* have to pull out the Lightly brow this early in the morning? "If you didn't want me in here, you could've locked the door. Or kicked me out last night. I assume you're assuming I'll be in trouble for not sleeping at the school? Sorry to disappoint, but Gigi let us get rooms at the motel again last night. Even she doesn't want us dying of mold inhalation before the inspection she's agreed to, probably because I convinced her it was her idea to not get another notch on her going-to-hell checklist by murdering her family with lung poisoning. I'll be in trouble for not sleeping at the motel, yes, but it's not as bad as not sleeping at the school."

I wish I could see his jaw behind that beard. I want to know if it's as cut as the rest of him. And if I'm making it tic.

Even if he had steam coming out his nose, it would probably get immediately swallowed into his mustache, so I couldn't see that either.

"Sleeping on my deck was not an invitation to come into my house."

"Afraid I'll find the dead bodies in your closets? Don't worry, Teague. I have enough of my own that I won't say a word."

His gaze flits to the wall over the dining room table, then back to me.

A wave of heat washes through my chest.

I know what he's saying.

I don't trust you to be good to my kid.

I wouldn't trust me either.

And maybe that's a sign that I, Phoebe Lightly, actually *do* have room for improvement. I swallow one more gulp of coffee and pretend his angry scrutiny isn't getting to me. "You can dial down the fury, Mr. Overprotective. Bridget might not be my favorite person in town, but that's only because she has Tavi-worship problems, and also, none of you in this town will ever be my favorite. I don't care what her name is or what gender she identifies as."

His nostrils flare like he doesn't believe me, which isn't a problem we'll solve this morning. Actions speak louder than words and all that.

And I've seen actions in my life that tell me he's justified in his reaction.

I've *done* actions in my life that tell me he's justified in his reaction.

But the thing I'm not prepared for this morning?

In addition to the shame of realizing Gigi was right—yes, I *am* the person who was mocking the size of my ex-boyfriend's penis in the *Post*—and that I don't want to be the person Teague doesn't trust around his daughter, his overprotective papa-bear act is turning my hormones into firecrackers, lighting them on fire, and shooting them into the sky with that brilliant canvas of stars from last night.

Teague Miller is turning me on while I'm having a painful realization about myself.

Several, in fact.

The next of which is that I don't think anyone in my own family loves me enough that they'd consider tossing someone out of a tree house at the merest suggestion that an insult might be flinging my way.

"Your family needs to fucking *leave*," he growls.

And it all clicks.

His worry over Tavi's social media feed and pictures. His forceful questions at the idea that someone else from New York would invade his sanctuary. Selling Gigi that horrific school building to use as a home and letting me fall in the lake and planting a freaking *raccoon family* in the school.

He's not chasing us away because he's a grumpy loner lumberjack.

Or at least that's not the *only* reason. He also wants us gone to protect his daughter.

And what about the rest of the town?

Are there other people in this town that he thinks he needs to protect from us? Do people in small towns have secrets just as big as the secrets that are kept in my social circles?

How many people here would suffer unexpected consequences if some of the nosier paparazzi started poking their heads around and asking questions that *I* know not to answer, but they might not?

And he's standing between us and them with those broad shoulders and that *you'll have to get through me first* glare.

I didn't even think I actually had ovaries, yet there they are, sighing and swooning like Lola Minelli over a full-size suite at the Ritz.

I sip my coffee again, hoping it'll hide the gamut of emotions wreaking havoc on me this morning, while I watch him pace the small space like a trapped, wounded animal deciding how long he'll let me stand here before he tears me to shreds.

"You and Shiloh get along," I say slowly. High five to me. I'm remembering people's names, and I'm almost positive I've got them and their relationship right. "Necessity, or do you actually like each other?"

"I'm not discussing this with you. Go. Away."

"I'm stuck in this hellhole until I learn to be a better person. You're clearly the kind destined to live on a throne among the stars when you have a heart attack on your boat and drown in your lake, so please. Indulge me. You get along with your ex-wife and threaten to feed me to your goats if I say one bad word about your daughter, when I don't think my own mother even likes me."

Dammit.

This isn't new information, and it's nothing I've never thought before, so why is my voice suddenly cracking?

And why does he have to notice?

Don't tell me he doesn't. His eyes go laser focused on me, sweeping over my face as though he's an expert lip-quiver and shiny-eye detective. "Who says Shiloh's my ex-wife?"

I suck a breath in through my nose and blink twice to get the hot-eye situation under control, distracting myself with a thumb hooked back at the wall of pictures. "Educated guess. Vegas? Accidental pregnancy? Or was it an open sperm donation?"

"I sincerely dislike you."

If that were true, his shoulders wouldn't be relaxing, and he'd be chasing me out of this tree house. I'm baiting him hard core here. And yes, it's as much a distraction for myself as it is for him. "The feeling is mutual."

In other words, I don't dislike him either.

He crosses his thick arms over his chest. "What matters to you?"

I open my mouth, then close it.

Blame it on the stargazing showing me exactly how inconsequential I am in the cosmos.

Blame it on exhaustion after working harder than I've physically worked a single day in my life and knowing I'm facing more of the same for the foreseeable future.

Blame it on Teague Miller's incomparable talent for asking the right questions to pick at me right down to my bones.

But I can't answer that question.

After his inquisition last night, the part of my brain that should be able to answer that question is still preoccupied with asking myself if I *want* to work for Remington Lightly or if I simply like being the Lightly heir who works for a living.

And do I?

Do I *really* work?

Or is my title ceremonial? I've never set foot on a factory floor. Only the executive-level offices. When I travel to various factories and plants, I get a driver to pick me up at the airport and only talk to the highest-ranking workers in each place. I don't even use most of Remington Lightly's products.

I truly am a terrible person with a terrible family, doing a job for money first, power second, and appearances third, because I don't know if I'm actually capable of the kind of love that Teague has for his daughter.

I don't know if I'm capable of having the kind of life that people in this town clearly value.

Hello, Saturday morning. Nice little existential crisis you've given me today.

"I *have* to get home," I mutter.

That papa-bear glower fades as he watches me. "The day Shiloh told me Bridget identified as a girl, you know what my first thought was?"

"I honestly have no idea."

"My first thought was, *At least picking a college major will be easy after this.* What to do after high school was the hardest decision I'd ever faced in my life. My daughter was born in the wrong body, but she knew herself well enough to know it. To own it. Despite all the ways it could complicate her life. She is who she is, and she knows who she is, and she owns who she is. That's courage. Supporting her while she figures out who she's supposed to be? Fuck. That's the easy stuff. Go clean your school, Phoebe. Go clean your school. Steal your coffee. Turn your nose up at tonight's fish boil under the Ferris wheel. You're gonna have to figure out who you are and what you want on your own. Nobody else can do it for you. In the meantime, get the hell out of my house."

He slips back to the hatch in the floor and slides down the ladder, leaving me alone in his kitchen with his coffee and no earthly idea how to actually leave this tree house.

But more, I'm standing here with no earthly idea who I am if I'm not Phoebe Lightly, in-demand socialite and workaholic heir to the Remington Lightly fortune.

Here, I'm nobody.

Or maybe, here, I can actually finally be *somebody*.

And not just any fancy rich somebody.

Maybe here, I can be somebody who learns to do *true* good.

And that thought—that I've wasted thirty years of my life living as a shell of the person I could be, because it was easy and convenient since I was born into a family that will want for nothing until the end of time—is more earthshaking than anything else Gigi could ever throw at me.

Chapter 9

Teague

Tickled Pink's end-of-school fish boil is usually one of my favorite events of the year.

All the occupied shops around the square, from Café Nirvana to the Pink Box to Ladyfingers to the grocery store, are closed early, and everyone's brought dishes to share near the shuttered land formerly set aside for the *Pink Gold* amusement park that never got off the ground.

Bridget and her friends are running all over, laughing and plotting summer plans and debating if they're too cool for cornhole or ladder golf this year. There's fried cheese curds and fish, and everyone's brought at least one dessert and maybe a side dish too.

And then there are the Lightlys.

I'm manning the cheese curds—won't fry themselves, and they're best fresh—when Tavi and Margot stop at my table. My shoulders immediately twitch for wondering if Phoebe said anything to them about her snooping this morning.

I know my daughter can handle herself, but I wouldn't be doing my job as her father if I didn't worry, and these people are more than she's ever faced before.

"What . . . is this?" Margot asks.

"Mom, they're fried cheese curds." Tavi points at the sign. "See?"

"I can read, Octavia. But that doesn't answer the question, does it?"

I dish up a scoop of fried curds onto a plate. "Only way to find out is to eat 'em for yourself. Dig in."

"Oh, I'm vegan." Tavi's wearing her sunglasses, so I can't tell if her smile is genuine.

Her clothes are.

Genuine not-fit-for-the-park clothes, that is. She's in hot-pink pants, a sparkly silver halter top covered with a cropped jean jacket, a sparklier headband-scarf thing, more bracelets than the jewelry store stocks here in town, and shoes that are doing a good job of aerating the grass.

"Me too," Margot says quickly. She's dressed for either a garden-club meeting or a funeral with those black pants and the complicated floral-print blouse that might be a poncho. The hat and the sunglasses suggest she's aiming for Rich Old Lady in Witness Protection, though. And don't ask about her purse. It's . . . something. "I am most definitely vegan. Where's the fish?"

"Mother," Tavi hisses, "try the damn cheese curd before Gigi sees you turning it down."

"I'm allergic."

Tavi flashes her smile at me. "Do you have any dairy-free cheese curds? And is that free-trade, ethically harvested, organic olive oil you're frying them in?"

Olive oil? Is she serious? I flash a smile right back at her. "It's bacon grease."

It's not, but the lie is worth it for their reactions. Margot puts three fingers to her mouth as though someone's just told her that she'll have to take a regular limo instead of the stretch Hummer limo to her next fancy gala, while Tavi's lips part like *bacon grease* is the same as *fried babies.*

The horrors.

These people make me twitchy, and that's before worrying about how they'll treat my friends and family here in Tickled Pink and the unintended consequences of them being here.

Weird to know I'm feeling slightly better about that after laying it all out for Phoebe this morning and watching her reaction.

It's like she might have a soul hiding under all those fancy clothes and haughty looks.

And if Ms. Boss Lady can have a soul . . . maybe there's hope for the rest of them too.

Maybe.

"Well, thank God you're vegan," Margot finally says to Tavi. "The things all that fried food would do to your hips. Such a shame you didn't get Phoebe's metabolism."

These people. Jesus.

"How about your dog?" I point to Tavi's fancy purse with a fuzzy little mini dog poking its head out. "It vegan too?"

I mean it sarcastically—dogs need meat—but Tavi's face lights up with one of her beaming smiles when she answers me.

"Completely. Pebbles loves her kelp-and-kale kibble. Don't you, sweetheart? Yes, you do. Yes, you do!"

The dog barks.

I gawk at them. She can't be serious. She *cannot* be serious.

She ignores my expression, pulls out her phone, and lines up herself and her dog for a selfie with the Ferris wheel in the background, and both of them make duck lips.

Not kidding.

The purse dog is making duck lips too.

The half-finished wheel in the background of her picture is covered in ivy, though it's still early enough in the season that it's not yet swallowed by all the greenery. "Smile for the camera, Pebbles. That's such a good—*Phoebe. Move.*"

Phoebe stops behind her sister. She almost fits in with the locals in her jeans and the Chucks and the long-sleeve, gauzy ivory blouse, and while she's also wearing sunglasses, I can tell by the way her lips tighten that she's irritated.

Join the club, Phoebe.

"Like this?" Phoebe asks, getting squarely between the back of Tavi's picture and the Ferris wheel.

Tavi scowls and shifts.

Phoebe shifts too.

Huh.

Didn't think I'd be on the verge of smiling while surrounded by this family, but look at that.

Every time Tavi tries to get a shot, Phoebe moves.

Margot throws her hands in the air. "Would you two please stop acting like two-year-olds?"

"I'm not—" Tavi starts.

Phoebe interrupts her as she shifts to block another selfie. "I was never this fun when I was two."

"*Oh my God*, go away. *Go away!*"

Phoebe obliges—kind of—and steps around her sister and takes the plate I've been holding out for her family. "Thank you, Teague. I feel my soul improving already for using my manners and trying foods that I wouldn't offer to a street rat in Brooklyn."

"Oh my God, you've been to Brooklyn?" Tavi says.

"Where did I go wrong?" Margot fans herself with her hand as though the idea of any of her family going to *Brooklyn* is enough to make her faint.

But I'm not really watching them.

I'm watching Phoebe, whose nose wrinkles as she pops a fried cheese curd into her mouth.

She chews twice and stops, and then the weirdest thing happens.

She lifts her sunglasses and peers at me.

There's a heady mix of distrust and wonder staring out at me from those bright green eyes while she slowly resumes chewing, like she likes the fried cheese curds, but she knows she's not supposed to, and she's wondering what sort of dirty tricks I'm playing here.

It's like she's never lived before.

Never had to.

Just wandered around in her uppity life, getting by on everything being taken care of for her, delivered on silver platters, being told she was better than the simple things, which are really the best things.

I'd know.

She finishes chewing and pushes her sunglasses all the way up. Her blonde hair's slicked back in a simple ponytail at her nape, so her sunglasses aren't fighting for space up on her head the way Tavi's would be.

"What, exactly, is a curd?" she asks.

"Leftover bits from making cheese. Not aged. Fresh."

She points to the plate. "And you *fry* them."

"Beer battered and fried up in pure canola oil. Better with peanut, but you can't do that with allergies floating around." I jerk my head to the next table. "You like these, try the fish and Jane's garage beer. Anya and Ridhi's chana masala can't be beat too." I eyeball her mother and sister. "Might be vegan. Have to ask them."

"But does it have sugar? Hidden sugar will go straight to Octavia's hips."

Margot's asking me the question, but she's staring at Phoebe the whole time.

Tavi's watching Phoebe too. And if she doesn't like Margot's jabs at her metabolism or figure, she hides it well.

Phoebe bites into a second cheese curd, her eyes sliding shut as a moan emanates from the back of her throat, and I get the weirdest sensation that the gawks from her family aren't horror.

Not from the uppity society mama, and not from the vegan either.

Do these people ever eat food that tastes good? Or do they just stick to the food that looks good for them to eat?

I give myself a mental shake.

Not my business. Not my business at all. Especially since watching Phoebe's lips close around my favorite Wisconsin snack while she groans in pleasure again is causing some trouble for me below the belt.

I dig into the bin of fresh curds. "Here. Try one not fried."

Her face doesn't twist in disgust, though Margot takes a step back. "Dear God, it's like a pasty, swollen worm."

"It's *cheese*, Mother," Phoebe replies as she leans in and bites the curd as I'm still holding it.

Fuck.

Not what I meant.

Two points to the Manhattan lady boss.

Two more points when she makes that throaty purr of approval in the back of her throat again.

What the *fuck* is going on with my junk that I'm getting hard over *Phoebe Lightly*?

"Is it supposed to squeak?" she asks.

I nod and try to clear my throat without making it obvious that I have to. "That's how you know it's fresh."

"They're delicious."

"Or all that bleach you used scrubbing toilets today has fried your nose and taste buds," Tavi murmurs.

Phoebe smiles and aims it straight at me. "Also possible. And now Carter has a *clean* bathroom to do with what he always did in high school."

"For the love of Kate Spade, Phoebe, not in front of other people," Margot says.

"Are you talking about the weed or the jerking off?" Tavi asks.

Margot huffs.

"Both." Phoebe grabs an older plate of curds that has been waiting for one of the teenagers to claim it. "These are surprisingly delicious."

"We backwoods folk finally figured out taste buds too. Fancy that."

My sarcasm only makes her smile wider.

Is she playing me, or is Phoebe Lightly actually considering honestly giving small-town life a chance?

Maybe she's just glad to not be scrubbing toilets again.

"Do you ever dip these in ranch dressing?" Phoebe asks.

"Phoebe, *gross.*" Tavi's lower face twists, and I can only imagine what's going on behind her sunglasses. "Are you doing this on purpose? You're only enjoying yourself to gross the rest of us out, aren't you?"

"Girls," Margot chides.

"Mom. You're not vegan. *Or* allergic. Try this." Phoebe holds the plate out to her.

Margot grimaces.

I think.

Her forehead doesn't move, but her mouth is definitely grimacing. "Phoebe, I really don't—*ah!*"

Water explodes against her back and sprays my curds and my deep fryer, making the hot oil pop and sizzle and shoot out everywhere. *"Dammit!"*

Lid.

I need the lid.

"Try the damn cheese curds, Octavia," Estelle yells from somewhere behind her granddaughters.

Another water balloon explodes, this one all over Tavi.

More water.

More water in my deep fryer.

More hot oil exploding out and splattering everywhere while people shriek and scatter in the flying frying oil.

"Stop!" I bellow back at the old lady.

Where the hell is my lid?

"Dad!" Bridget shrieks.

"Teague! Here!" Shiloh dives to my side, does a ninja roll, and comes up with the lid, slapping it over the pot as one more water balloon explodes, this one coating Phoebe, who's trying to duck in plain sight to hide from the water and oil, and splattering Shiloh and me in the side splash.

Shiloh grabs my arm. "You're burnt."

"I'll heal."

"First aid tent. Go." Spoken like a true fire chief in training.

"I'm—"

"Teague Andrew Miller, *go to the damn first aid tent and set a good example for your daughter.*"

I open my mouth again, but I take my eyes off the old lady.

Bad move.

Means I get a water balloon upside the face.

"I got the cranky lumberjack!" Estelle crows.

"Stop ambushing us!" Phoebe shrieks.

"This is how the movie goes!" Estelle shrieks back.

"It is *not!*"

"It's the closest we'll get to—" She cuts herself off as a balloon explodes on her chest. Swear on my tree house, her eyes ignite like the demon inside her is coming out to play as she turns a glare on her son. "What—" she starts as another balloon nails her in the chest.

"Don't throw water balloons at my wife, you old witch!" Michael yells.

"Don't call your mother an old witch, you ungrateful little leech!" Estelle yells back.

Tavi drops her purse, tells her dog to stay, and sprints full-steam, on her heels, to the coolers holding the town's water balloons.

We usually save them for the end of the night—you know, *after* the hot oil and other foods are put away—but the Lightlys are digging into the water balloon fight like they've been needing to do this all their lives.

"Dad! Dad, are you okay?" Bridget skids to a stop next to me.

I loop an arm around her shoulder. Gonna have a few blisters for sure, and Shiloh's right—I should get to the first aid table—but it's not easy to look away from the train wreck. "I'm good."

"I can't believe that old lady ambushed Tavi like that!"

"She's probably lucky it didn't happen while she was sleeping."

Tavi has good aim. She's firing water balloons at her brother and parents and grandmother like a beast. Phoebe's at her back, the two of them pulling a gunslinging-partners routine, moving together and taking out their family, though Phoebe's aim isn't as good.

Not that it matters.

Neither is anyone else's.

But the insults?

It's a sight to behold for sure.

"And that's for making a nanny raise me!"

"That's for insulting my grandmother's silver!"

"You don't believe in my career!"

"You sing like a frog stuck in puberty!"

"I am so tired of being the only person in this family doing any damn work to keep your trust funds full, and for what? For you all to be a disrespecting group of louts!"

"How *dare* you insult my baby boy!"

"You are such a stuck-up snob!"

"You look like a poser when you wear Stella McCartney!"

"You don't know the difference between Limoges and limoncello!"

I choke on air at that last one and slide a glance at Shiloh. "Think your mother would approve of her favorite movie being used to inspire this?"

She smiles. "I think this would be her favorite part of everything that's happened since Estelle Lightly emailed you to ask about the school."

"Are they going to leave any water balloons for the rest of us?" Bridget asks.

No one else is joining in, though all of us locals are watching in fascination, some holding their phones up, recording or taking pictures. The Lightlys are showing no signs of slowing down.

Apparently they have a lot of issues to work out.

"And I know you don't believe in my designs, but joke's on you, because my business is doing *fabulous*."

"I will never forgive you for calling me a waste of oxygen!"

"You missed my starring role in *Mamma Mia!* my senior year!"

"Oh, poor you. *The maid* took me to school for my first day of kindergarten!"

"That wasn't the maid. That was your father's mistress!"

"Whoa," Bridget whispers. "And I thought you guys had problems."

I squeeze her shoulder. "See how lucky you are? You could have rich-people issues instead."

"Or siblings," Shiloh adds.

Bridget snorts and rolls her eyes.

I wince.

Phoebe takes a water balloon from her grandmother square in the chest.

"And that's for almost letting me die!" Estelle shrieks. "I would've gone to hell and never had the chance to redeem myself if it were up to you!"

"You're welcome!" Phoebe shrieks back. "You never would've known you were an evil old witch if I hadn't almost let you die!"

Yep.

I'll take my own little family's brand of dysfunction over this any day.

Chapter 10

Phoebe

My shoes are squishing. The mosquitoes are biting. I have never been so tired in all my life.

And I keep bumping into Tavi as we make our way back to the motel for our last night before moving into the school because I can't stop staring up at the stars.

I run into her again, lift a heavy arm, and wave a finger at the sky. "Don't they make you feel like all of our grievances against each other are completely and totally insignificant?"

"You make me feel insignificant," she mutters.

For the first time in what feels like decades, I stop and look hard at my little sister.

Not that I can see her well. It's super dark out here. I don't know if we're standing next to the nail salon slash bait shop or the café slash auto shop. I actually don't even know if we're headed the right direction. Once we'd thrown all the water balloons at each other, I dug into the boiled fish, Mom left in tears, Dad left with a glare at Gigi, Carter left with a woman passing through on her way home from college, and Tavi and I walked around pretending we didn't look like drenched society ladies before participating in another balloon fight with the townspeople once someone showed up with more balloons for the kids.

Mostly, we let other people throw them at us, though.

Seemed like we deserved that.

Gigi, meanwhile, sat and discussed her near-death experience with Ridhi and Jane, a Black lady around my age who apparently makes that beer *in her garage*, which the county health department approved since she put the right food-grade equipment in it.

Small towns mystify me.

"How do I make you feel insignificant?" I ask Tavi.

"Are you serious? Ms. Perfect GPA, Ms. On Her Way to Being CEO of Remington Lightly, Ms. Good Metabolism and Natural Size Six, Ms. Always Has the Gigi-Approved Boyfriend—"

"Yes, Fletcher Barrington was an *excellent* choice. And Charles before him?"

"But Gigi still set you up with both of them. *She approved.* At least, until she didn't. She hates my boyfriends."

I clamp my lips shut. No sense in pointing out the obvious. *Because you pick vapid losers.*

Or possibly this is exactly why we're here.

Because I shouldn't judge. I have no idea how hard it is to be a B-list movie star, or a bassist in a band that only opens for small acts, or a TikTok star, or a surfing champion.

Or a fishing lumberjack, but that's not really relevant. Teague Miller is *not* in the same league as Tavi's usual choice in boyfriends. And I'm not getting irrationally irritated at that thought.

Be the better person, Phoebe. Be the better person.

Also, quit having ridiculous lumberjack fantasies that involve fried cheese and the way his lips parted when he fed it to you.

"I didn't have a perfect GPA," I tell Tavi. It's a surefire distraction for my libido.

"Um, yes, you did."

"No, the geek that I paid ten thousand dollars to do my homework for me had a perfect GPA. And Gigi found out. And she's sending me back to college while we're here."

Tavi stops, which I only realize because I veer into her again as I'm staring at the stars.

It's so weird.

I know I'm not drunk—I only had one red Solo cup of that Jane's Garage beer, and I can usually drink three bourbon sours and barely get a buzz—but I feel completely wasted.

"That's why you're here? Because Gigi's not letting you go back to work unless you earn your college credits yourself?"

"No. I'm here because I almost let her choke to death when I was supposed to be eating with her and I apparently have a long-neglected guilt complex. The college classes are an added bonus."

I don't know why I'm telling Tavi this.

Wait. That's not true.

I know exactly why.

Part of me hopes she'll tell me why she's really here too. We've been sisters since she came along when I was thirteen months old, but I know so little about her. And despite being completely out of my element here in Tickled Pink, I feel buffered from the pressures that would keep me from letting *any* vulnerabilities out in public.

That confession?

It would get me eaten alive in Manhattan.

Here?

Here, it's like I'm in this space where it's okay to not be perfect.

Also? For the first time since we got here, I didn't spend the day wanting to grab my phone to check email or text messages or voice mail.

I spent my day with my arms buried in disgusting sinks and toilets. But that wasn't why I didn't reach for my phone.

It's like I'm breaking the habit and I'm past the shakes stage.

The world didn't stop spinning just because someone took New York from this girl. Even all the stuff with Fletcher feels like it's on hold.

Like not getting messages from him every day, coupled with being so busy cleaning the school, is convincing my brain that he doesn't exist.

And now that I'm not distracted by my calendar and social life and the appearances I keep up anymore, I'm dismayed by what I'm seeing.

I really do want to do better.

Self-improvement is a new mountain to climb. One that might actually be more worth climbing than I would've considered if Gigi hadn't dragged us here.

The thing about having someone look you in the eye and tell you that they don't like you because of who you are is that sometimes, you realize you're not so sure you like yourself either.

It's like Teague Miller *knows* that when I'm at a fundraiser or garden party or brunch or gala, my joy comes from knowing I'm in a place others can't be, not from feeling like I'm among true friends that I could tell anything to.

I don't know how he knows. He's a freaking fishing lumberjack in a rural hell that he seems to enjoy.

Maybe I'm projecting.

But I'm not wrong in realizing that I could be a lot better than I am.

"You're seriously retaking your entire degree this year?" Tavi's horrified.

And not fake horrified like when a paparazzo catches her on film reacting to a story about a bunch of puppies being forced to eat grocery store kibble. Like, *real* horrified.

"Just algebra, biology, and two English lit classes."

"You can't do algebra?"

"I can do algebra." I think. It's so stupid, though. I have a calculator on my phone and an entire computer at my disposal during the day job. I know how to use a spreadsheet.

Mostly.

And what I don't know, I have an assistant for.

Why do I need anything else? *That* isn't the kind of self-improvement I'm talking about.

For the record.

Tavi starts walking again. She's barefoot but not complaining about the uneven cobblestone street. Probably because she's made of fairy wings and magic and is actually immune to stubbing her toe on uneven bricks in the ground. "So why didn't you do your algebra the first time?"

"Because I was dating a senior who was really good with his tongue, and if I went to class, I didn't get tongue, since it was the only time he wasn't booked. Probably with other women, but I didn't care."

She cracks up. "No! You seriously skipped class for sex? *You?* No. No way."

"It was *so good.* Do you know how few men actually know how to treat a clit?"

"Sadly, yes. Was he from money?"

"He made me see stars."

"So that's a no."

"Exactly."

We lapse into silence for a moment.

It's weird.

Almost comfortable.

"Do you ever wish you hadn't been born a Lightly?" I ask. How is it that a week ago, this question never would've crossed my mind, but since Teague asked me who I am, it's all I can think of?

It's her turn to bump into me. "When I was younger, I wished I was related to Alexander Bentley, but then I realized if I wasn't a Lightly, I probably wouldn't get to pick another rich family. So if my options were having money and a crappy family or having no money and a good family, why not keep the money and look for a different family along the way?"

I start to laugh, then realize she might be serious. "But what if the money keeps you from being the kind of person who'll fit in with a good family?"

"Or what if our family actually *is* a good family, but our own teenage angst and then normal human conflict scarred us into thinking it wasn't, and now we can't see the good for the habits we formed in our thoughts and actions when our brains weren't yet fully developed?"

I glance at her, which is silly—I still can't see more than her profile—but she's clearly looking up at the stars too. "Dad cheats on Mom all the time. She lets him because she likes all the comforts of Lightly money and connections, plus we pretend he doesn't and that we don't know. Carter's a spoiled brat who'd probably be in jail if we didn't come from money. Mom always consults her tarot cards instead of dealing with anything head-on, and Gigi rules with terror. You really think that's not awful?"

"To people here? Probably. But where we're from . . . we're lucky that's the worst of it. Carter's not in rehab, Mom and Dad seem to each get something beneficial out of their arrangement, so long as the details about Dad's mistresses don't leak to the press, and no one ever tries to cross Gigi or blackmail her, or if they do, they don't succeed, so we don't have to deal with the blast radius. The worst we have is Uncle You-Know-Who."

Right.

Life on the Upper East Side. The crime isn't the crime. The crime is getting caught. Our uncle got caught, and he and his wife and kids no longer exist.

At least to Gigi.

Not even here, where she's trying to save herself from hell, even if I'm beginning to question her methods.

"And it helps that you're Mom's favorite," I say quietly.

I'm not bitter.

Nope.

"Um, hello? Are you serious? Do you know you're all she ever talks about? *Phoebe got a promotion. Phoebe wears that business suit so well. Phoebe's hair is such a lovely shade, and it's all-natural too. Phoebe knew what she was doing when she picked* that *boyfriend. Phoebe doesn't have to watch her diet. Phoebe has such a lovely natural shape. Phoebe Phoebe Phoebe.*"

"She does not."

Tavi emphatically nods in the dark. "She *does.*"

"But you two are practically attached at the hip whenever you're in New York. And she's not seriously fat-shaming you, is she? You're— you're *gorgeous.* And strong. And healthy."

"And curves aren't cute anymore, and she takes me because she can't have you."

I'm so floored I can't form actual words. "That's—that's—this is *not* my natural hair color," I finally blurt.

"I mean, duh. But the point, Phoebe, is that she wants to *be* you. Her business sense is crap, she knocks off other designers and hasn't turned a profit in four years—repeat that and you're dead—and here you are, on the path to being the first Lightly to run the whole damn business since Great-Grandpa Horace died."

I start walking again.

If Tavi's right, why wouldn't my mother tell *me* that?

Because you're a ruthless bitch like your grandmother, idiot, a voice that sounds unfortunately like Teague Miller answers for me deep inside my own head.

I don't like being a bitch.

Driven, yes. Confident, yes. A winner, yes. And I do sometimes cut corners.

But I don't know the line that marks ruthless-bitch territory.

Still, I'm realizing there might be a balance, and I've been walking on the wrong side of the line.

I make a soft noise, a hum that wants to be a grunt of frustration. "Why can't we just talk to each other and say these things?"

"Because we're too busy being fabulous and making more money. Admitting to vulnerabilities would impede our forward motion."

Who *is* this woman? "That's—"

"Not something we talk about?" she finishes for me. I know she's flashing an ironic smile that the rest of the world will never see on her social media feed. I can *hear* it.

Takes me back to the year we did a reality show together in college, when we'd have a stupid argument on camera and I'd tell her she had to cut it, and she'd tell me we had to keep it in because *ratings*.

And no, Gigi wasn't a fan, and yes, she pretends it never happened. But it was free advertising for Remington Lightly's new Kangapoo skincare line that year—again, *horrible* name, but it makes money—so she didn't make a fuss.

Overtly.

"I was going to say *insightful on an uncomfortable level*," I admit.

"It's that too."

I trip on a sidewalk. Or is that dirt? Why do I smell animals? Is that me? "I'm not opposed to being a better person, but I'd like to do it without all of this . . . this . . . *pain*."

"Your journey, your rules."

I make a gagging noise. That's such a Tavi tagline.

And she laughs.

My sister. Walking in the dark with me, soaking wet, no cameras around, no selfies flashing, mosquitoes vampiring the hell out of us, and she's laughing.

"Do you miss Wi-Fi?" I whisper.

"Yes," she whispers back, but there's a pause.

There's a freaking pause.

"You're getting Wi-Fi!"

"Dial down the drama, Lady Boss Queen. I got like *one bar* when I ran ten miles out of town for my workout this morning, and it wasn't enough to download a single text message. Gigi did something to our phones. Swear she did."

"So help me, Octavia, if you're lying to me—"

"Why? You really want to get to all of your emails?"

I sniff delicately. "Of course I do. I have important things waiting for me."

"Like what?"

I open my mouth, a list ready to pour out, but it doesn't come. No *production reports are late* or *forecasts are down* or *the management chain is objecting to integrating bamboo into paper products.*

None of it.

This town has zapped my ability to function as an executive. Less than a week from being *somebody* to being *nobody*, and pretty sure I'll never be the same.

We make it another half a block, my brain misfiring every time I try to put words to the things I should be doing back in the city right now. Bugs and birds and I-don't-want-to-know-what-else are making noises in the night. And then there's a goat.

There's a *goat* making noise.

Oh no.

Oh no no no.

Did I take us *this* way?

Tavi bumps my shoulder. "What emails do you have waiting for you? Or are you not answering because you don't actually want to think about the company?"

"I—how can you ask that? Aren't *you* exhausted? Don't you need six weeks in Tahiti to recover before you start thinking about posting pictures on your socials again?"

She's staring at me. Not that we can see each other in the darkness, but I can *feel* her staring at me. "You don't want to run the company?"

Pebbles barks in her carrier like she, too, is mildly astonished that anyone would think I didn't want to live up to my legacy when I'm the one who declared it to be my legacy practically as the first words I ever spoke as a toddler.

I jerk my head around, trying to peer through the darkness to make sure we're *not* where I think we are. "Oh my God, where did that come from?"

"Seriously? Do you hear yourself? It's all over under everything you're saying."

"It is not. I do. I want to run the company. I think. I've always— this damn town. It's making me feel—"

"Not yourself?"

There's a wry irony in my sister's tone that says she knows.

She feels it too.

"I want to go home." My mouth says the words, but something deeper is asking, *Do you? Do you really?*

"I want to go to the Seychelles and Paris and French Polynesia."

"Didn't you just get back from Paris?"

A weird vibe hangs in the air for a pause, but it's gone so quick with Tavi's laugh that I must've imagined it. "There's never enough time in Paris."

I try to steer us around to go the *other* way. "What do you even eat there? Aren't the pastries slathered with butter? And there's cheese on every corner. It's like here, except—"

"Except it's Paris." She sighs. "Salads are universal, Phoebe. And Parisian salads are *delicious.*"

Parisian *salads*? I blink, and then I'm doubled over laughing.

"What?" she asks. "Have you ever had a salad in Paris? They're so fresh and exquisite and different and . . . and . . . delicious!"

I can't talk. I'm laughing so hard I can't even force out a mocking *I go to Paris for the salads.*

She sighs while more goats bleat nearby. "*Fine.* Laugh away, Ms. *I Eat Fried Cheese Curds Because a Handsome Lumberjack Offered Them to Me.*"

And now I'm laughing while a delicious shiver—the *Parisian salad* kind of delicious, obviously—snakes down my back.

I'd argue he's not handsome, that you can't even see half of his face for his beard, except his eyes—*oh*, his eyes.

They're expressive and layered and exactly what Lake Carezza in Italy would look like if it had gold nuggets sprinkled throughout its green depths. They're like—they're like priceless dragon eggs.

And his body—if he takes half as much care with a female body as he's clearly taken with sculpting his own physique, I would happily let Teague Miller do whatever he wanted with his tongue.

Including verbally spar with me first.

Okay.

Not laughing anymore. "He's a pain in the ass."

"Not so much that you weren't willing to spend the night at his house last night."

I try to hush her, because if he's home, he might overhear us. "I was negotiating a truce since he seems to enjoy dunking me in lakes so much."

"That's it? You spent the night just to negotiate a truce to keep yourself from hitting the *Tickled Pink Papers* again? So, like, you wouldn't care if I asked him out?"

My shoulders hitch, and I clamp my mouth shut to keep from hissing at her.

Hissing.

Like a demonic snake or something.

What is *wrong* with me? "We need to get out of this town if that's what you're thinking of asking out." As if leaving Tickled Pink would help. I have no job to go back to since Gigi told the board about my educational deficits. At least, not until I complete my four classes this summer and fall.

I could fight Gigi's requirements, but not while she's wearing me out just trying to keep up here.

"There's no leaving, Phoebe. We're stuck, unless we don't want to be Lightlys anymore. Why are you shoving me?"

"Because—"

"Just can't stay away, can you, Ms. Lightly?" Teague Miller's deep voice says behind us.

Tavi makes a startled noise, and then she's gone.

Poof.

One minute, I'm guiding her to turn around, and the next, she's not there.

But I can hear her laughing somewhere below me. "Oh, wow, that's embarrassing."

There's movement rustling in the dark, then a clean, lemony pine scent, and suddenly *two* bodies are close. "Up you go," Teague says. "Break anything?"

Pebbles barks.

Teague makes a noise.

And Tavi giggles again. "Thank you *so much*. Oh my God, I can't believe I just tripped on air. Wow. You are *really* strong."

"Quit flirting with him."

Did I just snap that?

Wonderful.

Now I sound like a jealous harpy.

"I'm not going to catch the small-towns, Phoebe," Tavi says. "And it's only polite to thank gentlemen who pick you up off the ground when their presence makes you swoon."

Teague makes another noise. My blood pressure shoots so high I can no longer tell if those are actual stars or if I'm about to pass out.

Be the better person, Phoebe. Be the better person.

No, screw that. "*Swoon?* What is this, a historical-movie set?"

Tavi ignores me. "You have goats! Do they have names? I love goats. I did goat yoga on Vancouver Island once last year, and it was, like, *the best* yoga I've ever done in my life."

"No," Teague replies.

"Do you milk them?"

"Yes."

She claps. "Oh, *fun*! For soap?"

"Sometimes."

"Is your field organic?"

I grab Tavi's arm before she can also ask if he asks permission from the goats before he milks them. *Why* am I picturing Teague murmuring, *Okay if I grab you here, Fluffy? I promise it'll make you feel better,* and tugging at a goat tit, and *why* is that somehow both hot and adorable? And why am I also on the verge of asking if those were *goat* cheese curds and also if he could fry a few more for me? "We need to go."

Oh no.

Oh no no no.

That's not *Tavi's* arm I'm grabbing.

This arm is thick and beefy and causing an irrational reaction in my body.

Hot flash? Check.

Tightening nipples? Check.

Suddenly achy clit? Double check.

It's *that* achy.

Belatedly, I snatch my hand away. "Excuse me, Mr. Miller. My sister and I are lost, and—"

He grips me by the shoulders and applies pressure to my right side, and the next thing I know, I'm facing the opposite direction. "Three-quarters of a mile straight," he says in my ear, his breath tickling my neck.

My skin erupts in shivers from my scalp to the soles of my feet and everywhere in between. "To the motel?" Uh-oh. I've become breathless, flirty Phoebe.

"To the school."

"We don't move in until tomorrow. I picked the principal's office for my bedroom."

Tavi stifles a titter of laughter. "She's a naughty, naughty girl."

Teague shoves.

My feet engage, and suddenly Tavi's arm is looped through mine while Pebbles whines, like she, too, wants to stay and make a fool of herself in front of the fishing lumberjack.

"Thank you, Teague," Tavi calls over her shoulder. "Who knew it was so easy to get lost in such a small town?"

"We're not lost," I hiss at her.

She laughs again. "I know. You *totally* wanted to see him on purpose."

"I did *not*."

"Your Natalia did."

"My *what*?"

"Your Natalia. I just named your vagina. Mine's Scarlett."

"If yours is that red, you should probably see your gynecologist."

She laughs again, and the big green jealousy monster—let's call him Dick—rears his head.

I don't laugh.

I don't laugh.

I don't laugh at work. When I laugh in social situations, it's forced, because it's what's expected, but the jokes are never funny. I don't laugh with my family, five minutes ago being the exception.

Tavi's all superficial, getting paid ridiculous sums of money to take pictures and videos with products sent to her from around the world, with no clear purpose in her life, always bouncing place to place, relying on her trust fund instead of making something of herself, because this influencer thing *will* dry up when she gets a few wrinkles, but she *laughs*.

I want that. I want to laugh. I want to be happy. I want—

I just *want*.

All the money in the world, the perfect job, the enviable social life, and I still *want*.

That's probably not the lesson Gigi wanted me to learn here, but it's what I've got.

Chapter 11

Teague

There are very few days when I regret moving to a little town in the Northwoods of Wisconsin to live in a tree.

Today is one of them.

It's been three days since I last saw Phoebe Lightly.

Three days since I heard Phoebe Lightly discussing an ex-boyfriend and his oral skills.

Snarling at her sister for asking me out.

Admitting to feeling lost in her life.

Being *Phoebe Lightly*.

Intruding on the peace and solitude of my fishing, my goat milking, my hiking, and my bingeing of *Queer Eye* with my kid by living rent-free in my head twenty-four seven. There's literally nothing that doesn't make me think about Phoebe Lightly and the way she looked at me over cheese curds.

Jesus.

Do I even hear myself right now?

Cheese curds are good, but *I'm fantasizing about Phoebe Lightly and cheese curds.*

And right now, that fantasy is front and center, in the flesh, in front of me.

Kind of.

All I had to do was walk past the black Honda Pilot sitting at the curb in front of the old high school on my way to drop off Bridget's book that she left at my place last night, and my streak of thinking about her without having to see her would've continued.

But did I?

No.

And now I'm sticking my nose in where it doesn't belong, knocking at the back window of the SUV, because my name is Teague Miller, and I have a type.

Thought I got over this twenty damn years ago.

Phoebe jumps, reaches for the door, frowns at it, and finally, after an eternity in which I could've made it the three blocks to Shiloh's house and back, pops the door open. "What?"

She's in a dress today, but it's not a power suit. It's a striped blue sundress that she's topped with a white cardigan, and it makes her look less like a bulldozing executive in training and more like the girl next door, especially with her hair in that simple low ponytail again.

"You didn't know how to open the door, did you?"

"I was trying to roll down the window. I know how to open a damn door."

My conscience gives me a swift kick in the balls. *Don't antagonize a lady who's trying.* "You know you sit in the back seat of a car long enough, it'll get hot enough to fry you, and then the *Tickled Pink Papers* will be the least of your worries?"

She grimaces, then lifts her purse—a small black number today—to cover her face. "Oh God, are the cameras out again?"

"What cameras?" I whip my head around. We've had a small uptick in tourists, mostly semilocals coming out to gawk at the Lightly School of Hard Knocks, as Shiloh, Ridhi, and I have started calling it, but I haven't seen reporters or cameras.

"Whatever cameras got that shot of me with my ass in the air when I tripped trying to carry that bookshelf off the moving truck yesterday. I'll fund Bridget's entire college career if you tell me who prints that damn gossip page, and I don't care if she switches majors seventeen times and takes twenty-five years to graduate."

I stroke my beard and pretend to contemplate the offer as I realize she's talking about Tickled Pink's homegrown gossip page, which I should've known, but that's not where my brain goes. "Sell my daughter's future for the pride of a socialite . . . nope. No can do."

"Is my grandmother already funding every kid's college career in this town? Is her million-dollar scholarship bribe over keeping us off the Wi-Fi enough to do that?"

Huh. Phoebe's stink eye is weirdly adorable.

Must be her makeup.

Or else someone spiked my breakfast.

"Not quite," I drawl. "I'll ask her to add a couple zeroes to that figure next time she needs help thinking of things she can do to inspire you and your family to become better people. She was out at the park last night bemoaning the fact that you all still irritate her."

"Clearly you didn't take advantage of the fact to suggest all the reasons she should give up this ridiculous plan of hers."

"Oh, I did. I laid out why you're all hopeless causes and how she'll get to heaven faster if she feeds you to the wolves, then moves to Tibet to join a monastery."

She briefly closes her eyes like she wants to roll them but doesn't want me to witness such a juvenile move on her part, and I can almost smell her desperate need to know if I'm telling the truth.

I am, in case you're wondering.

The part about telling Estelle what she should do, anyway. She's too haughty to admit her family was bothering her, but it's clear she's displeased that things aren't going according to her plan.

"Do you need something, Mr. Miller?" Phoebe asks.

"Nope. Mostly just to make sure you didn't die. It'd be about the most excitement the Tickled Pink Fire Department has seen in a while, after your grandmother trying to explode a vat of frying oil with water balloons the other day, that is, but Shiloh gets pretty mad at me if I don't stop bad ideas before they get off the ground. Prevent forest fires and all that." I pause. "What *are* you doing?"

"Waiting for my driver."

I look up at the school.

Then back to the Pilot.

Then fully back at Phoebe.

"Oh, *fuck*," she whispers. "There's not a driver."

The hairs on the back of my neck stand up at the images flashing next in my brain.

Not Phoebe dying in the back of a car because she overheated. It's a sunny seventy degrees, so the car *could* get hot, but I don't think she would've sat here much longer without going in search of her driver.

Or at least popping the door open.

No, it's the image of Phoebe wrapping the car around a pine tree between here and Deer Drop that has me concerned.

I know where she's going. It was all over the *Tickled Pink Papers* yesterday.

School.

She's going back to school because she cheated her way through the first time.

The designer backpack beside her doesn't exactly confirm it, but it doesn't contradict my theory either.

I growl softly to myself as she shifts to get out of the back seat.

Yeah.

This is apparently what I'm doing with the rest of my morning.

"Sit," I order.

She peers at me, her lower lip caught in her upper teeth.

"Sit," I repeat.

"I can drive."

"But do you know where you're going?"

Her lips part.

And then they tremble.

Dammit.

I dive for the front seat, lean across the wheel, and—*thank fuck*—the key fob is in the cup holder.

Means I don't need to go have a heart-to-heart with Estelle Lightly this early in the morning.

"Sit," I mutter one last time.

I pop back out of the car long enough to pat my back pocket—no sense getting pulled over without my own license on me, and there's a reasonable chance that would happen if any of the county deputies spotted Phoebe in the back seat, just because they're almost as big of gossips as Shiloh and her buddies at the fire station. Then I shut Phoebe in the back seat again and hop in to play driver for the day.

"Sparrow County Community College?" I ask after adjusting the seat.

A soft sound escapes her lips.

I adjust the rearview mirror, and *shit shit shit.*

She's about to cry, and I don't know which one of us is more horrified by that.

Drive, Teague. Drive. Don't talk. Eyes on the road.

I clear my throat while I put the car in gear and pull away from the curb. "I've gotta drop off this book for Bridget—"

"I don't have any of my own books!"

It's not a shriek. More like a sobby gasp, like she's trying to hold it back but her body won't cooperate. "Uh . . . you can buy your school-books at the college."

"My fun books!"

"We've got a good county library. And there's a little bookstore in Deer Drop—"

"And my sheets! My silk pillowcase! I don't have my silk pillowcase, and my hair can *feel* it. And my hair. *My hair!* My roots are showing. I know you don't care about my roots, but I haven't had a decent cup of coffee since before we got here—except for that one I stole from your house—four of my favorite outfits are ruined, my Louboutins are *still* at the bottom of the lake, Carter kept us up all night last night wailing away with his guitar, and he was smoking weed in the bathroom, and *Gigi cooked us oatmeal for breakfast today!*"

The last bit comes out on a shriek.

But I'm not wincing at the tone.

I'm wincing at the idea of what Estelle Lightly might've done to ruin oats.

I clear my throat. "Um . . . that's very kind that she's worried about you getting a healthy start to the day."

"*It tasted like glue!* And it had the consistency of slime. I've had oatmeal for breakfast. I like oatmeal for breakfast. But *that was not oatmeal.* And my mother's reading her tarot cards again and told me that I'm doomed to fail my classes and I might as well just go find a job being a farmer in Nebraska or something, and that was *after* my father nearly walked in on me naked because he wasn't wearing his glasses and got confused and thought he was walking into the men's shower room. And it was a *cold* shower because—because—because . . ."

She doesn't finish.

Doesn't have to.

It's a cold shower because the water heater at the school hasn't been replaced yet.

I try to ignore the sympathy and outright guilt creeping into my gut, but Phoebe's sobbing in the back seat, mumbling about spongy bread and drugstore sunscreen and canned spaghetti, and I can't do it.

I cannot squash the guilt.

I did this.

If I'd told Estelle Lightly to pound sand instead of trying to get the best of a rich old lady by showing her a school building unfit for occupants, she would've gotten over herself a different way, and Phoebe would still have her big New York life.

But I wanted to shove it to her.

I'm apparently still seventeen myself for all the maturity and self-improvement I've done in the past twenty years.

I slow the car in front of Shiloh's house, pause at the mailbox, and slip Bridget's book inside. She pops her head out and gives me the quintessential *why is my dad such a weirdo?* look.

Later, I mouth to her.

"Oh my God, your kid's watching me melt down!" Phoebe moans. "And I smell chocolate. Do you smell chocolate? I smell chocolate, and *I can't have chocolate because I can't stop crying.*"

"I have hot water," I blurt. "Just . . . just . . . take a deep breath, and after school, you can use my shower. Okay?"

"My Oribe Gold Lust," she sobs.

"I have no idea what that means."

"My *shampoo.* I want *my shampoo.* But it leaked all over my luggage and I can't get on the internet to order more and there's no good coffee in a twenty-mile radius without stealing it from you, and we know, because Tavi runs *all the damn time* and she hasn't found any drinkable coffee *at all,* and I haven't lifted weights or done Pilates in what feels like forever and my arms are starting to flab and I'm thirty and *I'm old* and I wasn't named in *Forbes's* Thirty under Thirty list, but *Tavi* was, and now I don't have a chance again, and *Carter was the shoe in Monopoly and he refused to give change in ones.*"

I'm sweating.

Bridget's had her fair share of meltdowns.

Hell, I've had my own fair share of meltdowns.

But Phoebe Lightly having a meltdown in my back seat because of something foisted on her that she doesn't think she has any control over—and why would she?—is different.

I steer us out of Tickled Pink proper and into the Tickled Pink unincorporated area around the lake road, which is dotted with houses that would've been much more comfortable for the family.

Aren't any big enough for sale out here, but Estelle Lightly wouldn't have let that stop her.

She's a special kind of beast.

She would've knocked on the doors and offered ridiculous sums of money to the people living wherever she wanted to live if she wanted her family comfortable.

"So the water balloon fight didn't clear the air?" I ask.

I can't see her in the rearview mirror—not with the way she's lying in the back seat—but I can hear her ragged breath.

Every little gasp is a knife to my heart.

She doesn't answer my question.

And now I feel like an even bigger asshole for my part in this.

It was one thing when they were random rich people invading my town and potentially drawing attention to my family and making my friends' lives hell and subjecting us to shit we don't want in our little slice of heaven.

But whatever my first impression of Phoebe Lightly might've been, she's human.

And she works hard.

I have no idea if she's earned her position in her family's company or if her heritage is giving her a boost.

But I do know what it's like to face the hard questions and have to decide where your path lies when everything you've taken for granted implodes around you.

"Thank you for driving me," she says, sniffling.

If you need me, I'll be dead. Five little words from a woman who most likely wasn't raised to use them, and she's sliced my heart wide open.

"Welcome," I mutter.

She sits back up and meets my gaze in the rearview mirror.

Her skin is blotchy and her eyes are red, but whatever she's using for mascara held up to the waterworks.

It's her lips that are the real problem, though.

Plump and still trembling.

I'm not a hero. I'm not a hero. I'm not a hero.

Nope.

Not working.

My biggest problem with Phoebe Lightly?

She's not what I expected.

I don't know if she's even what *she* expected.

But I know one thing.

Whoever she is, she's more today than she was when she fell in the lake trying to make it bend to her will last week.

And I don't think she's done.

Chapter 12

Phoebe

Teague Miller is my knight in flannel armor.

Not that he's in flannel today. He's in a deep-green performance T-shirt that hugs his chest and lumberjack biceps, shorts hanging off his hips, and he's leaning against Gigi's Honda Pilot when I exit the community college building that is *not* falling down and which does *not* smell vaguely like rotten fish the same way Tickled Pink does, except for those few minutes this morning when it smelled like chocolate.

Make no mistake: I won't be writing all my friends in Manhattan about the college building's architecture—it's a big metal-and-glass rectangle, as if the architect said, *What's the most boring building we can make? And . . . go!*—but it's functional and smells faintly like Lola Minelli's mother when she tries to be a rose herself at the Minelli family's garden party in the Hamptons every summer, and the restroom sinks have actual hot water.

Were I not a Lightly, there's a high probability I would've stripped and bathed in it.

Yes, the tiny sink in the restroom.

I would've made myself fit.

Swear I would've.

But Teague told me I could use his shower.

I don't know if it was a ploy to get me to stop crying—and yes, I'm mortified at letting him see me upset—or if he meant it, but if he takes away the offer, I might cry again.

He nods to me when I reach the car. "How was class?"

"Boring. Especially the part where my nineteen-year-old classmates kept whispering and pointing their phones my way. I'm considering sleeping with my teacher to get a good grade and then paying him to not tell Gigi."

His beard moves like he just clenched his jaw hard enough to bite through a macadamia nut shell.

I smile. "Kidding. Though it was still horrifically boring. And unnecessary. I have to do forty pages of algebra homework on a computer that I can't connect to the internet so that I can turn it in. Thank you for waiting for me. You didn't have to do that. I could've hitchhiked home."

His beard twitches again.

Why do I get the feeling I'm the butt of a—

A ringing cell phone from somewhere behind me cuts off my train of thought, and I drop my backpack.

I actually drop it.

It's a three-year-old Margot Lightly original design, not Louis Vuitton or anything, so I don't feel *too* bad, but it's still out of character for me to do something so drastic. *"I could get a cell signal here."*

Teague's brows lift.

So do the corners of his mouth.

I glare at him. "Oh my God. If I'd remembered to bring my phone, *I could've gotten cell signal here.*"

"Good chance. BarriTel put in a server farm—"

"BarriTel services this area?"

Dammit.

Dammit.

I'm shrieking again.

"You prefer AT&T?"

BarriTel.

BarriTel.

Fletcher Barrington's family's empire.

If I want cell service here, I'll have to pay *him*. If I'd brought my phone with me today—which I didn't, because it's more or less a brick good for nothing more than dwelling on my old life, and I didn't think about the fact that I was leaving the black hole of cell service—I'd be connecting to his network, rented by other companies.

Dammit.

I grab my backpack, march to the SUV's back door, glare imperiously at Teague, remember I'm being a better person and that I need to open my own door, and chip a nail trying to grab the handle.

He slides two paces to his left so that instead of leaning on the driver's door, he's leaning on the door I'm trying to open. "You really have a license?"

"Yes."

"When's the last time you drove?"

Don't twitch, I order my eyeball.

It ignores me. "I . . . don't remember."

"Why'd you get it?"

He knows.

He knows it's completely unnecessary for me to have a driver's license.

I've lived in New York my entire life. Yes, my family owns cars, but we don't *drive* them ourselves. We hire drivers who open our car doors for us. And yes, I travel for work to various locations around the world, but I don't get rental cars.

I'm cringing to myself now, because I don't want to admit what I get when I travel for work.

It's not the same as my coworkers. And until a week ago, I'd never thought about why.

I just assumed they weren't authorized that expense by the company, because they weren't Lightlys.

I straighten. "I wanted a little more freedom when I was on vacation in the Hamptons."

"Is it expired?"

"*No.* I renewed it just last year, thank you very much." I had Antoinette renew it.

He holds out his hand, palm up, and gestures with his fingers. "Let's see it."

"No."

"I can't drive you to school every day of the week, Phoebe, and I'm not letting you drive yourself until you prove to me that you can drive."

I pull myself up to my full Lightly height, which is three inches shorter than I'd like it to be but still at least four inches higher than my doctor's records have on file. Or so it feels. And feeling is half of being, isn't it? "You won't *let* me?"

"My daughter walks on the road you'd be driving on. Friends and family too. Damn right I won't *let* you. Gigi likes me. Just a few little words—"

"*Fine.*" He is *such* an ass. I yank my backpack to my chest and dig into the front pocket for my wallet. "And how are you coming on convincing her we need to leave and she needs to lay off?"

"Patience, my dear Phoebe. We're getting there."

He's enjoying this entirely too much.

And *I* enjoy it entirely too much when our fingers brush as he takes my driver's license and inspects it.

One corner of his mouth hitches again.

I'm well aware that the photo is hideous. I also have an unfortunate smudge on my record since you're apparently not supposed to bribe the workers at the motor vehicle licensing facilities to retake your photo, and I forgot that *that* photo would be reused when Antoinette renewed my license online for me.

But I stare him down like I'm the bloody queen of England.

It doesn't faze him in the least. Neither my horrific picture nor my glare. "It's current, I'll give you that." He slaps the keys into my palm along with returning my license. "Hop up there, Phoebs. Let's see if you actually know how to operate this thing."

My skin prickles and my gut twists.

In my thirty years, I've been behind the wheel of a car long enough to acquire my license and then approximately four hours total since.

I might have once known how to drive a car, but I have zero confidence that I can still do this without embarrassing myself.

But he's right.

I still need to, no matter how bad I might be.

So I slide into the driver's seat, and I sit there staring at the dashboard, my legs at least six inches too short to reach the pedals with the seat adjusted for Teague's height, momentarily stupefied because there's no actual key on this key fob.

The whole SUV shifts when Teague settles into the passenger seat beside me. "If you're freaking out, I can drive you back to Tickled Pink and tell Shiloh you need driving lessons instead. In addition to being a firefighter, she's also a registered driving instructor."

"I'm not freaking out. I'm reacquainting myself." What do I do first? Why isn't there—*Oh.*

There's a button where the key should go.

Oh my God. I watched Lola do this on *Lola's Tiny House* right before I had that fateful dinner with Gigi. Lola couldn't figure out how to start her car either. But you push the button.

"My last rental car had a key," I say defensively as I smash the button.

The car doesn't start.

I smash the button again.

Still no-go.

And then I notice the message lighting up on the dashboard reminding me I need to press the brake if I want the engine to turn on.

Teague reaches across me, his large frame brushing against my breast, his breath on my neck, his sideburns tickling my lips and making me suck in a breath.

His whole body tenses, but he doesn't move away.

Nope.

The man grabs my left hand and guides it to a series of switches on the side of the seat. "Here." His voice is strained. "Adjust your seat so you can reach the pedals."

"I was getting there."

"Get there faster."

His words say *Hurry up*, but his body is still lingering across mine. And I'm oddly okay with this.

No, *okay* isn't the right word.

I like this.

He smells how Remington Lightly's ads for our Kangapoo-brand body-care line claim to make a man smell. Woodsy and strong with a hint of salt and lemon. Capable. Like he's just come in from chopping down a tree at the edge of the ocean and is now getting ready to grill a steak for his lover.

I inhale deeper, and his body tenses harder against me before he jerks away. "I have an appointment to make clay pots with Bridget at the local art teacher's house in two hours. Let's get a move on."

Right.

Learn to drive the car again.

With Teague serving as my consultant.

I like him. He's honest. Not angling for anything other than to get us to leave.

Is he?

I shoot a side glance at him while I hit the right switches to move my seat forward. "Is my grandmother offering other financial incentives to the town for you to tolerate us?"

His lips purse. "No."

"The million-dollar scholarship to keep us off the town's Wi-Fi? What about the profit off of selling her the school in the first place?"

"That scholarship will help at least four more kids a year go to college than would've otherwise, if we manage it right, and that bridge we drove over on the river between Tickled Pink and Deer Drop? That's where the school profit's going. If there's leftover, it's helping tear down the Ferris wheel. Or patching some of the cobblestone roads on Main Street. We don't want you here, and we're not asking for handouts, but we're not turning down any of the cash she's dropping around town until we're rid of all of you." He points to the steering wheel. "Press the brake and then hit that button to start the car."

"I know how to start the car."

"You wanna tour around the parking lot a bit first?"

That's probably a good idea. "Teague. *I can drive a car.*"

"Thank you, Teague, for taking time out of your schedule to make sure I can take care of myself the next time I'm waiting for a driver."

The man should *not* do falsetto.

Mostly because it's an eerily accurate representation of what I sound like when I listen to interviews of myself. Has he memorized my speech patterns?

"Thank you, Teague."

I scowl at him.

He grins back.

My nipples sit up and sniff like Tavi's dog getting a whiff of prime rib after subsisting on carrots and spinach for months, heat streaks through my core, and I no longer have to worry about having children, because that grin just made my ovaries implode, which *surely* has broken them permanently.

I start to fan myself, realize he's still watching, and grope for the steering wheel instead.

Unfortunately, I miss and hit a lever, and the wipers go nuts across the windshield. It's a frantic *squark squark squark!* as they whip across the dry glass.

"Oh, good," I stutter, and I lunge for the lever again and try to figure out how to make them stop. "I needed to know where that was."

He leans over me again, and *sweet holy Oprah*, his shampoo or his soap or his beard oil is saturating the air around me, swirling and mingling with the new-car scent in here and teasing my senses, and my brain is in danger of going the way of my ovaries.

How am I supposed to drive when he smells like this?

"Your lights are here." He flips a knob at the end of the lever on the left side of the wheel, and I spare a brief hope that he's lived in a town that smells like rotten catfish so long that it's dulled his own senses so he can't smell how my body is reacting to his body being so close.

My panties are soaked. My nipples are diamonds. And I want to know if the back seat of this SUV is big enough for me to ride a lumberjack.

"Phoebe?" He leans back and peers at me again, and *oh God*, his eyes. They're like dragon eggs, layered and flaked with the colors of priceless emeralds and yellow sapphires, rich and textured.

Are they getting darker?

Are his lids heavy because he's turned on or because he's irritated?

Is he staring at my mouth?

"Are we leaving anytime today?" he asks.

I jerk my attention back to the wheel.

Again.

"Yes. Headlights. Windshield wipers. Gas pedal. Brake. I've got this."

"Seat belt?"

I'm intoxicated on hormones and should definitely not drive this car.

Especially since Teague Miller is the source of my hormonal intoxication.

What has this town done to me?

Introduced you to people who have to work for what they have, love each other without doubt through hard times, and do kind things for you despite you and your family being spoiled, obnoxious, terrible people who have shown very little respect for them.

I don't think this is what Gigi expected when she brought us here—not really—but I'm realizing more and more every day that I don't like myself.

The New York Phoebe? The one who's so important, in meetings every day, chewing out the people beneath me, stepping on people at my level to get above them, neglecting the simple manners my nanny taught me all those years ago when grabbing my coffee or demanding my assistant order me lunch, worrying more about if Sophia Cho would show up in the same designer that I wore to a gala than if my charitable donations actually helped the organizations they were meant to support?

I don't like her.

And for years, I've hidden my self-loathing behind a full calendar and an entitled sense of being better than everyone around me simply because I happened to be born rich.

But why was I born rich, if not to enjoy it?

Do you, Phoebe? Do you really enjoy it? Are you happy?

We came here because Gigi said we needed to be better people, and she thought re-creating a movie would be a shortcut. I'm playing the game so I can get back to my life.

But "getting back to my life" feels like going back into a haze, and I don't know if that's the effect of almost a week so far removed from normal or if I'm truly waking up for the first time since I was born.

Teague sighs heavily and scrubs a hand over his face before lounging back in the passenger seat, crossing his arms, and staring at me.

"I'm driving, I'm driving," I mutter.

Maybe Gigi's right.

Maybe I *don't* deserve a hot shower yet.

Chapter 13

Teague

Phoebe is correct. She can drive.

If by *drive* you mean *not kill someone along the way.*

Can't kill a person if you don't go more than ten miles an hour and ride the brakes the whole time while hunched over the wheel, squinting at the road.

"Can anyone else in your family drive?" I ask her as we lurch to a stop a quarter mile from the rickety bridge separating official Deer Drop land from the farthest reaches of Tickled Pink's outskirts.

"There was a squirrel."

"That was a shadow. And even if it was a squirrel, if there'd been someone behind us, you would've gotten rear-ended."

She scowls and hits the gas, actually gunning it this time and flying through scattered stick debris.

I reach for my *oh shit* handle. "But if you *can* avoid crap in the road, do it, because—"

"I know how to fucking drive, Teague. Okay?"

Dammit.

Dammit.

This is why Shiloh says I'm not teaching Bridget how to drive either. I have zero patience for incompetence.

But there's no way Bridge would be the same kind of menace that Phoebe is. Phoebe is all arrogance and snarls and gorgeous breasts and sexy determination and—

And the car's front right tire is thumping.

Thank fuck for that distraction. *Sexy determination?* I need to spend a night or two hooking up with someone in Deer Drop and get over this. "Pull over."

"I'm not pulling over!"

"You have something stuck in the tire. Pull. Over."

She *hmph*s.

I *hmph* back.

She yanks the wheel and slams on the brake, and we end up sitting with the back end of the Pilot sticking out into the road while the front end stops in a thicket of weeds perilously close to the edge of the Deer Drop side of the bridge. The sides of the road are lined with more of the pines and sugar maples that are prevalent up here, and there's no small part of me wanting to disappear in the forest and hike myself into oblivion.

Instead, I yank my door open and climb out, cursing myself for wearing shorts.

She scrambles out behind me, and I glance back in time to see her staring at the ground like she's contemplating kissing it.

Mental note: ask Shiloh to suggest to Estelle Lightly that her whole family take driving lessons if she's buying them a damn car.

Not that the car will be a problem for a while.

The front right tire's flat, and even in the weeds, it's pretty easy to see why.

My eye twitches.

Can't entirely blame her, even if I want to. I would've driven through that crap myself if I'd been driving alone.

She joins me on my side of the car and gives the tire a dubious eyeball. "Is that a flat?"

"Yep."

"So we need to get towed."

"Nope."

"You can drive on flat tires?"

"No, you replace the flat tires with the donut to get you to the tire shop."

Now that dubious eyeball is aimed directly at me. "You're going to make me change a tire, aren't you?"

"Yep."

"And lecture me about how leaves and sticks in the road can break tires?"

I squat and point to the piece of bone sticking out of the front of the tire. "No, but antlers can."

Her lips part, and she angles closer to me. "Antlers?"

"Antlers. Off a deer."

"I know what antlers grow on."

I could bait her, but I'd like to get back home. And it's freak happenstance that a part of an antler was in a pile of old sticks and leaves in the middle of the road. Probably blew off an old pickup truck. Can't fault her for not knowing it would be there.

Takes just a minute to find the owner's manual in the glove box and identify where the spare is, with Phoebe peering over my shoulder the whole time. Few more minutes to get it out with Phoebe insisting the whole time that she can do this if I just point to her what to do.

I let her try to undo a lug nut, get so turned on watching her muscles bunch while she squats in the weeds in that dress without complaint that I tell her she's doing it wrong and make her move.

I also ignore her indignant protests when I pop the tire off, replace it with the donut, and tighten the lug nuts back down. "Got places to be," I grunt at her.

She can do it herself next time.

But for now, the worst of it is feeling her eyes on me while I'm working.

She's fallen quiet.

Remarkably quiet.

The same kind of quiet she went when I was helping show her how to move her seat and where her light switch was.

Making me sweat, if I'm being honest.

Boss-lady socialite Phoebe Lightly?

Completely resistible.

Human Phoebe Lightly?

Intriguing.

Phoebe Lightly trying to improve herself as a human being while looking at me with undisguised lust after brushing her arm against mine and leaning into my space and smelling like stardust and maple syrup?

There's only so much a man can handle before his cock starts doing his thinking for him.

I'm tightening the last lug nut when she gasps. "Did you hear that?"

"Hear what?"

"Something *moved.*"

"It's the woods. Something's always moving. Or it's the wind."

"Oh my God."

I give the wrench one last tug, rise, and turn to face her. "Phoebe. It's nothing."

"Don't move," she whispers. "It can see us."

"What can see us?"

"Shh!" She flings an arm across my chest, staring into the wilderness. "Don't you hear it?"

"All I hear is your ass getting into the passenger seat so we can get back home before—"

A crashing and rustling makes me break off, and then, yeah, I do see it.

There's a deer running full-steam through the timber.

"Aaaaah!" Phoebe screams and leaps on me.

The deer pivots and lunges in the opposite direction, disappearing deeper into the woods.

I stumble back against the car. "Can you—"

"It's going to eat me!"

"It's not going to eat you!"

"You don't know that!" She tries to climb me like a tree, legs and arms wrapped around me, wiggling while I stagger to get my balance, until she's almost sitting on my shoulders while I twist and spin and reach for the car.

"Would you please—"

"Aaaah!"

"Dammit!"

I can't do it.

I can't stay upright.

We're tumbling into the brush, my arms flailing, her with one leg hooked over my shoulder and another around my ribs while she smushes her breasts in my face, which should be a fantasy, but instead, it's a nightmare of bramble scratches and trying to not land on her while we go down.

"Oof."

"Ow ow ow!"

I can't get out from under her because I'm somehow both trapped and also trapping her. "Are you hurt? What hurts?"

"My pride, Teague. I hurt my damn pride!"

Jesus. "Tell your damn pride to get over it!" Why can't I get her leg off me? "And would you—*oof.*"

"Oh my God! Did I just punch you in the gut? I didn't mean to do that. Can you please get off my foot?"

"I can't get off your foot. Your body's in the way."

"Ow. Something just bit me!"

"*Stop moving.* You're rolling in a damn sticker bush, and you'll have things biting you in all the places you never knew things could bite you until kingdom come if you *don't stay still.*"

Her gaze connects with mine, eyes wide, lips parted, as she finally stops her thrashing. "What's a sticker bush?" she whispers.

"It's a damn bush with burrs, and I'm gonna be picking them out of my ass for the next week," I snap.

Her tongue darts out to swipe her lower lip. "Is that thing going to eat me?"

"The deer's gone, Phoebe. You scared it more than it scared you."

"A deer tried to eat my face off once when we went to the Hamptons when I was little."

"It did *not* try to—"

She shoves my shoulder. "*You weren't there, Teague Miller.* It did too. I was wearing a flower crown at this fair that my mother insisted we go to, and there was a petting zoo, and there was a deer, and it tried to eat my face off."

"There was a *deer* at a petting zoo in the Hamptons." I squeeze my eyes shut. "Of course there was. Money can buy anything."

"It wasn't a money thing. It's always there, and *anyone* can go to it."

"Anyone who can get to the Hamptons."

"What's your problem? Hm? I'm trying here. I'm trying *so hard*, and nothing's good enough for you, because you think I can't be rich and also be a better person today than I was yesterday. What, exactly, do I have to do to prove to you that I'm a woman doing her damn best in a situation that's so far out of my element that I wake up every morning wondering what sort of torture awaits me today, but I still make myself get out of bed every day anyway in the hopes that it actually *will* make me into a better person?"

I freeze.

Hard freeze.

I know those words.

I know those words all too well. Maybe not in that order, and definitely not in the same setting, but the sentiment counts.

I swallow. The next words aren't so easy, but they're necessary. "I'm sorry."

She blinks, and her body tenses.

Jesus.

I'm tensing too. "You're right," I add.

Pretty sure she couldn't go back to flailing around again right now even if she wanted to.

I'd bet my tree house and every last one of my goats that *I'm sorry* and *you're right* aren't phrases that she hears from anyone beyond people who are paid to say it to her.

Her grandmother saying sorry?

Not a chance.

Her parents?

When pigs fly.

Her siblings?

And where would they have learned that being wrong is okay?

I know her world.

I don't want to remember that I know her world, but I do.

Apologies are for the weak. Do something wrong, you double down that you're right until everyone around you believes it too.

I fucking *hate* her world.

She licks her lips again. "I wish you wouldn't do that," she whispers.

"Do what?"

"Make me like you more."

Before I can let myself begin to process what that means, Phoebe Lightly does the last thing I would've expected a week ago and the first thing on my list of *Events I'll Regret Tomorrow.*

She angles her lips to mine, and she kisses me.

And I do the last thing I would've expected of myself a week ago, and I let her.

Let her.

Fine.

I'm lying. I'm not *letting* her.

I'm meeting her halfway.

Of everything I thought kissing Phoebe Lightly would be—and yes, unfortunately, I *have* thought about kissing Phoebe Lightly—*soft* was not the first word that would've come to mind.

Soul sucking, yes.

Angry, definitely.

Controlling.

Manipulative.

In charge.

Unpleasant all around. *That's* what I expected from kissing Phoebe Lightly.

But soft? Tentative? Curious?

From the woman who tried to make an entire lake bow before her, who meets every challenge with such headstrong will that she'd probably leap out of a plane without a parachute just to prove she could fly?

Never.

Yet here we are, with her lips asking permission from mine for this to be something more.

Like she needs this kiss to assure her that no matter who she is or who she isn't, she's still worthy of simple human affection.

Fuck.

I like this kiss.

I like soft Phoebe.

I don't care if I have a sticker burr poking through my shirt too close to my armpit or if a wild boar's about to leap out of the woods and trample us.

She tastes like cinnamon and a fresh spring morning. Like sipping chai in the sunshine after the rain. Her fingers dance across my neck, like she's afraid to touch me but unable to resist at the same time. Her lips part, and *God*.

Soft, vulnerable, sexy Phoebe.

I'm such a sucker for a lost soul. Especially when that lost soul is doing so damn much work to find herself despite all the reasons she doesn't have to.

A horn honks, and she leaps back as much as she can with us tangled on the ground like this, gasping, eyes wide for a split second before she tumbles sideways, getting me in the gut once again with her elbow. "I didn't—we didn't—that didn't—"

"Hello, there," Deer Drop Floyd calls. "You folks need a hand? Oh. Teague. It's you."

Fucking Deer Drop Floyd.

"Just a flat tire," I tell him.

A flat tire, blue balls, and a blossoming obsession with one unexpectedly and inconveniently attractive socialite lady boss.

"We fixed it, thank you." Phoebe's managed to get untangled enough to rise without assistance—naturally—and she's smoothing a hand over her not-so-fancy, but still undoubtedly expensive, dress and cardigan.

She doesn't look at me.

Deer Drop Floyd lifts his sunglasses and sets them on top of his ball cap, squinting at her, then at me, then back to her. "Aren't you—"

"Getting back to Tickled Pink now," I interrupt. I grab Phoebe by the elbow and point to the passenger seat. "I'm late to see my daughter. Later, Floyd. Thanks for stopping."

"Couldn't hardly not, what with your bad parking job."

Phoebe flinches.

I mentally flip off the asshole who stole Ridhi's coconut-pudding recipe. "Thanks, Floyd. I'll put that in my self-improvement bucket."

That, and *no more kissing Phoebe Lightly.*

She's a blip. And not the kind of blip I need to have a fling with, no matter how much progress she makes on her own definition of being a better human.

Chapter 14

Phoebe

Teague Miller broke me with a kiss.

Yes, yes, I know. Technically, I kissed him.

I could argue he made me do it by being so kind and competent and patient, except I'd be lying to myself.

One, he's not patient. And two, he didn't make me do anything.

Nothing I didn't want to do, that is. And this morning, less than twenty-four hours after the sticker-bush kiss, listening to Gigi's analysis of the scene in *Pink Gold* when Whitney Anastasia realizes that Tickled Pink is actually the golden gates to heaven and that she can't pass through town to go see if her son made it to heaven until she's done enough good deeds to even her balance sheet, I'm realizing that Gigi can't make me be a better person.

Gigi doesn't inspire me.

She terrifies me.

For a long time, that was okay. It was what I *wanted*. Learning to be as terrifying as Gigi, as unstoppable, as determined—that was how you made it in life.

But I was wrong.

And I'm still not sure what to do with that.

But now, she's being Gigi, terrifying me in this exact moment, as a matter of fact, as we're sitting in the cafeteria after having a breakfast of cold reheated pancakes—trust me, yes, that's possible—and wilted fruit salad, which, yes, is *also* possible.

"We're hosting a meal for the townspeople of Tickled Pink," Gigi announces.

"Mother, I don't think anyone here wants to dine with us after what we did at the last community function," my father says.

"And who would we hire to cater it?" My mother shudders as she flips her next tarot card. "That woman who runs the café? I didn't know it was possible to damage coffee beans the way she does. Look. The Sun is upside down. If we hire that woman, everyone will hate us for the damage to their taste buds. Plus, she does *not* know how to cook anything vegan. Tavi needs to watch her figure, but she doesn't need to starve. There's a balance."

"Shut up, Mother," Carter mutters.

"Don't disrespect your elders," my father snaps at him.

I shoot a glance at Tavi, who's playing with a green screen app on her phone while taking selfies of herself and Pebbles. She's wearing her sunglasses inside again and pretending she doesn't hear a thing.

"Anya and Ridhi cook better than we can." I lift my *Pink Gold* fortieth-anniversary commemorative refillable coffee tumbler, which I bought with my coffee at Café Nirvana this morning when I signed up for their monthly coffee subscription with my quarterly oil changes, and which I felt honor bound to buy after having my ass—and the Pilot's—saved by Teague and the tire guy who works in the other half of Café Nirvana's building. "And this coffee is better than anything any of us have tried to make."

The actual truth?

This coffee isn't *better* than anything we make ourselves. It's *good* today.

Either the coffee is as good as Ridhi and Anya want it to be depending on the customer, or Teague Miller isn't the only thing that's broken parts of me.

I'm tolerating the coffee here.

No, I'm *appreciating* the coffee here.

Also, why am I craving fried cheese curds at eight in the morning? And lumberjack kisses?

It's not the coffee. It's me. I'm broken.

"You poor thing," Mom says. "Estelle, Phoebe needs a week off at that detox spa in Arizona to get her taste back."

"No one's having a detox week." Gigi lifts her nose and digs in her heels again. "We're hosting a family dinner for the entire town, and it will be delicious."

"How?" Mom demands. "Who's catering?"

"We'd do all our own cooking," I tell my mother.

Her lip curls and her eyes go wide in horror as she reaches for her next card. Is that a new deck? *Another* one? "Holy sweet Kate Spade. We're murdering the entire town with food poisoning, aren't we? Look. *Look.* This card rarely means literal death, but I think it's making an exception today. Estelle. Is this your plan? Ride through the pearly gates of heaven once you've taken out Tickled Pink? You *know* that movie was fiction, don't you? And even if it wasn't, you can't rewrite the ending. Or change the fact that *Whitney Anastasia was dead* the whole time. Oh my sweet Coco Chanel. We're dead, aren't we? *We're all dead.*"

"Phoebe is correct." Gigi gives me an approving nod. It's similar to her disapproving nod but with less displeasure. To get a *true* approving nod, you have to do something more than easily anticipate the worst possible torture she could inflict on everyone around her. "We'll be learning to cook so that we can serve our friends and neighbors and show them that we're no better than they are."

"I can cook," Carter mutters.

Tickled Pink Floyd moans.

No, really. It startles us all when the *wooooooooo* reverberates through the ductwork, followed by mutterings of *ungrateful louts* and *pompous teachers think they don't need to pick up their own shit either.* The noise and mumblings have happened at least twice a day since we moved in, and even though I'm sure it's old pipes settling and overactive imaginations, it still makes us jump.

Damn ghosts.

Tavi turns her head briefly toward the noise, then wrinkles her nose as she looks back at Gigi. In addition to the sunglasses, she's hiding out under a massive pink straw hat that she picked up at the Pink Box two days ago while she waited for a hair appointment at the Gold Palace. "Even a questionable small-town salon shampoo is better than cold-water rinses of shampoo, and dry shampoo will only get you so far," she whispered to me when we ended up in the second-floor girls' bathroom at the same time to brush our teeth before bed last night.

Gigi tried to replace the water heater herself with Dad's help yesterday.

It didn't go so well. And the local plumber is apparently working a big job somewhere outside Tickled Pink and can't get to us for a while, but we were able to get water back.

It's bad when you're *grateful* for the cold shower.

And yes, I'm actively ignoring that invitation from Teague to use his shower yesterday.

I . . . haven't earned it yet.

"Gigi, do we need some kind of approval from the health department before we cook for a lot of people?" Tavi asks.

"Only if we're *selling* the food. We aren't selling anything. We're being good neighbors and giving it away *for free.*"

"Because it'll be awful," my mother murmurs over her cards.

"Will we have vegan options?" Tavi asks.

"I can cook," Carter repeats.

I start to ask if he can also *shut his damn music off* before three in the morning, remember I'm trying to be the bigger person, and take a deep breath instead. "I didn't know that, Carter. What's your favorite dish to cook?"

He shifts suspicious brown eyes my way. "You don't believe me."

"Mom and Dad can't cook. Tavi can't cook. I can't cook. I assumed you couldn't either. I apologize. I shouldn't make assumptions."

The entire cafeteria goes silent.

Rule number three: *A Lightly never apologizes.*

It's a sign of weakness. Poor character. An admission of a lapse in judgment, which a Lightly should never have.

Not if she wants to stay a Lightly.

Just ask Uncle George and his plea deal.

I refuse to shiver under the weight of my family's shocked astonishment at my blatant disregard for the rules. "Good people apologize when they're wrong. We won't become better if we don't acknowledge when we're wrong, will we? And if we're never wrong, are we truly good people? Or is this all for show? Do we *all* get to honestly improve, or do we just throw money and cleaning products and paint and temporary common-person hobbies at the problem until we forget that we lie, steal, cheat, insult, and stroke our own egos all the way to the top?"

No one answers.

Not even Gigi.

I rise. "I have to get to class. If one of you could be so kind as to leave me a note about the menu and what you need me to do and when we're hosting this dinner, I would very much appreciate it. I'll start painting the entry hallway when I get home. Or pulling weeds out front. Or whatever other task you need to assign me for having the gall to do something so beneath a Lightly as to *apologize*."

I don't have to get to class.

Class isn't for another two hours today.

But I don't want to sit in this cafeteria another minute.

Not when it all feels so fake and when I'm starting to question if we've always *been* fake.

Also—possibly I *should* leave for class now. Especially if I'm driving myself.

Teague drove me straight to the auto shop connected to Café Nirvana yesterday, and the SUV has a brand-new tire now. The kind gentleman there delivered the car back to the high school for me so that I wouldn't have to pick it up.

Or more likely, the reason that Teague was on his phone while I was making arrangements for payment was because he was texting the man to suggest he deliver the car back where it belonged so that I didn't take out any fire hydrants while avoiding squirrels in the road for the whole *two-block* drive from the square to the high school.

Whatever.

The most important part of my plan to leave for my classes early, though, is that I have a charged phone *and* a charged tablet, and unlike yesterday, I'm taking them to school today.

Gigi can't prevent me from using the community college's Wi-Fi.

In the interest of being a better person, I won't lie and say I'm not also leaving because I desperately need to reconnect with my real world, even though I can't think of a single person in my office who I actually miss or a single acquaintance in my social circle who I want to talk to, considering they'll want all the gossip about Gigi and her breakdown and this ridiculous situation in backwoods Wisconsin.

Wait.

Why do I need to connect with my real world again?

Oh. Right.

Because Antoinette might think I'm dead. I need to assure my personal assistant that I'm not dead.

Actually, she might be glad if she thinks I'm dead.

I woke up in a cold sweat two nights ago after realizing I'd given her an outfit for her dog for Christmas two weeks after it had died. I had her place the order to send herself her own condolences flowers, and I asked an administrative assistant in another department to order the dog's outfit in a rare bout of recognition that asking Antoinette would ruin the surprise.

Oh my God.

I need to apologize to Antoinette.

Can I do that?

I'm so deep in my own head at the stark realization that the Phoebe I'm becoming here might not line up with the Phoebe I am in New York that I don't realize there's a shadow outside the frosted-glass door I'm shoving open to get outside until it bounces back off a boulder.

"Oof," Teague says.

Not a boulder.

A lumberjack.

"Oh my God, watch where you're going," I gasp.

He straightens and glowers at me as a hint of chocolate tickles my nose, making me question for the second time today if my taste buds are broken. One more sniff, and I get his pine-lemon scent again.

"I mean, I'm s-sorry," I stutter. "I d-don't need a ride to school today." I didn't stutter in front of boys who wanted their drivers to pick me up for school when I was seventeen, so there's absolutely no excuse for stuttering in front of a grown man when I'm thirty.

Yet here I am, half-incapable of forming actual words.

He steps to one side and eyeballs me with all the suspicion that he probably should. "Your grandmother wants a tour of office space."

"There's office space in Tickled Pink? Why does she need office space? What's she planning on doing with it? We have sixteen empty classrooms here. Why would she need *more* real estate?"

"Do I look like an Estelle Lightly expert to you?"

He rubs his forehead, and an unfamiliar feeling slashes through my chest.

Guilt.

I've stifled it for so long I don't readily recognize it for what it is, despite the number of times I've felt it since I got here. "I'm sorry."

I'm saying that a lot today. Would I if I were still in New York? Would I mean it? I mean it now. "I saw your shadow. I should've slowed down."

He sighs.

It's a far cry from the grin he flashed me yesterday in the car.

Back before I killed a tire and then things got weird and we both pretended we weren't making out in bug- and biting-plant-infested weeds.

I found another of those sticker burrs in my hair this morning while I was taking a cold shower.

He lifts his chin past me. "Your family needs a doorbell. Is everyone decent? Your grandmother's expecting me."

"Yes. Cafeteria. Family meeting." I start to walk past him, get another whiff of chocolate, then pause. "You're not actually setting her up with office space, are you?"

He smiles.

Teague Miller *smiles*.

It makes those multifaceted, dragon-egg jewels in his eyes sparkle while his shoulders relax and his lips—no.

No.

Not thinking about his lips.

Just his eyes twinkling is enough to steal my breath.

I swallow hard to make sure he can't hear it in my voice. "Is the office space condemned too?"

"Oh, Phoebe. So much to learn about all the ways real estate can be wrong."

God help me, I'm smiling back.

I'm *enjoying* this. "Is it as bad as the motel?"

"What's wrong with the motel?"

"Funky smell, 1980s decor, and I would *not* use a blue light in any of the rooms. Do they wash the bedding? Ever? Never mind. Don't answer that."

"There's no bedding in the office space." He tilts his head. "Probably."

"*Probably?* What are you selling my grandmother?"

"Waste not, want not, Ms. Lightly."

"You *are* still working on convincing her to leave, aren't you?"

He grins wider. "You clearly haven't heard yet what she signed your family up for."

"I know we're hosting dinner."

"Did *not* know about that one. I'm busy."

"I sincerely hope everyone in town is busy."

I'm standing on the steps of a high school flirting with a man who offered to let me use his shower yesterday.

Not that I was willing to take him up on it after the tire-kiss thing, but him smiling at me this morning?

Like we're friends?

Or maybe not friends but at least not mortal enemies?

This is new.

And not just with Teague.

It's new *in my life.*

I don't flirt with men. I proposition them when their reputations, experience, and bank accounts are good complements to mine. Relationships in my world are based on success probabilities and expanding empires.

Feelings have nothing to do with them.

But going from a place where all Teague would do was growl at me to a place where he's smiling and conspiring with me?

I like this.

And you have a real life to get back to, Phoebe, that sinister little voice in the back of my head whispers.

She sounds like a cross between Gigi and my father.

I frown. "Wait. If you didn't know we were hosting dinner, what *do* you know about that I don't?"

His grin goes even brighter before it disappears completely, his gaze darting behind me.

It's the only warning I get before the door rams into my back, sending me tumbling straight into Teague with an unladylike "Fuck!" slipping out of my lips.

Funny thing about fishing lumberjacks, though.

They're remarkably solid, and they make good catchers.

Two rock-hard tree trunks wrap around my ribs, and I get a heady whiff of pine and toast and something with just a hint of spice, like he had cinnamon and cloves in his morning coffee.

Also, his T-shirt is the softest fabric I've ever felt in my life.

And it's warm.

Warm with all his body heat.

"Dear God, Phoebe, please tell me you're not so desperate for attention that you're throwing yourself at the local riffraff?" my mother says behind me.

I tense.

But when I straighten and cast a glance at Teague, he's not visibly offended.

If anything, he looks . . . *satisfied*? "I believe the phrase you're looking for, Mrs. Lightly, is, *I'm sorry, Phoebe. Are you okay?*"

Mom's nose lifts.

"He's right, Mom," I murmur. "We're in Tickled Pink. The gate angels are watching."

Her forehead doesn't move—that's what Botox is for—but her lips purse. "I'm sure they are. Phoebe, how do you feel about a mommy-daughter shopping day in . . . that other town."

"Deer Drop?" I prompt.

One of her eyelids flutters low. "If we truly wanted to help the people here, we'd rename that place."

"Good bait shop over in Deer Drop," Teague says. "Best live worms around. And the Farm-'n'-Fish has overalls on sale. Not sure what other shopping there is to do, but the Deer Droppers are good people. Bet they could teach you a thing or two about being good people. Except Deer Drop Floyd. Avoid him. He'll try to get in your pants."

"Stop," I whisper to him, wanting to smile but also realizing that if I do, I'm undoing all the good I've done for my personal progress. I should *not* take joy in my mom's suffering. "She's not ready for you."

"Can we help you?" Mom asks Teague.

"Got a meeting with your matriarch at nine."

Mom and I both look at our watches, see that it's 9:02, and suck in the same breath of horror.

"Go!" Mom cries. "Go on. You're late!"

I nod. "You really don't want to be late."

But Teague studies us both like *we're* the crazy ones. "Maybe if Estelle wants to get into heaven, she should try to learn the world doesn't revolve around her." He tips his baseball cap at us and steps between us. "Enjoy your morning, ladies. I'm off for a leisurely stroll through the halls of someone else's youth."

He slips inside the building, his shoulder brushing mine and making goose bumps erupt all over my skin.

I look at my mom.

She smiles, clearly oblivious to what Teague's body apparently does to mine. "As I said. We should have a shopping day."

I don't ask if she's supposed to be working.

She has fifty-five years of not working under her belt. At least, not doing the kind of work Gigi wants us to do here. And despite the random sketches I've seen at the occasional meal since we arrived, I don't think she's doing much to expand her fashion empire either.

"I have to go to class."

"Oh, Phoebe, skip class! You're brilliant. You'll still pass."

"Gigi's donating five million dollars to the school on the condition that I don't skip class." Somehow, she's managed to make actual moral dilemmas for me.

If I skip class, I'm not just hurting myself.

I'm hurting the people who stand to benefit from Gigi's donation.

I won't call it kindness or charity—Gigi could drop $5 million daily for the rest of her life and still die a billionaire without so much as glancing at the trust funds she controls for the rest of us—but it's still a massive infusion of capital for an area that doesn't get a lot of donations like this.

"Maybe after school we can grab lunch and hit the Deer Drop gift shop?" I offer Mom.

Her eyelid does its irritated flutter again. "Fine, fine. We can play this game. I'll drive."

"Mom—"

"Of the two of us, dear, I'm not the one who tried to kill the car yesterday."

She loves you most, Tavi's voice whispers right near the part of my brain that's inspiring all these feelings of guilt the past few days. And has Mom always been so harsh on Tavi about her weight?

I should talk to her about that.

Mom, I mean. She probably doesn't realize she might be hurting Tavi's feelings.

I reach into my clutch and pull out the keys. "When's the last time you drove?"

"I drive all the time at our country estate in the Catskills."

Her fingers twitch impatiently.

But I hold the keys just out of reach. "Mom? Why are you here?"

"To support your grandmother, dear. It's what you do for family."

She's lying. There are very few things that I know with 100 percent certainty in my life these days, but I know without a doubt that my mother is lying.

Not your journey, Phoebe.

So I nod and hand her the keys. "That's great, Mom. And thank you for spending the day with me. It'll be really good for both of us."

It will.

Won't it?

Chapter 15

Phoebe

Dear sweet internet.

Oh my God, dear sweet internet.

I get a signal as soon as we hit the community college's parking lot, and after having zero signal since we got here and then forgetting I could bring my phone with me yesterday, it almost feels surreal. Mom and I both hear my phone explode with text and voice mail notifications, and she bursts into sobs and almost takes out a squirrel that has no idea the parking lot is suddenly a danger zone.

"Oh my sweet Wi-Fi," I gasp when I enter the password the school gave me yesterday too.

I barely notice the SUV lurching to a stop or Mom rustling in her handbag beside me for her own phone, also exploding with notifications. "I'm so sorry, baby," she sobs. "Mommy will never abandon you again."

"Mom, you didn't—"

"Shh. I'm talking to the internet. Let me have my moment, Phoebe. *Let me have my moment.*"

I'd be offended, except *oh my God, the real world.*

There are messages from friends asking if I'm still alive. Invitations to galas and fundraisers and parties. A notification on my private email that—*"What?"*

"What *what*?" Mom's scrolling through her phone like she's having her first gin and tonic after crawling through the Sahara without water.

"She disabled my work email. *She disabled my work email!*"

I switch over to my Remington Lightly corporate app, and *oh my God.*

She did.

She completely locked me out.

I can't access my work email. I can't access my files. And it's not that someone's changed my password.

My username doesn't even exist.

And while I'm having a next-level crisis here, Mom's already on the phone.

"Hello, Rosita? This is Margot Lightly. I'd like to book a full spa experience, please, but I'm going to need you to bring the spa to me, because my mother-in-law is having a late-life identity crisis and she can't be left alone. No, no, no need for services for her too. But if you could pack an extra therapist and massage table, I'll treat my daughters as well. I—excuse me? She did *what*?"

Mom goes as pale as my favorite shade of platinum blonde.

One guess what's happening here.

Estelle Lightly. My grandmother. Ruler of our universe.

She's blocked us from any chance at connecting with our real world.

"Yes, thank you. I'll simply make arrangements with a different spa. One who caters to their clients' actual needs."

She hangs up, gripping her phone so tightly that I wouldn't be surprised if she launched it out the window next. The lines at the corners of her mouth are stark white, lips pressed together so hard she could probably crack a macadamia between them. "Your grandmother—"

"You should go home, Mom. *Home* home. To New York."

I didn't think it was possible for her to get any paler, but her entire complexion is so pasty I actually feel the need to touch her to make sure she hasn't morphed into a ghost.

She snatches her hand back from my grasp. "What kind of mother would I be if I abandoned my babies to the whims of that psychopath? I blame myself for letting her have any influence on you at all, you know. Phoebe, you're so—you're so bright. And such a hard worker. You could succeed anywhere. There's no reason for you to take this treatment by your grandmother. I'll slip you money, sweetheart. I have a little hidden away. Save yourself. Run away and save yourself."

My phone dings again, and I glance down to see a notification from Fletcher.

Ignore me one more day at your own peril, Lightly. I've already turned half of Manhattan against you.

Before Tickled Pink, I wouldn't have hesitated to reach into that secret folder on my phone and send him the same picture I could send to any gossip rag in the city to remind him who he's playing with.

But I can't do it.

Not because I have any qualms about destroying Fletcher Barrington. He's a scab on the crust of humanity.

No, it's because I'm picturing someone sending photos and gossip regarding Teague Miller's daughter to a tabloid. I'm feeling the wrath that would come from Papa Bear at anyone attacking Bridget for who she is.

Fletcher's lover is married with kids.

It's not my place to ruin his life too.

"Phoebe—"

"Why are you here, Mom?"

She looks me square in the eye, and for that moment, everything hangs still.

I know Gigi has dirt on all of us. She probably knows everything from why I didn't get the promotion I wanted to where Fletcher's grandfather's watch is right now to when I lost my virginity and how many times I *have* leaked damning pictures to the press.

Sometimes pictures of my friends.

Sometimes pictures of colleagues.

Sometimes pictures of former friends and lovers.

I'm no angel.

None of us are.

I know my mom has skeletons too.

But I don't know what they are.

She breaks eye contact, looking back down at her phone. "I'm here because I could never let my children endure this alone."

My dad's always said that I'm the spitting image of my mother. Watching her profile, the way her lips move subtly as she scrolls her phone, the curve of her ear, the soft indent in her cheek that's not quite a full dimple, the line of her nose—I realize he's right.

I am completely my mother's daughter.

And I always thought it was only on the outside.

I like fashion, but I had no desire to go into that business. I like parties, but not to the degree she does. I like travel, but I'd never drop everything to jet off to Monaco on a spur-of-the-moment girls' trip.

But I *would* drop everything to head to a corporate retreat with company-provided spa treatments. I would give my Louboutins to be able to stroll into Persephone Richardson's engagement party tonight. And while my mother's handbags and shoes haven't reached the level of success that she pretends they have, probably because her true talents don't lie in designs and her pride won't let her admit that, I have no doubt I got my business sense—not my drive but my *sense*, the instincts to leap on trends to sell things and the ability to adapt when necessary—from her.

God knows my father has none, despite what he tells his buddies on the fairway, where he spends more time than he spends in the office.

But I still don't know why Mom's here.

I want to. I want to know why she's here. I want her to trust me enough to tell me.

I want to be worthy of that trust.

Gigi's methods might be heavy handed, but she's right. We're not good people. We do terrible things.

I can't make my family be better, but I can make *myself* be better.

"Mom, I need to call my assistant and reply to a text quick, and then how about we get coffee?"

"Forget the coffee, darling. Mommy needs a vodka."

She flips her phone around so I can see it, and *oh my God* again.

That's me.

In full color.

Being dragged to shore by Teague last week.

On the *Post*'s website.

Forget the vodka.

I need a complete and total new life.

Chapter 16

Phoebe

What's the word for when you're hiding from one task you don't want to do by pretending to do algebra homework that looks like it's written in Greek?

There has to be *some* language that has a word for that. Like that German *grief bacon* word.

I'd look it up as I'm procrastinating on my algebra homework Friday afternoon, except Anna—*Anya*, dammit, still working on that—steadfastly refuses to give me the Wi-Fi password here in Café Nirvana, which is probably for the best, even if I don't want to admit it.

The internet has not been kind to me.

At all.

Is there a word in any language that means *the feeling one has when she realizes she has no idea who she is or what she wants, but she should definitely not ask that question of the internet when the people who love to see her fail are talking all about all the ways in which she's failed spectacularly?*

Mental note: look up that word tomorrow.

Or maybe I'll invent it.

Excellent plan, Phoebe. Your legacy shall be new, complicated words that will be so much clunkier in English than they would be in any other language.

Now, what's my favorite letter?

I gaze out the window, eyes roaming over the ivy-covered half–Ferris wheel across the square as if it can answer my questions, instead of doing homework or heading back to the high school to help dig up the floor in the gymnasium, since it's apparently rotted and needs to be replaced before a visiting paparazzo breaks into the school through the basement, gets scared by Tickled Pink Floyd's ghost, and crashes through the subfloor and into the slimy, wet mess left when the other day's fix on the water heater didn't work.

Everything in this town is falling down.

I keep hearing whispers about increasing tourism, but tourism for what?

A ghost town?

The closed high school's a disaster, and it's not like anyone else will move in when we're done. *Or* want to visit a memorial to my grandmother. The half-done Ferris wheel has been reclaimed by nature. The shops all need a fresh coat of paint, especially the empty ones. There's a gaping empty hole in the square where there used to be a fountain, and I heard whispers that people are hoping we'll find the original golden gates from the *Pink Gold* film when we finally clean out the rest of the junk in the high school.

It's like this town is what my family would've been if my great-grandfather hadn't mortgaged his house to the hilt when Remington Lightly's first product—intended to be a new kind of linen paper for poets, scientists, and businessmen—failed on the market, leading to a complete rebranding campaign that launched a new kind of toilet paper instead.

Yep.

We got rich on accidental toilet paper in a big gamble that paid off.

Yet here we are, looking down our noses at people who work hard every day in the shadow of what could've been, because their big gamble didn't pay off.

And what am I gambling?

Nothing.

Nothing.

I live well because my great-grandfather accidentally invented a better kind of toilet paper a century ago. But I won't leave anything behind. The world won't be talking about my contributions, my successes, my legacy, or anything else when I'm gone.

Not at this rate.

"You know, most people get their homework done by putting the pencil on the paper and doing the work."

Even if I didn't recognize Bridget's voice, I'd recognize the speech pattern.

The apple didn't fall far from the tree with that one.

I grip my coffee cup and lift my gaze slowly until she's had to wait for my attention. Old habits and all. Plus, I'd do the same to her father.

It's half the fun. "Can I help you?"

She tilts her head and studies me with her brown eyes flickering over my face. "Is that supposed to be an intimidation tactic? You shouldn't try so hard. Just paint your lips and nails bloodred and wear a few more of those suits like you did when you first got here, and you manage it naturally. Actually, maybe if you did that, your homework would've bowed to your demands and done itself by now . . ."

Anya makes a noise that's most likely a stifled laugh behind the bakery counter. "Bridget. Don't talk to adults like that."

"Even Phoebe?"

There's that noise again. "Yes, even Phoebe."

Bridget rolls her eyes.

Anya's face twists like she's trying not to laugh, and she goes back to restocking those Café Nirvana tumblers that are crazy effective at keeping coffee hot. I took three of them with me this morning, and the last one was still piping when I finally opened it after lunch.

Anya's shelf was full when I left this morning, which means the tourists who were gawking at the high school must've bought some.

Thank Oprah for curtains. One was trying to look into my bedroom window.

I lean back in the booth and gesture for Bridget to sit opposite me. "You're in school."

"I'm on summer break."

"But you've been in school more recently than I have. You have more recent practice at good homework habits."

She squints at me, then looks over her shoulder. "Aunt Anya, Phoebe's buying me a coffee. Can I have one of those *fancy* coffees, please? The one that tastes like crème brûlée? Oh! Or one of the s'mores lattes? Or both?"

I don't twitch as I nod my agreement to Anya. It's a *good* thing they don't give us the best, fanciest, most delicious coffee here, even though, despite what Anya told me the first day, they clearly make it.

They're wearing us down.

Making us want to leave.

That's the plan, right?

"Whatever she wants," I agree.

Ridhi pokes her head out of the kitchen. "*One* coffee, Bridge. Remember what happened the last time you overdosed on caffeine?"

Bridget rolls her eyes again. "No one got hurt."

"What happened the last time you overdosed on caffeine?" I ask her.

She flashes a grin that has so much Teague in it that I subconsciously lean forward.

Stop it, Phoebe. Stop liking the lumberjack, and stop trying to get close to him through his kid.

"Tickled Pink secret," Bridget says. "I'd tell you, but you haven't had your initiation yet."

Oh, for Oprah's sake. "That's fine. I'll make up my own version."

"Can it involve fairy wings and a sparkly clutch and diamond-crusted heels and me saving Prince Charming from a flock of baby bunnies that we adopt afterward?"

"There's nothing embarrassing in that."

"You can have an embarrassing story about me and keep fumbling through your algebra homework, or you can spread a rumor to all the New York tabloids that I'm the catch of the century, and I'll show you what you're doing wrong with that polynomial equation."

"So you want your father to kill me." I slowly sip my own coffee, contemplate how it doesn't taste like it was made with dead fish today, and wonder if that's on purpose. Have *I* passed some kind of initiation right here? Have I leveled up my coffee? It was legitimately good yesterday too. *Good* good. With a shot of caramel and a dash of milk, even.

Maybe Fridays are good-coffee days.

Or maybe, just maybe, there's more to this town than I thought.

"Actually, I want a job," Bridget says. "It gets *so boring* here in the summer, and I'm getting my driver's license next year, and I want a car so I can go hang out in Deer Drop."

"Deer Drop," Anya sneers to herself behind the counter while Ridhi pokes her head out of the kitchen to frown at us again.

Bridget slides me a sly smile.

I'd bet my Louboutins—the ones *not* at the bottom of the lake—that she's baiting her aunt and stepmother on purpose.

"You know algebra?" I ask her.

"I'm a genius. If we were in New York, *I'd* be running your family's company. Not that I want to. I'm going to engineer the next generation of solar panels when I graduate college."

"Today," Anya murmurs as she hands Bridget a small coffee cup. "Tomorrow, you'll be plotting how to be queen of a small nation."

"Tomorrow, Deer Drop; next week, Canada," Bridget replies. "Thank you for the coffee, Aunt Anya. Now, Phoebe, tell me what *x* is supposed to be here."

If she weren't hounding me about my homework, I might honestly appreciate this teenager. "Do you ever wonder what you'll use algebra for when you grow up?"

"Who cares? It's fun when you're good at it."

"Is algebra itself fun, or is mocking others for not knowing algebra fun?"

"I'm not mocking you. I'm building your character. There's a difference. Do you want help or not?"

What I *want* is to pay her to do my homework for me. But Gigi would find out.

Gigi knows all.

That's the one trick my grandmother has that I haven't yet learned.

"I would love help. Thank you."

Her whole face lights up like this is the biggest gift she's ever been given, which is interesting.

When we got here, I was sure seeing Tavi was the biggest gift she'd ever been given. And then learning about her own journey—I would've thought having supportive parents was her biggest gift.

But she's clearly excited about algebra.

So excited, in fact, that she's leaning toward me, pointing at the equation scrawled across the top of my paper, rambling in a foreign tongue.

I stare at her blankly with the same look I use—no, *used to use*—on my underlings at Remington Lightly when they'd start going into the weeds on issues I didn't care about.

She pauses midway through her lecture and cracks up. "Oh man, you're really lost, aren't you? Is this a Friday-afternoon thing, or are you always bad at math?"

"I haven't been in a school mindset in a decade. This takes time."

"A decade? You were twenty-eight when you graduated?"

My grandmother's essence floods my body, and I feel myself levitating off the bench. "I am *not* almost *forty*, you—you—"

"Wow, Dad's right. This really is easy."

Anya visibly stifles another laugh. "Bridget, be nice. It's hard being off your normal game."

"I was just testing the theory, Aunt Anya. This was scientific. I swear."

The bells jingle on the door, and five people I don't recognize peek their heads in. "Oh my gosh, this is just like the picture on Tavi's feed," one whispers.

Bridget rolls her eyes and sticks her tongue out. "Deer Droppers," she whispers, like we're friends and she wasn't baiting me moments ago.

"How the *hell* did Tavi update her feed with pictures from this place?" I whisper back, since her baiting me doesn't matter if there's a secret method of getting Wi-Fi.

Bridget smirks. "Ten bucks for that information."

"I bought your coffee."

"Not yet, you haven't. For all I know, you'll stiff my stepmom and my aunt."

"It's not like they don't know where I live to come get payment if I do. Or maybe you'll invent a love interest for Tickled Pink Floyd's ghost so that we have to hear extra moaning and mutterings all night long. Or maybe you can torture us by intentionally sending us plumbers who keep booby-trapping the hot water in the school. Or *maybe* you can just give me the damn Wi-Fi password like you did for Tavi."

"Bluetooth transfers still work even without Wi-Fi, so she transferred the pictures to me, and I sent them to her publicist. Need anything sent to your people? I'm super affordable."

"I'll buy you a car myself if you pass algebra for me. *And* quit helping Tavi cheat."

"Your grandmother would probably buy me a house *and* a car if I told her how much you guys are all skirting the corners of your assignments on being better people. Lucky for you, I don't like manipulative beasts, though, so I won't tell. At least, not today. Although do you know what I *will* do for you?"

It's a trap.

Whatever this is, it's a trap. "What?"

"I'll be your private tutor to help you get through algebra."

I gesture to the paper. "News flash—I can't understand a single word you just said when you were trying to explain this to me. And I'm not hiring a tutor who speaks in demonic tongues instead of English."

"Okay, okay. Here. Start again."

"Oh my God, is that one of them?" I hear one of the tourists whisper.

My shoulders want to bunch, and my face wants to get hot.

I'm a Lightly, dammit. I can handle this.

Bridget squints at me. "They can't hurt you, you know. Not if you don't let them. The only person whose opinion matters is you and anyone you choose to let in."

"That's—"

"Easy for me to say?" She quirks a grin. "You really are sheltered, aren't you?"

I suck in a deep breath.

I don't think I'm sheltered.

I think I've just never had the kind of support that this kid has.

"We're solving for *x*," I remind her.

She rolls her eyes with a laugh. "Okay, lake lady. Let's do this."

Chapter 17

Teague

Lake's crowded today, like it is most Fridays, Saturdays, and Sundays through the summer, but the fish are biting, my cooler's loaded down with Jane's Garage honey-wheat ale and another round of cold roast-beef sandwiches, I like everyone on the boats around me, and Estelle Lightly actually went a shade of horrified as I was showing her the best office space Tickled Pink has to offer the other day.

Wins all around.

"That a bass?" Willie Wayne calls to me as I unhook a four-teen-incher and toss it back into the lake late afternoon.

"Largemouth," I call back.

He grins. "Those are biting on- *and* offshore, aren't they?"

"Shush your mouth before that Lightly woman quits throwing money at us," Jane says.

Don't really want her money.

Took it all right the other day, though. Again. And I know the town'll put it to good use.

But I also chased a reporter from Madison out of town this morning when I caught him snooping on the overgrown football field behind the old high school, and there's no telling how many have sneaked in when I wasn't looking.

"What'd the older Lightly guy want at your house last night?" Willie Wayne asks Jane.

She tips her head back and laughs. "Wants to know how to make his own beer. He's thinking he'll put Tickled Pink on the map with Michael Lightly Brews."

I wince.

Willie Wayne winces.

Even the Deer Droppers out on the lake close enough to overhear wince.

You don't walk into Jane's garage and assume that because she does it, anyone can. She's been perfecting her recipes for years.

And if Michael Lightly's planning on brewing the way he was sweeping floors that first day that we all pitched in to help clean the high school—which is to say, shortcut after shortcut when he wasn't trying to bribe someone else to do it for him—it's safe to say his beer would taste like bear piss.

"You gonna teach him?" Willie Wayne finally asks her.

"Oh, I'll teach him something."

"Can I be a fly on your wall when you do?"

"I'll do you one better and let you be a guest lecturer."

I snort with laughter, even though we're starting to get dirty looks. Undoubtedly for scaring the fish.

But the idea of having Willie Wayne try to explain how to brew beer is on par with the idea of having Jane try to make Ridhi's oatcakes.

Neither one's gonna work out well.

"Hey, Teague, that one of them Lightlys over with Bridget?"

Jane nods to the shore, and I straighten and look over my shoulder.

And then I pull my hat off and scratch my head, because that definitely looks like Bridget shoving off in a boat with Phoebe perched at the other end. "Huh."

Not sure how I feel about this.

On the one hand, Phoebe's tolerable.

Hot, you mean, my brain corrects.

I mentally flip myself off and get back to the other hand.

And the other hand is that I don't want her setting examples for my daughter.

Probably.

She *did* apologize for running into me last time I saw her. Know that had to take a lot.

"She looks a lot different in lake clothes," Willie Wayne muses.

"She came to see me yesterday too." Jane kicks back in her boat and casts out away from me. "Asked if she could buy a beer off my doorstep and then asked personal questions."

Don't ask. Don't ask. Don't ask.

Willie Wayne does it for me. "Personal questions?"

"Yeah. She asked if I'd ever had to get revenge on an ex for being a twatwaffle and if I think hell really exists."

Now he's scratching his head too. "What'd you tell her?"

"That she has to earn the story about Deer Drop Floyd."

Willie Wayne and I both nod. Fair answer to both questions.

"She thanked me, asked if it was appropriate to leave a tip for garage beer, and then told me she hoped that her family descending on my town was the worst of hell for me."

Phoebe's trying. I'll give her that.

I'll give her that every day of the week right now, matter of fact.

But what I don't know is if it's an act to satisfy her grandmother or if she's actually having a personal reckoning with her life.

I reel my line in and wait for Bridget to motor to a stop near me. My boat rocks softly over the little wakes, and I can't stop shooting looks at Phoebe.

She's sitting at the helm, facing backward, legs tucked under her like royalty, wearing casual pants and a tight raspberry-colored tank top under an open white oxford shirt knotted at her waist, and she's holding a white bucket hat to her head.

There's a hint of a smile touching her lips as she tilts her head to the sky, but her eyes are hidden behind her sunglasses, so I have no idea if she's enjoying the day or if she's plotting to drop a bomb in the lake and scare all the fish into never biting again.

Or maybe send her grandmother scuba diving.

That'd do it.

Those fish would go so far into hiding they'd never come out again.

She's also talking, though. Like she's saying something to my kid, who's grinning in response while she slows the boat, holding it not too far away but not getting close enough for an accident. She's in her usual—a crop top T-shirt with a giant floating Lady Gaga head, ripped jeans, and the bright, neon-green sneakers Ridhi got her for her birthday. "Dad! Can I tutor Phoebe in algebra?"

"No."

"*Dad.* She's not paying me to take the class *for* her."

Phoebe's smile is demure amusement. "Learned that lesson already."

"But she's really bad at math when it doesn't involve dollars and cents, and I could use a few more dollars in *my* bank account so I can go see the Neon Panic concert when they're in Milwaukee, *and* she says she'll fund the cat shelter for the next *year*, plus teach us to fundraise ourselves so we're not as strapped for cash all the time when her donation runs out. Besides, isn't the world a better place when one more person knows basic algebra?"

I flick my gaze over both of them.

Bridget's giving me the mulish *don't be a stick-in-the-mud* teenager look, despite the fact that I know she's lying about why she wants money, which is probably because Shiloh and I are in complete agreement that she's not getting a car when she turns sixteen, and even if we weren't, Ridhi feels so strongly about it on her own she'd overrule us like she's the Estelle Lightly of the family.

Phoebe lifts her sunglasses, which aren't at all necessary given the cloud cover rolling in and the fact that it's nearly six, and she stares right back. *Go on. Tell me I have to fail on my own when your kid is brilliant and the whole town would benefit from my bribe.*

Willie Wayne coughs. Jane leans our way like she's afraid she'll miss something good if she leaves.

Bridge lowers her face and bats her eyelashes at me. "*Please*, Dad?"

"Good lesson in character building if you do it for free," I tell her.

She gasps.

Phoebe's lips twist.

"Or if you find something else you want that doesn't cost anything. Maybe Phoebe should agree to pose for you as a model for your painting for every hour you spend tutoring her. Or . . . huh. Phoebe, what else are you good at?"

Bridget scowls. "That is *not* fair."

"In addition to knowing how to milk money out of people, I'm an excellent fashion consultant," Phoebe says.

"If you teach my daughter how to manipulate people, your grand-mother will be the least of your worries."

Her mouth twists into an amused smile. "Wow. That really *was* easy."

One point to Phoebe.

That won't do, and don't let the fact that I'm struggling to not smile fool you. I'm not amused. "As to your other offer, your fashion sense is lacking. Bridge, you want to work in an office all day and spend your nights going to parties with people you don't like?"

Phoebe tugs her ponytail back over her shoulder. "That's very pre-sumptuous of you that my knowledge of couture would be limited to professional and formal attire."

"No offense, but he's right," Bridget tells Phoebe. "Your aesthetic really doesn't vibe with my personality. I'm gonna be a marine biologist who plays in a grunge-rock band on the weekends."

Today, anyway.

Last week, she was going to be a social justice warrior, and the week before, she wanted to be a band teacher.

The music part's consistent. I'll give her that.

Phoebe's not deterred by Bridget's initial rejections. Naturally. "I thought you said you were going to be a solar panel engineer."

"Hello, I can do *all* of them."

"Do you play an instrument?"

"I'm learning guitar."

"So's my brother."

Bridget cracks up.

"Hot damn, she's funny?" Willie Wayne says.

"I'm multitalented, Mr. Johnson."

"Jorgenson," he corrects.

Her nose wrinkles. "I have name blindness. My apologies."

"That's not a thing," Jane mutters.

"It depends on your social circles, and I'm trying to get over it," Phoebe tells her. She turns back to me. "If I can't pay for tutoring and I can't barter for services, then are we out here for nothing, or are you merely enjoying the fact that I've once again had to get in a boat to come negotiate with you? Not that I mind. Your daughter is a *lovely* conversationalist, and she knows so much about the town."

And you is the unspoken rest of that sentence.

Shit.

What's Bridget telling her? How long have these two been hanging out today?

And why am I enjoying this more than I should? "You could volunteer at the cat shelter with Bridget."

"Oh, *swag*, you *could*," Bridget squeals. "We have kittens. They're *so* cute. You'll love them. We have to play with them so they get socialized right."

Phoebe's eyes narrow. "*Volunteering* entails playing with kittens?"

"And cleaning up litter boxes," I offer.

"And finding them forever homes," Bridget adds. "You could totally call your friends back in New York and introduce them to homegrown Wisconsin kittens that they *need* in their lives."

Phoebe's smile goes tight. "One would think."

Huh.

Wonder if she's been checking her emails when she's in Deer Drop and isn't liking what she's seeing.

"Dunno, Bridge," I say. "Seems Tavi has the better platform for that."

And there it is.

I have finally poked the bear.

Idiot, my good shoulder angel says.

Pass the popcorn, my bad shoulder angel replies.

She's hot when she's pissed, my crotch chimes in. *And you know we like her hot. Like in that dream last night.*

Phoebe's straightening slowly, like she's stretching before a good fight. "Mr. Miller, are you aware of exactly *why* my grandmother needed space in that abomination of a closed-up community hall you showed her the other day?"

Unfortunately, I do. "She's trying to buy her way out of hell?"

"She's conducting interviews for biographers, screenwriters, and directors to tell the story of her near-death experience."

Can't deny that news gave me pause.

But even if all the Hollywood and literary types invade Tickled Pink, too, it usually takes years to get projects off the ground, and there's no way in hell anything's getting filmed here.

We're known for *Pink Gold.*

There's not a person in this town who would rather it be known for Estelle Lightly. *That,* we won't let happen. And I'll be leading the charge to stop her.

Means doing things I haven't done in years, things I swore I'd never do again, but there's something about having the Lightly family in town that's making it hard to deny who I am at my core.

Not today's problem, though.

Especially since, unlike with the school, Estelle's calling in actual contractors to fix the old community center.

I lean back in my easy chair and pop the footrest, even though the clouds approaching and the dipping sun are telling me that it's about time to head back to shore for the day. "Tell you what, Ms. Lightly. You want Bridget to tutor you, you'll volunteer at the cat shelter two hours a week, pay her whatever Shiloh says is a fair rate, *and* you'll make sure none of those literary and film people your grandmother wants to bring to town show up."

"You're being unreasonable," Bridget tells me. "Having an educated population is good for all of us, and Phoebe's working on her education."

I tuck my hands under my head. "If I was being unreasonable, I'd just say no."

"You know I could tutor her in secret."

That's my kid. Arguing with me over ways she can help someone else.

Definitely got that from her mother.

"She worth the risk of lying to your parents?" I ask Bridget.

"She's not offering me drugs or teaching me how to lie, steal, and cheat my way to the top, Dad. And I know she's a great example of what *not* to do. We haven't had this many *Tickled Pink Papers* printed since I was like eight."

Phoebe's shoulders tense, but I only notice because I'm watching.

Or maybe her boat rocked wrong.

But there's no denying the way her lips tightened too.

Probably because I'm grinning. Bet Jane and Willie Wayne are too.

Not every day someone prompts the gossip page to run with the same thing two days in a row, but Phoebe did it.

Except this time, instead of giving herself a flat tire, she ran into a mailbox.

The one right in front of the Tickled Pink fire station, matter of fact.

"My mother thought she saw someone wearing Tulip Pendragon and temporarily distracted me" was her excuse.

She's not making excuses now, though. "Your daughter clearly knows better than to follow my lead on anything, if you're worried about me setting a bad example."

Bridge nods. "Seriously. Did you see what she picked for her last boyfriend?"

"Psychopath," Jane mutters.

"Entitled ass," Willie Wayne agrees. "Hope we don't get that tower fixed now."

Now I'm pissed, and I don't know why.

All right, fine.

I *do* know why.

If she has bad taste in men and she's flirting with me, what does that say about me?

That's not why, you liar, my good shoulder angel says.

My bad shoulder angel doesn't chime in. He's fallen off laughing.

Because I know why Willie Wayne doesn't want the tower fixed.

It's because Phoebe's last ex-boyfriend is the heir to the telecommunications company that owns it, and I don't want to think about her ex-boyfriends.

It's also because Phoebe's last ex-boyfriend is spreading rumors through the tabloids in New York that she got caught sleeping with a married man while trying to work her way up the corporate ladder, and Phoebe's name is mud in her home social circles right now.

I'd claim I only know that because Bridget's been digging into the gossip pages, but that would also be a lie.

I've been digging into the gossip pages.

Phoebe Lightly is addictive, and if I can't be verbally sparring with her, driving her around, and kissing her, then I want to be looking at gossip about her.

My name is Teague Miller, and I have a problem.

"So we're agreed then," Bridget says. "Thank you, Dad. I'll ask Mom what's a fair rate."

"I didn't—"

Phoebe smiles at me. "You're a really great father, Teague. I wish my father had been half as supportive and attentive to my influences as you are to Bridget's."

And now I'm getting hot in the cheeks, because that almost sounded sincere. "That's not—"

"Bridget, can I drive the boat?" Phoebe asks.

Bridge points the *stay in your seat* finger at her. "No. You're a nuisance. No offense, I mean, but your driving record basically speaks for itself."

"You can't get a flat tire in a boat."

"No, but you could hit another boat, and they could all sink. Or the Tickled Pink Monster could leap out of the water and eat you."

"The *what*?"

"The Tickled Pink Monster."

"Scotland has Loch Ness," Jane says.

Willie Wayne nods. "We have the Tickled Pink Monster. Used to be Tickled Pink Floyd's pet lizard."

He takes off his hat and falls silent.

Bridget puts a hand to her heart.

Jane pulls off her hat, too, and gives me a look.

So I pull off my hat too.

"Sad tale," I mutter.

Bridget shoots me a death glare. "We don't like to talk about it."

"Just like Tickled Pink Floyd."

Phoebe's gaze wavers as she sweeps it over the four of us. "You're telling me the ghost of the high school had a giant lizard that now haunts this lake?"

Bridget flaps a hand at her. "Shh. We're having a moment of silence."

And everyone's worried about *Phoebe* being the bad influence.

"Back to fishing," Jane declares. "Go quiet on your way in, Bridge. Got a feeling I might catch me a big one quick before the storm rolls in."

"Or another shoe." Willie Wayne lifts a fancy heel.

Phoebe gasps and lunges. *"My Louboutin!"*

Bridget squeaks and reaches for her, but she's too late.

Deer Drop Lake, two; Phoebe Lightly, zero.

Chapter 18

Phoebe

I should've gone down with my Louboutins on that first day here in Tickled Pink.

That would've been easier.

Instead, I'm groaning with every step as I descend the high school's musty-smelling staircase to the basement, shower caddy in hand, wrapped in my bath towel, to the sounds of Carter wailing the same two lines over and over again—*you don't love love love me like the moon moon moon, you don't light light light me like the moon moon moon*—his amp dialed up high enough that they can probably hear him all the way up in the Milky Way.

I'm wearing noise-canceling headphones, and I'm *still* in danger of going deaf.

At least Carter's wailing is canceling out the sounds of Tickled Pink Floyd moaning and muttering in the air ducts.

I glare at the vent at the bottom of the stairs. "Come out and fight me, you asshole ghost. I'm in a mood."

The ghost doesn't materialize.

Naturally.

Because it's a ghost.

Except it's not, because ghosts aren't real. It's probably a Bluetooth speaker hidden somewhere deep in the vents that someone in town is using to try to scare us away.

I'd give them a high five of appreciation—hell, I'd give them a billion dollars—except the ghost ploy isn't working to scare Gigi away. And on top of not working, it's waking me up at night.

If I actually fall asleep in the first place, that is.

My mattress is hard as a brick. Gigi ordered two-hundred-thread-count, scratchy cotton sheets for our new beds, and I forgot to order myself new Matouk percale sheets and new silk pillowcases when I was on the internet at school this week. And my body is so very tired and sore in places I didn't know it *could* be tired and sore after days of painting, cleaning, weeding, mowing, and hauling junk.

Hence the groaning.

Except, in the middle of the night, I'm not always sure the ghost *isn't* real. I *swear* I saw something ghostly when I got up to try a yoga routine to help me fall asleep the other night, and I swear it was carrying a heavy scent of chocolate with it.

Possibly it was the ghost of my pre–Tickled Pink life.

The one dying a slow death in the gossip pages in New York right now while Fletcher threatens to fly here himself to retrieve the watch that I told him I gave to a charity drive at work, *despite* all the ammunition he's giving the tabloids.

Bonus tonight?

A thunderstorm's rolled in, which means everything inside this depressing high school is dark enough to require that we have the lights on already, and they're flickering from the pull that Carter's amps are putting on the electrical system.

No problem.

Wanna know why?

Because I'm about to take a cold shower to wash all the lake water off me.

Again.

Because it's "good for character growth." We haven't *earned* hot water yet.

Not if all our attempts at fixing the plumbing have failed.

And they have.

Spectacularly.

It's a sign from God, Gigi says.

I march around the corner at the base of the steps, trudge past a row of empty trophy cases marked for donation to a school somewhere else, since Gigi wants the trophy cases in the Estelle Lightly Memorial Exhibit for Good to be hand carved by some artist she knows back in New York, and stomp into the girls' locker room.

I don't know where Tavi is. Probably hiding in her room, or maybe she's waiting out the storm somewhere. She's exercising like a fiend when she's not helping around the school, and she's rarely here when we have time off. I literally don't know how she's not dying right now, considering her diet is basically like three chickpeas, cucumber water, and undressed spinach.

Mom's hiding in her room, no question, which is a nice break from her offering to do breakfast, lunch, dinner, and shopping with me every day this week.

She wants out of Tickled Pink like most people want vegetables to taste like ice cream, and I'm the only family member officially authorized by Gigi to leave the town's boundaries.

I'd like to have more patience for her efforts to get to know me better again, except I feel as though it's all for show.

Like *I'm* her secret project from Gigi.

Maybe Tavi was right. Maybe Mom *does* want to have a better relationship with me, and that's the only fault Gigi can find with her.

It's not like she'd be kept out of heaven for knowing her husband cheats on her and doing nothing about it or for being a second-rate designer, and Mom fully owns every way she's ever blackmailed, manipulated, and insulted everyone around her.

You can't make a person grow a soul if they don't want to.

Which would mean Mom cares about me more than I thought she did.

If I'm her project.

And suddenly I'm not sure of anything at all again.

Dad's painting the cafeteria. I'm assuming Gigi found out about his trip to see Jane yesterday and is threatening to tell the Remington Lightly board that Dad's infidelity is grounds for dismissal, not just a leave of absence.

Probably also that she'll revoke his membership to the Bergamot Club if he doesn't paint the cafeteria, which might be the bigger threat. I don't know if he loves golf most or if he loves being a member of the golf club most, but I know it's the worst thing she could threaten him with.

I also know he'd rather be mowing the grass, but he can't do that while the storm is raging outside.

I have no idea where Gigi is, but I'm sure it's somewhere plotting ways to make all of us suffer while she watches and declares that management of other people's improvements is good for her soul.

Or that her new mission in life is to write a book and commission a movie about herself in the name of warning other socialite heirs and heiresses against the horrors of living an indulgent life like she has.

I snort.

I snort.

I don't *snort.* I'm a damn Lightly. We huff delicately. We look down our noses. We purse our lips in distaste. We don't *snort.*

Yet here I am, doing my best angry-bull impression, marching into the damn community showers, where—*"Aaaaaahhhh!"*

Gigi spins in the shower, giving me a full frontal.

But that's not the worst of it.

No, the worst of it is that *there's a naked man in here with her.*

A familiar naked man.

An *old*, familiar naked man.

"Aaaaaahhhh!" I scream again.

She says something back at me, but between Carter's music and the headphones, I can't hear it.

All I know is that my grandmother's not even trying to cover all her lady bits, unlike her companion with his liver-spotted hands cupping his manhood and his wet gray hair sticking up like she was running her fingers through it.

Gigi has assumed her regal, nose-in-the-air, shoulders-back, hands-on-hips, *I will chew you up and spit you out for daring to walk into this bathroom right now* position while her hair drips down her makeup-free face, and *my grandmother is Gollum.*

My grandmother is that freaky, weird character from *The Lord of the Rings* when she's naked, with just a little more hair and saggy old-lady boobs.

"You didn't put the sign on the door!" I screech.

I'm screeching.

At Gigi.

It's like asking to have my food poisoned. Not enough to kill me, mind you, but enough to remind me that what Gigi hath given, Gigi can taketh away, and a Lightly doesn't embarrass herself with repercussions of food poisoning in public.

Her companion—*oh my God, it's her butler.*

Gigi's getting it on *with her butler.* She brought in a booty call from New York.

She's doing the nasty with a man she pays on the regular.

Gigi's butler is her gigolo.

Oh my sweet holy Oprah.

He slips a hand onto her shoulder and leans in to whisper in her ear while water streams out of the middle locker room showerhead, letting *his* dangly bits show, *just like Whitney Anastasia having an affair with the neighbor next to the post office in the movie,* and *oh my God,* I cannot.

I *can't.*

Not anymore.

Gigi's still lecturing down her nose at me as my legs finally engage to turn on their own and carry me back out of the locker room.

I don't head to the stairs.

Not when I know I can get out of the building through the janitor's exit on this level.

It takes me moments to push through the crowded room, overflowing with ancient equipment that we haven't begun to dig through yet, to get to the door leading to the half stairwell up into the pouring rain, and a split second to decide what I want to do next.

It's dumb.

It's *so* dumb.

I'm wearing *a bathrobe and slippers.*

They're Versace, but they're still a bathrobe and slippers.

Probably all the more reason that I shouldn't.

But I still march away from the school, my slippers slapping on the cobblestone street, which I can hear reverberating through my body, past Café Nirvana, past the Pink Box, past the square and the place Tavi got a questionable shampoo and blowout yesterday, past Carter's new favorite bar, until the businesses fade and the bass beat of my brother's synthesizer fades and I'm in a residential area that leads to a goat farm three blocks down.

Thunder cracks around me, cutting through my headphones, which will probably short out on my ears in the rain, and is that really a bad thing?

Here lies Phoebe Lightly, a woman on a mission to get her life back when it was cut short by her wireless headphones serving as the lightning rod to take her out of her misery.

I don't think that's actually possible, but I still yank them off and toss them to the goats once I've climbed the fence.

And as I realize the goats aren't actually out in the rain, I remember that I don't have to climb the fence.

There's a damn staircase on the connected tree house on the other side.

I'm soaked to the bone. I probably look a little like Gollum myself. My robe might be ruined. I just stepped in wet goat poop in my $500 slippers. I'm still clutching the ridiculous shower caddy I bought myself so that Carter wouldn't steal my shampoo, which I miraculously found at a drugstore in Deer Drop yesterday, and now I have to pick my way through the field to the gate or climb back over the damn fence to get to the steps.

Don't cry, Phoebe. You are a Lightly. Lightlys don't cry. We fight. We manipulate. We overcome. But we do not cry.

Fuck it.

I'm going to cry.

Again.

And that's before the elevator drops from the tree house. "Need a lift?" a deep voice says.

A deep, sexy, dry voice that says he'll be happy to pick at me until I'm back to being myself so that I don't have to cry in front of him, and that very act of kindness itself is enough to make my eyes burn.

I don't answer him.

Instead, I throw myself into the crate, lock the little gate, and pull my knees to my chin, huddling against the cold, wet summer evening while he uses those lumberjack arms to tug the ropes so quickly that I'm suddenly on the second level of his tree house.

I didn't realize the elevator went up this far.

"C'mon, Phoebe. Shower's this way."

I pull myself to my feet, my eyes so hot and my throat so thick I barely trust myself to speak. "Tell me I look like a drowned rat."

"That'd be insulting to the rat."

He follows the line with a twitch of his lips and kind eyes that say he's only insulting me because he knows the normalcy will make me feel better, and the next thing I know, I've hurled myself at him and am trying to suck his tonsils out of his mouth.

I'm angry.

And I'm tired.

And I'm lost.

Kissing Teague is the lifeline that I don't understand but that I *need*. He's somehow become my friend, and I *need* him.

I like sparring with him. I like baiting him. I like that he keeps me on my toes.

I like that he's a good man underneath it all.

And I like that he tastes like peppermint tea, smells like raw power, is built like Thor, doesn't suck up to my grandmother, and is still willing to let me kiss him.

His deficits clearly include a lack of taste in women, but that will hardly stop me now.

Not when those powerful arms are scooping me up while he kisses me back.

Chapter 19

Teague

I'll regret this in the morning.

Hell, I'll regret it long before morning.

But does that keep me from carrying a soaking-wet Phoebe Lightly into my house while I'm kissing her like the fate of the world rests on the two of us getting it on?

Nope.

Not a chance.

She's shivering like she's lost all the protective layers that used to keep her from the knowledge that she's no more special than anyone else, and she's kissing me like she needs me to fix it.

I'm a damn sucker for a damsel in distress.

And Phoebe is once again dripping with water, her blonde hair stuck to her face, her robe so soaked it squishes with every step I take, soaking my T-shirt too.

Her hands grip my ears, holding my head in place while our tongues clash, not letting go even when I set her on the desk.

If anything, she grabs on more, twisting so she loops her legs around my hips, her robe falling open. The shower caddy she was carrying tumbles to the floor.

And she keeps kissing me.

I know what this is.

It's stress relief. It's a distraction. A blip.

And I'm on board.

No better way to get this woman out of my system than to find out she's just as uptight and demanding in the sack as she is when she's walking around Tickled Pink with her nose in the air.

Liar, a little voice whispers. *You're not getting her out of your system.*

She's tugging on my shirt, pulling it out of my jeans, so I push her soaking-wet robe off her shoulders.

She shimmies, helping it along, and breaks the kiss long enough for a short "Oh God, *yes,*" and then she's rising up off the desk, pressing her body against mine.

I'm still fully dressed.

She's bare-ass naked, with cold, wet skin to boot, getting so close I wonder if she's trying to crawl inside my body.

"You're a disaster," I say against her lips.

"Yes. *Yes.*" She tugs at my pants. "Can we just bang this out already?"

That's the hope.

Bang it out.

Get over her.

Get back to chasing her and her family out of my town. "Finally realized you need me, did you?"

She huffs out a short laugh. "So sure you're Mr. Irresistible?"

"You're not all that yourself."

Her breasts aren't small, but they each fit inside my palms, and when I push them up and thumb her hard nipples, she doesn't reply to my jab.

Instead, her eyes roll back in her head, and she lifts her chest into my touch while she nips at my lower lip and pushes my shirt up.

My cock, already hard as steel, strains harder.

I abandon her breasts long enough to rip my shirt over my head. She shoves my pants down my hips, my cock springing free, and her soft "*Oh*, come to Mama" makes my hard-on bob.

And that's before she grips me in both hands and strokes.

Her hands should not feel this good, but the chill of her skin against my hot, aching dick is lighting up my nerve endings, and I'm hissing out a breath as I struggle to keep control. "I'm gonna regret this in the morning."

"Same. Tell me you have a condom."

I grab my wallet and flip out the spare I put in there three days ago, then shuck my pants the rest of the way.

She's still sitting on her soaked robe while she rips the condom open and rolls it down my length.

That won't do.

Not planning on treating her like a princess, but I'm not planning on giving her any excuse to say I let her sit in a cold, wet pile of soiled cashmere while I fucked her either.

Thunder crashes while she wraps her legs around my hips. I grip her under her thighs, lift, and turn to lower her to the floor. "Oh, no," she gasps.

I freeze.

"*I'm* on top."

Is she—an unexpected bark of laughter slips out of my lips, because she is.

She's serious.

She's shoving my shoulder and shimmying around until she's straddling me.

Of course she is.

"Oh God, don't do that," she says, her voice breathy and desperate.

I flip her onto her back again. "Do what?"

"Laugh. *Do not* laugh. I can't take it today."

Before I can press her on exactly what that means, she shifts her hips, rubbing her pussy all over my cock, and my eyes cross.

It's been too long if Phoebe Lightly is doing this to me.

Or you like her too much, one of my shoulder angels tells me.

Warns me.

Whatever.

My dick's driving this show, not my shoulder angels.

And Phoebe.

Phoebe is definitely driving this show, and she demonstrates by nipping at my lip again while she executes some kind of ninja move that has us rolling over once more, crashing into the bookcase, her poised on top of me, leg trapped between me and a row of engineering textbooks, her breasts sliding against my bare chest, and then she's sliding onto my dick while she does a magic trick with her tongue in my mouth.

Fuck, she should not feel this good.

She's tight and slick and demanding around my cock and desperate and hungry in her kisses.

She's eager. Engaged. Bossing me around without saying a word.

I know she's using me. I'm an escape. A tool. A means to forget where she is and why and with who.

And I don't care.

I thrust up to meet her rolling hips, and she breaks the kiss with a curse.

Her eyes roll into the back of her head like my cock's the best cock she's ever had, like I'm doing the same thing for her pussy that her *magic-tongued* asshole boyfriend did for her in college.

Fuck. I have to forget I ever overheard that.

One cure.

And that's showing her that yes, yes, I am the best she'll ever get.

She lifts her hips and lowers them again, pulling me deeper, squeezing me tighter.

Taking back all the control.

I don't think so, boss lady.

I twist, and I'm on top again.

"You aren't easy, are you?" She strokes a hand down my chest while the other teases the rim of my ear, and she smiles.

She *smiles*.

Her wet hair is plastered all over her face. She has no makeup. No jewelry. Fine, pale eyelashes. Her nose is just a smidge too big for her face, her chin stubborn, her cheeks naturally round.

If she weren't rich, no one would call her pretty.

But when she smiles, she's the sunshine cutting through the thunderstorm raging outside.

No, not the sun.

She's the moon. Lurking. Hiding. Phasing in and out, waiting to positively glow until she finally escapes out of the shadow of her normal world.

She tilts her hips again, squeezing her inner muscles around my cock, and *fuck*, she feels so good.

I pump into her.

She meets me thrust for thrust, arching her hips and shoving me so we're rolling all over the floor while we're rutting like wild animals, my balls aching with the need for release, her pussy so tight and slick, her gasps and moans and kisses and touches and eager participation driving me wild.

Of course she's driving me wild.

She's Phoebe Lightly.

She doesn't do *anything* halfway.

Including stress-relief fucks.

"Oh my God, Teague," she gasps as I get her beneath me once more and slam deep inside of her. "I'm coming. *I'm coming.*"

Her legs clamp around my ass while she tilts her pelvis hard against mine and squeezes my dick so tightly with her pussy that I couldn't hold out one more second if the fate of the entire universe depended on it, and suddenly I'm coming, too, wild and deep and desperate, groaning in relief into the crook of her neck while her fingers dig into my back and her glorious body spasms and clenches around my cock, coaxing my release so thoroughly that the strain pulls in the pit of my gut.

Jesus.

Fuck.

One time will *not* be enough.

Holy hell.

Phoebe Lightly is a damn witch. A goddess. A goddess witch who knows how to use her body to play mine until all time and space are suspended, with nothing but this desperate need to bang her all over again, before I've even finished the first time, surging through my veins.

Her legs fall away, her head thumping to the floor as her inner walls release their grip on me, and I ride the last waves of my own climax while trying not to collapse on top of her.

"Fuck," I whisper.

I can't lift my head.

Can't look at her.

If there's even the slightest chance she's feeling half as satisfied, as happy, as *right*, as I am in this exact moment, despite all the ways this is wrong, I don't want to know.

I *can't* know.

Phoebe Lightly is a distraction.

She's not real.

She's not my future. She shouldn't be my present.

But she's seeping into my bones, and I don't dislike that nearly as much as I should.

Chapter 20

Phoebe

Marriage is something I used to think I'd only consider for the right man, with the right name, the right genes, the right look, the right job, and the right inherent respect for the fact that I would be the one who wore the pantsuit in the family.

But I'm fairly certain I would marry Teague Miller just for his bathroom.

Never mind all the awkward lack of eye contact when we finally made it off the floor a little bit ago, when he pointed me to a door I hadn't noticed, hiding a bathroom so small that you can practically shower, sit on the toilet, and wash your hands in the sink all at the same time, and grunted something about fresh towels, like he, too, was overwhelmed by what we'd just done and in no shape to deal with it.

I would 100 percent marry Teague Miller right now.

Just for his shower.

Yep.

Not at all for the way he just *gets* me. How he knows when to spar. When to provoke. When to be kind. When to bang me so good that one hard, hot lay changes my life.

Which is ridiculous.

It wasn't *that* good.

Not like this shower.

Really.

It's only the hot water that's confusing me, because the awkward aftermath was 100 percent real—and 110 percent a bad sign for anything resembling a real relationship forming from this.

"*Oh my God*, this is so good," I groan while I stand in the dinky little shower, steam rising all around me, my body flushed with both sexual satisfaction and the pounding of hot water against my skin.

I will never take hot showers for granted again.

Never.

Ever.

Ever.

Again.

I try to hug the water droplets. There's nothing complicated about how they make me feel. "I love you, hot water. I love you so much."

There's a knock at the door. "Do you have clean clothes?" Teague calls.

"I don't need them. I'm never leaving your shower."

The door cracks open.

I peer through the foggy glass surrounding me, but I don't see him stick his head in.

Which means he's trying to chill me out.

Amateur.

Okay, *fine*. Maybe he's considering joining me.

And maybe I want him to, even if I don't know where he'll fit, except possibly inside me again.

But I can't say that.

Can I?

"You can let the steam out all you want," I call. "I'll make more."

He doesn't answer.

He doesn't have to.

The scents of chocolate and vanilla mixing with my steam answer for him.

Oh my God.

He's making chocolate chip cookies.

Is *that* why I've been smelling chocolate here and there all over Tickled Pink amid the lake-fish smell? Because he makes chocolate chip cookies all the time?

My mouth floods, and I suck in a bit of drool before it can slip down my chin. No one's here to witness it, but I'd know if I drooled in the shower.

"You're playing dirty," I call. Is it possible to love a man who keeps making me fall into lakes, who doesn't take any of my shit, who wants me to leave his town, and who lives in a tree house?

"Only way *to* play," he calls back.

Dear sweet Oprah, I am falling so hard for this man.

And the weird thing is, when the water shuts off on its own—like he's turned off the water valve to the bathroom—I like him a little bit more.

Not that I'll admit that to him. I *can't* admit that to him. *"Did you just steal my water?"*

"Save some for the fishes." He sticks a hand into the bathroom and drops a pile of clothes into the sink. "Don't think Bridge will mind if you borrow these for a night. But bring them back clean."

His towels are thick and warm, and I take my time drying off. I didn't bring my hair dryer, and I can't find one in the tiny bathroom, either, so eventually, I leave the room with damp hair, wearing baggy green pants that remind me of nineties rap artists and a button-down polyester shirt with what I initially think is a black-and-white houndstooth pattern but turns out to be itty-bitty alternating black and white kitten faces.

My intention is to head back to the school. It's getting close to family dinnertime, which we always eat late, and if I'm not there, Gigi will probably declare that I need to be the one to clean the bathrooms in that community center she's fixing up now too.

But the sight of Teague sitting on a simple navy-blue love seat, sweatpants-clad legs propped up on a coffee table that was *not* there when we were rolling around on the floor, a plate of fresh chocolate chip cookies in his lap, and a dark Sparrow County High T-shirt hugging his chest and tree-trunk arms, gives me pause.

What would it be like to sit here and just *talk* with him, like we did in the car when he drove me to school?

Could we have a fling? Do this friends-with-benefits thing until it's time for me to leave town? "Thank you for the shower. And the Halloween costume."

"Not a Halloween costume." He bites into a cookie.

My stomach drops. In the good way, I mean. The *does the man know how sexy it is to watch him lick chocolate off his lips?* kind of way.

If I'm not careful, I'll jump him again. And I wonder if that's his endgame.

I should leave. I should really, really leave.

You definitely need to leave, my heart agrees. "Does Bridget actually wear this outfit in public?"

"Every Tuesday. Make sure it's back by then."

I start to offer to have Tavi talk to Bridget about fashion, but then I catch it.

The eye twinkle.

Teague Miller is baiting me.

Again.

My clit pulses. Does he know how much I like a good challenge? How much I enjoy verbal sparring and mind games? "If it's easier for me to walk home naked, I can do that instead. Wouldn't be the first time."

His sweatpants tent. "Wouldn't be the first time I did a citizen's arrest on a naked woman in town either."

It's so damn natural to sit down next to him, prop my feet up, and help myself to a cookie. It's like he *gets* me.

I'm not here because I wanted to use his shower.

I'm here because he's come to represent a weird place where I can be myself, even when I don't exactly know what that means. But I know I'm safe while I figure it out. "When was the first time?"

"Eight or ten years ago? Church group came through to feel the power of the heavenly gates. One of the ladies got drunk at Ladyfingers, old Tickled Pink Floyd told her that the fountain in the town square was the *real* gate to heaven, but she had to leave this earth the same way she came into it, in her birthday suit, and next thing you know, she was stripping down and diving in."

I can't tell if he's making this up or not. "And you arrested her for trying to get to heaven."

"Nah, I arrested her because it was ten in the morning, she was naked, and the preschool was out on a field trip. Hell. Bridget was in that class. Must've been closer to twelve years ago . . . Jesus." He swipes a hand over his face. "And now she's working on getting her driver's permit."

"And *not* letting you dress her in horrific fashion choices?" I lift a leg and point to the green parachute pants. "If you want your daughter to like you, don't drunk-shop for her birthday presents."

His full grin appears.

Oprah have mercy.

"So what broke you tonight?" he asks.

I grimace before I can stop myself. "I actually like you too much to subject you to this story."

"That bad?"

Not going there. I'm blanking it from my memory. Instead, I point to the built-in bookshelves. "You're a reader."

"All decoration."

"People who live in tiny houses don't keep books for decoration."

"Not that tiny."

I bite into another cookie.

Know how many times I have cookies at home?

Never.

Never times.

Know how good this cookie is?

On a scale of hot shower to explosive orgasm, it's right up there.

It's so good I can't even hear my mother's subliminal messages about where all that sugar and fat will end up on my body.

I let my eyes wander around the rest of the room. There's a desk beneath a window overlooking the goat field, as well as the fuzzy rug we were just rolling around on between the desk and the bookshelves. The walls are plank wood, and charming white lace curtains are tied back on either side of the windows. Instead of family pictures, these walls are decorated with black-and-white photos of covered bridges. The room isn't large, but it's not so small that two people can't breathe in here either. "Did you build this?"

"The cookie?"

"Your house."

He slides a look around, too, like he's deciding how much he's willing to tell me. "Yep."

"And you live here year-round?"

"Yep."

"All by yourself?"

"Bridget stays over when she wants to. Used to get her on the nights when Shiloh was on shift at the fire department, but now, we let her pick her schedule."

"Do your parents come visit?"

Those hazel eyes shift my way like he's wondering just how much more I'm willing to dig into his life.

All the way, Teague Miller. All the way.

"That would be impossible. And what about you? You making progress on being a better person?"

Oh God, he's an orphan. I wonder if he misses his parents or if he's more like me, and they were a function of his life and comfort level without being his entire world. "I've made *all* the progress. Look at me, sitting here in a fashion-disaster outfit, threatening to walk naked to get back to my monstrosity of a temporary home so that I can tend to the souls of my family."

He grins again. "Hate to tell you, Phoebs, but suffering doesn't automatically make you a better person."

"You're only saying that because you've never suffered enough."

He opens his mouth like he's going to divulge just how much he's suffered in his life and let me in on all his deep, dark secrets, but instead of Teague's voice, I hear something completely different.

Gigi.

"Hello? Mr. Miller? I know you're home, because there's nowhere else a man with your social life would be tonight. Have no fears. I'm here to improve your evening."

He glances at his crotch, which is suddenly no longer tented. "Wow. That was effective."

I snort-laugh, get a cookie caught in my throat, have a flashback to Gigi choking to death on the floor of her town house dining room, and am still unable to stop laughing through coughing up crumbs.

"Mr. Miller?" Gigi calls again. "Is that my granddaughter with you? I sincerely hope you didn't allow her to shower here."

He rolls his eyes and hands me the plate of cookies so he can stand and stroll to the window. "Go away, Estelle. I've had enough of you this week."

"That's hardly polite."

"Okay, pot."

Gigi sucks in a breath so loud I can hear it over my own snort of laughter.

"Did you just call *me* impolite?" she demands.

"If the Louboutin fits . . . or do you wear Margot Lightly shoes? You don't, do you? Lovely of you to support your daughter-in-law."

"She's only in business because I paid for her to be in business. I don't need to wear the shoe to do the time."

"Never even considered it, though, did you? Yep, you're definitely on your way to heaven." He does a slow clap. "Now go away."

"I need to discuss snowshoe baseball strategy with you. Don't pretend you won't love every minute of watching my family eat dirt. You're going to hell with us, Teague Miller."

"Maybe, but I won't be dying with regrets."

I can't decide if I'm horny or horrified, but I know that I suddenly want to strip Teague naked and do him all over again.

He's talking back to my grandmother.

And he's living.

So far.

"Let down the elevator," Gigi orders.

Teague doesn't answer.

Instead, he stands there, arms crossed, legs wide, glaring out the window like she's the Wicked Witch of the West and he can use the powers of his mind to make a house drop on top of her.

It's not an entirely fair comparison, but this has been a rough week.

"You know I could pack up my bank account and leave this town?" Gigi says.

"Got by just fine for years without your bank account, and we will again once you're gone. We're not here so you can buy your way into heaven, Estelle. There are no shortcuts."

She sucks in a breath.

I'm not laughing anymore either.

Gigi might be terrifying, but she's also the one who saved me the day that deer tried to eat my head. She taught me that you can't succeed in business if you show fear or weakness, no matter what you're feeling inside. She brought me a flashlight in case the power went out during a long two weeks one summer when Tavi, Carter, and I were moved into her town house with our nanny while our own house underwent renovations. We were supposed to be in Spain on vacation but had to skip it because Dad had thrown out his back and needed surgery for a slipped disk.

Mom went to Spain without us.

And suddenly I realize that must've been one of the times Mom caught Dad cheating on her.

All the little innuendos about *how* Dad slipped a disk in his back over the years, Mom's flat glare anytime it comes up, Dad's discomfort—it all clicks.

He was.

He was sleeping with another woman when he threw his back out.

Gigi isn't perfect.

But she cares in her own way.

And that counts.

"Do you know what, Mr. Miller?" Gigi says.

"I have no earthly idea what, Mrs. Lightly."

"You might be good enough for my granddaughter after all."

I suck in another breath.

It's like she *knows* that giving her seal of approval is the worst possible thing she could offer.

Worse?

Teague doesn't tense. He doesn't growl. He doesn't leap back in horror.

Instead, he lifts a hand and waves like he's dismissing her. "Love the mind games, Estelle. Don't ever change."

Oh. My. God.

Is this what swooning feels like?

Is this—is this honest, primal lust for a man who's not afraid to play my grandmother right back?

He shuts the window and turns to me. "Same time next week?"

My lips part.

The last time a man said that to me, I was in a hidden alcove on the terrace above where my mother was hosting a post-fashion-week gala, with a man I'd hooked up with because our families had similar goals but we'd yet to form a formal alliance.

That fling lasted four months and led to Remington Lightly acquiring a cleaning-products line in exchange for our flailing office-supply division.

I foresee many more orgasms in this arrangement with Teague, even if my heart's shrinking a little at the realization that for him, this is just a way to kill time while we go about the business of getting both of our lives back to normal.

And that's how it should be.

Just because I'm infatuated with a man, not for what he can do for me and my family but because he's honestly attractive, doesn't mean I get to have a real relationship. So I should appreciate this for what it is.

I give him my best seductive smile, even though a small part of me is dying a little inside.

I like him.

I like him.

And friends with benefits? A weekly arrangement?

It's not enough.

But it's something. A start. A possibility of more. "I'll put you on my calendar."

Chapter 21

Teague

Phoebe Lightly is hot in baseball pants.

Should've seen that coming. Especially since I saw her naked five days ago.

Nearly down to the hour.

Not that I'm counting. Or obsessed. Or wondering why the *fuck* I suggested waiting an entire week to see her naked again for a scheduled booty call on the calendar. Who does that?

Wait. Don't answer. I don't want to go there.

But I wouldn't mind talking her out of those baseball pants tonight.

"Somebody told the old lady uniforms weren't necessary, didn't they?" Dylan Wright says beside me.

Tickled Pink's resident plumber has finished his massive job over in Deer Drop, and he's back to play the part of the Tickled Pink Gold Stars power hitter in our snowshoe baseball game tonight.

I snort softly and clap him on the shoulder, grateful for the distraction from Phoebe's ass. "You've missed a lot."

"I can see that."

The Tickled Pink Gold Stars have been playing snowshoe baseball every summer for the past fifty years—long before I arrived in town, and long before they were called the Gold Stars—but to the best of my knowledge, we've never had uniforms before.

Team T-shirts, yes.

Uniforms? Not like these.

I didn't think I'd like them, but every time Phoebe bends over to adjust her snowshoes, I am 100 percent on board with having uniforms.

And it's not just that we had sex.

It's also that I walked into Café Nirvana three days ago and found Bridget doubled over with laughter while Phoebe was having a magnetic-eyelash malfunction, and instead of growling and glaring at my kid, Phoebe was laughing with her, shrieking like a teenager herself over her algebra book.

I overheard her asking Anya for tips on how to brew coffee when you're starting with water that smells like a fish that ate too many fried cheese curds, which should've been annoying, except she delivered the line with this twinkle in her eye, like she knew she was being a pain in the ass but was impressed with her own creativity in describing the water. Plus, she listened and asked more questions as Anya answered her, like she cared about Anya's opinions and experience.

She complimented Willie Wayne's catch as he was showing it off onshore yesterday.

She apologized to the Tickled Pink Fire Department for the cooking disaster that led to the alarms going off in the school, and thanked them for their prompt response.

If you didn't know her when she got here, you wouldn't know she was anything more than a sophisticated small-town woman with expensive taste and good manners.

"The colors are . . . something," Dylan says, drawing my attention back to the uniforms and Phoebe, bent over to fiddle with the laces on her snowshoes once again.

"The whole uniform is *something*." Willie Wayne rolls his shoulders like he can't get the shirt to fit right. Or maybe like he's not comfortable in a baby-pink jersey decorated with gold stars that somehow managed to be positioned right at nipple level for everyone. "This is snowshoe baseball. Not a fashion show."

"Who cares what we look like if we get our asses kicked," Jane mutters beside him.

"Sweetie, you're going to play great tonight." Gibson pats her shoulder. They're the newest married couple in Tickled Pink. Though they got hitched four years ago, they're still our resident newlyweds.

Which is what makes the rumors about Michael Lightly flirting with Jane all the more funny.

Not that any of us doubt that the rumors are true.

Jane's hot. Of course she's the first woman Michael Lightly would go for.

Plus, we all couldn't wait to see the look on his face when he realized Jane is married to a six-foot-four brick wall who looks like the Rock, but with hair.

Yeah, I know. We're assholes.

Not that Gibson would hurt him. He's spent the past month photographing bugs in South American jungles for a science magazine. Guy's less dangerous than Tavi Lightly's dog.

But it's fun watching the double takes coming from the Lightly family.

"Would you *please* tie my shoes, darling?" Margot snaps at Michael.

He whips his gaze back to his wife's feet while Carter rolls his eyes and Estelle tests her snowshoes on the field, which is piled high with sawdust.

We're on the ball field between the old high school's football field and the area roped off for the abandoned amusement park, with the half-done Ferris wheel covered in ivy looming across the grassy meadow behind home plate, gearing up for one of my favorite summer traditions.

Snowshoe baseball is exactly that—baseball played while the players wear snowshoes. The sawdust layered almost a foot deep over the field is to make it more challenging. And so we don't get *too* hurt, we play with a ball a little bigger than a softball. All the towns around have at least one team.

Tonight, we're playing the Mighty Dusts, and they've brought their own cheering section.

It's nearly as big as the crowd of busybodies from Deer Drop, which has three teams contributing to the league.

Both sets of cheering sections are larger than the pool of reporters in from various places around the state—and I heard a writer for one of the big sports magazines is here, too—but the reporters are still giving me indigestion.

I'd have indigestion if there were only one reporter.

This is *not* how I want to spend my snowshoe baseball game.

But the good news is, there's no reason anyone will be paying attention to anyone other than the Lightlys.

Anya and Ridhi have their refreshments table set up, piled high with monster cookies, cream puffs, and cupcakes to sell to the onlookers. Tonight's proceeds are all going to the local library.

Estelle's butler, who she's rumored to be having an affair with, also has a table of baked goods set up.

His are labeled with fancy placards that say things like *scones* and *crumpets* and *English biscuits*, but most everything looks like hockey pucks.

To be fair, some are brown or tan hockey pucks, but those crumpets would definitely be mistaken for a real hockey puck.

And they're charging double normal snowshoe baseball refreshment rates.

"Premium comes at a price, darling," Estelle said to me when I questioned if she was trying to fleece our friends.

"What's edibility cost?" I threw back before Bridget shushed me in a rare reversal of roles.

Dylan chuckles next to me. I slide him a look, remember I'm in my hat and sunglasses so he can't see me looking at him, and nudge him instead. He's about my height, white, brown hair, a few years younger than me, and the ladies in my life tell me he looks more like a high school quarterback than he does a plumber.

They also tell me he behaves much better than a high school quarterback.

And that's usually when I tell them all to stop talking.

"What?" I ask him.

"All the fancy people in Tickled Pink. Think it was like this when they were shooting the movie all those years ago?"

"No."

Willie Wayne chuckles. "Don't mind him, Dylan. Got a burr up his butt because he doesn't like that he likes one of 'em."

"Which one?" Dylan asks.

I shake my head at them. "None. None of them."

Willie Wayne nods. "That's why he keeps dropping by the high school to tell them not to leave the doorframes out in the football field overnight when they're painting."

They're ridiculous. "If we're repurposing the building into a museum for the movie when they're gone, we don't need to be sanding bug guts off the doors and repainting them again ourselves."

"He's only been helping Phoebe, though," Willie Wayne stage-whispers to Dylan.

"Ah. The taller one." Dylan flips his baseball cap around and tilts his head at them. "What's the story on the other granddaughter?"

"Social media influencer." Jane follows the pronouncement by spitting in the dirt.

"Don't trust her," Willie Wayne adds. "She's too nice."

"Definitely an angle," Jane agrees.

"Like she's luring us in."

"She's a worm on a hook, and we're the catfish."

"Probably planning on writing an exposé."

"Or painting herself as the victim of small-town life."

"Not our fault her grandmother keeps trying to fix the plumbing herself."

"And forgetting to put a sign on the door when she's doing the nasty with her butler in the locker room."

I cringe. "Can we *not* talk about that? Does anyone need that mental image?"

As if she's psychic, Phoebe turns and looks directly at me.

Rumor made it around that the reason she was out in that thunderstorm was that *she* was the one who found her grandmother in the shower, naked with the butler, and that it was the straw that finally broke her.

And I can't stop thinking how grateful I am that she turned to *me* when she needed comfort.

Been too long. It's not that I like Phoebe Lightly. It's that—all right, *fine*.

I like Phoebe Lightly. *And* she's sexy to boot.

"Mr. Miller, could you please explain the rules of this game to us one more time?" she calls. "We seem to have different understandings of the goal here."

"Goal's to win," I call.

"Yes, but we need to define *win*." She's fucking hot when her eyes narrow in determination like that.

"It's like she knows we win if her family face-plants in the sawdust," Jane murmurs.

Willie Wayne nods. "She's the smart one."

I angle over to the bench like I haven't been itching to come this way since I set foot on the ball diamond. The rest of the Lightlys are watching me with undisguised suspicion.

You get used to it after a while.

Helps that they *should* be suspicious. Tonight? Playing snowshoe baseball?

This is one more step in my plans to convince Estelle Lightly that she's not built for small-town Wisconsin life.

"Goal's to score the most runs," I tell Phoebe.

Tavi curls a lock of hair around her finger. Her dog's also in a uniform, sitting on the bench beside her, its leash tied around the leg of the bench. "Do you get extra points if you make it around the bases without falling?"

"Nope."

"Told you," Carter mutters. "They just want to see us covered in sawdust."

"And eating it too," I tell him.

Phoebe frowns at me.

I grin. "What? We all eat it eventually."

"Thank God I'm management," Margot says.

"You're playing with the rest of us, Mother," Carter replies.

"The team that eats dirt together . . ." Phoebe frowns deeper. "I actually don't know what we do to celebrate eating dirt. Teague?"

Why does my name on her lips sound like an invitation to strip her out of those baseball pants? "Sawdust. The team that eats sawdust together . . . sprouts . . . new trees. Together."

The entire Lightly family looks at my crotch.

"Oh my God, Dad, stop talking," Bridget mutters. She's in her own uniform shirt, with jean shorts, her bright sneakers, and a rainbow tie-dye ball cap with her ponytail falling out behind it. She gives me one last glare before turning her entire attention to her team and clapping her hands. "C'mon, team. Time to go. We have home field advantage, which means we're out in the field first. Dad. You're pitching. Willie Wayne. First base. Jane. Shortstop. The rest of you . . . gah. Okay. Carter, take second base. Mr. Lightly, right field. Mrs. Lightly, left field. Mrs. Grandma Lightly, center field."

"Excuse you, young lady," Estelle says with a sniff. "Exactly who do you think you are?"

"Team manager. I have mad coaching skills."

"She does," Jane agrees. "We let her pretend to be a grown-up and boss us around on snowshoe baseball nights. She's a strategy goddess."

"Thank you, Jane," my kid says with a confidence that should be terrifying but always manages to reassure me that she'll be fine. The world, maybe not, but my kid, yes. She nods to the Lightly women. "Tavi, how's your arm?"

Tavi lifts her gloved hand and flexes. "I can be a *beast*, Bridget!"

My daughter, who would've gone speechless two weeks ago in the presence of one of her social media idols, questionable as I find that, sighs. "Um, you can lose the glove. We play without them. And how about your throwing arm?"

"She threw Carter's amp across the theater this morning," Phoebe says dryly.

"I did *not*. It slipped."

"While you had it over your head and were aiming it at his bed."

Bridget turns a nose-crinkling frown on Carter. "So is your bed, like, on the stage in the theater? Don't you worry about people spying on you from the light booth? Or like, about Tickled Pink Floyd plopping down in a chair and watching you sleep?"

Tavi rises, almost trips in her snowshoes, and steadies herself with her arms spread wide. "He's a vampire. He doesn't sleep."

"And the ghost of Tickled Pink Floyd isn't real," Phoebe adds.

Bridget's brows go up. "Okay. You're catching, by the way. Go squat behind home. Dylan? Can Phoebe borrow your catcher's mask?"

"Sure thing, short stuff."

"Call me that again, and you're benched."

"*Bridget.*" While I cringe at my daughter's power trip, Dylan grins the grin that I've been told he used to full advantage back in his younger years.

"I'm already benched, Coach," he says.

"Only until one of the newbies inhales too much sawdust."

Tavi smiles at Dylan. "Is there a trick?"

"Don't fall for it, man," Willie Wayne whispers to him. "She smiles like that at all of us. I'm telling you, it's a trap."

Dylan turns his own grin on Tavi. "Trick's to not fall down."

"Y'all officially meet Dylan yet?" I ask the Lightlys. "He's a plumber."

Tavi jerks her sunglasses down and stares at him with undisguised lust. "*You're* a plumber?"

"Oh my God, *my savior.*" Phoebe throws herself at him, trips in her snowshoes, and ends up face-planting in his crotch.

I growl and reach for her, but her arms are flailing as she tries to straighten herself, and my hat and sunglasses get knocked loose before I, too, fall into Dylan's crotch.

"Dammit."

"Whose idea was it to wear these ridiculous—*oof.*" Phoebe winces as Tavi, too, lands on top of us.

Carter doubles over laughing.

Margot attempts to assist us and trips over Tavi's dog, who snarls and leaps back, while Michael tries to help Margot and ends up on top of her instead.

"For the love of Kate Spade, Michael, *what are we doing here?*" she shrieks.

"We're becoming better people, Margot."

"If I wanted to be a better person, I'd have my martinis neat instead of dirty, and I'd actually take the advice that my tarot decks give me! Estelle, I swear, I—" She cuts herself off as she spits sawdust.

"Don't talk or inhale," I tell Phoebe and Tavi.

"How are we supposed to—oh. Ew. Bleh. *Bleh bleh bleeeeecchhhh!*" Tavi tries to wipe her tongue on her uniform sleeve.

Her dog is going nuts, barking up a storm.

"Our asses are toast." Bridget heaves a sigh loud enough to drown out Carter's wheezing laughter.

"Don't say *ass*," I remind my kid.

"I don't know which of you to help first," Dylan says.

I grab Phoebe's arm in one hand, Tavi's in the other hand, and I haul them both up while Dylan stands there with his arms in the air.

"Nice," I tell him. "Appreciate the help."

"Not real keen on getting featured in the *Tickled Pink Papers* with my hands holding any one of you to my crotch, man."

Dammit.

My sunglasses.

And hat.

They fell off and are now covered in sawdust, and there's a row of photographers and locals aiming cameras and phones our way.

"The family that plays together eats sawdust together," Estelle says from her spot down the way. Her butler came running—in regular shoes—to make sure she didn't fall too. "But you're all still a long way from having souls worthy of heaven. Let's get this ball on the road."

"*Play ball*, Gigi," Tavi says between spits.

She's straightened and is balancing much better on her snowshoes now.

Phoebe's still leaning into me, which feels like fucking heaven. I haven't had a whiff of her hair or a brush of her hand in five damn days, and I want to toss her over my shoulder, take her back behind the Ferris wheel, and work her out of my system again.

"If you can get me an appointment with God while we're here so I can check that *be a better person* box and move on from the torture, I'd appreciate it," she murmurs.

"Around here, I *am* God," I reply.

Dylan cracks up.

Jane doubles over like Carter.

Willie Wayne laughs so hard he trips on his way to sitting down.

"Sorry, Phoebe," Bridget says. "I clearly haven't done my job right if he still has *that* much ego left."

Phoebe nods, but she doesn't seem in any great hurry to move away from me either. "Clearly you have work to do. Let's start with having your normal catcher play instead of me. I'm *positive* that'll help your father's ego."

Bridget lifts an eyebrow in a terrifying impersonation of Phoebe impersonating her grandmother. "And I'm positive that I eat whiners for breakfast. Get your ass on the field, Lightly. All of you. Play ball. Make me proud. Or at least not so embarrassed that I have to drop out of high school."

Phoebe nods. "We'll do our best, Coach."

"Don't say *ass* if you want to not be grounded," I tell my daughter. Again.

She turns that damn eyebrow on me. "Win first. Then we'll discuss what a coach should and shouldn't say to a ragtag team of hooligans."

Is my eyeball twitching? I think my eyeball's twitching. "You're lucky you're funny."

She grins. "Still have no idea where I got *that* from."

Phoebe laughs softly beside me. She's coated in sawdust already, yet there's a smile lurking both on her lips and in her eyes.

Like she's seeing the same things I saw when I landed here sixteen years ago.

Community. Friends. Family. Fun.

A place to belong.

Get out of your head, idiot. She's not here to stay.

The weird thing is, for the first time since Estelle Lightly invaded Tickled Pink, I'm not desperate for all of them to leave.

No matter how much that row of reporters out behind center field is making me twitch.

"So the goal is staying upright *while* you win?" Phoebe asks me.

Her fingers brush against mine in that *no one would think anything of it if they noticed* kind of way, and her question seems tame enough, but the way she says it—I want to pull her under the bleachers and do things with her that would embarrass even God himself.

"That's the goal," I agree.

She flashes a smile so blindingly bright, so *real*, that I go light headed.

"What is it you say around here?" she asks me. "Oh, right. Hold my cheese and watch this. I'm gonna play the hell out of winning this game."

Chapter 22

Phoebe

Ladyfingers is hopping tonight.

The bar is nothing like the bars I frequent in New York, but it's so Tickled Pink that I can't imagine it being any other way.

I don't *want* it to be any other way.

Jane and her husband—*ha ha,* Tickled Pink, *Jane has a husband?*—are at our table, along with Willie Wayne and *his* wife, Akiko, who apparently runs the library at the high school. Several other locals are laughing and joking with them. Most of the tables in the small establishment are full, too, and not just because my entire family is here.

The entire town has come out to celebrate our horrific loss in snowshoe baseball.

The bar is gleaming white, like it's a cloud, which is the only nod to the heavenly part of Tickled Pink. The stools are all full with out-of-towners who stayed after the game for more festivities. The white Formica tables all have chipped tops, and most are unsteady. The walls are covered with signed photos of celebrities who've been here over the years, though most are dated, mixed with movie posters for *Pink Gold*. Dollar bills with notes in black Sharpie coat the ceiling.

"What's the story there?" I ask Teague.

I don't know if he sat down next to me or if I sat down next to him, but since our epic argument in the third inning over which one of us was responsible for catching balls thrown to home base to tag out runners—I said me, because I'm the catcher, and he said him, because I'm terrible at snowshoe baseball—I've been desperate to get close to him again.

Okay, *fine.*

Since he serviced my lady parts more thoroughly than I usually eviscerate my ex-boyfriends, I've been desperate to get close to him again. And I don't care which of us was right or wrong on the ball field.

It just felt good to be poking him.

He doesn't look up at the ceiling. "Are you *sure* you're okay?"

Yes.

Teague Miller isn't poking me. He's asking if I'm okay.

Possibly the snowshoe baseball game *did* get a little out of hand. "People have been surviving black eyes for millennia, Teague."

"Gotta hand it to you, Phoebe—I didn't take you for a badass that first day you rolled into town." Jane lifts her beer to me.

I try to clink and miss, because it turns out holding an ice pack to one eye messes with your depth perception. "*Badass* is my middle name."

Her husband, Gibson, grabs the edge of my glass and guides it until we clink. "Didn't see that wild pitch coming. Really didn't."

"It was *not* a wild pitch," Teague mutters.

He's right. It wasn't. The batter tipped it wrong, which took off my protective face mask, and when she spun to help me, she clobbered me in the face with her bat.

Accidentally.

Everyone agreed it was an accident.

But everyone's also blaming Teague, and I get the feeling this is normal.

Part of me wants to drag him out back and kiss him and assure him that there are no hard feelings for my lack of sports dexterity—and assure myself that things have only felt weird between us every time I've seen him this week because there have always been other people around and neither of us wants anyone else to know we bumped uglies.

Another part of me wants to sit here and soak in this feeling of being a part of something, where all of us are coated in sawdust and sporting various bruises and injuries, sharing in the pain of loss, except it's easier, because we're together.

And another part of me hopes Teague will do that thing where he loops his arm around the back of my chair like he's just resting it there. I haven't seen him much since I sneaked out of his tree house almost a week ago, and I'd convinced myself that my afterglow and a hot shower were what I was reacting to in thinking that I *liked* him, except I *do* like him.

He's this amazing mix of honesty and reluctance and grouchiness and kindness. He's good at everything he does, which means either he's some kind of alien or he knows who he is and what he wants and only does the things he excels at, which is enough to fill his days.

Despite all his grouchiness, everyone around here adores him.

And he's leaning into me, our shoulders brushing, occasionally sending me searing private looks that mean he wants me.

Me.

High-maintenance, workaholic, out-of-touch, doesn't-know-who-I-even-am *me.*

Like he's seeing something in me that no one else would've cared to recognize before.

Something *I* don't even recognize in myself.

"I'm very proud of you, Phoebe," Gigi says, which catches my attention like nothing else would. "You've actually given this a real shot. I'm far less concerned about your soul tonight than I was the night you nearly let me die."

And *there* it is. The dig buried in the compliment.

"If only we could say the same about you, Estelle," my mother says brightly.

"Stop it, Margot," my father mutters.

Carter rises. I'm starting to understand why he always looks like a constipated hedgehog.

It's us.

We turn him into a constipated hedgehog. "Need another beer, Phoebe?"

"No, thank you, but I could use some fried cheese curds."

He holds my gaze just long enough to let me know he knows I'm baiting Mom and Tavi both.

Not that Tavi's paying attention. She's just bolted out of her seat to join the attractive plumber guy at the bar. "Hi, I'm Tavi," I hear her say. "I wanted to meet your face and say sorry for trying to meet your crotch first."

Every single person at our table turns to watch with way more curiosity than my sister hitting on a guy deserves to be watched with.

"Is he married?" I whisper to Teague.

His lips twitch. "Now, why would you ask that?"

"Don't play innocent. Not even your bear-in-witness-protection outfit could hide how amused you were to introduce my father to Mr. Jane."

"She's been wearing a wedding ring this entire time."

"You clearly don't know my family well enough yet."

"You ever sleep with a married man?"

I try to shove him, miss—stupid lack of depth perception—and almost fall in his lap instead. "What kind of a question is that?"

"The kind that says I know your family well enough to ask that question."

Thank Oprah for ice packs.

This one's suddenly working overtime.

"Shh," Jane hisses at us. "We can't hear what kind of sexual favors she's offering Dylan for his services."

Jane just got herself moved to the very top of my holiday-card list.

Not that I've ever had a holiday-card list before, but she's definitely on it now.

Dylan—*not Duncan, Phoebe, not Duncan*—is flashing dimples and warm brown teddy bear eyes at Tavi as he holds out a clean hand. If this man is a plumber, I'll—

Wait.

I was going to say I'd eat dirt, except I've already done that plenty tonight.

"You're the plumber, right?" Tavi's saying.

"That's me. Living the pipe dream. Nice catch out there. You've played before?"

"Oh, no, I just dabble in sportsing. I guess maybe I'm naturally athletic? But let's not talk about me. Tell me about *you*. I've never met anyone in your profession before, and you are *nothing* like what they show on TV." Her lashes flutter.

Jane snickers. Willie Wayne giggles. Their spouses smile indulgently at both of them.

Me?

I'm a one-woman cheering section in my head right now.

My sister has 100 percent of my support in whatever she needs to do to this man's monkey wrench to get us into hot water.

Quite literally.

"He's every bit what you see on TV," Teague calls.

"Shut up, Miller," Willie Wayne snaps.

"Ignore him," Jane calls to Tavi and Dylan. "Carry on. We're not listening in."

"We are," Teague replies. "Also, Tavi, you should know that Dylan is competent, full of corny jokes, and booked solid for the next six weeks."

I whimper.

I do.

"*Completely* solid?" Tavi's gaze flits between Dylan and Teague, her lashes and brows combining to make a face I've never seen on her before.

I think she's trying for sexy, but she's missing the mark, and it's not hard to guess why.

Six more weeks of cold showers interspersed with the occasional bout of a fix when Gigi finds a good YouTube tutorial that we're willing to tackle?

That'll mess with anyone's flirting game.

Enough of that bullshit. First thing in the morning, I'm heading to Deer Drop for school, but I'm stopping by a store for a stink bomb, a set of Bluetooth speakers for my own special kind of made-up haunting, slime, strobe lights, and fire extinguishers.

I don't yet know what I'll do with all of it, but I have every intention of chasing Gigi so far out of Tickled Pink to find help for performing an exorcism that we'll have time to kidnap Dylan and pay him scads of cash in exchange for hot water.

"I keep pretty busy," Dylan tells Tavi. "I can probably squeeze—"

"A lemon and make lemonade!" Jane interjects.

"—you in," Dylan finishes.

"We are fixing the plumbing in the school *ourselves*," Gigi declares.

I gasp.

Everything suddenly makes perfect sense.

Gigi's controlling the hot water in the school.

Was there steam that time that that thing happened that I've blocked from my memory? *Was she showering in hot water?* Is she turning it off when the rest of us get in?

"Relax," Teague murmurs to me. "You're on his calendar next week. Saw it myself. Plus, took this long to get the parts in. But Jane threatened things I can't repeat if he tells you that."

That doesn't mean my grandmother hasn't been adding extra layers of torture.

The worst of it?

She doesn't even realize just how much torture this is.

Not the living-in-Tickled-Pink part.

But the part where it's so glaringly obvious that I don't belong. And I'm starting to want to.

Here.

Not in New York.

Here. Where people ask how you are because they care and not because they're hoping you'll expose a chink in your armor. Where they'll laugh if you fall in the lake but also hand you a towel when you get to shore and maybe even dive into the lake themselves to make you feel not so alone. Where they'll let you play on their snowshoe baseball team, even if they know it means losing, just to humor an old lady who thinks it's the path to heaven.

I know the locals are getting something out of us being here. I've heard whispers that tourism is up. My grandmother's money doesn't hurt. And we're apparently the most entertainment they've had since "the boar incident," whatever that is.

But even Mr. Grumpy Lumberjack smiles when he sees me. Anya keeps serving me better and better coffee. Jane dropped off a growler of beer with my name on it after my algebra pop quiz. And a woman named Patrice, who apparently used to run the spa, bought my lunch at the little sandwich shop yesterday because "I know you can afford it, but that doesn't mean it's not nice to let someone else show they care in the little ways every now and again."

I don't believe they're working an angle.

I think they're genuinely nice people who appreciate what they have and don't have to pretend they're anything they're not for fear of someone else taking it from them.

Tickled Pink?

It's eye opening.

And *I like it*.

I'm not saying I'd sign up to stay forever—who am I to think they'd *want* to tolerate me forever?—but I like it.

"Excuse me," Bridget calls over the noise. She rings a cowbell, and everyone cringes and claps their hands over their ears.

Bridget grins. "I can't say this was the best start our team's ever had, but I *can* say we set records for how badly we sucked sawdust tonight."

The locals mutter to themselves.

"If my children would've listened to me about how to hold a bat—"

"Margot, are you the coach here? No? Then sit down." Bridget points to my mother as though Bridget's the teacher and my mother is the kindergartner whining about someone else getting a turn with her favorite doll.

I should be horrified that a teenager is talking to my mother that way, but my mother's incapable of saying anything nice about anyone these days, and it's grating on my nerves.

Teague half rises. *"Bridget."*

There go my nipples. Apparently his authoritative dad voice does it for me too.

Bridget huffs. "She's not the coach."

"And I could impose early bedtime and curfew if you don't check your attitude."

"And *that* is how you parent," Gigi murmurs to my father.

"You shouldn't claim to know how to parent when you never did it yourself, Mother," he replies.

Bridget slides a look away from Teague, who's still giving her that *I don't have to allow you to learn to drive if you don't check yourself* look, and she clears her throat. "As I was saying, I'm really proud of how you all played, even if I wish some of you actually knew the rules of baseball before you set foot on my field tonight."

Gigi's still giving my father the stink eye. "Whitney Anastasia went *bowling*," she says. "If this town had the bowling alley as advertised, my children and grandchildren would not have embarrassed you so much."

Bridget gives her the same *I am teacher, hear me roar* look but otherwise ignores her.

Probably because Teague's still treating Bridget to the *I will send you to bed early without dessert and make you write book reports on the most boring books I can find* look.

She huffs softly. "For the newbs, here's the deal. Every game, win or lose, wipeout or sellout, one player on the team is awarded the Gold Star halo for skill, effort, and heart."

"That's so kind of you, Bridget." Gigi rises. "I accept."

"Sit down, Mrs. Grandma Lightly. My grandmother's halo doesn't go to players who have their butler carry them on and off the field and do their batting for them."

Teague makes a noise.

"It goes to someone not afraid to get his uniform dirty," Jane interjects, like she's trying to save the teenager from an ass chewing for saying something all the adults were thinking.

"Someone who did their best," Willie Wayne joins in.

Ridhi nods, though she's also giving Bridget the side-eye. "Someone who exemplifies all that Tickled Pink stands for."

"And someone the team agrees on," Bridget finishes.

"What?" Mom rises. "I didn't get to vote."

"Sorry, Mrs. Younger Lightly," Bridget says, not looking the least bit sorry. "Temporary honorary team members don't get to vote."

Translation: *You're not part of the team.*

I didn't get to vote either. I'm not on the team.

I'm never on the team. I have my own goals. My own ambitions. My own dreams. I pretend to be a team player when it suits my purposes, and I undermine things when they don't. That's life when you're a Lightly. Love and acceptance come from performing well, not from being a team player.

But I want to be on the team.

I want to belong.

Tavi's face twists like she wants to laugh at a teenager continuously getting the best of all of us. Like she's not doing the hard soul-searching while we're here.

Or maybe, considering she got the brunt of Mom's corrections about how to play, she's glad someone's on her side. *No, Tavi, keep your eye on the ball! Oh my God, you have to CATCH it, Octavia! Catch it and TAG THE RUNNER! Have you been eating sugar again? Your concentration is off.*

Even Carter's giving us both the *could she please shut up?* look.

And I don't think he's making that face about Bridget.

"Who won, Bridge?" Anya calls.

"Don't keep us in suspense!" Dylan agrees.

It's obvious who'll win. I mean, it's Teague. He's a great pitcher, and he was the only person on the team to help score two points.

Runs.

I mean runs.

If not Teague, definitely Jane. She's a badass, *and* she was the last to fall in her snowshoes.

"As coach of the Tickled Pink Gold Stars," Bridget says dramatically as she pulls a bejeweled but slightly bent halo out from behind her back, "it gives me great pleasure to announce that our first Star of the Year award goes to . . ."

I nudge Teague. "How much do you pay her so that you win every week?" I whisper.

"Phoebe Lightly!" Bridget cries.

Teague smirks at me while the whole bar erupts in cheers around us. "A lot. So much money. And this is how she repays me, the backstabber."

"Is that *Whitney Anastasia's heaven halo*?" Gigi rises again.

Bridget ignores her. "C'mon, Phoebe. Speech!"

I don't move.

I'm afraid if I move, I'll cry.

"But I sucked," I whisper.

"You did," Teague agrees. "You put your whole damn heart into sucking. Mad respect, Ms. Lightly. You earned this one."

I swallow twice—which is twice more than should be necessary, because I *am* a Lightly, dammit, but again, *he's being nice to me.* I fumble over pushing my chair back, knock it over, spin to grab it, and trip on the leg before I get my bearings, rise, and force a very hot-faced smile at Bridget.

The applause gets louder.

For *me.*

Bridget settles the movie-prop halo on my head—and yes, I'm 100 percent sure this is the old movie prop from the scene when Whitney Anastasia finally gets her ticket to see her son in heaven—and then the teenager holds out a hand. "C'mon up here, Snowshoe Halo Queen. It's tradition. You have to give a speech."

Two months ago, I could've given a speech with both eyes tied behind my back.

Wait.

With one arm closed.

Dammit.

Oprah help me, there's a table of reporters in the corner, and I'm about to put myself back in the gossip pages.

I set my ice pack aside so I can use both eyes to climb onto the table with Bridget, grateful this isn't one of the wobbly tables. I'm not feeling my Lightly enough to will it into staying steady.

Bridget hops down.

Willie Wayne whistles while the clapping continues.

My eyes get hot.

I don't know if they're mocking me or accepting me. I probably deserve the mocking. Not so sure I deserve the acceptance.

"Quiet, quiet," Bridget calls. "Let her talk."

The bar settles into a rough silence, the kind that suggests it could get raucous and crazy at any second all over again.

Gigi's glaring at me.

Mom looks embarrassed.

Dad—he's *smiling*.

So is Tavi.

Carter's clapping. He's not smiling, but he's not grumble-glaring either. He nods, and *oh my God*.

That's *respect*.

I blink, and now he's rolling his eyes.

But there was respect.

I saw it.

"C'mon, Phoebe. We *know* you can talk," Bridget prods.

The bar laughs but quickly settles again.

I touch the halo, don't think about how many other heads it's been on over the years, and struggle to get my face to cooperate. "Ah, wow. Thank you. This is what you give the people you don't want to play anymore, right? So I can't fuck up the rest of your season too?"

They laugh again.

At me.

And *I like it*.

Phoebe Lightly, self-deprecating entertainer of the year.

"In all seriousness," I continue, completely unsure what's about to come out of my mouth, "thank you for letting me make all the mistakes. This halo was worth the price of losing my Louboutins to the Tickled Pink Monster."

And I'm going to cry.

So I hop back down, start to turn in to Teague's arms for a hug, remember that I'm not ready for public displays of affection with a guy

227

who only wants to schedule me on his calendar for weekly booty calls, no matter how friendly he's become in the meantime, and instead, I dart out of the bar.

"I didn't want this," I whisper to the looming shadow of the half-finished Ferris wheel. "I didn't want to grow. I didn't want the pain."

The Ferris wheel doesn't answer.

It doesn't have to.

One, because it's a freaking Ferris wheel.

But two?

I think that half-finished Ferris wheel totally gets where I'm coming from.

Chapter 23

Teague

It doesn't matter how many times I tell myself I shouldn't care, that this is a temporary infatuation with the wrong woman, all I want to do is follow Phoebe out of the bar and find out what's wrong.

But if I follow her, everyone will notice.

Estelle Lightly might have her suspicions about whatever this relationship is, but that doesn't mean I'm ready for the whole town to be talking about it.

I still feel like a massive asshole by the time I tell Bridget I'm taking off. Both because I'm abandoning my daughter while she's having fun and while she still needs an adult to remind her to watch her mouth, and because I didn't take off sooner to make sure Phoebe's okay.

Know the last time I had an internal conflict between staying with my daughter and going to see another woman?

Never.

Never.

This isn't good.

Bridget perks up over her root beer. "Hold on. Let me tell Ridhi I'm coming with you."

Shiloh's pulling a two-day shift at the fire station, which is rarely what prompts Bridget to change her mind on where she's sleeping. And any other night, I'd be thrilled to have her join me. But she'll expect to go home, and I want to head in the opposite direction.

"You can stay—"

"Dad. Don't be dense, okay?"

Either she wants something, or I'm not doing a very good job of hiding that I have somewhere else I'd like to be, and she's trying to save me from myself.

Or possibly she needs to tell me where my own game sucked but doesn't want to do it in front of anyone else.

She flits off to hug Ridhi and high-five Willie Wayne and snap a selfie with Tavi, and then she claps Carter on the back. "If you'd put half as much effort into writing songs as you put into resisting having fun, I really can't see why you won't be, like, the best rock star on the entire planet someday."

"You need to remember your manners," I tell her while we leave the bar behind, the high school also at our backs farther down the street. "Don't bait grown-ups. You don't have enough life experience to back it up yet, and it's not your place."

"I'm not baiting anyone. I'm dropping truth like it's glitter. But don't worry. I won't truth-glitter Mrs. Grandma Lightly. She'd take it out on you and Mom, and then I'd feel bad."

I loop an arm around her shoulders. She's a few inches shorter than me and ten times kinder. "We can handle a cranky old rich lady."

"Do you think Phoebe's okay? She's not, like, worried that Mrs. Grandma Lightly will try to steal her Gold Star halo in the middle of the night, is she?"

I sigh. "I don't know."

"That's not the way to heaven, but I know it's hard to break three hundred years' worth of bad habits."

I cough to cover the snicker that flies out of my mouth. "Bridget."

She flashes me a grin as we stroll under a streetlight. "What? You know it's true. Hey, can I go to the Dells with Mei and her family for a few days next week?"

"You want to leave Tickled Pink to go amusement park hopping? Ew, *boring*."

"Dad."

"When I was your age, I didn't have a fishing lake and pet goats and boredom and the most awesome dad in the world to hang out with and load my e-reader all summer long. And here you are, wanting to go have fun with roller coasters and swim parks and—"

"Dad."

"What? Home isn't heaven for you?" I ruffle her hat.

She ducks away, settling it back down again. "You are really irritating when we lose. Some people would use this as an opportunity for character growth."

"The world couldn't handle me if I got any more awesome."

She stares at me a beat before doubling over laughing.

I turn and watch her, but I'm actually peering beyond, at the outline of the high school, lit by the moon, but without any visible lights on inside it.

The principal's office—Phoebe's bedroom—faces the football field, which means I can't see her windows from here.

But if she were at the school, there would be other light shining through the building.

Wouldn't there?

"C'mon, old man." Bridget straightens, still giggling, and loops an arm through mine. "Let's get you home and tucked in for the night so I can sneak onto your computer and look up ways to run away."

The good news is, she wouldn't actually tell me if she were planning on running away, which means it's not in her plans for the summer. God knows we have our angsty days, and we have to work on that mouth of hers, but on the whole, I don't worry she'll pull a—

Well, a *me*.

"How many more weeks do we have to let the Lightlys play on our team?" she asks.

"*Gasp*. You don't want to play with Tavi anymore? But you took such *fabu* selfies. They were totally *swag*."

"Oh my God, you are in a *mood*. Is this because Phoebe didn't fall into your arms and kiss you senseless when I haloed her as the Gold Star of the game?"

"*Bridget.*"

"What?" She sweeps ahead of me, dramatically putting the back of her hand to her forehead. "It's what Whitney Anastasia did when Guy Pierre crowned her the bowling queen in the movie."

"So you *were* making fun of me," a quiet voice says in the shadows.

I leap.

Bridget yelps.

We both spin, looking for the source of the voice, tripping over ourselves and each other.

"*What?* Oh my God, Phoebe, no," Bridget says.

"You put your heart—*oof*—into the game," I add as Bridget straightens but gets me with an elbow to the gut.

"We don't mock people for doing their best."

"Unless they're only pretending to do their best."

"Which we know you weren't, *right*, Dad?"

Ah.

There Phoebe is, tucked into the trees near the easy entrance to my house. She's fingering the halo crown, brows furrowed as her eyes flit from my daughter to me and back.

"That's why you left?" I ask quietly. "You thought we were making fun of you?"

"I—yes."

She's lying.

If not lying, then not telling the whole truth.

"Phoebe!" Bridget tackles her with a hug. "Oh my God, I would *never*. I mean, I would, and I have, but not, like, actually because I wanted to hurt you. I make fun of myself all the time too. It helps with the self-improvement."

Phoebe's lips part, and her arms flap around a moment before she figures out how to hug Bridget back.

And when she does, she squeezes her eyes shut so tightly my heart squeezes hard enough to suck the air out of my lungs.

Phoebe Lightly needs Tickled Pink.

She needs hugs. She needs unconditional acceptance. She needs to know sometimes, trying your best is enough, and it's okay if your best is literally curling up in a ball and hiding under a blanket fort on occasion.

And I want to put my fist through a tree at how fucking familiar this is.

"Heart counts for more than skill around here," I tell her. "And you put your heart into it."

"That wasn't heart. It was refusal to fail. Lightlys don't fail."

"You cheered for everyone," Bridget says.

"So did Tavi."

"Yeah, but that comes naturally to her. It doesn't to you. And you did it anyway. You made the conscious effort to do something good for someone else."

That's my kid. Brilliantly insightful.

"You should come in," she adds. "Dad has to check on the goats, but I have nowhere to be and nothing to do, and I'm on a root beer buzz."

"I shouldn't—" Phoebe starts, but Bridge cuts her off with a snort.

"What? You'd rather go take a cold shower at the high school? I have some spare pajamas that'll fit you. And they're *not* former theater costumes either."

Phoebe peers at me, laser focused, like she's asking me a million other questions, starting with *Is this okay with you?* and ending with *We are definitely not getting an early arrival on our nooky date, are we?*

I'm paraphrasing.

Pretty sure Phoebe Lightly wouldn't put the question quite like that.

"C'mon, Phoebe." I gesture to the stairs leading to my entry room. "Unless you want to keep getting eaten alive by the bugs out here?"

"Oh, are there bugs? I barely even notice now that they're biting on top of all the other bites."

Bridget claps. "Oh my gosh, Phoebe, the Gold Star halo *and* peak mosquito evolution. You're, like, a real Tickled Pinker now. C'mon. I won't tell your grandma if you use our shower again."

While Bridget heads up the stairs, Phoebe pauses next to me. Her hand brushes mine, and my cock goes hard in an instant.

She's not what I'm supposed to be attracted to, but I can't seem to help myself.

Probably because she's more than I thought she was when she arrived.

She might even be more than *she* thought she was.

And that's one more thing we have in common, even if she'll never know it.

"This place isn't half-bad," she says quietly.

I nod and loop a finger around hers. "It's magic."

"I can see why you wouldn't want outsiders."

"Yeah?"

"Too many people like us—we'd ruin it."

"You're not ruining anything."

She lifts a brow at me and steps closer. "Is that the grumpy fishing lumberjack talking or the horny guy who's plotting ways to send his kid to check on the goats while he joins me in the shower?"

When she puts it that way, I'm not actually sure what the right answer is.

"Dad! Phoebe! C'mon, before you get eaten alive."

I don't move.

Neither does Phoebe.

"Thank you for letting me feel like I fit in," she whispers. She goes up on tiptoe, brushes a kiss to my cheek, and then drops my hand to ascend the stairs. "Bridget, does this Gold Star award come with a free hour of Wi-Fi?"

"Wi-Fi will rot your brain," my daughter replies.

Phoebe laughs.

And that sound, of her enjoying herself here, fitting in here, *laughing* here, more than anything, is dangerous to my heart.

Chapter 24

Phoebe

It's one in the morning. I have to leave for class in eight hours. I smell like someone put chili-cheese dogs under my armpits, my eye still aches, and my skin is so gritty with sawdust I'll never be clean again.

Also, I'm getting my ass handed to me by a fifteen-year-old in Yahtzee, I'm snacking on Cheetos and drinking root beer, I'm still wearing the Tickled Pink Gold Stars halo, and I don't want to leave.

Ever.

Teague's passed out cold in one of the easy chairs on the first level of his tree house, one foot propped on an ottoman, one arm resting on his stomach while his even breathing provides the background music for our game.

"Yahtzee!" Bridget whisper-shrieks. "That's *two* this game. Swag."

"Cheater," I hiss. "Also, what does *swag* even mean?"

"I'm lucky, not a cheater," she retorts as she does a little dance with her arms. "The dice gods adore me. And you're too old to get *swag*."

"I get *swag* all the time. Stuff We All Get? SWAG? I have so much swag it needs its own room in my town house."

"I have so much swag that it can't handle the *-ger* on the other end."

We stare at each other for a beat before Bridget snorts with laughter the same time I crack up.

Teague snort-snuffles, then bolts straight up. "Wha—hell. What time—*Bridget.* Bed."

She rolls her eyes.

I roll my eyes.

She falls back on the rug with another shriek of laughter. "Phoebe! You look like your mom when your grandmother was up to bat!"

"Oh my God, *I thought you liked me!*"

"You two realize the entire earth is trying to sleep?" Teague grumbles. "Bridget. *Bed.* Phoebe. *Go home.*"

"You know you'd have a much better social life if you weren't so cranky and all *go to bed, go home, let me snore in peace* all the time."

Teague stares at me like I'm a remote-controlled zombie alien while Bridget bangs a hand on the floor and hoots. "She's not wrong, Dad."

"What did you put in that root beer?" I ask her.

"Sugar, Phoebe. It's *sugar.*" She straightens, still giggling. "Does Tavi ever have sugar? Like, for real, when no one's watching? Because I would auction off this tree house to pay to watch that."

"Bridget—"

She rolls her eyes again at the tone in Teague's voice. "Yeah, yeah, yeah, go to bed, blah blah. It's not like I'm doing anything before noon today."

"Goats won't milk themselves."

"That's why you have—"

She cuts herself off with a glance at me.

"What?" I ask. "What does he have?"

"Teenage labor," he replies. "Lightly. Ass up off the floor. I'm not carrying you back to the school, and you're not staying here tonight."

"Why not? I'm a very quiet sleeper. You wouldn't even know I was here."

"He doesn't have sleepovers with *girls* while I'm staying the night," Bridget says. "And you're, like, way too old to have a sleepover with a teenager without being creepy. I mean, even twenty would be too old, but you're like forty-*mmph!*"

For the record, that's not me clamping a hand over her mouth.

That's her father.

And her eyes are sparkling like she's enjoying this more than she enjoyed watching my entire family fall in sawdust all night and then kicking my ass in every game we've played since they got home and invited me in, and his eyes are tired but equally amused, like the two of them *like* each other, and he's very much looking forward to the day when she's old enough that he doesn't have to chastise her for being mouthy anymore.

She says something unintelligible behind his hand, and the next thing I know, he's released her so she can tap my halo. "Night, Phoebe. Sleep well so that we don't have to do algebra homework all weekend when you get it wrong the first time." She swings around to the ladder in the corner and scurries up it while Teague gestures me to the door.

"I can walk myself—" I start, but I get the eyeball of doom, and I shut up.

But not without another unexpected snort of laughter slipping out of my mouth.

"No more root beer for you," he mutters before looking over at the ladder and raising his voice. "Bridget. Teeth and bed. Not kidding. I'll be back in twenty minutes."

"Yes, Your Holy Emperor-ness," she calls from upstairs.

Teague puts his hand on my lower back and guides me to the door.

I wonder how slowly I can walk back to the high school.

Or how quickly, if he knows any good dark alleys to slip into in Tickled Pink. There's a nice dark alley behind the café, isn't there? Or maybe one near the Ferris wheel?

I'm really starting to like the Ferris wheel.

It has potential.

Like me.

"Feeling better?" Teague asks me as he guides me out of the door, his hand on the small of my back.

"Since you went all po-po and broke up my party? Depends on if you're offering another kind of party." I bump his hip.

"Are you drunk? Were you slipping my kid vodka while I was sleeping?"

"No, Mr. Rules. She was getting me high on root beer. Am I old if I say I'll be feeling this tomorrow?"

"Yes."

Once again, I crack up.

I don't know if it's funny because it's late and I should be sleeping, too, or if it's funny because it's funny, but I do know one thing without a doubt. "I don't laugh like this in New York."

He pauses and glances at me in the soft yellow light, and before I can question what he's doing, he's grabbed my hand and is tugging me up the exterior stairwell.

"Why are your stairs outside? And why is your foyer—"

He pulls me against him and clamps a hand over my mouth. "Shh."

Oh.

Right.

Bridget can hear us, and if I'm getting booty call time, I need to be *quiet*.

I giggle again.

"Are you slaphappy?" he whispers.

"I'm *free*," I whisper back. Wow. It's odd to say that out loud.

And he's gazing at me in the dim light as though it's even odder than I think it is.

I open my mouth to expand on that, but he taps a finger to my lips again and then tugs me along, up all four flights of steps, all the way to—"Oh, wow."

His tree house has a rooftop terrace, and it's so high in the trees there aren't any branches blocking the view.

"Where did the stars go?" I whisper as I lean into his solid body, my face aimed at the heavens.

There are a few, but not as many as the night they were glittering the sky. Yes, *glittering* the sky.

"Moon's too bright," he murmurs in my ear.

I shiver.

Not because it's chilly outside but because I have a feeling being up on this rooftop terrace with my grumpy lumberjack will make tonight even better.

I inhale deeply, and there it is again—that subtle whiff of chocolate.

It's one more bit of hidden goodness in this town that I thought I'd hate.

I'd still sacrifice a small child for an hour with my massage therapist, and I miss wearing Armani, and I would willingly starve myself for four days if the reward were a night out at any of the city's Michelin-starred restaurants.

I wouldn't be picky.

But I'm also happy to be *here*.

I shift to look at Teague, and something else catches my eye. "You can see the Ferris wheel from here."

"You can see the whole town from here." His large hands slide over my belly, and he pulls my back against him while I turn to take in the rest of the view.

Lights twinkle below.

Not many but enough. And the light of the moon shows off everything from the square to the school to the community center with Gigi's new office to the old neighborhoods and the lake.

I relax into his arms, all my sugar-fueled energy dipping behind a hum coming from my lower belly. "What would it take to rebuild the Ferris wheel?"

He tenses. "Why?"

"It's pretty, but it could be so much more." I frown. "Sort of like me. And it's fine that Gigi's fixing the school and the community center, but no one will come to Tickled Pink to see an old high school building. They'd come to ride the Ferris wheel and watch snowshoe baseball and toss coins into the Fountain of Everlasting Eternity and to get taffy from the candy shop and ride cloud boats on the lake."

"We don't have a candy shop." His voice is rough, his body getting more rigid with every word I utter.

"Tourists aren't the devil, Teague. They won't descend on the town and try to tear Bridget apart. She's awesome and she knows it, and I think *you* know all that too. And everyone else around here with secrets—so what? You're the kind of people who accept each other, good and bad. So why not let Tickled Pink grow back into what it was supposed to be? With a little—*ah!*"

I'm no longer facing the town.

Instead, my back is to the railing, and I'm lost in the most intensely serious gaze I've ever seen on Teague Miller's face.

"You want to fix Tickled Pink."

Not a question. A statement. Yet there are so many layers hiding in the tone of his words, the biggest being *why?*

He doesn't stop me, so I let my fingers trail down his thick chest as I speak. "Tickled Pink isn't broken. It's crusty on the edges and worn down and tired in places, but it's not broken. It just needs a little love to bring it back to its full potential. In a way people would actually appreciate. No one wants to use an old school. But a Ferris wheel? All the kids would want to ride the Ferris wheel."

"You get it." He's staring at me that way again. But I don't think it's that he finds me incomprehensible.

I think—I think this is *awe.*

I suck in a surprised breath, taste chocolate again, and then Teague's kissing me.

Not because we have an appointment on a calendar.

Actually, I don't have a clue exactly why he's kissing me, but I won't argue.

Not when his lips are coaxing mine apart and he's sliding his large hands over my hips to cradle my ass. Not when he tastes better than a bourbon sour after a long day of work and feels like a shield between me and every insecurity I've discovered since landing in this unexpected little town.

And not when that hard ridge of his erection is pressing insistently into my belly.

Teague *likes* me.

He knows who I am. He knows my faults. He doesn't put me on a pedestal because I'm a Lightly.

If anything, that's the part of me that repels him the most.

Yet he's kissing me like I matter.

Like I'm special.

Like he can't resist me despite who I am, like my faults are what make me worthy.

Like I have nothing I need to hide.

No matter how bad it is.

I break out of his kiss with a gasp. "I tried to seduce a married man to get a promotion."

Oh my Oprah.

I just said that out loud.

He squeezes his eyes shut, then drops his forehead to mine. "Okay."

Shut up, Phoebe. Shut up. Shut up and kiss the man. "And I frequently make the people under me put together presentations so that I can present them to my bosses like they're my own, but I throw them under the bus anytime something's wrong."

"Phoebe—"

I can't stop. I've started, and I can't stop. "And I blackmailed a former boyfriend's ex-girlfriend into spilling all the tea she had on him from his time at rehab so that he wouldn't tell the gossip rags that I got super drunk at a Christmas party and threw up all over the back of his limo."

"Would you do it again?"

I freeze.

No is the right answer.

But if I were in New York, I don't know that I'd do anything differently. "It's so much easier to see right and wrong here."

He makes a noise I can't interpret.

High five, dummy. He is so done with you.

Fuck that.

I go up on tiptoe and smash my mouth to his. "Talking over."

"Phoebe."

"Kissing only."

"Phoebe."

It's seriously hard to kiss a guy who keeps giving you a mouthful of beard. "I was just kidding."

He grips me by my ears and gets right up in my face. "You can't undo a lifetime of habits and values just like that, like you're flicking a switch. But you're doing the hard work anyway. That's fucking hot."

Speaking of hot, someone appears to have lit a match behind my eyeballs. Why is simple acceptance so hard to take? "You're fucking hot."

"Dammit, Phoebe, I'm serious. You're—"

"Dad? Where's my spare toothpaste? I just ran out, and I hate this stuff you use. Ew. Oh, gross. Are you guys making out up here? Big yikes. Could you, like, get after it somewhere else?"

Bridget's top half is sticking out of a hatch in the floor.

"We're not making out. Your dad's helping me straighten my contact."

"Did you look in the drawer in the bathroom?" Teague asks his daughter.

"No. That would've been too easy." She sniffs. "Why does it smell like chocolate? Are you eating cookies up here? When did you make cookies? Why don't I have cookies?"

He twists farther away from me. "We're not having cookies."

"Clearly," I mutter.

I get a look.

Two looks, actually.

And they're exactly what you'd expect from a cranky lumberjack and his outspoken yet unexpectedly endearing daughter.

But that's not the weirdest part.

The weirdest part is that I want to stay.

And I don't just mean tonight.

Chapter 25

Teague

Forever.

It's been *forever*—or maybe a week—since Phoebe landed in my tree house for some good old-fashioned cheering up, and now, minutes before I expect her to arrive again, after what feels like freaking months of missed opportunities, Bridget is banging on my door.

I love my daughter.

But I swear *she knows*.

She knows I have plans to get Phoebe naked and do naughty, naughty things to her, and she's here to stop me.

I swing the door open, ready to tell her I need some quiet grumpy dad time, and instead, every protective instinct in my body roars to life as I catch sight of her tear-streaked face.

"Who?" I demand. I can't get out *did this to you?* I'm too busy preparing to kick some ever-loving ass for her.

"Mom won't let me have ice cream for dinner."

My lips part.

"Don't make that face," she sobs. "I don't *feel good* today, okay? I just *want ice cream*."

I slip an arm around her shoulders and pull her in for a hug.

I know three things for absolute certain.

One, Shiloh wouldn't reject a rare night of ice cream for dinner without a reason.

Two, Bridget wouldn't come crying to me if she had any other options. Not because she doesn't trust me but because she's fifteen.

And three, this is definitely not about ice cream.

My phone buzzes in my back pocket, and Bridget lets out another sob. "Don't listen to her," she says. "She's wrong."

Awesome.

"She" will undoubtedly be Shiloh, and I'm about to get the rest of the story.

I pull my phone out to check, and sure enough, there's a message from my ex-wife.

> Is B with you? Caught her trying to sneak out to a party with the seniors.

The seniors.

Code for, *They were going to go drinking and smoking, and I don't care if our daughter has the maturity of a thirty-six-year-old some days. She's still fifteen, and I'm not interested in picking her body parts out of a pine tree if she gets in a car to go joyriding.*

Sometimes I think Bridget got screwed in having a firefighter for a mother and me for her father.

Too bad.

I'm on Team Mom for this one.

> Got her, I reply.

I pause.

Is it wrong to ask my ex-wife to track down my booty call and ask her to reschedule?

Maybe not wrong but definitely awkward.

"C'mon, Bridge. Chocolate milk in the kitchen." And then I'll figure out how to signal Phoebe to hold off on those plans.

"I don't want chocolate milk."

"Paint your nails?"

She glowers at me.

I scrub a hand over my face and turn toward the ladder. "Your mom's not—"

"Hey, big guy, you want a piece of—*oh my God!*"

The door slams against the wall a second too late to warn me it's open, and I spin in time to see Phoebe hunching in on herself, trench coat hanging open, red lace bra barely visible, in sky-high stilettos that make every spare drop of blood in my body—and some not so spare—rush to my cock.

I can't decide if I'm hoping she's blocking our view of the matching red lace panties or if I'm hoping she's wearing short shorts.

Either way, I know that this is a problem.

This is definitely a problem.

"Oh my God, ew ew ew!" Bridget shrieks.

"Kidding!" Phoebe shrieks back. "I would never—that's gross—ha ha, your faces!"

She dives back out of the door.

Bridget's shaking her hands like that'll help erase the mental image. "Why do *you* get to have private naked parties, and *I* can't even hang out with like three friends with our clothes on? *Ugh.*"

"It's not—we're not—" I start.

She rolls her eyes.

"Because I'm a damn grown-up," I finally say. "Go get chocolate milk."

"I'm not a baby!"

"I know, Bridge, but you're not—"

"Ugh." She ignores me and heads for the ladder to the upper levels of the tree house.

I dart out the door and start to loop my deck. "Phoebe—"

"We're good." She flaps a hand, too, from her spot inside the tree house elevator. The flappy hands are going around. "Could you please lower me so I can go die of mortification among the goats? They'll eat my remains once I'm good and dead, right? I'd do this myself, but I'm actually too busy being embarrassed to remember how this lever system works, and *I don't do embarrassed.* I once had food poisoning in the middle of a very important high-level meeting at work, *with my boyfriend's father present,* and there were some seriously unfortunate side effects, and *I still owned it like a boss.* But do you see me? Here? Now? *I'm embarrassed.* What's happening to me?"

"Just—stay. Let me make a phone call, and—"

"No, no. I'm good." She blows out a breath. "I just needed to get that out, and now I'm going to go back to being rational, good-hearted Phoebe who wouldn't have blinked if I'd busted in on you in the middle of poker night with your buddies. This is *only* because your kid saw me nearly naked."

She's hot as hell. I don't know what she did to her hair or her makeup, but the whole thing put together—it's like she planned a night of role-playing "sixties call girl comes to visit the tree house man."

I subtly adjust my boner and hope Bridget isn't watching. "You ever sneak out to parties when you were fifteen?"

"Fifteen?" She huffs. "Try eleven."

"*Shh.* Jesus. Pretend you're the parent here."

"Oh." Her eyes go wide. *"Oh."*

Her skin is gorgeous. And when her mouth goes round like that, the ideas that form in my head—

"Bridget! Hey! Rematch on that Yahtzee game?" Phoebe says.

"Ugh."

I know that *ugh* too.

That's the *ugh* of *I thought you were on my side and I could sneak away out of the other side of the house while my dad was distracted staring at your cleavage.*

Fuck.

"Did you walk all the way over here in that?" I ask Phoebe after verifying with a quick glance that Bridget is, indeed, heading back inside again.

"Would that turn you on more?" she whispers.

"Yes."

She licks her lips.

Not good not good not good.

I literally cannot remember the last time a woman licking her lips made me this hard.

"No," she finally says. "I changed in your weird little fishing storage foyer at the top of the stairs. I just dived into the elevator because it was closer." Her brows twist. "Oh my God, this town has truly broken me."

"And yet, I like you so much better this way."

"Hm."

I should not be smiling at this woman, but her clear befuddlement with apparently liking that I like her is irresistible.

It's like we're both having identity crises.

"Stay," I start, but she shakes her head.

"Give me the town's Wi-Fi password, and you can text me when it's clear to come back."

This feels like a trap.

All of it.

Every bit.

"Did you convince Bridget to ruin our plans so that you could get the Wi-Fi password?"

God, she's hot when her lips purse out.

Actually, is there *anything* she does with her lips that isn't hot?

"Brilliant and devious as that would be," she finally says, "I would've just paid her for the Wi-Fi password and then let you service my loins."

"*Oh my God*, could you two *please* stop talking?" Bridget shrieks.

I scratch my beard. "At least I know where she's at . . ."

Phoebe smiles. "You know where to find me if she happens to decide to pout at someone else's house instead."

"Hitting on Deer Drop Floyd because you're desperate?"

"In the principal's office, Teague. *In the principal's office.* Now, if you're not going to give me the password, let me down so I can go finish dying of mortification in peace."

"You don't need to be embarrassed."

"And you don't need to book an appointment on my calendar to see me naked. Okay? Just . . . drop by and tell anyone who sees you at the school that you're there about the electricity."

I glance up at the next level, where I'm fairly certain Bridget is listening in on every word. "Noted."

She glances up too. "Does she want a party?" she whispers.

And that's how my booty call turns into an evening in the cafeteria of the old high school instead, with Phoebe mixing virgin drinks for me, my kid, my ex-wife, and her current wife, while Carter Lightly—sorry, Carter *Hardly*—attempts to provide musical entertainment to go with our charades game.

But my ex-wife still pulls the ultimate cockblock at the end of the night. "You staying with your dad?" she asks Bridget on our way out, when I'm hoping to turn around and sneak right back in.

Bridget nods. "He'll let me sleep in."

"Will not," I declare.

"She's up at five if she stays with us," Shiloh says with a smirk.

"Bakery help," Ridhi agrees.

"After she helps us wash the fire trucks."

I glare at both of them.

They snicker, attack Bridget with hugs and kisses, link hands, and stroll off into the night.

"I could go home by myself," Bridget tells me.

Not with that twinkle in her eye, she can't.

I look back at Phoebe, who's leaning in the school doorway beneath the giant **Boys** sign etched into the concrete overhead.

Wi-Fi, she mouths.

"Dream on," Bridget says. "If the town gets that million for keeping you off the network, I'm using my part of the scholarship money to study landscaping so that I can put the Fountain of Everlasting Eternity back in, but better. I've missed the crucial part of childhood where I frolic in fountains while my parents either take pictures or shriek at me to get out before I freak out all the other people who are watching."

Phoebe frowns. "That's a thing?"

"You were truly raised by wolves."

And I am truly not getting laid tonight.

Tomorrow, I mouth to her.

"You should come over tomorrow night, and I'll explain everything that you missed in your childhood," Bridget says. "I'm staying at Dad's again. Just feel like it."

Phoebe and I both look at my kid, who smiles like the terrible little cockblocking devil that *she* is too.

This is going to be a long, long summer.

Chapter 26

Phoebe

It's like I can't stop finding out everything I knew in life was a lie.

The latest: that cats are evil and will eat your soul.

That is *such a lie.*

"Phoebe. For heaven's sakes, can you please act a *little* dignified?" My mother punctuates her sentence with a sigh as she sits perched at a table in the corner of the small playroom at the shelter, flipping tarot cards.

I'm on the floor, on my back, letting six kittens crawl all over my body. It's the most affection I've had in *days.*

Why?

Because Bridget and her mothers are devious, devious people who have figured out my weakness and want to make sure I suffer greatly enough to become a good person *without* the stress relief of sex with a hot lumberjack.

The worst part?

I actually *like the cockblockers.*

Shiloh's funny. Ridhi's cooking rivals some of my regular haunts on the Upper East Side, which I would deny if I were in New York, but I'm not.

Also, no waiting, and no making my assistant call and bully anyone for a reservation.

And Bridget?

Bridget is this massive ball of energy who'll basically love anyone who throws her a bone but doesn't tolerate bullshit.

She's a human puppy with mood swings and an intense desire to prevent the adults in her life from having sex.

"They need to be socialized, Mrs. Lightly," Bridget says. "But Phoebe, she's right. Get up. Quit cheating. There's more litter to be scooped."

"You'd deny these poor babies their playground? *For shame.* Also? Who's the grown-up here? I get to issue orders."

"New plan. *I* act as their playground, and *you* scoop the litter, because your soul needs it more." Bridget tries to scowl at me the same way Teague does when I'm intentionally getting under his skin, and I have to resist the urge to look at the clock to see how close we're getting to when he's coming to pick her up from our volunteer time here at the shelter. "Or I can tell your mother about that little incident with your homework?"

I gasp as if that's a horrific threat. "Oh my God, Bridget, play dirty, why don't you? But you know I'm right. *Cookies* are the long-lost algebraic relative of pi, and whoever took cookies out of math is pure evil."

"Don't eat cookies, Phoebe, dear," my mother says as she shuffles her tarot deck. When she heard I was doing volunteer work, she insisted on coming along, "because my soul needs improving, too, if I'm to ever get out of this hellhole." "It'll impact your figure, and you have such a lovely figure."

Bridget makes a gagging motion.

I suppress a smile, then try to untangle myself from the six little kittens still sniffing and crawling all over my body.

It's not as easy as it sounds. But it involves a hella ton of laughter, so I'm okay with the extra trouble.

"Your tools, madam," Bridget says, presenting me with a bag and a litter scooper before she dives to the floor to pet the kittens too.

I strangely don't mind the litter.

Sure, it smells a little, but the more I do for other people, the more connection I feel with them.

When I was in New York, I'd buy lunch for a friend, or I'd pick up the tab on spa day, or I'd send flowers or chocolates—or both—to someone if I perceived I'd slighted them somehow and cared to make amends for social or business advantages.

We'd air-kiss.

We'd discuss which vacations we intended to take next.

We'd gossip about who wore what at a function.

But I couldn't tell you if Lola Minelli actually had her heart broken by that actor-comedian she was dating before she started doing *Lola's Tiny House*. I never paid attention to people's names if they didn't appear to be people who would be useful to me. I *forgot* my assistant's dog had died. I have zero idea if Tavi actually likes her job or if she does it because it's easy.

If I were in New York, there's no one I could talk to about the smack-in-the-face realizations I've had here about the way my actions impact other people and about what matters.

Or about how I feel like a hypocrite for only caring about other people as I realize just how much I don't know about myself. And how much I want to figure out who I'd be if I hadn't been born Phoebe Lightly.

"Oh dear, Ziggy, you've gotten the Lovers." Mom peers at the card, then at the kitten, who's older than the other kittens. He's like a second-grade kitten as compared to preschool kittens. Bridget told us Ziggy's a spotted silver tabby, and he can't seem to walk a straight line. He needs a kitty massage or something to loosen up some tense muscles in one side of his back. "You have difficult choices coming up. Is this a kill shelter?"

"Mrs. Lightly," Bridget gasps.

"Don't yell at me, young lady. I merely interpret the cards. Between the Hanged Man and the Lovers, I daresay this cat is in danger."

I pause in scooping litter to frown at her. "Mom. Stop. You can't read a cat's cards. He has no self-awareness."

"All beings have self-awareness, Phoebe."

"But he still can't speak English or discuss his inner turmoil, even *with* a licensed therapist, which you are not."

Mom lifts the cat and stares into his green eyes.

Or tries to.

The cat's squirming in her grip, looking for a way out.

"Mom. Let the cat go."

"Shh, child. I'm having a telepathic moment with him. He needs to know he's in danger if he doesn't change his ways."

"Huh." Jennifer, the woman in charge, pauses on her way through with a stack of paperwork in hand. "Ziggy's the one we keep finding hanging from the top of his cage like he's trying to *Mission: Impossible* his way out of it."

Mom gives me the *told you so* look.

"He's *a kitten.*"

"He's on a path to eternal damnation. Look. The cards say it clearly. He's willfully ignoring the choices he needs to make to have a happy life." She sets the cat down, and he scurries to leap into a box of newspapers, which he instantly begins clawing like he's trying to dig through them.

Bridget's staring at my mother. "That's really not a nice thing to say about a cat."

"The cards say what they say. Talk to the deck. In the meantime, you should stop eating all of those carbs. They're terrible for your figure, dear."

"*Mother.* Stop. *Now.*" I roll my eyes at Bridget. "Ignore her. Clearly, avoiding carbs hasn't improved *her* life any. Or her soul."

"Phoebe Sabrina Lightly, would you like me to read *your* cards?"

"Not with that deck."

"This deck said that Starlight there will find a home with two daughters who will dress her up and love her and treat her like a princess and that Hank over there will live a long and healthy life as the resident cat at the catfé that some enterprising soul will open in Deer Drop."

"Since when do the cards get that specific?"

"When the participant is willing to give more feedback, their future becomes much more clear." She eyeballs the cats. "Now. Which one is Fluffball? He's next on my list."

"Fluffball is a they/them," Bridget says.

"My apologies. Where are they?"

"Hiding from your ridiculous cards, because they have no tolerance for malarkey."

"Malarkey?" I ask the teenager.

"I'm bringing the 1930s back. The cool parts, anyway. *Ziggy!* Don't pick on Elmo! You know that never ends well."

Ziggy leaps away from a very upset black-and-white kitten with a fluffed tail and flattened ears, backs into a calico kitten, who hisses at him, and then leaps away from another calico kitten, who bats at his face, before Bridget finally snags him.

She cuddles him close while he tries to escape her grasp. "I know, I know. You just want someone to play with, but none of the other kittens like the way you play."

Ziggy meows.

A memory flashes hard at the front of my brain, of me sitting in the foyer of Gigi's brownstone, second grade, crying to my mother about how Alexia Cordelia had declared me "not a very good friend" at recess, and how the rest of the girls in my class had snubbed me for the rest of the day, leaving me to get picked to play on the boys' team for dodgeball in gym, and how they'd all thrown their balls harder at me that day, and my heart melts into a puddle for the little cat.

"Phoebe, you are a Lightly," Mom said to me that day. "When someone hits you, you hit them back twice as hard. Now come. We're going to make Alexia Cordelia rue the day she dared cross you."

Her plan worked, of course.

She sent me to school the next day as the first kid in my class to carry a Louis Vuitton purse, and all the girls who'd been on Team Alexia Cordelia the day before became card-carrying members of Team Phoebe instead when I let them touch my purse.

Looking back, I can see why the victory felt so empty.

Those friends weren't *friends*.

I could've used a real friend.

Just like Ziggy could now.

He just needs someone to love him unconditionally.

To accept him for who he is without demanding that he change.

I'm not sure I've ever loved anyone unconditionally like that.

But I'll damn sure give it my best. "Jennifer, how do you adopt a cat?"

She slides her brown eyes over me, then glances at Bridget, then my mom, before finally looking back at me. "Paperwork and a fee and a home check."

"Excellent. Bridget, could you please be a dear and fetch me my handbag?"

"Of course, Mrs. Grandma Lightly," she mutters.

I blink at her once, realize I sounded *exactly* like my grandmother, and clap my hand over my mouth with a horrified inhale.

Litter dust shoots down my throat, and *ick ick ick*. "How do cats— *gack*—do their business—*blech*—in this?"

"They don't inhale," Bridget says, which makes it worse.

I'm now laughing and coughing so hard at the same time that drool—actual, literal drool—is sliding down my chin, and I can't wipe it off because I'm coated in litter dust.

If Jennifer's on the *Tickled Pink Papers* committee and snaps a picture of me like this, at least I'll know whose house to burn down.

Kidding.

Kidding.

But I will *totally* snap a picture of her midsneeze and submit it anonymously to the gossip page if I get the chance.

I try to wipe my chin with my shoulder while I'm still coughing and bump into the wall by accident.

"That's what you get for thinking about adopting a cat," my mother mutters—loudly—while I cough and sputter and contemplate the vodka sour I'll need after this to cleanse my digestive system.

"I'm adopting Ziggy," I inform her between coughs.

"You know a cat is a lifetime commitment?" Jennifer asks.

She has the most amazing hips. Tavi has curves like that, too, but she works out so much that you can't always tell.

"Until the cat or I die, yes, Jennifer, I'm aware. Also, where do you get nondusty cat litter? I need to make a very large donation of cleaner cat litter to save you all from lung poisoning."

"There are self-scooping litter boxes, too, if you're rolling out the checkbook," Bridget says.

I know I should remind her that she's a teenager, but I love her honesty and her chutzpah. "Done."

Jennifer winces again. "Phoebe, no offense, but no matter how much you donate to the cat shelter, even if the school passes the home check, I'm not entirely certain—"

"That I can follow through with my commitments to an animal?" Oh, hell yes, I'm utilizing the Lightly eyebrow. "I know we don't know each other well, but the one thing you really need to know about me is that I do *not* fail. At *anything*. Including loving the shit out of a cat currently living in a—in a—"

Oh my God.

I'm choking up.

I'm choking up and I'm going to cry because the cat is not where he belongs. "—in the wrong environment."

Mom's gaping at me like alien earthworms or something have taken over my body.

Bridget's eyes are shiny.

And Jennifer's frozen in place.

I've broken everyone by having feelings.

Awesome.

"Phoebe, have you actually . . . touched . . . Ziggy?" Jennifer finally asks.

And there I go with the Lightly eyebrow *again*. It's like my face has a mind of its own.

But I'm completely in charge of the rest of me as I dust my hands off on my pants—my thousand-dollar Valentino jeans, for the record—rise, and cross to where Bridget and Ziggy are hanging out near the cat tree that three other kittens are climbing all over.

Ziggy clearly doesn't want to be left out of the climbing, because he's attempting to scale Bridget's face.

"Ziggy, would you like to go home with me?" I ask the cat.

He pauses with one paw on Bridget's ponytail holder and another on her ear, and he meows at me.

"See?" I say triumphantly. "He wants to come home with me."

Bridget squirms and gently grabs the cat under the ribs, tugging him off her head while he tries to pull her hair out of her ponytail. "Here, Phoebe."

My eyes get hot again.

What if he doesn't like me?

What if I drop him?

What if I really can't do something as simple as care for a cat?

What if I'm making a complete and total fool of myself here?

Bridget rises. "It's okay," she says quietly. "He might bite. Or he might scratch you. But you'll heal. Probably."

"I don't know that you're helping," I tell her.

She grins. "Well, yeah. Go on. Hold him for a minute. And he really might scratch or bite, but kittens sometimes do. They grow out of it."

I hesitantly reach for the cat she's offering. Thus far, I've just let the rest of them romp all over my body, and I haven't actually picked one up.

But as soon as my hand goes under his little rib cage, he starts vibrating, and a massive purr resonates around the room. I suck in a surprised breath and pull him close to my chest.

He's *really* furry.

And so tiny.

He shouldn't feel so tiny—not next to the rest of the kittens, who are half his size—but he does.

And he's so light. Like, even smaller than Tavi's dog.

If I drop him—*no.*

No, I will *not* drop this cat.

He's soft and fluffy and squirmy, and he's trying to climb my arm. "Whoa, kitty."

"You can squat near the ground if it makes you feel better," Bridget tells me. "That way if he jumps, he doesn't have as far to go."

"But I don't want him to jump! If he jumps, that means he doesn't like me. Doesn't it?"

"Cats pick their owners," Jennifer says. "If you really want a cat, we can wait until—"

I drop to my ass on the floor as Ziggy claws his way up my arm, onto my shoulder, and then to the top of my head, his little pinprick claws digging in like mutant mosquitoes attacking my skin everywhere he climbs.

Bridget cracks up and pulls out her phone. "Hold just like that, Phoebe. I have to send this to the *Tickled Pink Papers*."

"It's *you*! You're the one who keeps—*ah!*"

I reach for Ziggy, who's wobbling on my head like it's a beach ball floating in a pool and he can't find his balance.

"She's not very maternal, is she?" my mom murmurs to Jennifer.

"Not exactly her fault she started at a disadvantage there, is it?" Bridget fires back.

"Bridget," Teague suddenly says from the doorway in that super hot, super displeased, disciplinarian dad voice, making all of us jump, which makes Ziggy fall off my head.

"Ziggy!" I shriek.

The kitten squats on all fours and shrinks back, and I clap my hand to my mouth again. "I'm not yelling," I whisper to him. "I'm worried about you."

He shakes his little head and prances off to leap onto Fluffball, who executes a ninja roll and pounces right back, making Ziggy rear back and run away.

I haven't been chosen.

He doesn't want me.

"At least the cat has some sense," my mother mutters.

"I think the cat has basic instinctive needs to be a cat," Bridget replies. "Don't take it personally, Phoebe. If he's not supposed to be your cat, he's actually saving you a lot of heartache in not leading you on first."

"Are you sure you're fifteen?"

"Sometimes I think I'm a time traveler who got caught wrong in the space-time continuum, and it gave me a concussion when I was dropped into this body, but one day soon, I'll wake up with my full memory intact and the knowledge of how to return to my home planet."

I look at Teague, who's smiling at his daughter like she's the very light of his life, and I realize, once again, just how insignificant I am.

"If you want your sushi while it's fresh, you'll get it in gear," he tells her. "Also, apologize to Mrs. Lightly. You're being mouthy again."

"Sushi?" The desperation in Mom's voice is evident, and I can't blame her.

"Sushi?" Yeah. Mine's the same. I would give my left kneecap for good sushi.

Teague nods. "Fresh caught out of Deer Drop Lake this morning. Bluegill and trout."

Mom rears back in horror so fast that we can hear her back crack, which scares the four closest kitties, who scatter like my ex-boyfriends when my grandmother walks into a room. Elmo leaps onto the table, lands on Mom's tarot deck, and pushes the cards off one by one while he tries to scramble away.

"My cards!" she shrieks.

"Make sure he doesn't pee!" Jennifer shrieks.

But it's too late.

Elmo is peeing all over the table and Mom's scattered tarot cards. And Mom.

She lifts her gaze to me as the kitten lets loose, and the utter horror on her face makes me forget all about the little digs.

She doesn't belong here.

She's not adaptable. She's not flexible. She has the friends she wants to have back in New York, and she's completely isolated and missing them.

And her brunch dates. And her spa appointments. And probably some of her business stuff too.

She's made a few sketches of new design ideas, but she's been complaining for a few months that she's just not as inspired as she used to be.

And that, as much as anything, makes me mad all over again that Gigi demanded we all be here.

Who is she to tell us who needs to be a better person?

The only person she *should* be in charge of is herself.

Teague's moving swiftly through the room, coming to play savior to my mother, who looks on the verge of tears.

Bridget's staring in abject fascination at all of it.

And Jennifer looks like she wants to go hide in another county.

"She has seventeen more sets of cards at home," I murmur to the shelter manager.

"Phoebe."

I'm Pavlov's dog, and Teague's voice saying my name is my bell. I don't think. I don't pause. I just turn.

"Hold this."

My hands go out, and suddenly I'm holding Elmo.

He's a little black-and-white bundle of softness, and just like Ziggy, he instantly starts purring.

But unlike Ziggy, when I pull him to my chest, he hooks a claw into my *Pink Gold* commemorative T-shirt right above my breast and holds on.

Bridget's shoving paper towels at Teague, who's attacking the cat's mess as though it'll burn the building down if he doesn't. Jennifer's hustling over with a garbage can.

Mom's standing helplessly on the other side of the table, letting everyone else do the work while she plays the ultimate victim.

And this little ball of black-and-white fluff vibrates against my chest while I softly stroke his fur with my free hand.

"Hi," I whisper.

He lifts his little gray-green eyes to study me, then rubs his face on my shirt.

"Phoebe," Bridget suddenly whispers. "I think you've been chosen."

There go the blowtorches behind my eyes again. I blink hard to get it under control, which makes me mad.

"Oh, Phoebe, surely not," my mom says.

"Margot, don't be a dick," Teague replies.

Forget trying not to cry.

Now I'm trying not to laugh too.

I think I've found myself a hero.

Chapter 27

Phoebe

I have the best cat on the entire planet.

He doesn't do tricks, but he does hit the litter box, and he's content to sit in my lap while we binge the three episodes of *Lola's Tiny House* that I downloaded to my tablet when I was at school before my shift at the shelter.

He's also an excellent distraction from thinking about missing New York and Giuseppe, my massage therapist, and yes, I miss him enough to remember his name.

But Elmo's not quite enough to distract me from questioning where I fit in the world.

In New York, I knew I wouldn't get married for love. I knew I used people. I knew I broke other people's moral codes to get ahead, and I didn't care.

It was what was expected to fit in. As a Lightly, I very much fit into that part of my society.

Here?

Here, I care. Here, I have regrets for things I've done. Here, it matters to me that a cat might judge me for my character. It matters to me that my algebra tutor is struggling with having a crush on a boy who she's afraid "won't like someone like me." It matters to me that the not-so-cranky lumberjack who just *knew* which cat to hand me was so very, very kind the entire time he was at the shelter with us but still left with nothing more than a gentle squeeze to my shoulder and a "Good job, Ms. Lightly."

"What does that even mean?" I ask Elmo.

He looks up at me and makes the most adorable meow I've ever heard in my entire life.

And then he settles back in the midst of my crossed legs, activates his little vibrating purr box like if he doesn't purr he'll die, and turns his attention to my tablet screen once more, and I realize I've missed half this episode.

I could turn the volume up or even go play it on the projector Gigi had installed in the cafeteria for our twice-weekly viewings of *Pink Gold*. Carter's out somewhere, or possibly he's gone into hibernation after not sleeping for the first few weeks we were here.

Tavi keeps disappearing. Probably going to wherever her secret Wi-Fi server is located, and yes, I know she has one. I keep hearing around town that her socials are all updated with pictures of her running in front of the Ferris wheel, or doing yoga by the lake, or drinking weird vegan smoothies in front of a bunch of trees that look Tickled Pinkish, or cutting vegetables in Shiloh and Ridhi's kitchen—the one in their house, not the café's kitchen—which is easily the most gorgeous kitchen I've ever seen.

I don't even cook, and I have kitchen envy.

Tavi has other new pictures and videos, too, from Italy and Sweden and Argentina. I've seen her every day, so I know she's posting content she's had saved up, but I also know she has to be negotiating with Gigi to get back out to her travels so the exotic half of her vegan-lifestyle brand doesn't dry up.

If Gigi's in the school tonight, I don't want to know. She's picked the art room on the third floor as her bedroom, and her butler is staying in the classroom across the hall from her.

None of the rest of us go to the third floor.

Ever.

I don't ask what anyone else's reasons are, but mine revolve around Bridget whispering to me during tutoring the other day that Niles told Anya that he's been Gigi's secret boyfriend for years, and he took the job as her butler so he could be closer to her.

It makes me both sad and happy for them.

Happy, because why shouldn't people be with the people who make them happy?

But also sad, because wherever Niles came from, he clearly doesn't have the pedigree he needs for Gigi to claim him in public.

I don't know where Dad is, either—it's too late for him to be obsessively mowing the grass on the old football field like he's done for the past four days—but I know Mom was planning to "have mommy time," which is code for *pop a Xanax and sleep off this nightmare.*

The Pink Box has started stocking random new tarot decks twice a week.

Pretty sure they're getting them off eBay and marking the price up, since it's a given that Mom will insist she needs them.

Mad respect to the proprietors.

But it all means that Elmo and I are totally alone.

Bridget's stayed with Teague every single night since Friday night, which I know mostly because I've been that lame, desperate woman who's taken up evening walks around the town for exercise as an excuse to see if he's free and available to service my lady parts.

I try to force my attention back to the show, but it's hard to watch Lola navigate tiny-house living without thinking of Teague's tree house.

Teague's tree house makes Lola's tiny house look like a dump. Maybe it's because Lola's house is blinged out with designer everything, clearly the producers' method of making more advertising dollars, and Teague's house is comfortable almost in an old-money kind of way— buy classy quality once, and you'll never have to buy it again.

Or maybe it's that Lola films in her tiny house, and Teague *lives* in his tree house, and it's the people that make the home.

And maybe I need to quit fantasizing about him.

He's still just a man. And I'm starting to suspect my grandmother is slipping his kid bribes to stay with him all summer.

And the ghost is knocking on my door.

I frown. .

Elmo meows and looks at the window.

Tickled Pink Floyd moans, then mutters something about spilled cafeteria food.

And someone raps at my window.

Not my door.

My window.

"Are you ready to scratch their face off if it's a tourist?" I whisper to my kitten.

He gives me puppy dog eyes. Swear he does.

I set him on my bed. "Stay. Let Mommy handle this."

I kill the lights and pull back a corner of the curtain as the rapping at my window comes a third time.

And as soon as I realize who's out there, I almost squeal with joy.

Teague's outside my window.

I throw the curtains the rest of the way back, fumble with opening the creaky old thing, and finally shove it open. "What are you doing here?" I whisper, even though I hope I know.

"I really didn't want to like you."

I smile despite the grumpy scowl on his face. "You don't say."

"But you, Phoebe Lightly, are a new surprise every day, and I think I'm addicted."

He pushes up into the window frame, and then Teague Miller, my first enemy in Tickled Pink, my partner in crime for figuring out how to convince my grandmother this hell was a bad idea, the man who saves me from lakes, thunderstorms, and punctured tires and who introduced me to cheese curds and the simplest ways to be a better human being, is suddenly devouring my mouth while climbing into my bedroom through a window.

"Shuh winnow," I gasp in the midst of kissing him back.

He interprets perfectly, slamming my window shut behind him.

I yank the curtains closed again.

And then there's no more thinking.

No more worrying.

No more frustration.

It's just me and this bear of a man touching, kissing, tearing each other's clothes off, and tumbling into bed.

But not before he sets my kitten gently on the floor. "Close your eyes," he orders Elmo. "You're too young for this."

I start to laugh, but then his mouth is on my breast, sucking my nipple and sending the most intense jolt of pleasure from my chest to my pussy and making me gasp instead.

"I've been dreaming about this," he murmurs as he shifts to my other nipple.

"Why?" *Oh my God*, I need to shut up. I need to shut up *right now*.

"*Why?* Because you're annoyingly sexy and I want to see you come again." His hands roam over my body. "Jesus. Your skin is so damn soft. And gorgeous."

Oh my God.

I don't think I can do this.

I don't think I can have sex with him unless there's a chance he actually likes me.

Who the *fuck* am I, and what have I done with my badass self?

I tense, and he lifts his head. "Phoebe?"

"Do you like me, or am I just a passing novelty?" Why can I not shut up?

Why?

Those soft lips of his turn down, and his eyes narrow again. It's like I can see him cursing to himself about the crazy chick who wants to talk about if I *like* him like we're in high school.

"I like you."

It should be enough. It should really be enough. *"Why?"*

"Because you're trying. You're bullheaded and stubborn and not all that great at small-town life, but you're *trying*. And that—that says more about who you are *here"*—he taps my heart—"than anything you wear or where you work or what your name is."

"Oh."

He swirls his tongue around my nipple, then blows on it, making me squirm in the best way.

"Your turn," he murmurs. "Do you like *me*, or am I a way to blow off steam?"

I lick my lips.

This is harder on this side.

Didn't expect that.

"I like you," I whisper.

"Why?"

"Because you push and you don't make it any easier on me than I make it on you. Because you don't give me a free pass just because this is hard, but you're not actually a total dick. Because you care about everyone around here, and even knowing you want us to leave, you do things to make us more comfortable while we're here. Because—because it's like I *know* you. And can you *please* make me shut up now? I'm feeling *very* naked."

"You *are* very naked."

"But I don't often *feel—ooh*."

The man's fingers—and his mouth—and his tongue—and he's sliding down my body, which is *not* something my lovers normally do.

But Teague—Teague is dipping his tongue into my belly button and lifting my leg over his shoulder and *oh my holy sweet Oprah*, he is going *there*.

He sticks his nose between my thighs, licks my seam, and I'm singing.

Maybe not singing, but that isn't a sound that's ever come out of my mouth before.

And when he swirls his tongue around my clit, my hips come up off the bed. "Again," I order.

He chuckles against my sensitive flesh. "Bossy."

"You knew who you were coming to see. Do it again."

My hands are tangled in his hair, and his beard is tickling my inner thighs, and Teague Miller, the stubborn lumberjack who probably would've rather let me go the way of my Louboutins in that lake the first day I met him, gets down to business with his mouth on my pussy until coherent thought is impossible.

I'm a writhing bundle of pleasure and throbbing nerve endings until he sucks my clit while he slips two fingers inside me, and suddenly I'm coming so hard and fast that I'm drowning in euphoria, chanting his name, mewling—*mewling* in utter rhapsody.

Forget diamonds. Forget shoes. Forget spa days.

That's all trimmings and trappings.

This?

An orgasm so hard and deep and intense that I'm seeing colors I never knew existed?

I have found the meaning of life.

My body sags against the mattress as the last of the spasms fades away. "Oh my God," I whisper.

"You don't do anything halfway, do you?" Teague shifts, moving back up my body, pressing soft kisses over the quivering flesh of my belly.

"I don't—I've never—it's not usually—"

He lifts his head and smirks at me while he moves his chin just right to brush his beard over my breastbone. "You don't say."

I fling an arm over my eyes, but I'm laughing.

Laughing.

In bed.

With a man.

Who *very* clearly knows his way around my body, and who very clearly seems to be enjoying himself almost as much as I am.

"Don't hide," he says softly. "I'm not done with you."

I'm pretty sure that orgasm turned my bones to magic pixie dust, and my muscles have never been more relaxed and jellylike in my life, but I still find the strength to twist beneath him and roll until I'm on top. "Excuse me, sir, but I believe *I'm* not done with *you.*"

He smiles.

It's not a smirk or a sneer or a triumphant *gotcha.*

It's a soft, affectionate, *I know your game, and I don't mind if it takes you a while to see what's right in front of you* smile. "I like you naked."

I don't think he's talking about *physically.* "You should. I'm hot."

God, his laugh is an aphrodisiac. I rub my very satisfied lady parts over his hard cock. "I'm glad you're here," I whisper to him.

"I'm glad *you're* here."

It's raw honesty from both of us, and it's scary, but it's also so easy.

Vulnerable isn't my favorite state of being.

But I'm *safe.*

And that's what makes rolling my hips to take him inside me so much more than it's ever been before.

This isn't a power struggle. It's not a negotiation. It's not for social gain.

It's basic, simple affection, yet it's also the most powerful force I've felt in my life.

His eyes roll back in his head. "Fuck, you feel so good."

"Just wait until next time, when I go down on *you*."

He growls, rolls, and once again, he has the upper hand as he thrusts into me. "Big promises."

I'm a *shut up and just fuck me* kinda gal.

But not with Teague. I want *all* of him. "We are—*oh my God, there*—not waiting another *seventeen fucking years*—you are *so good* at this—to do this—*aaaah, yes*—again."

"You count—*fuck*, Phoebe, do that again."

I clench my inner walls around his cock while he pushes deeper into me. "That?"

"Minx."

"You didn't count?"

"I counted seconds. *Real* time. And it was longer than seventeen years."

He's hitting all my favorite spots deep in my core, and he's making my chest glow at the same time. I'm not convenient. I'm not easy to live with. And yet, he missed me.

I could get addicted to this kind of affection.

He links his fingers with mine and pins my hand to the bed, his gaze locked on me while he pumps into me, stroking my already-over-sensitive nerve endings.

And I surrender.

I don't need to be on top. I don't need to be in control. I don't need anything beyond this unexpected gift of being here, with him, tonight, letting our bodies do the talking.

The *I like you*s.

The *I believe in you*s.

The *I support you*s.

I don't know how it's happened, but being here, getting to know this man—he keeps making me want to be *more*. To do better. To reach higher.

I don't know how to do the same for him, but he's gazing at me like I already have.

And that's what pushes me over the edge.

Not the insanely delicious feel of his hard-as-marble cock rocking inside me but the whole experience of being with him.

Of being with someone who sees the good in me in a way no one ever has before.

My second orgasm hits, and I cry out so loudly they probably hear me in Deer Drop.

Teague groans and buries his face in my neck, and I realize he's coming too.

I want to do this again.

I want to give him as much pleasure as he's given me.

For as long as he'll let me.

Chapter 28

Teague

I should leave, but I'm too comfortable in Phoebe's bed.

No, check that. The bed's not all that great.

I'm too comfortable *with Phoebe*.

We're tangled in the sheets, her on her back, me splayed half across her, drawing lazy figures over her bare belly while her kitten tries to help.

If I were feeling masochistic, I'd ask myself why I'm so attracted to her, but I don't want to dwell on how very, very similar we are.

Old memories have been haunting me enough lately.

I just want to lie here, with her fingers threading through my hair and lightly scratching my scalp, her heart beating strong beneath my ear, one rosy nipple in view every time I open my eyes, and just *be*.

No complications.

No past. No future.

Just *now*.

"I always wanted to do something naughty in a principal's office," I murmur against her skin.

"The office is my closet. This is actually the secretary's room," she replies.

"I always wanted to do something naughty with the school secretary."

Her laughter gives my soul wings in a way I haven't felt since—

Nope.

Not talking about that either.

This?

This is temporary and fun, and my brain can shut up if it wants to go anywhere else. Or we can talk about *her.* "You're baiting the Tickled Pink gossip brigade on purpose."

She gasps. "I would *never.*"

I angle my head to eyeball her, and there it is.

That twitch of her lips that says she's lying.

One more thing I didn't expect to like about her, yet here we are. "Admit it, Phoebe."

"I admit nothing."

"Who are you protecting by taking the brunt of the gossip?"

She sighs and looks up at the ceiling. "Maybe I like all of the attention."

"Including from the gossip rags in New York?"

And there's the wince. "The night Gigi choked on her dinner and almost died, we were having an argument over a very public breakup I'd just gone through, and I told her there was always someone else waiting in the wings to make more drama. That it passes and people forget."

"Only until it's convenient for them to remember again," I mutter.

Her laugh isn't quite as lighthearted as it was a few minutes ago. "You learn quick."

Shit. "People aren't all that different no matter where they come from. And you're avoiding the question."

"It's a silly question."

"It's proof you're a good person."

She falls silent, and I angle another glance at her.

It should be weird how comfortable it is to just lie here with her, but it's not.

"I'm not a good person when I'm in New York," she says softly. "Here, it's like—it's easier. When this year's over . . . when it's time to go back . . ."

She trails off as my pulse kicks up. "One day at a time, Phoebe. That's a long way off. Also, do you always let in the strangers who knock on your window in the middle of the night?"

Her body relaxes beneath me again. "Only the ones who look like serial killers. They give the best orgasms."

Smiling isn't my normal expression. Bridget says I have resting twitch face.

Yet here I am, a near-perpetual smile on my face, because of Phoebe Lightly. "Only to the women we enjoy torturing the most."

She sighs, but it's not a frustrated sigh or a snorty sigh or a stuck-up sigh.

It's a content sigh that comes with her fingers drifting down to trace my ear, making my cock stir again.

"Why is it so easy to just have fun with you?" she asks.

"I'm a fun guy."

"You're a grumpy fishing lumberjack."

I lift my head and attempt to do that eyebrow thing she's always doing.

She laughs softly while she keeps stroking my ear. "I know, I know. I'm a bitchy socialite workaholic."

"Are you?"

She sighs again, and this one isn't nearly as content. "I thought I could *win* this thing Gigi has us doing if I played her game and did a good job with it, except . . . I think I've done *too* good of a job. I can't see myself going back to New York, to my job, to my social life, to my—to my past, and falling into the same habits without feeling like I'm giving up something that I never realized would matter to me."

"Your . . . principles? Or just your principal's office?"

She doesn't laugh at the joke. "My soul."

And that's exactly why I like Phoebe Lightly more than I thought I would.

She has no idea how much we have in common.

I've made my own mistakes in life. Wondered about my own soul. Dug out of finding out I wasn't the person I wanted to be.

Watching her choose the same for herself—it's like having a front-row seat to a butterfly emerging from a cocoon after going in as a snake.

"I don't know if I believe in heaven," she says to the cracked ceiling. "I don't know if there's an afterlife. But I know—I know I've taken too much for granted. I have more money than some small nations operate with in an entire year. I have connections to high-powered people all over the world. I have access to personal assistants and consultants and concierges who can make nearly anything happen in the blink of an eye. And when I'm gone, they'll all breathe a sigh of relief that they don't have to deal with me anymore. They won't miss me. They won't talk about how I made their lives better. They'll remember that time I gave them a watch so that I didn't have to give it back to an ex-boyfriend, or the time I tried to sleep my way into a promotion, or the time I couldn't be bothered to learn their names because if they didn't fold my sheets right, I'd tell my personal assistant to fire them and find someone else who would."

"It's the world you live in."

"There are good people in the world I live in. I've chosen to not be one. And I can't go back home without choosing between who I can be and who I used to be."

I open my mouth, intending to ask her who she wants to be, to ask her *where* she wants to be, but before I form the words, a scream rips through the air somewhere nearby.

Phoebe leaps up so fast that even my reflexes are impressed. Her cat scrambles for a corner. I pick myself up off the floor and dive for my jeans while she shrugs into a robe and takes off at a run toward the scream as it echoes a second time.

"Mom?" she cries.

I hit the hallway running while I'm still zipping up my jeans. There's yelling now, coming from the floor below, echoing through the hallway.

I'm halfway to the right hallway when I realize what's going on.

"Who the *hell* are you?" Phoebe's saying.

Shit.

I freeze, and someone barrels into me, sending both of us tripping down the last few steps.

"What the *fuck*, man?" Carter shoves me and takes off for his sister and mother.

I follow more slowly.

I know what's around the corner, and it has my gut twisting in a way I haven't felt in almost twenty years.

"Headlock him, Phoebe," Margot Lightly cries. "Tie him up and show him what happens to people who sneak into our home!"

"I'm sorry, you're *who*?" Phoebe says.

"Stand back and let me handle this asshole," Carter growls.

I turn the corner. "Let him—" I start.

No need to finish that sentence.

Phoebe's releasing her grip on Floyd's collar and stepping back, arm out to block Carter. Her head turns slowly—so slowly—until she's glaring at me with enough ice to douse the sun itself.

I swallow once.

Twice.

Contemplate what I should probably start texting to Bridget and Shiloh as the last communication of my life.

"Tell 'em, Teague," Floyd says as he shirks back toward the janitor's closet. "Wasn't to do no harm. And ya told 'em I was here. Ya did tell 'em, didn't ya?"

"We did," I agree.

"*Phoebe*, he's getting away!" Margot shrieks.

I'm a dead man.

"What the *fuck* is he talking about?" Carter asks. "Mom—go to bed. You don't need to see what's about to go down."

"No. Violence." Phoebe points at Tickled Pink Floyd without looking at him. "You will leave this building and *never* come back, but you will *also* write me a long letter detailing every last secret passage in this building so that I can use it to haunt my grandmother's ass every single day for the rest of our time here, and you'll leave that letter with Jane, and yes, I mean home-brewing Jane, because I trust her, and I also know how to ruin her beer when no one's looking. And *you*." She swings her finger to point to me. "*You* are operating at a level closer to Upper East Side than backwoods Wisconsin, and we are going to be having a *very* serious discussion about *exactly* where you learned *to try to smoke us out with a fake-real ghost* just as soon as I can get within four feet of you without wanting to rip out your jugular."

"What in the *hell* is going on here?" Margot wails.

"That's our ghost." Phoebe swings her finger once more to Tickled Pink Floyd, who's so close to freedom that I can taste it for him. "He's not *a ghost*, despite what our friends and neighbors would've liked us to believe."

We didn't say he was a ghost is definitely the wrong thing to say right now.

Technically, we never lied.

Floyd *does* like to still hang around the high school. And he did used to have a pet lizard.

"You could hire him to be the janitor again," I say instead. "He loves it here."

"Best home I ever had," Floyd agrees.

"Oh my God, I *cannot*," Margot gasps. "Carter. Take me to my room. I'm *done*. And you—you—*where is your shirt?* For the love of— oh my *God*, Phoebe, *are you sleeping with the lumberjack?* But Elijah

Richardson is due back in New York soon, and you two would've made such an adorable couple!"

I step aside as Carter leads Margot up the stairs, the older woman muttering and fussing and leaning heavily on him.

He's glowering at me, but if he thinks he's scary, he really doesn't know his sister.

She's so livid her skin is splotchy. Arms crossed over her robe, her fingers drumming against her opposite biceps. I want to stalk down the hallway and kiss her senseless, but guilt won't let me.

"*Warning*, Miller. I wanted *warning*."

I swallow.

Hard. "Good one, though, wasn't it?"

She sucks in a massive breath through her nose.

And that's when it happens.

The twinkle.

Fuck me, she's sporting a damn *twinkle* in her eyes.

And now I wish she truly were going to kill me, because this?

Phoebe Lightly matching my game with more game of her own?

This will be what kills me.

Her wits. Her game.

Her respect.

"That thing you did a little bit ago?" She gestures to her crotch. "There will be more for reparations. Understood?"

I cross my arms too. The hot and cold sensations battling through my body are giving way to something else.

Intoxication.

I could fall in love with this woman. I really could. "Dunno, Lightly. You might be getting the better end of the deal there."

"I'm still furious with you."

"But you respect the lengths I'll go to for the sake of victory."

She licks her lips. "I can do both."

"Phoebe? Are you down there? What is all of this undignified shrieking?" Estelle turns the stairwell corner, and her eyes narrow. "Mr. Miller. Scaring my family with your half-naked physique? How unoriginal."

Do not twitch, Miller. Do not twitch. "Yes, ma'am. I know. You did it first."

Phoebe makes a strangled noise, then points at me again. "*Out.* I'll deal with you tomorrow."

"Promise?"

And there goes her eyebrow.

It shouldn't make me smile, but it does.

Chapter 29

Phoebe

I have an algebra test this morning, Gigi's called an emergency family meeting, and Elmo, my kitten, keeps trying to sneak into Carter's bedroom, but are any of those things at the top of my worry list?

No.

No, they're not.

Why?

Because Teague Miller is currently occupying the top forty-seven spots on my list.

I'm furious with him for the Tickled Pink Floyd ghost prank last night.

I'm also hella jealous that I didn't think of it myself.

That was devious.

Devious on a level that rivals some of the things my family's done. It's beyond what I would've expected of anyone in Tickled Pink, and it's making me realize just how little I know about Teague.

Yet I would still very much like for him to crawl through my window and service my cooch again tonight.

"What's this about, and how long will it take?" Tavi asks as she sits down next to me at the cafeteria table. She's carrying Pebbles and wearing sunglasses, and her entire posture is hunched like she's battling some kind of bug.

"Look who finally decided to come home," Carter says as he sits on my other side. "Up late servicing the plumber again?"

"*Oh my God*, could you be a little more crude? I'm not *servicing the plumber*."

"He's beneath you?" Carter asks.

I shove him. "She just *said* she's not servicing the plumber. Of course he's not *beneath* her."

We stare at each other for half a second, and then I crack up.

Me.

Phoebe Sabrina Lightly.

Making a joke about my sister having sex and cracking up.

Oh my sweet Oprah, I think—

"I need to go home."

That's exactly what I was thinking, but those words did *not* come out of my mouth.

"No one's leaving, Margot," Gigi replies as she strolls in from the kitchen, her butler-boyfriend following with a tray laden with this morning's monstrosity.

I can't believe I'm actually grateful for *real* cafeteria food, but I am 100 percent stopping at the community college's lunch counter for a yogurt parfait before class starts. Niles is growing on me, despite Gigi still not claiming him as anything more than her butler, but he has the cooking skills of a Lightly.

Which is to say, none at all.

"Yes, Estelle, I'm *leaving*," my mother snaps.

I turn in my seat, and *holy shit*.

She's packed.

All eleven suitcases.

And Tickled Pink Floyd is right behind her.

"Our 'ghost' is giving me a ride to the airport, and I'm going home."

"Margot—"

"Shut up, Estelle. Phoebe, I'm sorry you have to find out like this, but your real father is a pool boy who used to service our grounds at our estate in the Adirondacks. I cheated on Michael. *I cheated.* And I've regretted it every minute of my life since, but I will *not* be held captive by this—this—this blackmail coming from this black-hearted and black-souled black widow of a venomous creature who likes to call herself your grandmother. But do you know what I realized after our ghost turned into a real man again last night, Phoebe? I realized I'm not related to her, and *neither are you.* You don't have to take this abuse either. You're not a Lightly by blood. She can't hold you here. So come, darling. You can come home with me, and we can build ourselves a better life than the one this old hag is holding us to."

I blink at her.

I hear her words.

I comprehend their meaning.

Except—*"No."*

What is this?

How is this?

She's not serious.

I'm a Lightly. *I'm a Lightly.* It's who I am. It's who I've always been.

But—

"Margot," Gigi hisses.

"No, Estelle. I am *done* letting you run my life and my children's lives. They deserve better. Phoebe. Octavia. Carter. Let's go."

I look at my father.

He's head down over a newspaper like this isn't new information.

Like he doesn't care.

"Mom?" I whisper.

"I'm sorry, baby," she whispers back. "I should've taken you and run as soon as I realized that witch knew my secret. I'm so sorry."

I swing around and look at Gigi.

Never—*ever*—have I seen her face those shades of red and angry.

"We agreed we would *never* speak of this," Gigi says. "Phoebe has a future because of me, and you're trying to throw it all away."

"Phoebe has a *leash* because of you."

Oh my God.

She's serious.

Tavi grabs my hand, and I realize I've gasped. Carter leans in close, like he wants to hug me but doesn't know how.

"We are so fucked up," he mutters.

My whole body is numb.

Brain? Numb.

Legs? Numb.

Mouth? Numb.

Lungs?

I don't even know if I have lungs.

Is anything real?

Is anything not a lie?

Who am I?

"*Phoebe.*" Mom claps her hands. "Octavia and Carter too. Chop-chop. We're leaving."

I stare at my father again.

My father?

Not my father?

What makes a man a father? It's not like he was there for my school functions or family dinners. He wasn't there for my high school graduation. My college graduation.

Because he knew I wasn't really his?

Or because he's a shitty father?

All those things he did for Tavi but not for me—*oh my God*.

"Phoebe, you'll stay exactly where you are, and nothing will change," Gigi announces.

Carter growls softly. "She's such a fucking asshole."

"Where do you want to go?" Tavi asks me. "Name it. We're there. Like, yesterday."

Oh my sweet holy Oprah.

I'm not a Lightly.

I'm not a Lightly.

And that's what does it. That's what makes me snap.

I rise.

"Finally," my mother says. "Hurry up, dear. It's a private plane, but I'd still like to get on it posthaste."

Gigi squares her shoulders and lasers in on me. "Phoebe Sabrina Lightly, if you walk out that door . . ."

"I'm not a Lightly," I whisper.

"Don't be ridiculous. You were raised a Lightly, and *no one* beyond this room will *ever*—"

"Shut up, Gigi," I snap.

She sucks in a breath.

Tavi sucks in a breath.

"That's my girl," Mom says. "Now—"

"Shut up, Mom."

I don't know who I am.

Not because I'm telling people to shut up but because *I don't know who I am.*

Nature versus nurture. Genetics versus environment. I was *raised* as a Lightly. I was *born* to be a Lightly.

But I'm *not.*

And after everything I've learned, everything I've realized here in Tickled Pink, finding out my father isn't my father is the cherry on the *who are you?* sundae.

"Phoebe, if you walk out that door—"

I don't listen to the rest of whatever Gigi feels she has to say to me, because it doesn't matter.

Look what she did to Uncle George.

She abandoned him for a lot less than being the illegitimate kid of a daughter-in-law that she never liked.

I'm not a Lightly.

I've never been a Lightly, no matter the fact that I believed for my entire life that my sole purpose was one day walking in the footsteps of my great-grandfather.

When he's not actually my great-grandfather at all.

I could walk back into the cafeteria, play along, and be a Lightly.

The question is, Do I really want to?

And if I don't . . . who will I be next?

Chapter 30

Teague

Bridget took off with Shiloh for a day of clothes shopping first thing this morning, and I have no idea if Phoebe's still pissed at me, so I do what seems like the safest thing to do after taking care of my goats, and I head to the lake.

I'm about to hop in my boat and shove off when the sound of shoes crunching over the gravel near the pull-in catches my attention.

Phoebe's found me.

She's in a sundress and a short jacket, with flats on her feet, sunglasses on her face, and all her hair swept up under a bandana that would make Bridget look like she was planning on spending the day with her hands buried in cupcake mixes, but on Phoebe, it looks like she's just using it as one more place to hide a weapon.

I brace myself. "Morning, sunshine."

"Does this thing have a second seat?" She nudges my boat with her toe, keeping her hands in her jacket pockets.

"If I say yes, are you getting in?"

"Yes."

"If I say yes and you get in, are you planning on murdering me and dumping my body out there?"

"No."

She's pale.

Too pale.

Her shoulders are shrunken in, her eyes are hidden behind her sunglasses, and she keeps pulling one hand out of her pocket to lift it to her mouth, then snatching it back down, like she wants to bite her nails but has been trained better.

Something's wrong.

Something's very, very wrong.

Good morning to you too, protective instincts. "Bring your own lunch?" I ask.

"No."

"All right then." Boat's half in the water, so I wade out and flip the extra seat up. Bridget doesn't come out with me near as much as she used to, but I still keep her seat at the ready. Just in case. "Climb on in."

She takes my hand without a word, still keeping her other hand in her pocket, trusting me to help her navigate to the seat, and then she plops down like her legs couldn't have held her another minute.

I shove off, hop in, and paddle out until it's deep enough to drop my motor and head to my favorite fishing spot.

We're not the first out here today. Won't be the last.

Damn near the tensest, though.

Won't make for good fishing.

Still gonna try.

So when we hit the middle of the lake, I kill the motor, drop the anchor, and dig out a pole. "You want to give it a go?"

She doesn't look at my pole.

My fishing pole or my cock, for the record.

"Who would you be if you found out you weren't yourself?" she asks.

I drop the pole. "That's . . . a very specific question."

"My mother left."

I wince and rub my neck. "Tickled Pink Floyd is more harmless than—"

"She was only staying because my grandmother was blackmailing her with threatening to tell me that my father isn't my father if she didn't come make herself into a better person here."

I open my mouth, then shut it again.

"All my life, I've wanted to follow in my great-grandfather's footsteps. I wanted to run Remington Lightly because it was in my blood. Except it wasn't. It's *not*. So now I'm right back to where I was that night after we got here when you asked me who I was. Who I am. And do you know what? It's fucking terrifying. *I don't know who I am.*" She finally twists her head to look at me. "I don't know who I am."

Tell her, dumbass, my good shoulder angel says.

She's a fling, my bad shoulder angel replies.

I ignore them both and reach into my cooler, coming up with two bottles of False Hope IPA. Don't really care that it's barely nine in the morning.

Definitely need a drink right now.

I pop the top on the first one and hand it to her. As she leans forward, a kitten sticks its head out of her pocket.

"Jesus."

"Don't start. Elmo wanted to come. I don't know much, but I know he needs me, and that's the thing I'm clinging to right now, okay?"

"You have an algebra test today."

"Screw algebra. *I don't know who I am.*" She drops her head between her knees. "Oh, fuck. Gigi won't give the school that donation if I miss class."

"Your grandmother is a damn menace."

"She's not actually my grandmother."

I didn't pack enough beer for this. "Phoebe—"

"Don't you dare mansplain family to me. I know blood isn't everything. But I—"

291

"You always thought you could blame biology for why you're fucked up."

She lifts her head and her sunglasses, and she stares at me like it's inconceivable that I just explained to her exactly what she's struggling with.

"*Yes,*" she gasps.

Elmo meows.

I scrub a hand over my face. "Who do you *want* to be?"

"The person who's already answered that question and done all the work to make it happen."

For the first time since I left the school last night, I smile.

That's the most Phoebe thing she's said all morning.

"Start easy," I tell her. "Who do you want to be friends with?"

"That's not the easy part, Teague."

"You are who you surround yourself with."

She frowns at the lake again. "But who would want to be friends with me?"

"I would."

"Do *not* be nice to me."

"Don't let your grandmother's expectations of relationships define what you're willing to settle for when it comes to yourself. And for the record—I *like* difficult Phoebe."

"But you're a little off yourself."

"And I like *honest* Phoebe, even when she's wrong."

"You're a grown man who lives in a tree house, has no discernible job beyond occasionally selling questionable buildings to rich old ladies, spends his days fishing, isn't fazed at all by being surrounded by women, including women who were born in male bodies, or by his ex-wife leaving him to marry a woman, knows his way around a woman's clit, and your favorite game involves eating sawdust. *You're a little off,* Teague."

"You forgot the part where I love my ex-wife's new wife's parents. They've been in Florida for the winter but should be back soon."

She lifts her kitten to her face. "Elmo, we've let a crazy man take us on a boat ride."

"You're here *because* I'm a grown man living in a tree house with weird complications in my life. They make your problems seem normal."

She slouches back in the chair.

If we weren't on a boat, and if she hadn't fallen into this lake twice already, and if she weren't carrying a kitten, I'd be crawling over to her, pulling her sunglasses off her face, and kissing the hell out of her.

I rub my neck. She's not the only one facing hard things this morning, apparently. "Everyone's a little lost sometimes. You might feel like your 'lost' is *bigger*, but people are people are people. Doesn't matter if you own the earth, the moon, and the sky or if you don't have two nickels to rub together. What matters is realizing that who you are is who you *want* to be and that you surround yourself with the people who help you get there. You're—you're in the best damn place you could be right now. Tickled Pink won't judge. They'll just be here while you figure it all out."

My heart's pounding more than it should be, and it doesn't help when she flicks her gaze back to me, peering at me over her sunglasses as though she can see through me, right to the heart of how much I know what I'm talking about here.

I look back over the lake. "You're more than your last name, Phoebe. You're proving it every single day here."

"Mom wants me to go back to New York with her."

My heart clenches, and no amount of *she's temporary, idiot* will convince it to not panic.

Nor will *she's not the kind of life you want.*

"What do you want to do?"

"I want to build a new Ferris wheel right next to the old one, just so I can go for a ride and pretend I'm seven years old again, at a fair, asking to go on a Ferris wheel and being told yes this time. That's what

I want. But that's a really stupid reason to build a Ferris wheel in a town that I might not even stay in much longer."

"Always wanted to take Bridget up on that Ferris wheel," I say softly.

Her gaze swings back to me, hidden behind those damn sunglasses again.

"So instead of telling myself no, I should say yes for other people."

"Might not know who you want to be, but that doesn't mean you can't know what you want to do."

Her lips quiver. "I told you I made my own way in the world, but that's a lie. Everything I've ever done, everything I've ever been, it's all based on my last name. I don't know—yesterday, I could've made a single phone call to put things in motion to build a damn Ferris wheel. And today—today, when I can finally see *why*, I can't see *how*. I know there's a *how*. Gigi's not taking my trust fund. It's mine. But it's . . . it's *not*. Am I making sense?"

Fuck it.

I lean forward in my seat, go down on my knees, and angle closer to her, getting rid of those damn sunglasses. "Phoebe Lightly, I don't think you've actually met anyone in this town yet if you think your trust fund is the only way to get something done."

"Because so many people here are sitting on secret nest eggs worth billions?" She gives me half of that damn eyebrow tilt, like she thinks it's not hers anymore. "You can't squeeze juice out of a rock."

"But we can squeeze juice out of Deer Drop."

A laugh bursts out of her, like it's surprising her, too, but that's all I need.

Just to know she can still laugh.

On impulse, I lean in and kiss her.

Can't help myself.

I *like* her. I like her drive. I like her wit. I like her devious side, and I like watching her discover her soft side.

I like that she trusts me enough to take me along on her ride.

And I very much like that she's gripping my shirt in her fist and kissing me back.

Which isn't something we should do right here in the middle of the lake where anyone can see, even if I'm pretty sure none of the *Tickled Pink Papers* spies are out and about today.

So I reluctantly pull back, for both our sakes.

"I don't want to leave," she whispers.

"So stay. Do good. Find you. One day at a time. You're having a lot thrown at you. It's okay to take a while to figure things out. Do it where you feel safe and loved."

She relaxes her grip on my shirt but doesn't quite let go while she blinks quickly against shiny eyes. "Thank you for being a good friend."

Friend.

I have half a clue what that word means to her.

And I hope I'm worthy of it.

Chapter 31

Phoebe

One day at a time.

That was an excellent idea.

It's been just over a week since Mom dropped one more bombshell on the family. I'm still occasionally numb over the revelation, but my life hasn't stopped, and I'm slowly coming to grips with what I want my life to be.

With *who* I want to be.

I've spent half my nights at Teague's place, and even when I've stayed at the school, I've had actual, honest-to-God, regular hot showers, thanks to Dylan the plumber.

But even better? Which I can't believe I'm saying, but it's true—this *is* better than hot showers.

Tavi and Carter and I have started talking.

Like real people who know how to have real relationships.

Carter's still annoying and basically purposeless, and I still don't fully understand why Tavi's only goal in life is to look pretty on camera until she ages out of the influencer system, but I don't need to understand.

I think that's half of what I needed to learn here in Tickled Pink.

Sometimes, you have to go on blind faith that the people around you have your best interests in mind, and you have to have their backs, too, even when you don't understand them.

So I don't ask where she's disappearing to every single night while pretending like she's not. And while we continue fixing up the school like we're not a bunch of dysfunctional menaces to society, I ask Carter questions about where he learned to cook and what his dreams are, and I try to understand and practice accepting that no one is who they seem on the outside.

I'm screwing up as much as I'm getting right, but for the first time in my life, I'm trying.

And now it's time to *try* with someone else.

After my last class of the week, instead of heading to the coffee shop to meet Bridget for tutoring, I head back to the high school. I have a bound proposal printed on linen paper, the knowledge that I'm walking into a meeting with the devil with the gate to my heart swinging wide open, and a grumpy lumberjack expecting me in two hours with no idea that I might be a total disaster.

But I need to do this.

Not because it's the mission Gigi set out for me after she choked on that steak but because I *want* to do this.

For me.

And for Tickled Pink.

When I get to the school's third floor and turn down the corridor leading to the art room, I discover Gigi isn't here.

Niles is, and he's painting.

Not the walls but a canvas.

He's making art.

I tilt my head and study the landscape on his easel. He's captured the square in Tickled Pink with a gorgeous mix of colors that makes the town seem basked in a sunset inspired by heaven.

This place.

It eventually gets to everyone, doesn't it?

"That's beautiful," I say softly.

"Aaaah!" He leaps sixteen feet in the air, dropping his palette and flinging his brush across his canvas and smearing a bright-blue slash over the square.

I have momentary visions of giving Gigi's lover-butler a heart attack, and I drop everything to rush into the room even as it strikes me that Gigi picked the art room because her secret boyfriend is an artist. "Don't die! Oh my Oprah, don't die!"

He tilts a furry brow at me, clearly annoyed, as he bends to grab the paint palette smearing all over the art room floor. "I'm not that old that a little fright will take me out."

I might be. My heart is threatening to pound out of my chest. "My apologies." It's getting easier to say those words. Helps that I *feel* better in ways I didn't expect when I offer them. "I thought you heard me. Or that you would be as paranoid as the rest of us about Gigi sneaking around and seeing things she shouldn't."

There's that *ignorant child* look again. "Your grandmother's a cream puff."

I snort.

Yes, me, Phoebe Sabrina Lightly. *I snort.*

It's literally the *only* appropriate response.

"She is," he insists. "Nobody sees it, but she is. You think she calls you her granddaughter because she didn't want anyone to know Margot's indiscretion? She calls you her granddaughter because family's more than blood. She has her faults, but she knows it wasn't your fault how you were born, and she admires the hell out of you."

Heat prickles over the usual parts of my body that go numb when I remember every goal I ever had in life until recently was around what I believed to be in my DNA. "How long have you been dating her?"

He could be glaring at me for ruining his painting, or scowling at me for asking the question everyone else has wanted to know for weeks, or angry with me for leaving her alone to choke on that piece of Kobe beef, but instead, he gazes at me with nothing but sincerity as he wipes his hands on a paint rag. "In love with her."

My face twists.

I can't help it.

And he smiles.

Smiles. "Can't help who you love. And love's never made the world worse, has it?"

"But she keeps you a secret."

"Ever occur to you that I'm the one asking her to keep us a secret?"

My lips part.

And that question is still on my brain when I finally locate Gigi in the basement of the school, personally picking through the piles in the janitor's office, with Tickled Pink Floyd beside her.

"Why on earth would *anyone* keep so many worthless pieces of junk?" she demands of the old janitor.

"Lack of shine don't make it junk, just like polish don't make it good hearted," the old janitor replies.

I clear my throat before Gigi can slice him open with her tongue for the subtle insult. "Excuse me, Gigi, could I please have a minute of your time?"

Her gaze lingers on Tickled Pink Floyd for a long moment before she turns to me. "Of course. Anything for one of my grandchildren."

That's how it's been all week. *Anything for one of my grandchildren.*

No mention of the fact that I'm not technically related by blood. Just pretending the drama never happened, much like everyone did for the thirty years before this.

The difference is *I* know now.

But is Niles right?

Does she actually love and admire me for who I am and not because I was raised a Lightly? "Do you call me that to keep up appearances or because you truly feel it?"

Floyd makes a noise and disappears under a pile of junk. Part of a wall moves.

So *that's* how he sneaked in.

I'm exploring that secret passage later.

If I still live here later.

Gigi's narrowed her eyes at me again as though *I'm* the one she's planning on eviscerating for displeasing her. "How long have we known one another, Phoebe?"

"The answer to that question is entirely too complicated to unpack in a single sentence."

She's wearing a white blouse again, though this one is streaked with dirt, and her hair is mussed in a way that's unusual. Maybe Gigi *is* human. "We've known each other long enough for you to know that I don't suffer fools, and were you not worthy of being my granddaughter, you would not currently be standing before me."

"That's not the compliment you mean it to be."

She flinches.

Heat floods my face and chest as I realize I've actually struck a nerve.

She *does* care.

Niles wasn't blowing smoke. She cares. She *does* think of me as part of her family, regardless of where I came from.

But she doesn't know how to show it. She doesn't know how to be anything other than a badass, terrorizing everyone around her to keep herself from feeling—

Well, probably everything I've felt since we got here to Tickled Pink.

She's had a few more years of practice having to hide her vulnerabilities than I have.

And honestly?

Feeling sucks sometimes.

I wish I didn't *feel* several times a day lately.

"I have a business proposal for you," I say in the unusual silence that she hasn't rushed to fill.

"And you wonder if you're truly my granddaughter," she says with a subtle sniff. "Nurture over nature. Always."

Is it wrong that *this* is what finally snaps me out of this *who am I?* funk that I've been in all week?

But it does.

It *completely* does.

Because you know what?

I would not have chosen these people. Gigi has her strengths. She has her weaknesses. She's nurturing in her own way, and it's helped me become the person that I am, but I don't want to be all of that person anymore.

Especially the Gigi-est parts.

And I don't have to. I can *choose* not to.

I toss the business proposal in the trash. Linen paper and all. There's no way in hell—and I know hell at this point—that I'm asking for another dime from her.

That's the easy way to get what I want.

Screw easy.

I'm doing this the right way.

"You can't be a better person if all you're doing is investing money in a small town to make them worship *you*," I tell her.

She chokes on air.

Yep.

I'm making my grandmother choke again.

And *yes*. Yes, she's my grandmother. Nurture. She's right. She's helped make me who I am, the good parts and the bad parts.

My DNA doesn't matter.

I *am* a Lightly. They chose me, regardless of how or why.

It's time I lived back up to my Lightly heritage. *My* way.

"This school? The community center?" I continue. "What are you *really* using them for? And if you're going to tell me it's really so that they can put up shrines and plaques to you like you said Tickled Pink should've done for Whitney Anastasia in that damn movie *that you still miss the point of,* then you're hopeless. You have to do the things you'd do if you didn't have money. And you're still using your money, except you're using it to manipulate people who might not be perfect but who were probably all better off before we set foot in this town. You want to be a better person? Fix the school so it can be a museum about the town and this area, not you. Fix the community center and fund it so that it can be a place where kids go to hang out after school and know they have food and hot water available to them. Donate that five million to the college over in Deer Drop without stipulations. Fund the town's scholarship without stipulations too. For Oprah's sake, Gigi, *do real good.* And claim your boyfriend in public while you're at it. If he's willing to be publicly associated with you, that is. And if he's not, fuck him."

She's trying to aim the eyebrow at me, but it's not working, because I'm about done with the damn eyebrow and it's lost its effectiveness, but also because her eyes are getting shiny. "I suppose that, considering you've completed your assignment here and I no longer have to worry about the state of your soul, I can allow a small amount of grace for your attitude."

Dammit.

Now *my* eyes are getting hot. I jab a finger toward her, hitting only air while my kitten brushes his furry body around my ankles. "*I* get to decide when I've become a better person. Because *I* know my heart and my soul better than anyone. So *thank you* for the compliment, but I am *not* done, and you don't get to decide for me."

Her lips settle into a satisfied smirk. "I *have* done such a wonderful job with you, haven't I?"

"This is all me, Gigi."

"Does it truly matter in your heart, Phoebe, who gets the credit, or does it matter that you have that satisfaction of knowing you've become a better person?"

My eyeball is twitching.

I feel like Teague watching Bridget tell off a group of adults, except I can't muzzle my grandmother like he can muzzle his daughter.

Or try to, at least. There's basically only *trying*.

Where both Gigi *and* Bridget are concerned.

"I'm leaving," I tell her. But I don't mean I'm leaving Tickled Pink.

I *like* Tickled Pink. I want to stay in Tickled Pink.

Do I have a few things to clear up still in New York? Like dealing with Fletcher and finding some closure with my mom over her secret?

Yes. I should do those things.

But I'll get there.

Right now, I'm leaving the school. I have homework, if I want to do it, and I will, because I like to finish what I start, even if I don't take another class.

Plus, there's a fishing lumberjack I might catch herding some goats in mosquito-infested air, and I need a good partner in crime since I just blew out of the water all my funding plans for my next big goal in life.

"C'mon, Elmo," I murmur to my kitten as I scoop him up and head out of the janitor's closet.

"Are you completely moving out of your room?" Gigi calls after me. "Because if you are, I'm expanding my services to a few acquaintances of mine whose children need some improvements to their soul, and I might need the space."

Elmo meows in horror.

"Don't listen to her, sweetie," I whisper to him. "She loves making idle threats when she doesn't get her way. And sometimes when she can't handle that she did get her way too."

"I'm serious, young lady," she calls after me. "I *am* bringing souls back to the Upper East Side."

Gigi still has a long way to go.

But she also has a lot more years to make up for.

And that's okay.

We all do our best. It's what we've got.

Chapter 32

Phoebe

Almost six weeks to the day after we arrived in Tickled Pink, my family is out on the freshly cut football field behind the school, tables lined up in rows, tents set up to cover the food we're trying to protect from the mosquitoes, though it would probably be better if we let the mosquitoes eat it.

They'd die of food poisoning.

My family did, after all, make this food. I'm not certain our *thank you for welcoming us* dinner will have quite the impact we want it to.

Unless we kill the mosquitoes. Then we all benefit from not getting eaten alive.

"Are we sure this is edible?" I hiss to Tavi as I spot the first brave souls approaching from the parking lot.

"If it's not, they'll leave sooner," she hisses back.

"Quit being sissies," Carter mutters. "You literally had to cut a watermelon."

"I made a three-bean salad, Carter, and *it was hard to pick which beans*," Tavi shoots back.

My watermelon and I decide to stay out of it.

Cutting fruit is not yet one of my hidden talents, and we know better than to insult Carter's fried chicken.

Yes.

Fried chicken.

My brother, the worthless not-quite-one-hit-wonder rock star, made fried chicken for five hundred people. And yes, it smells delicious.

Tavi suddenly spins so her back is to the gathering crowd. "Have you heard from Mom?"

"With what cell signal or Wi-Fi?" Despite my suspicions that Gigi will be announcing tonight that she will, in fact, fund the promised scholarship for the town with no additional requirements on the locals, we're still banned and blocked from access to the outside world.

I think she's also announcing that she's fixing up the community center to give back to the town as a working community center with massive improvements.

Niles talks a lot when you get him hyped up on caffeine, and my grandmother might've been doing more soul-searching than I was giving her credit for, and she really doesn't know how to be a kind person in public. She's still battling her own walls.

"You're going to school three days a week," Tavi says. "Mom might've emailed, and I know you check your messages there."

"Have you seen the *Tickled Pink Papers*?" I reply.

Her cheek twitches. "Phoebe. You know you can't believe everything you see in a small-town gossip page."

"Except for the part where everything else they've printed is true." And now they're reporting that the gossip pages back home in New York are saying Mom's checked herself into a spa.

A special kind of spa.

The kind of spa that rich people go to when they need to recover from nervous breakdowns.

And that said nervous breakdown was caused by rumors hitting the *Post* about my proposition of my boss's boss in my attempt to get a promotion earlier this year.

I'm well and truly ruined in New York, and I don't care.

I wasn't happy there.

Not like I am here.

"I'm off email, and I'm off phone, and I'm working on *me*. I don't even have my phone on me. Teague's holding it until I'm ready to face it."

Also, Teague would 100 percent let me use his Wi-Fi if I asked him for the password.

We've moved past *I want to torture you any way I can* and into *I like you, I know you're struggling, and I'm here to support you for whatever you feel you need* territory.

He definitely has the harder job in our relationship, though he's fooling himself if he thinks I'm not doing *anything* for him.

He's expanding his viewpoint on outsiders and coming to realize that not everything outside the Tickled Pink borders is inherently evil. And he's welcome.

Dylan, the plumber, approaches our table.

Victim number one.

Volunteer, I mean. Volunteer number one.

This is good. He knows toilets. He can fix anything that breaks as a side effect of masses of people eating our food.

The townspeople probably coordinated this.

"Hey, Tavi." He nods to me, too, while Tavi makes the tiniest noise of acknowledgment beneath her *oh my God, hide me* face, her back still to the table. He keeps talking like she's not actively ignoring him. "Carter. Phoebe. You playing snowshoe baseball with us next week when we take on Deer Drop?"

"No, I'm running the dunk tank," I tell him.

His forehead wrinkles when his brows go up. "Dunk tank? That's new."

"You didn't hear? Shiloh found her mom's diary, and there was an entry about a deleted scene in *Pink Gold* where Whitney Anastasia let the townspeople try to dunk her in a dunk tank, and they raised money to fix the town's septic system that way, so Gigi's letting us put her in the dunk tank for twenty bucks a pop."

Teague is an evil genius for convincing Shiloh to "find" that.

I could love the man.

I really could.

And the way he's been teaching me to throw so that I can hit the target and dunk Gigi myself, with a promise that he won't miss even if I do?

I might start believing in heroes.

Dylan looks at where Tavi was standing a moment ago.

She's crawling in the grass under the table like she lost something now, and because we have tablecloths, he can't see her from his side.

But I can.

"Is that dunk tank what that *Deer Drop Gossip Sheet* was about that I found in my driveway?" Dylan asks.

I make an innocent face. "I have no idea what you're talking about. Also, I didn't know you live in Deer Drop. Or that they have their own gossip sheet."

"I'm a Tickled Pinker through and through, but sometimes Deer Drop forgets where the town lines are. And I've got a feeling it wasn't Deer Drop who started their gossip sheet." He grins. The man truly is adorable.

I'm not saying I'd break the hot water at the school again just to have an excuse to call him out, but I wouldn't be sad at the eye candy if the sink in the kitchen were to break.

And yes, I said that in front of Teague yesterday, and yes, I had a hard time getting out of his bed this morning after how very satisfied all of my body felt while he reminded me who's the more attractive of the two of them.

Poor man still doesn't always catch on when I accidentally on purpose have those little slips into being the old version of me.

"Clearly, Deer Drop heard how popular the *Tickled Pink Papers* are and wanted to cash in themselves," I tell him.

"With free flyers dropped on everyone's door over there claiming that your grandmother thinks that Deer Droppers are the least intelligent Wisconsinites?"

"They really don't know how to do gossip sheets, do they? Poor things. I wonder if they'll be mad enough to spend twenty bucks a pop to try to dunk her . . ." I'm betting they will. And it'll be used as seed money to start the fund to build a new Ferris wheel.

And if dunking Gigi is as popular as I hope it is, we might have some money left over for a down payment on a candy shop.

I am putting Tickled Pink back on the map as everything it was supposed to be.

Tavi whimper-coughs under the table.

Dylan squats down, lifts the tablecloth, and peers at her. "Hey. There you are. Lose something?"

She pats her chest. "My voice," she rasps out.

"And you think you'll find it down here?"

"Never know," she whisper-grunts.

"Fried chicken?" Bridget says as she and Teague approach our table too. "Is that actual edible fried chicken?"

"I didn't make it," I say as my heart flutters.

Flutters.

Just seeing the big bearded lumberjack is enough to put a goofy grin on my face and butterflies in my chest and swoony dreams in my head of snuggling up next to him in his tree house during the first snowfall of the year.

I have it so bad.

And I have zero regrets.

Teague gives me a secret smile that says he's glad to see me as well but won't make a fuss, because he's not a fuss maker, before he bends over and looks under the table at Tavi too.

"She's looking for her voice," Dylan says.

Both men straighten.

Dylan is poker faced in a way that suggests he's not an idiot.

He knows Tavi's avoiding him.

He might even know why, which is information I'm unfortunately not privy to, despite the number of times I've asked her why she's avoiding him.

But I don't really care when Teague looks at me, and my heart melts into what's usually left over from my feet after a night out dancing in the wrong shoes.

Something squishy and unrecognizable and a little painful but also totally doing its job and on its way to its own personal growth.

I like him.

I like him *a lot.*

"Be patient with yourself, Phoebe," he's said about six million times lately. "Change hurts, but it's worth it."

He never says more, but there's something in his voice that tells me he's been there.

He's turned into my safe space. And for the first time in my life, I want to return a favor, not because of what it'll gain me but out of sheer gratitude.

"You two are so disgusting," Bridget mutters over her chicken. "Oh, *swag.* Whoa. I was totally sus, but this is, like, *good.* Dad. Dad, *try this.*"

She shoves a chicken leg in his mouth before he can object, and his eyebrows shoot up in surprise.

"Carter made it," Tavi says as she pops back up from under the table.

Teague shoots a glance at Dylan, who's gotten distracted by the boiling pot of water that my father is trying to use to cook corn at the next table over, then swallows before grinning at Tavi. "Found your voice?"

"Right where I put it."

She glances at Dylan's retreating backside, too—is it disloyal of me to say that I'd think he was a professional sportser instead of a plumber if all I saw was this angle?—and oh, hell, he said bye, and I was too busy making teenage moon eyes at Teague to say bye back, wasn't I?

"Hate to break this to you, but he's not actually falling for your charms," Teague tells Tavi. "And he doesn't bite, so you don't have to hide."

"I have no idea what you're talking about. Why would you assume I'm flirting with a plumber, and why would I assume he'd bite?"

Bridget pulls a face that makes me laugh. "Has she always been a terrible liar?" she asks.

"Bridget. Let the poor thing alone." Shiloh descends on our table, too, with Ridhi and a few of her fellow firefighters behind her. "Unless you'd like us to talk about—"

"Shh! Zip it! No. I don't know what you're talking about."

Teague's left eye twitches. Ridhi heaves a sigh.

"You cut this watermelon yourself?" he asks me.

I hand him a spoon. "I was channeling my inner artist. We're still getting acquainted."

He grins, and *oh my heart*, I love it when he smiles. His eyes light up, and small forest animals sing, and random grinches around the world suddenly have the urge to kiss babies and eat Christmas dinner with their enemies.

Yep.

I have it *so very, very bad*.

"Mr. Miller, you should come try our rolls," Gigi calls from her table, where Niles has donned an apron and is holding a set of tongs for distributing the homemade yeast rolls that I'm positive she had flown in from her favorite chef in New York.

"Is she still insufferable?" Shiloh murmurs to me.

"Worse every day, though she's occasionally having breakthrough lucid moments of true kindness. We're getting near the end of her reenacting the movie."

"I hope your dunk-tank plan works."

"It won't make her a better person, but it might give us what we need to fix the Ferris wheel."

It's weird to be friendly with my boyfriend's ex-wife.

Actually, it's weird to think of Teague as my boyfriend, but I don't want to call him my lover.

That's too Upper East Side.

And he *is* my friend, which isn't something I would've ever said about my previous boyfriends.

He looks at Gigi, then back to me, then back to Gigi. "Did you make them?" he asks her.

"That was the point, Mr. Miller."

"You think you're above your own rules, Estelle. It's a fair question."

She lifts her nose. "You're hardly suffering for any of what I've brought to your town, now, are you? Phoebe, please instruct the gentleman to come try one of my yeast rolls."

"I'll give you a hundred bucks if you keep everyone from her table," Carter mutters to Teague.

"If we're going to have to listen to her complain about being snubbed, you need to pony up at least—*mmph*!"

Bridget stops talking as Teague covers her mouth with his hand.

"Quit sassing everything that moves," he tells her. He lifts his chin to Carter. "I'll make a phone call and get you a gig down in Appleton if you convince at least thirty people to throw her rolls at her, but you have to donate all tips to the Ferris wheel fund."

"Done."

"I can hear you," Gigi says.

"Can I go first?" Bridget asks.

"No," Teague, Shiloh, Ridhi, and half the firefighters all reply together.

"Dish me up some watermelon, Phoebe," Jane says as she, too, approaches our table with Gibson behind her. "I hate it when it's all those uniform cubes or one of those watermelon baskets with the balls. No personality, and I don't trust the person who cut it to not be a serial killer."

This.

This is what I crave. Beneath all the sass and banter, these people love and accept each other. "I could've made a basket out of the watermelon?" I ask Jane. "People can do that?"

She spears me with her eyeballs, but Teague speaks up before she can finish me off with what I suspect is a good *some people can, but not you.* "Phoebe, pretty sure if you'd tried, it would've looked like a mass murder gone wrong."

"So he peeked in the kitchen," Carter says to himself as he hands a plate of fried chicken to someone I don't recognize.

"Deer Droppers," Teague murmurs to me. His eye twitches again. "And a few reporters."

"Not bad for tourism," Shiloh reminds him.

There's that twitch once more, but he nods like he's accepted this will be part of his life. He's the only one in Tickled Pink who's not thrilled about the national attention, and he's coming around.

My family and I spend the next several hours holding our breath and hoping no one drops dead on the spot. Tavi's bean salad is an unexpected hit, and Dad's boiled corn is edible, but neither can touch Carter's fried chicken.

Who knew?

I wouldn't have if not for Tickled Pink.

I'm heading back out of the school with a wet rag to clean the last of the serving tables shortly after dusk when Willie Wayne rushes me. "Phoebe. Phoebe, I need you to tell me if that's who I think it is."

He points over the field to a tall guy in a cowboy hat who's currently talking to the ladies who run the Pink Box and the nail salon.

They're all giggling.

The ladies, I mean. The cowboy is smiling, but I can't make out much more than that with dusk settling over the field.

"Who do you think it is?" I ask him.

He leans in and whispers, "Jonah Beauregard."

I choke on air and try not to laugh. "Willie Wayne. *Why* would Jonah Beauregard . . ."

Wait.

Hell.

No, she didn't.

My grandmother did *not* actually invite more people from our social circles here to become better people . . . did she?

Willie Wayne grunts. "She told us all she wanted to buy that community center to host her biographers and whatever you call the people who make movies about people. Documentarians? I dunno. But I *do* know she hasn't had a single visitor, and I'm thinking it's because she doesn't want to tell us her real plans, and I think her real plans are probably way more terrifying, and I think Jonah Beauregard has something to do with them."

He's right that Gigi was making up the story about her biographers, but I think he's wrong about her using it as an office for expanding her soul-improvement project.

She'd just move them into the school.

I eyeball him. "How do you even know who Jonah Beauregard is?"

Me? Of course I know who Jonah Beauregard is. We don't run in the same circles—he's old Texas oil money, and I'm old Upper East Side

Remington Lightly money, so we've never met in person—but any good socialite knows what's going on in other socialite circles.

It's the backup plan if your own life falls to shit.

Willie Wayne mutters something.

I give him the Lightly eyebrow.

"*Lola's Tiny House*," he repeats, louder. "Lola was talking about him on last week's episode, so I looked him up."

"There's a new episode?" I hiss.

His grin goes sly. "If you weren't so busy with the hanky-panky, you could have time for the watchy-watchy."

"*Watchy-watchy?*"

"Bingey-bingey?" He grins bigger.

I try—and fail—to not smile back. "You're ridiculous. Come on. Let's go investigate this supposed oil heir and find out if he's really who he says he is."

Gigi's overseeing a beanbag-toss game. Carter's propped on a picnic table, strumming his guitar. Dad's deep in conversation with some people from Deer Drop. Tavi's disappeared.

Naturally.

Right when it's time to clean up.

Bridget *was* playing the beanbag game, but she's disappeared too.

So has Teague.

Huh. Maybe they both had to use the restroom.

Willie Wayne and I approach the small cluster of women and the cowboy, who straightens and nods to me. "Ms. Lightly?"

Beneath the cowboy hat, he's wearing an Armani jacket over a white button-down, Tom Ford jeans, cowboy boots that I know nothing about—dating Texas money was never on my radar enough for me to learn boot fashion—and a belt buckle the size of the Milky Way.

He has a short beard, a noticeable scar beneath his left eye, and the confident air that comes with growing up in high society.

If this man *isn't* Jonah Beauregard, he's doing a damn good impression of the oil heir.

"Mr. Beauregard." I hold out a hand, intending to shake, but I get a gentleman's kiss to my knuckles.

"Call me Jonah," he says with a warm smile that catches me off guard.

Not because I think he's faking it any more than the people in my old circles do.

But because it's a weirdly familiar smile.

Total déjà vu moment here.

"Jonah." I extract my hand. "Please tell me my grandmother hasn't blackmailed you into being her next victim."

His smile grows broader. "No, ma'am. I'm here on personal business of my own."

"He's looking for someone," one of the women around us whispers.

"His long-lost brother," the other chimes in.

"Now, ma'am, I didn't say that I was—" he starts.

"Who else would you be looking for?" Willie Wayne interrupts. "Unless you're secretly in love with Tavi Lightly?"

"Excuse me," I interject like my brain hasn't just gone spinning, "but there are *two* eligible Lightly daughters here for a man to be secretly in love with."

All of them study me for a second.

"Nah, he wouldn't be crushing on you," Willie Wayne declares.

One of the women elbows him.

"He meant that in the nice way," the other woman tells me.

"Your personal business?" I prompt Jonah Beauregard again.

There's not an official rule number four of being a Lightly, but if there were, it would be *Never forget what you know about other members of the upper echelons of society.*

Didn't think I'd need it here, and I don't *want* it, but everything I know about Jonah Beauregard and his family is flashing through my brain.

Can't help it.

It's what I've been trained to do all my life.

Texas oil money. Whole family shunned not just in Texas but across the country, twenty or so years ago after their company was involved in a massive spill. Oldest son disappeared. Father caught in a love triangle. Grandfather suspected of embezzlement and tried for other criminal activity related to the spill but never convicted of either.

Not like Uncle George, who Gigi *still* won't acknowledge.

I wonder if she knows her soul will need to make peace with that if she's going to make it to heaven?

Jonah nods to me, his eyes narrowing as though he knows I know every dirty secret about his family. "You have a moment, Ms. Lightly?"

His voice gives me chills.

Not because it's frightening.

But because I suddenly know why it sounds familiar.

And everything I thought I knew about Tickled Pink?

And my favorite lumberjack?

I was wrong.

I was *so* wrong.

Chapter 33

Teague

When I realize Phoebe's disappeared from the surprisingly edible feast tonight, I start to smile.

Wonder if she did any shopping in Deer Drop this week.

Hope so.

Her last set of lumberjack lingerie, as she called it, made me so light headed I couldn't think for almost an entire day after she left.

I wait a few more minutes to see if I spot her again, then go for casual as I amble over to Shiloh and Ridhi. "I'm heading out. You got Bridget?"

They share a look.

No, a smirk.

And I don't care.

I have a date with a naked Phoebe.

"Your place?" she said earlier with a wink, and yeah. That's where I'm heading.

"You might want to try to be more subtle if you don't want to see Bridget's *I'm going to puke* face," Ridhi tells me.

"Somebody has it *bad*," Anya murmurs behind us.

Gleefully, for the record.

Don't much care. They're happy for me. They can give me shit all they want.

Because *I'm* happy too.

Happy in ways I never thought I could be.

All because of a mouthy, sometimes overconfident, haughty, but gold-hearted workaholic socialite.

The last thing I expected when Phoebe Lightly tried to penguin her way into Dylan's fishing boat was for me to fall head over heels for her, but it's impossible to *not* be attracted to those fascinating layers of sass and entitlement tempered with her growing self-awareness and kindness.

There's something irresistible about a woman fighting to shake off who she was to become even more than she ever thought she could be. It's fucking hard, and she's doing it, and I respect the hell out of her for it. That in the process, she would see my home the way I do—rich in what matters, defined by its soul instead of its outer shell—and want to help it the way we always help each other around here instead of just opening her checkbook and moneying her way out of it—I'm well and truly gone.

I think I've met my match.

I catch myself whistling on the walk from the football field back to my place, and once again—don't care.

It's very likely I'm not the same person I was, either, when Phoebe fell into the lake the first time.

And that's not a bad thing.

Not a bad thing at all.

There's a light glowing in the sitting room on my first floor. I open the door softly, wondering if she'll be exhausted from serving everyone all night and still in her jeans and fancy-ass blouse coated in streaks of watermelon juice, or if she changed into sweats, or possibly into something skimpy and silky that'll be no match for my fingers.

Don't actually have a preference.

I'm just ready to be alone with Phoebe for the night.

Her back is to me, a messy bun visible over the top of the chair, red-stiletto-clad feet propped on my ottoman. She's facing the windows overlooking the twinkling stars of town and the dark abyss of the lake, and I go hard so fast it feels like a punch to my gut.

Worth it. "Excuse me, ma'am, I think you have the wrong house," I tease, my voice husky, because that's what she does to me. She makes it so I can't breathe. Can't talk. Can't think.

"Do you know the problem with taking the girl out of the Upper East Side?"

Role-playing. *Yes.* I love when we play games. "No butlers to feed you grapes after a long day of chewing people up and spitting people out?"

"The problem is that you can never fully take the Upper East Side out of the girl, Richard."

My veins ice over, my lungs seize, my feet go numb, and I heave out as much of a gasp as I can as the name echoes in my small sitting room. *"What?"*

"It was never about Bridget or the town, was it?" If I think my veins are icy, they have *nothing* on the glaciers dripping from Phoebe's voice now. "It was about *you*. The whole time. About you hiding. You know Bridget can take care of herself and that she's loved here. You know everyone in this town would stand up and protect one another and send people like us packing in a heartbeat if they needed to, and you and I both know that that school and the bugs and all of those animals inside and out of the school are only the start of what you could've done to us. This was never about Tickled Pink and your family and what the media did to Shiloh when she was younger. You didn't want us here because you didn't want anyone to find out about *you*."

I can barely find my voice, but I *need* to. I desperately need to find my voice. "What the fuck are you talking about?"

She lifts her phone and flashes a website at me without turning around.

She's on the Wi-Fi. Someone gave her the password.

And that's a photo of me as a teenager, twenty-some years ago.

She knows.

She knows.

Panic overrides everything else in my brain, and I short-circuit.

All of me. I'm short-circuiting and reverting to an autopilot response that I once practiced so much I probably still sometimes say it in my sleep. "Who's that, and how's that related to anything?" I tell myself to shut up, but it doesn't work. It doesn't work, and I can't stop myself. "You drink too much tonight?"

"Edward Richard Montgomery Beauregard the Fourth," she says, each distinct syllable a physical slap in the face making me realize how much I have to lose in this exact moment. "The lost heir to the Greenright Oil fortune. I was barely in middle school when you disappeared. Right before your grandfather's trial for negligence in that oil spill, wasn't it?"

"I don't know what you're talking about."

Deny deny deny.

It's instinctual. My heart's running from a saber-toothed tiger, and my head feels like it's been put in a juicer. I need to breathe. I need to breathe, and I need to think, and I need to process that everything I've buried in my life is spilling out into the open in my private sanctuary.

"You might think Upper East Siders have no interest in old Texas oil money, but you'd be mistaken. We *always* have contingency plans for advantageous connections and marriages, and we'd rather marry big belt buckles with massive trust funds than have to shop at discount stores and wear anything of generic origin, and we can't have contingency plans if we don't know about the money in Texas and California and Seattle and—well, anywhere old and new money settle. *Everyone* knows about the no-foul-play-suspected disappearance of Edward Richard

Montgomery Beauregard the Fourth, and *everyone* has a conspiracy theory about where he went and what he's up to." She sweeps her feet off the ottoman, rises, and fuck me, there is *zero* doubt that this woman is Estelle Lightly's granddaughter.

She's in red. Red power suit. Red lipstick. Red anger seething through her deadly calm voice. Her messy bun is the *only* thing chaotic about her, and it adds an air of danger that a slicked-back corporate hairdo wouldn't. "In the interest of being the bigger person that I'm trying *desperately* to be, I'm choosing to believe you have a *very* good reason for lying to me about who you are, and I'm going to give you one chance to tell me what it is before I walk out this door."

This is not Phoebe Lightly, my girlfriend with a soul.

This is Phoebe Lightly, deceived socialite.

And I'm not Teague Miller, grumpy single dad in a small town in Wisconsin.

I'm *Edward Richard Montgomery Beauregard IV.* I'm seventeen fucking years old again, trapped, angry, and terrified, and I know exactly what a deceived socialite can do, because I was dating one when my world blew up, and I know how this ends.

I know *exactly* how this ends.

Time to leave.

Move.

Get Bridget.

Take what's left of my bank account, buy plane tickets, and go back into hiding somewhere they'll never find out who I am, where I came from, and what I did. "My name is Teague Andrew Miller, and if you don't believe me, the door's right there, princess."

Her green eyes narrow. "If that's the name you were born with, you'd be having one hell of a fun time role-playing being what you believe to be a fictional missing oil heir right now. Or you'd be rolling your eyes and asking if I hit my head while I was slicing watermelon or if I finally broke myself by stepping too far outside of my comfy little heiress world. But you're angry. And you're scared. And the only reason you'd be angry and scared is if I'm getting too close to a truth you don't want me to know. One more time. Why are you lying to everyone here?"

Fuck. Just *fuck.*

It's been a long time since I didn't know who I was, but in this moment, I do *not* have a clue who I am or what I want. All I know is that I've spent the past sixteen years putting this town above all else, and I'm suddenly terrified I've fucked it up so badly that I can't stay.

I can't stay.

My home isn't safe, *because of me.*

And on top of the fear that if Phoebe Lightly figured me out, my whole fucking biological family could find me, there's the sweat breaking out at what my friends and neighbors will do when they find out how long I've lied to them about who I am.

I've spent *sixteen years* lying to the people I love about who I am.

They'll never forgive me.

And worse, once it gets out who I am—and it *will*—the rest of the life I left behind will descend on this town and destroy it.

I can't stay here. Once again, I'm about to lose it all. And this time, it's not just me in danger.

This time, it's everyone who taught me how to love, how to live, and how to be the man I want to be.

It's everyone I love. *Truly* love. "I swear on the grave of the man I named myself after, if you do a single thing to hurt my family or anyone in this town, I will *bury* you. I don't give two shits how much of Estelle Lightly you have in you. You have *nothing* on me and what I'll do to protect the people I love, and you have *no* idea who you're actually up against."

"And who, exactly, is that?"

My fingers curl into my fists, and I feel like I'm sitting in an ice bucket on fire.

You're better than this, my good shoulder angel whispers.

You know better than anyone how little rich people can truly change, my bad shoulder angel counters. *Look at you, falling back into old habits just because someone said your old name. Do you really think Phoebe Lightly will let you get away with this?*

Fuck. I swallow hard and match her socialite composure with some repressed haughty privilege of my own. "I'm someone willing to go as far as I have to go to protect the people who matter."

Something flashes beneath her poise, and under all the adrenaline and fear and shock of having my past suddenly drop into my home, of having my past threaten my present and my future, my heart tries to kick me in the balls.

"And I'm not one of those people, am I?" she says.

I swallow hard, but I don't answer her.

I can't.

Upper East Side Phoebe Lightly is a threat to my entire existence—I knew that the minute she walked into my town—and this woman standing in my safe sanctuary isn't *my girlfriend*, the woman on a mission to be a better person.

No, this woman is 100 percent Upper East Side Phoebe Lightly.

She could destroy me. My family. This town.

And if not her, then someone from *my* past. Someone from *her* past.

A former lover. An angry employee. A disgruntled ex-friend.

If she knows who I am, who else has she told?

Who else *would* she tell?

Who else from her family will figure it out?

Fuck.

She could tell the entire Upper East Side.

The socialites would descend on my town without hesitation, looking to score a lost heir, which is *exactly* what I wanted to avoid. Tickled Pink deserves better than the life I thought I could shake off and leave behind.

The thing about change?

It's hard, and regression can happen in an instant. Especially with the kind of change that people like me—and people like Phoebe Lightly—have to make to be truly better people.

To walk away from who we were raised to be from birth.

I should know.

That regression is happening to *me* right now, and I have close to twenty fucking years of experience being who I *want* to be instead of the silver-spooned asshole I was until one of my family's ships leaking all over the damn ocean finally served as a wake-up call to who I was and where I was going.

She's had what, a *month*?

I want to trust her.

I want to tell her everything.

Of all the people in this world, I think she's the one who could get it.

But what if she doesn't?

What happens to my family—my *whole* family, this whole fucking town, *me*—if she realizes I'm no better at my core than anyone in her family?

And what will my friends and family do if she tells them?

How will they handle the fact that I've lied to them, and not about something small but about something big, the entire time I was building a life here?

They'll never forgive me.

I'll never be able to look them in the eye again.

I won't belong here anymore.

I probably never did.

My lie is up.

It's time to face the music.

Fuck.

"We were never going to work, were we?" she says quietly. *You're a dead man* quietly. "You're fine if *I'm* the one who needs all the work. But not if you have to let anyone in. *All* the way in. Is that why it didn't work with you and Shiloh? Because you didn't let her in?"

Basically. "You're treading on dangerous ground."

"Of course I am. We're spoiled rich brats who use trust funds to build tree houses and Ferris wheels and pretend that we're fine, because money can fix everything, when we're not. We're not fine at all, and there are so few safe spaces in this world to admit it."

"You come from people who wanted to make better toilet paper. I come from people who think it's just another day at the office when there's an ecological disaster that kills millions of sea creatures." *Jesus.* I just said that out loud.

I'm going to have to throw her off the balcony and make it look like an accident.

Fuck off, idiot, both of my shoulder angels tell me.

They know I don't have it in me, but I have *something* in me, and it's not pretty right now.

Phoebe's glaring. "So you ran away from home and changed your name to disassociate from them instead of taking a stand and publicly announcing you were cutting ties? Did you take your trust fund with you?"

If my face wasn't hot before, it's steaming now. That was low.

And accurate, a snide voice whispers in my head. "Get. The. fuck. Out."

"You did. You took the money and ran."

"I said—"

"Don't worry, *Richard.* I'm going. You have bigger problems. I might've figured out fastest why your brother's here and who he is, but I won't be the last to put it together. Tickled Pink isn't full of backwoods hicks. And they know *you.* They'll figure it out."

"If you—"

She makes a commanding noise, and my voice dies away.

If deadly calm Phoebe Lightly is terrifying, visibly angry Phoebe Lightly is something else entirely.

"I thought you were my hero. I thought you could see something in me that no one else could. I thought you were truly the bigger person stooping to my level to give me a hand up. But that's not it at all, is it? You didn't see what I could be. You saw your own old life, and you got off on watching me struggle in all the ways you don't have to anymore. In all the ways you never had to, because you got to do it in secret, without the added bonus of the public humiliation. Fuck off, Teague. Just fuck off."

She brushes past me, not touching me, but I feel like she slammed a bulldozer into my shoulder anyway, and when the door slams behind her, the noise is more than just a door slamming.

It's the sound of my carefully crafted life imploding.

Chapter 34

Phoebe

He lied.

On the surface, I'm not entitled to be mad about that.

How much have I lied about in my life? If I left New York, if I started over like he did, would I want to go somewhere that everyone knew who I was and what was wrong with me?

Not at all.

But of everyone in his life, he should've known I would've understood. Hasn't the past month meant *anything*?

And that's what has me stifling sobs and swerving through the streets of Tickled Pink in the dark, aimlessly wandering while I try to find a safe space to completely lose my shit, terrified someone will see me like this, utterly broken that I couldn't keep myself together enough to not look like a threat to Teague, and equally angry that *he lied to me*.

And not about the little stuff.

The man I thought I was falling in love with isn't the man I thought he was at all, and it turns out he doesn't truly believe I can change.

That I'm worthy of his trust. That I'll ever be good enough for him to let me all the way in.

He would rather cut me out than trust that I could be the person who stands beside him while *his* past comes back to haunt him.

But the worst part?

If Teague Miller, the gruff and grumpy single dad with a heart of gold, the man who's been my damn *hero*, the man who's been my model of everything I want to be, isn't actually who he says he is, then can I ever be who I want to be?

I thought he was a small-town single dad adored by his friends and family for the little things, but it turns out, underneath it all, he's just like me.

The *old* me.

What am I supposed to do with that?

I've been angry before when relationships fizzled and died. Furious. Pissed off. Determined to get revenge.

But right now, there's no rage.

There's simply emptiness.

I'm a hollow shell. I can't fit back in the socialite box, and I can't stay here, where I thought I was *home*, because my anchor is actually a trap.

I want my cat, but I don't want to go back to the school. I want to hug someone, but I don't want to see anyone.

I want a time machine. I want to go back in time to dinner with Gigi, when I thought Tavi was calling me, and I want to dunk my phone in my soup and take whatever it was Gigi had been planning to dish out, and then I want to have gone back to work the next day as the soulless snob that I was and never, ever know what I was missing in life.

I want to not feel. I want to not know why there was always an underlying hum of disappointment, of discontentment, sitting somewhere between that spot behind my ear and that place between my lungs always making me wish that I could go somewhere and scream until it went away. I want to go back to believing it was normal and that everyone felt it and you just had to live with it. Or that it was because

I wasn't climbing the corporate ladder fast enough. That it was because I was never quite good enough for Gigi, who had ridiculous standards anyway. That it was because the men in my circles were such a general disappointment.

I clap my hand over my mouth as another sob wells up.

The men are such a general disappointment.

Not Teague, I would've said just a few short hours ago. *He's proof that goodness exists in the world. That nothing is what it seems. That grumpy exteriors hide the kindest, softest underbellies. That I, too, can find happiness.*

That I, too, can be worthy of the kind of love, family, and community that Whitney Anastasia found in Pink Gold.

If this is happiness, I don't want it. If this is a soul, I'd like to return it, please.

Why does it have to hurt so much?

Because you grew a heart, Phoebe, Teague's voice whispers in the back of my head.

And that's what ultimately breaks me.

An old, closed-up church looms in front of me, and I sprint for it as unwelcome tears start gushing out of my eyeballs.

I don't want anyone to see me like this.

I want to be alone.

Alone with my own misery. Alone to put my shields back on. Alone to figure out how I'll deal with the fact that the sun will have the utter gall to rise again tomorrow morning, like my entire life isn't broken beyond repair.

But when I tuck myself into the corner of the covered doorway, I realize there's light peeking through in the slim opening between the double doors.

It's a church.

It's not used anymore, but it's open, and it has light.

I hurl myself inside, suck in a gaspy sob, and taste chocolate.

Chocolate.

Oh my God.

Is this church the gate to heaven?

Is the movie real?

Am I dead?

I blink through my hazy vision, stifling sobs and following the chocolate scent and the sounds of pop music coming from down a stairwell.

I want to be alone, but I also want chocolate. And a hug.

I want to be alone but have a hug.

Like always, I want the impossible.

I hit the massive community room at the bottom of the stairs, ready to pull my shit together and order whoever's down here to hand over the chocolate and warn that if they tell that they saw me like this, they'll lose whatever's nearest and dearest to them, but the sight in front of me is one more surprise that I absolutely cannot handle tonight.

Tavi's here.

Tavi's here, stirring something on the stove, shaking her hips to the beat of the song and shoving a gigantic cheeseburger in her mouth.

I gasp out loud, and her head whips around so fast, cheeseburger still in her mouth, that I'm surprised her skull stays on her neck.

She sucks in a visible breath, eyes going wide at the sight of me, and while I stand there staring at her in shock, her own surprise turns to something else.

She tries to speak.

Her eyes get rounder.

She tries again.

And then she drops the burger and clutches her throat.

Oh my God.

She's choking.

She's choking.

She does this *thing* with her head and makes this *face*, and *oh my God, now I'm killing my sister.*

Her eyeballs go round.

She's visibly trying to cough while she clutches her neck with one hand and pounds on her own chest with the other, and *oh my God oh my God OH MY GOD.*

First Gigi.

Now Tavi.

"No," I sob.

I can't see. I'm once again immediately crying so hard I can't see, but I stumble around my sister, grab her from behind, and pump my fist under her breastbone.

Over. And over. And over.

I made her choke on a cheeseburger.

Why is it always beef?

"Don't die," I sob. "Please don't die. I'm sorry. I'm so sorry."

"Phoebe," she rasps. "Stop. *Stop.* I'm okay."

"Don't die!"

I take a sharp elbow to the ribs, and I realize she's talking.

She's talking, which means she can breathe, which means she's not choking—was she choking? Did I save her? Or was she never choking? *Oh my Oprah,* I'm going to kill her with the Heimlich.

"Phoebe. *Sit.*" She shoves me to the floor. "What are you doing here? Why are you crying? What happened? Did Teague do something? If he hurt you, I will kick his ass from here to Mars and back again."

I'm sobbing so hard I have the hiccups.

My face hurts. My mouth hurts. My eyes hurt. My nose hurts.

And none of them—*none* of them—hurts like my heart.

No.

No.

Shut it down, Phoebe. We're a Lightly. We don't let other people break us.

Except I do.

I have.

I need to go back. I need to go back to who I was before.

I need to hold on to something other than all my pain and disappointment and feelings of absolute futility.

"I killed you," I gasp.

She shoves a cup into my hand. "Drink. I'm okay. And never eating again. But I'm okay."

I try to drink, realize it's just water and not vodka or tequila or liquid pot, which should be a thing if it's not, and almost spit it back out.

"You're eating a hamburger." At least, that's what I'm trying to say. I have no idea if my words are coherent.

"Oh my God, you're hallucinating." Tavi puts a cool hand to my forehead. "You poor thing. Did you eat too much of the fried chicken? Was it not cooked all the way through?"

I snag her hand and peer at her through blurry eyes as a tinny, feminine voice rings out separate from the rock music playing in the room. "Tavi? *Tavi?* Hello? You can't just tell me to combine lavender and hazelnut in next month's truffles and then *disappear.*"

I gasp again and try to glare at my sister through my blurry vision.

This is helping.

This is helping *so much.* "And *you have cell service.*"

I *know* that came out clear as day.

"Phoebe, that's the music," she says gently.

"Yes, the lavender and hazelnut," I call out in a terrible imitation of my sister's voice.

She blanches sheet white. Like, paler than the color of Lola Minelli's face when she opened the door to her closet in the first episode of *Lola's Tiny House* and discovered it wasn't a closet but the outside world, because tiny houses don't have closets.

My sister grabs my elbow and hauls me to my feet. She works out so much that she's a beast like that. "Phoebe. Come on. Let's go get some fresh air."

"Tavi? Are you still alone?"

I channel my previous self once more and draw myself as tall as I can get, glaring at her.

Considering my eyes are puffy, my nose is, too, and my lips feel like they have permanent crusty cracks, I don't expect it to be successful, but *I have rage, dammit.*

Or heartbreak that's trying really, really hard to be rage.

I can't find my rage.

It's broken.

"Phoebe, tell me he didn't dump you," she whispers, giving my arm a soft squeeze and nudging me toward the door, more firmly, like she didn't hear the person on the phone.

I scan the room.

There are plastic molds all over worn and cracked cafeteria tables. Bags of sugar. Chunks of chocolate. An array of spices and fruits and nuts that all look fresher than anything I've seen since landing in Tickled Pink. The ancient stovetop in the galley kitchen along the wall is on, and there's steam rising from a pan.

"Phoebe?" She pushes.

I dig my heels in. "Stop talking."

"So it *is* Teague."

The sound of his name slices my heart open and does some damage to my lungs as well, but *I'm a goddamn fucking Lightly.*

Except I'm not.

I'm a marshmallow. "Quit hurting me," I whisper.

"*Phoebe.* I don't want to hurt you. I want to know if I have to hurt *him.*" She nods to the back door. "Let's go take—"

"*You were eating a hamburger.*" I yank my arm out of hers and step around her, deeper into the kitchen, looking for something—*anything*—to latch on to so I won't have to face that I've just screwed up the best relationship I ever had, which wasn't a relationship at all if he'd keep something like *his basic identity* from me.

From *me*.

Who's so much more like who he was than anyone in this town.

That's what hurts the most.

"I—" she starts, but then I find the cheeseburger.

She tried to bury it under a towel next to the stove.

"Phoebe."

I sniff. *"This is real beef!"*

"Shh."

She snatches the cheeseburger, eyeballs a trash can, mutters, "Screw it," and then shoves another gigantic bite in her mouth while she reaches for her phone and hangs up on someone.

"You eat hamburger and cheese."

Tavi—my sister, Octavia Lightly, vegan fitness influencer who shames people who let their dogs play with stuffed chew toys *shaped* like meat, and who would never let a grain of sugar pass through her lips—is eating a hamburger drenched in cheese *and bacon* and talking to someone on the phone about truffles while she stands in a kitchen full of everything she needs to make a chocolate feast for an entire town of broken-hearted people.

She has a secret twin.

That's the only explanation. Our mother hid my father from me, and now I'm being *Parent Trap*ped.

*Sister Trap*ped.

Whatever.

She visibly swallows, takes a swig of water, and frowns at me. "Can we please not talk about this? You look like a feral raccoon who hasn't slept in four years and just had your stash of pizza leftovers stolen by the garbage truck, and I really don't want either of us to regret anything we're about to say, because I actually like you these days, and I don't want that to change."

"Don't be nice to me," I whisper, but it's too late.

The tears are coming again.

I don't *want* to be this version of me.

I don't *want* to hurt.

But she likes me. *She likes me.*

And the truth is, I like her. And I think I like her even more for eating cheeseburgers and playing with sugar-laden chocolate.

"Tell me what to do." She pauses a split second, and then my sister does something she's never done before.

She hugs me.

She hugs me, and it's everything I need, and it only makes everything hurt more, but also less, and *I don't know how to do this.*

"I don't know how to hurt," I whisper against her shoulder. "I don't know how to cope with all of the pain."

"Did he do this to you?"

Instead of answering, I hug my sister back.

"I am so serious right now, Phoebe. I will *end* him if he did this to you."

I could tell her.

I could tell her who he is. How he reacted to me finding out. That I probably handled it wrong, too, but *oh my Oprah*, I hurt.

And on some level, I still want to protect him. "Is that good chocolate?"

Her body tenses against mine. "It's all vegan and sugar-free."

"No." A sob escapes me, followed by a hiccup.

I can't help it.

"Okay! Okay! It's good chocolate! Just—just stop crying. Please. *Please* stop crying." She wrenches herself away, grabs one of the plastic mold things, pops out a chocolate, and shoves it in my mouth.

And *oh. My. Oprah.*

My mouth has found meaning in life.

The rest of me is still broken, but my mouth—my mouth knows where it belongs, and it's right here, in this dingy little kitchen, with my *lying* sister and her mouthgasmic truffle.

I don't know what spice that is, or if it's a spice or an herb or a drug, but I know that the chocolate is melting on my tongue in a soothing concoction of flavors and I will never be the same.

Fucking damn you, Tickled Pink.

Once again, I can't go back.

"What—" I start.

She lifts the mold thing over her head. "No questions. We're talking about *you*. You ask questions, I throw it away. Understood?"

"Who *are* you?" I ask around a mouthful of chocolate medicine.

It's not a cure for heartbreak, but it's closer than I thought it would be.

She takes two steps toward the garbage can.

"I take it back!" I shriek, dribbling chocolate drool down my chin as tears spill out of my eyeballs again. "I take it back! I didn't ask!"

She frowns a Gigi frown at me. "Good. Because I might've liked you these past few weeks, but I will absolutely destroy you if you so much as breathe a word of this to anyone. As far as you're concerned, this is the weirdest nightmare you've ever had, understood?"

I nod.

She hands me one more truffle. "Now. Tell me what happened and what you want me to do about it."

I study my sister. She has Dad's eyes. *Gigi's* eyes. She's a Lightly, through and through. Pushing ahead, forging her own path, keeping her own secrets, and probably feeling alone and miserable and like better times will forever be just out of reach.

Maybe I'm projecting.

Maybe I'm not.

I can't make her accept herself and own being herself the way I'm trying so damn hard to accept and fix myself, and screwing up every step of the way.

I didn't think Tickled Pink would do this to me.

I didn't think *I* would do this to me.

But here I am, eating sugar- and dairy-laden truffles that my vegan fitness-influencer sister made while she gnaws on a cheeseburger like a starving tyrannosaur contemplating that even after all the progress I've made since the moment Gigi choked on that piece of Kobe filet, I still don't know who I am or if I'm doing this for me or if I'm doing it because it made a man like me.

This truffle isn't as good as the last one.

I think I'm expecting too much of it.

"Tavi?" I whisper.

She lifts her brows, waiting.

"I don't know who I am, and I don't know who I want to be, and I thought I could figure it out here, but the truth is—I think I need a break from Tickled Pink."

Chapter 35

Teague

My brother.

It's the first thing that registers after the fog of fear and anger and hurt lifts when Phoebe leaves, and it's what has me racing out the door, making my goats bleat and freak out, while I realize the only person who knows where I need to go is the last person who'd be willing to give me the information.

Is this panic?

Or is this regret?

I don't know.

But I know I need to solve the biggest problem at the moment, which is making sure *my brother* doesn't hurt anyone here.

Or me.

Twenty years.

Twenty years of doing what I needed to do to build a life away from the damn cage I escaped from, and now it's here.

Here.

In my sanctuary. My safe place. My world.

Turning my happiness against me.

One person at a time.

Dammit.

I race to the football field, and there they are.

My family.

Bridget. Shiloh. Ridhi. Laughing over a game of cornhole like the entire world isn't on the cusp of tumbling over a cliff that we can't come back from.

So they don't know.

I can still salvage this.

I just have to find him.

Find him and make him leave before he takes more from me, and then make the whole damn Lightly clan leave too.

Ridhi glances up and makes eye contact. "Thought you had a hot date," she calls.

Bridget makes a face like she wants to puke.

And Shiloh—let's just say my ex-wife has a knack for knowing when I'm being a massive fuckup.

Jesus.

She'll hate me when I tell her what I have to tell her.

Is this the last time we'll have normal? *Ever?*

"Teague?" she says.

"You should all head in before the mosquitoes eat you alive."

And before my brother realizes who they are.

It's been twenty years.

I don't know if he's just like our grandfather or if he left home, too, or if he's his own brand of fucked up, but I know I want my family safe until I find out.

"Where's Phoebe?" Shiloh asks.

The question stings like a bear-size bee would. My joy, my hope, my *friend*—I've lost her, because I can't trust her.

Not with this.

And I don't know if it's because she's untrustworthy or if it's because I have trust issues.

340

Probably both.

Upper East Side Phoebe is a threat, not to my town, not to my daughter, not to my friends who I call family, but to *me*.

To the person I've lied and told myself that I've grown to be.

And it's easier to tell myself that she can't really change who she is inside than it is to face the fact that this might be my fault.

That she might have a right to be angry with me.

That I *do* need to face my past and come clean to see if there's any chance that the people I love can accept me with all my faults and forgive me for all my lies.

Later.

That's for *later*.

Right now, I need my family safe.

I need them—I need them to know that no matter my name, I love them, and I want to protect them.

Fuck.

I scan the football field, looking for any shadows that don't belong, while Shiloh tosses her beanbag to Bridget and crosses the short distance to me. I should be moving. Searching. Hunting. Protecting.

But instead, I stand there and wait for my ex-wife and her crossed arms and *don't you dare bullshit me* expression to reach me.

Probably should've done this years ago.

"What's going on?" she asks. "You look the exact same way you did when I told you I was pregnant."

I make a noise that's not entirely human.

Choke on it, really, while I try to shake my head, a discomfort settling in the pit of my stomach that I don't want to analyze too hard, because I don't know if it's hope or disappointment or outright terror at the idea of Phoebe being pregnant.

Terror.

I choose terror.

Have to.

Any other option is too damn painful right now.

"So?" Shiloh presses.

Jesus.

I look away, and not just because she's using the damn Estelle Lightly eyebrow to a much greater effect than anyone else in this town who's been trying it. "You see any strangers tonight?" I ask gruffly.

"Deer Drop strangers, or Estelle Lightly–type strangers?"

My entire body breaks out in a cold sweat. My heart's pounding furiously—has been, and no, I don't plan on stopping to consider all the reasons—and if I don't move, I'm going to bust out of my own skin.

"Spit it out, Teague," she says quietly.

Fuck. "You remember I told you once I had family I didn't keep in touch with because they were not good people?" The words keep sticking in my throat, and I catch myself popping my knuckles.

Old habit.

I hate it.

Haven't done it in *twenty fucking years.*

"It rings a bell," Shiloh says evenly.

Of course it does. *You have secrets, Teague Miller, and that would be fine if I weren't your wife.*

Those words—the exact phrase she told me when she handed me divorce papers when Bridget was four months old—have never left me.

Probably because I knew she was right.

Just like she was right about the damn goats.

I met Shiloh on a trip through Door County, a little peninsula sticking into Lake Michigan over on the eastern side of Wisconsin, about sixteen years ago when I was looking for a place to settle. Hadn't found it yet, but then I found Shiloh.

We kept bumping into each other all day long.

She invited me to hang out at her campsite. We had a casual hookup. Good times. Traded numbers. Went our separate ways knowing we wouldn't use the numbers, but then she texted a few weeks later.

I met her in Tickled Pink because I had nowhere else to be and nothing else to do, and going felt right, and I liked her.

And then she dropped the bombshell news.

Condom must've broken. There hasn't been anyone else.

We got married because she was pregnant and we both thought that was what we needed to do. Got to be good friends, even, and considered ourselves lucky that we could stand each other.

But she was right.

I didn't let her all the way in.

Not when she told me her own biggest childhood traumas (having her picture splashed in the tabloids when they discovered Ella Denning's daughter liked kissing boys *and* girls) or when she told me her biggest fears (that she didn't know how to be a good mother, because she was nothing like her own) or when she confessed that her biggest dream was to take singing lessons and star in *Annie*.

I crack my knuckles again. "They . . . might've found me."

She frowns, then instantly looks over her shoulder.

Checking on Bridget.

Probably Ridhi too.

"Can you—can you please take her home?" I hate the fear in my voice, but *dammit*. I can't sit with Bridget and Shiloh and also track down my brother.

"Where's Phoebe?" Shiloh asks.

I swallow and ignore the painful swelling under my breastbone. "No idea."

"Teague . . ."

I didn't keep everything from her. I told her I'd been expected to take over the family business, and my grandfather and I had had a big fight when I'd told him I wouldn't. I told her I never wanted to see them again. That they were what was wrong with so much of the world. I told her I wouldn't trust them around my kid and that I was working on being a better man than the examples I'd had growing up.

I never told her how big the family business was.

That I'd had a trust fund.

That I'd been born with a different name.

The hoops I'd jumped through to shed it all in those few years between leaving Texas and meeting her. That my birth certificate was fake, because money can buy new names and erase history when it has to.

"Can you please take Bridget home?" I repeat.

When Estelle Lightly uses that eyebrow, it's amusing.

When Shiloh does it, it's terrifying. "You owe me."

Three words she's never said to me in all the time we've known each other.

I swallow and nod.

She doesn't mean I owe her for the favor.

She means I owe her my whole truth.

She shifts her weight, still glaring at me. "You might check Ladyfingers. Heard Carter was heading that way with a new friend."

Dammit. "Thank you." I turn, then look back. "It's been twenty years. I didn't think they'd try to find me."

"It's been twenty years," she replies. "Whoever they're hoping to find, you're not it."

And this is why I'm friends with my ex-wife.

Short of one of us confessing to being a serial killer, we roll with whatever life throws at us.

I owe her the truth, but I know she'll process it, accept it, and understand.

Unlike Phoebe, who throws it back.

Because it matters to her, idiot. Because she knows you know exactly where she's at because you've been there, and you didn't let her in, and you never planned on letting her in.

I ignore the guilt, the anger, the guilt—yeah, it's there twice—and head to the bar.

And what I find inside makes my gut cramp.

Carter Lightly is sitting in a booth with a guy in a cowboy hat.

But they're not alone.

Willie Wayne's there too.

So is Dylan.

"Teague!" Willie Wayne waves to me. "We got us another live one wanting to dump money in the town to make him a better person. Isn't the old Olsen place by the lake still for sale?"

"No."

Dylan grins. Willie Wayne hoots. Carter smirks at me.

Does he know?

"Don't mind ol' Teague," Willie Wayne says to my brother. *Jesus.* My brother. "He gets cranky, but he was wrong about the Lightlys, and I bet he's wrong about you too."

A pair of dark-brown eyes that look just like my mama's stares at me from under the brim of that hat. My lungs contract again, my heart hammers, and my fingers twitch.

There's not enough oxygen or alcohol in the entire state for this.

"If you don't want to sell him the Olsen place, Deer Drop Floyd probably would," Dylan muses.

I scowl at him.

Willie Wayne too.

They both snicker.

"C'mon, D," Willie Wayne says. "Let's let Mr. Grumpy see what he can dig up on our new friend Jonah here. Lightly. Move your ass before we pass an ordinance outlawing you from opening your mouth unless you make us fried chicken every night."

They slide out of the booth, and Dylan claps me on the shoulder. "Go easy on him. Had a rough travel day. Not all rich people are inherently assholes, yeah?"

Willie Wayne cackles. "Nah, give 'em all Tickled Pink has to give. Might be nicer than Estelle Lightly, but that doesn't mean he's good for us."

Do they know?

Do they know?

Is that why they're clearing out?

Carter doesn't say a word.

Just stares at me like he has cell signal and got a call from his sister.

Fuck.

I never say *fuck* this much.

Not anymore.

Yet here I am, all the *fucks* flying all over the place.

I have almost as many *fucks* tonight as I have gallons of paranoia.

And that's before I look away from my friends and back to the man sitting in the booth.

He has a full beer in front of him, an untouched basket of onion rings, too, hands tucked under the table, nothing moving but his eyes as they flicker over me, and I don't know if those are questions or accusations or something else entirely behind the movement of his eyeballs.

Can't yell without making a scene. Can't make a scene without everyone asking what the hell I'm yelling for. Can't get out of explaining to the people who are my family—my *real*, chosen family—where I came from and why I don't want to sit down.

So I sit.

I sit with my throat clogging and a hot, thick, wet sense of shame enveloping me like that weighted blanket Bridget sometimes sleeps under.

Jonah was her age—fifteen—when I left.

He was old enough to look like a man but not old enough to *be* a man.

Hell, at not quite eighteen I was barely old enough to be a man.

Two of us always fought like snakes and honey badgers. Getting out, looking back—I know it wasn't us.

It was Grandpa Shithead and Pops, the second and third Edward Richard Montgomery Beauregards respectively, threatening to leave the company to one or the other of us if we didn't shape up and prove ourselves. Pitting us against each other in a war to see who was man enough to head up Greenright Oil. Telling me that Jonah was smarter. Telling Jonah that I had more common sense. He had the looks. I had the fists for fighting.

I don't know why Jonah's here.

And I don't like not knowing.

He breaks the silence first, clearing his throat, and then—"It's really you."

His voice is deeper. Twangy, too, like he never left Texas. Flashbacks fly fast and furious through the front of my skull, from rodeos to sunsets on South Padre Island to true Tex-Mex food.

Grandpa hollering about those damn tree huggers. Pops rolling his eyes and saying oil wasn't going anywhere. Ma sneaking chocolate chip cookies into the tree house.

"Grandpa's gone," Jonah says into the silence that I couldn't fill even if I wanted to. That's not a cat that has my tongue. It's a whole damn tiger. "Passed on early last year. Didn't know if you heard."

I shake my head once.

Didn't know.

Don't know if I care or not. Probably do.

Probably not as much as Phoebe would care if Estelle kicked the bucket, though.

Fuck.

"Board of directors kicked Pops out too." He's quiet. Soft spoken like Mama was. Big difference from the little brother who used to holler and yell at me whenever he couldn't find his baseball glove. "Didn't know if you'd care, but—I got the rest of your trust fund unlocked. Yours to do with as you'd like."

"I don't want any fucking money."

He doesn't smile.

Doesn't frown.

Just watches me while he nods slowly. "Pops tracked you, you know. Knew when you left the country. Knew about the millions you were dropping for disaster relief and wildlife preservation and on green-energy research. Didn't know—I didn't know if you'd want to finish what you started. That's all."

I drop my head and close my eyes.

Why is it so damn hard to breathe?

"No, that's not all," he says. "I missed you. I was pissed as a gator in a cage when you left, but I knew why you did it, and I might've spent some time being mad, but I missed you. That night you told Grandpa off—I knew you weren't the asshole. You didn't just talk the talk either. You walked away. You stood up for what you believed in. You could see where we were heading, what he was doing was wrong. But then you were gone. You were gone, and I hated you, but I only hated you because I missed you. Even when we were fighting—we were on the same side. Same side against Grandpa. Against Pops."

Someone's going to overhear, and I'll have to explain this, but I don't know if I care. I swallow hard and make myself look at my little brother.

I don't know if he's shorter or taller than me. I don't know if he's married. If he has kids. If he's ever had his heart broken or if he's running Greenright Oil. If he lives in Grandpa's old mansion or if he built himself his own tree house like he always used to say he'd do too.

If he's really still in Texas or if he just sounds like it.

"Can we start over?" He shifts and reaches a hand across the table. "I'm Jonah Beauregard. Been sitting in as the temporary CEO of Greenright Oil, but only long enough to find the right person for the job so we can live up to what our name's always implied we should be. She started Monday. Means I've got some time off to do what I think my big brother did a long time ago, and that's to figure out who I am when nobody's looking."

Fuck.

Fuck.

I squeeze my eyes shut again.

"Holy shit," Willie Wayne says somewhere nearby. "Not even Estelle Lightly made him cry, and she's a *lot* scarier."

The booth squeaks across from me. "Or I'll just leave my card. You want to talk, anytime, I'd like that. But it looks like you've got a good life here. Not my place to screw that up. I just—I saw your picture online, playing some kind of baseball game here. Wanted to see for myself if it was really you."

The Lightlys.

Snowshoe baseball.

It was all over the *Tickled Pink Papers* that we made the gossip pages around the country.

The one thing I was most afraid of, and instead of getting my grandfather raining fire and brimstone or my father showing up with outraged indignation that a Beauregard would walk away from our duty to family and settle in such a backward place, I have my little brother offering to leave me alone.

"Wait." I'm talking, but I'm not in control of my mouth. Not in control of opening my eyes to see him angling out of the booth either. I'm not in control of much tonight, it seems. "He's really dead?"

Jonah nods.

"And Pops—"

"Still yells, but he doesn't get around much these days. Funny how sleeping with his best friend's wife and trying to blackmail half the board can backfire on a person."

I shudder.

I *hate* that life. "And you?" I ask my brother.

His lips twist like he's considering smiling. "A wise man I once knew sneaked just enough money into a Swiss bank account to fund his way through college and, by all accounts, find himself. Turns out that might be a good option for me too."

"Where?"

He shrugs. "Wherever feels right."

It's a statement born of privilege, and I think he knows it.

I was there once too.

And what I discovered was that nothing much mattered until there were people around me who could accept me, flaws and all, until I was strong enough to accept them right back.

To know that I was giving as much back as I was getting in my community.

He glances down at the table, where he's left his card, and he starts to say something, but I cut him off.

"There's an old fixer-upper for sale on the lake. And this place—turns out it's really, really good for some people to find themselves. If you want to give it a try."

His eyes go shiny, and my brother—*my brother*—smiles. "I'll keep that in mind."

This isn't what I expected.

It's better.

I don't think he's lying to me. I don't think he's out to get me.

And even if he were, I have an entire town at my back. I hope.

Along with—*fuck*.

Not along with someone else just like us who gets it too.

Because I made sure that wasn't an option.

Chapter 36

Phoebe

I don't know where I am.

I know I'm at a lake tucked into rolling hills. There's a breeze, but I don't need a coat. I don't need to shed any layers either. It's just the perfect temperature. I know the staff at this private hideaway is well trained. I know someone's been watching me all morning, ready to dash out to satisfy my every whim.

But I don't know where I am.

And I don't care.

While my kitten stalks a flock of geese nearby, I'm sitting in an Adirondack chair inside a gazebo overlooking the lake, staring at the water and wondering if anyone's ever lost a pair of Louboutins in it, or if anyone ever uses it for fishing, or if it knows the answer of who I'm supposed to be.

When I told Tavi I wanted to leave Tickled Pink last night, she packed Elmo and me up in Gigi's Pilot, drove me to the nearest airport, and booked me a private jet to *somewhere*.

"You take care of you, and I'll take care of the details," she told me.

And she did.

A car met me at the airport when I landed. My room is stocked with clothes in my size. Breakfast arrived fifteen minutes after I woke up, and I couldn't find fault with a single offering on my tray.

I don't know if this is Tavi's way of buying my silence with her secret, or if it's her way of being a good sister, or some combination of both, and I don't actually care.

All I can focus on is sitting here, asking the universe if I have the strength to keep being a better me if I have to do it alone, or if I should cut my losses now, go back to New York, drop all the gossip bombs I have on every person who's said a single bad word about me, ever, and rise to my position as the most powerful Lightly to ever rule Manhattan.

I shake my phone and stare at the water. "Magic Eight Ball app, should I be the better person?"

I flip my phone over and consult the answer. *You will burn in hell for wearing white after Labor Day.*

"What the *hell*, Magic Eight Ball app?"

Someone steps into the gazebo behind me, and I slump back in the chair. "I'm not hungry for lunch," I tell them.

"That's my girl, but they won't let you out of eating here merely because you have a broken heart."

I sit up so fast I bang my elbow on the armrest and almost trip myself as I leap out of the chair. *"Mom?"*

Am I crying?

Again?

Oh my Oprah. I am. I'm crying. Again.

"Phoebe, darling, not the drama this early in the morning." She wraps her arms around me and hugs me tight.

Two hugs from my family in two days.

"What are you doing here?" I ask, my voice muffled and raw against the lush fabric of her morning robe. I'd ask why I'm crying again, but I know.

It's because every emotion I've squelched in my entire life has been unlocked by basic levels of affection that should be normal in a family.

"I'm hiding from reality, sweetheart, just like you."

Oh God.

Tavi sent me to a rehab facility.

She doesn't trust I'll keep her secret, so she's setting me up to look like a liar if I come back *saying crazy things* when I get out of rehab, and—*no*.

No, we're going to believe in the good of humanity.

Aren't we?

Yes.

Yes, we are.

Tavi sent me to a private retreat to help me find the space I need to think about what I want to do next. She's a good sister.

And if she's not, she'll regret the day she was born.

No, Phoebe, if she's not, we will still be the bigger person and move on with our lives.

Mom hugs me tighter. "I'm so sorry I left you there," she whispers. "I'm so sorry I lied to you. I'm so sorry I wasn't a better mother."

"Mom—"

"No, I wasn't. And that—that *place*. It made me feel things I've never felt. It made me want to be honest. And honest hurts. Phoebe, it hurts *so much*."

My heart feels like it's been hit with a shrink ray from that old eighties movie that I had to watch once when I got signed up for the wrong summer camp, and that much shrinkage that fast *hurts*. "I know, Mom."

She's still hugging me.

I don't think my mother has hugged me in at least seven years.

Maybe ever.

Not like this.

"Are you okay?" she asks me. "What do you need? How can I help? I don't know how to do this, Phoebe, but I want to be here for you."

It's so odd to feel completely broken but to also realize Gigi might've actually known what she was doing when she dragged the five of us to Tickled Pink.

Even if we don't know how to be better, we're all aware that *better* exists.

And that maybe, just maybe, we need *better*.

"Teague lied to me," I whisper.

"Oh, honey, that's what men do."

"But I thought we had something, and *it hurts*."

The lie is what hurts. Or maybe his distrust of me is what hurts.

Or maybe it's knowing that I'm still not good enough to have earned the truth.

Whatever it is, I know that telling my mom what hurts is akin to offering to split my chest open and hand her my heart on a platter. She could destroy it, or she could put a Band-Aid on it, kiss its boo-boos, and help me tuck it back where it belongs, and I don't know which she'll do.

She strokes my back. "This is what we call *his loss*, Phoebe."

"No, Mom. It's *my* loss too. I *ache*. I hurt so badly I can't see a future where I don't hurt. I don't want to dig deeper into his lie and expose him to the whole town. I don't want to hurt him back. And I don't know myself anymore if I don't want to hurt him back. And that makes me realize I don't know where I belong. How do you find where you belong when the one thing that made you belong is gone?"

I can't stop talking.

I can't stop pouring out my heart to my mom.

Never—*ever*—have we done this before.

"Oh, Phoebe. Sweetheart. I didn't have enough mimosas for this, but I'll try, okay? Mommy will try." She guides me back to my chair. "You love him too much to ruin him? Is that what you're saying?"

"I—"

Oh my Oprah.

I love him.

I do.

I love him. I want to know *why* he walked away from his family. I want to know how I can help him. I want to tell him I don't care who he was, because who he's become is a level of sheer, utter goodness that I can only hope to achieve someday.

I'm an achiever, and I don't know if I can ever be that good.

I want to tell him that he makes me want to be a better person.

And if I can't have him in my life, I don't care what happens to me, because I will never, ever be strong enough on my own to be all that I can be if he's not beside me.

Oh my Oprah.

I don't just love him.

I'm so madly *in love* with him that life is meaningless without him.

I stare at my mom in horror. *"Make it stop."*

"Darling, you can't control love."

"Yes, I can."

I shriek so loudly I startle a flock of geese, who erupt in honks and take flight en masse from their spot on the grassy bank. Elmo's fur stands up on end. His tail too. He hisses, then dives for the gazebo and hides under my chair.

"Oh, my poor baby." Mom strokes my hair. "I'm booking us a spa day, and then a champagne boat ride across the lake, and then a shopping trip."

"Will it make me feel better?" It sounds absolutely awful.

"No, my sweet angel. But it'll give you time to think in comfort."

I gasp.

"Love is awful, Phoebe. Time is the only thing that heals it. Time and getting back to normal. If you're up for it, we'll head back to the city in a few days. Everything looks different there. But heartbreak or not, I refuse to let you return looking like this. Your poor face. And your poor hair. And your poor aura. Don't worry, sweetheart. Mommy's here. Even if it hurts, you're not alone."

She's gazing out over the lake, and it's impossible not to see the sadness in her eyes.

I grab Elmo and snuggle him. I still have Elmo. I still have my kitten. "Did you love my biological father?" I whisper to Mom.

She flinches. "Irrelevant, isn't it?"

"He hurt you."

"Do you know the hardest part of being in Tickled Pink? The hardest part was seeing all of those people who were so *happy*. Married people. Single people. Grumpy people. They were *happy*. They didn't have designer clothes. They'd never eaten at a Michelin-starred restaurant or brunched with the rich and powerful. And Coco Chanel knows they wouldn't know a real facial if it leaped out of that lake and attacked them with the seaweed. But they were *happy*. They know something we don't. And I don't think I'll ever know it, Phoebe. I truly don't think I ever will."

"I was happy there." I bury my nose in Elmo's fur while he purrs against my face.

"Then go back," she says quietly. "Go back. Forgive him. Be happy."

I swallow against another tide of rising grief. "I don't think it's that simple."

Could I go back to Tickled Pink?

Yes.

I could go back. I could work to raise money to build a new Ferris wheel. I could have coffee at Café Nirvana and do lunch with Jane and volunteer at the cat shelter with Bridget (maybe) and buy a house and live with sixteen cats and have Tavi visit when she wants a hamburger (for however much longer she lasts in Tickled Pink), and I could know that I was doing something good and worthwhile with my life to help someone else.

But I'd know I was in Teague's territory.

I'd know I might run into him at the grocery store or while taking a walk along the lake or when we break ground for the new Ferris wheel.

He'd be the real estate agent working on my purchase of the adorable little building downtown that I plan to turn into a candy shop where we make our own taffy, and when I say *we*, I mean someone else, because I want to give Tickled Pink a candy shop but I shouldn't be trusted in a kitchen.

So maybe I need to find my own small town.

But Shiloh and Ridhi and Willie Wayne wouldn't be there.

They might not have a snowshoe baseball team or anything like it.

Elmo squirms.

I'm getting his fur wet with my tears.

"Oh, my sweet Phoebe." Mom strokes my hair again. "It really will get better. I promise."

"I think you're right."

"More often than you can admit, I'm afraid."

She's trying for a joke. I know she is. Another day, I might laugh at it.

"I need to go back to the city," I tell her. "There's not much left for me there, but whatever I do next, there or elsewhere, I think I need to tie up a few last loose ends."

She rubs her hands together and smiles brightly. "Are we going to ruin Fletcher? Destroying assholes always makes me feel better."

I wish I could say the same. "No, Mom. That won't make me feel better. But closure will."

"Can I destroy him after you have closure?"

"*Mom.*"

She sighs. "Fine. I just won't tell you."

"It won't make you happy either," I say quietly.

She's silent for a long time.

"That place really does change you, doesn't it?" she finally says.

"It really, really does."

Chapter 37

Teague

After a long night of sitting at the lake, catching up with Jonah, double-checking everything he told me with internet searches I haven't let myself make in twenty years, I start the new day staring at the old high school.

I owe Phoebe an apology.

You owe her a lot more than that, those annoying shoulder angels chime in.

She yelled at me first, I remind them.

They don't answer, because they're not real.

Or maybe because she had a right to be mad, and I let panic and fear override the man I want to be.

Funny thing about realizing everything you knew growing up was bad for you—it makes you question your own actions every time you catch your parents coming out of your own mouth or your feet or your hands or your facial expressions, and that self-awareness doesn't go away, even with twenty years of practice.

I know exactly what she's going through.

But while she laid out all her feelings and fears and struggles, I nodded and listened like she was the first workaholic socialite heiress to ever struggle with the questions of *who am I and can I be better enough to be worthy of happiness?*

I'm living, breathing proof that people like her—people like *me*—can change.

And I kept that from her.

I could say she used me as her personal therapist. That she got more out of our relationship than I did.

But that's not true.

She made me see *me* in a new light.

In a lot of ways, she's a fuck ton braver than I am. I got to go on my own self-improvement journey quietly. Away from gossip pages. Away from the constant reminder of who I'd been. Away from any preconceived expectations from anyone other than myself.

She did it out in the open, all over the *Tickled Pink Papers*, landing on her face in sawdust on the snowshoe baseball field, falling into the lake, knowing that everyone in her old life was laughing at her too.

And I thought I had any right to be mad at her for being smart enough and quick enough to put two and two together when she met my brother last night.

"Excuse me, but where the hell do you think you were all night, young man?" my daughter demands behind me.

I turn and give her the *watch your mouth* look, and her brows shoot up to her forehead. "Whoa. Sorry, Dad. I didn't—you look like shi—like you're sick. Are you sick? You never get sick. Do you want me to run to the store for chicken noodle soup and crackers? Or the library for a book? I can read you a book. You should go lie down. Has Mom seen you like this? You *cannot* let Phoebe see you like this. Death-Dad look is for, like, the seventeenth date. Or maybe not until after marriage."

"Phoebe's not here." Tavi strolls down the school steps under the **Boys** entrance, decked out in tight pink jeans, heels up to her knees, that idiotic boa strangling her neck and shoulders, sunglasses big enough to use in a pinch as an emergency alien-signaling device, and her dog poking its head out of her purse. "She's having private soul-reflection time. Sounds like she's not the only one who needs it."

She lowers the glasses and glares at me.

"Dad?" Bridget says quietly. "What did you do?"

"Yes, Teague," Tavi says, "what *did* you do?"

I don't know if the Lightly hellion is asking because she knows or because she doesn't, but I know my heart's suddenly not in my chest where it's supposed to be. "Where is she?"

"Not here."

"*Not at the school* here, or *not in Tickled Pink* here?"

"Tavi?" Bridget whispers.

She slides her glasses back up her nose. "Bridget, we are totes having coffee tomorrow. And nails next Tuesday. But right now, I can't stand the sight of your father, and I need to go puke in private. His presence makes me nauseous."

"Where—" I repeat.

She stops at the bottom step. Even in her heels, she's not tall enough to look me straight on. "I don't know if you know this or not, but a socialite scorned is *not* someone you mess with. And I'm feeling scorned by association. The *only* reason I'm not planning your evisceration is because she's asked me not to. Yet. But be warned, Teague Miller. If we decide to destroy you, we *will* destroy you."

Bridget looks between us as Tavi struts away.

I rub my eyes, because I can't reach into my chest, locate my panicked heart, and rub it. "You know how we talk about apologizing and forgiving each other?" I say to my daughter.

Her eyes are as wide as the Great Lakes as she nods.

"I need to do some apologizing. To a lot of people. Are your mom and Ridhi home?"

I come clean to my daughter, my ex-wife, and her wife over a few pots of coffee in their kitchen. After the initial surprise, Ridhi says what

I hope the other two are thinking. "Asshole move, thinking you couldn't trust us with that, but I guess you make up for it in other ways."

"How long had you been Teague Miller when we met?" Shiloh asks.

"Not long in the grand scheme of things."

"No wonder you knew how to change my name," Bridget says. "You weren't really born who you were supposed to be either."

I blink at her as my eyes get hot again. "Suppose I wasn't."

"So I have an uncle, and he's an okay person?"

I nod.

"And he's rich?"

"Bridget."

She looks at Shiloh, who's glaring. "What? Do you know how many kids at school talk about finding a rich uncle to buy them a car for their sixteenth birthday? This is like—it's like all of my birthdays and holidays rolled into one. Is he moving here? Is he staying in the tree house? Or—*oh*. Does Estelle need to monitor his soul for a while?"

That would be funny any other day.

But Shiloh's ignoring her to ask the next inevitable question. "And Phoebe knows?"

I wince.

Don't realize I'm rubbing my chest, too, until all three ladies in the room pointedly stare at my hand.

"Phoebe met Jonah and put two and two together, and . . . I didn't handle it well when she confronted me about my past," I finally say into the silence.

"How not well?"

"She left," Bridget whispers.

Heat flushes through my whole body.

Heat, shame, and regret.

I should've told her.

I should've just told her the truth, and I didn't, and now I don't know where she is or what I'm going to do about it.

"And how do you feel about that?" Shiloh asks me when I nod confirmation of Bridget's statement.

That's exactly what a therapist would ask, and considering we've had family therapy, I'd know.

I try to spear Shiloh with a glare, but it falls flat.

The three of them heave identical sighs.

"Out with it." Ridhi holds out a hand and makes the *give it to me* gesture. "What other deep dark secrets do you have hiding in your closet that you need to work out if you're ever going to be willing to open yourself up to being vulnerable in love?"

Hello, knife. That was a jagged rip to my heart. "I'm plenty open to love. I love all three of you."

"*Romantic* love, Dad." Bridget rolls her eyes. "Like, *soul mate* love. Like, *I would die for you* love. Like *Romeo and Juliet.*"

"Highly dysfunctional and overly dramatic," Ridhi says. "Don't be like *Romeo and Juliet*. Find a happy ending."

"Not everyone is meant to have *forever romantic soul mate* love," Shiloh says. "Maybe your dad's happier alone. With just his fish and his goats. And his tree house. Away from everyone else. Where no one can hurt him because they can't get close enough."

Bridget's face crinkles. "That's seriously depressing."

"If that's the life he wants to live, it's his choice. He's been perfectly happy being a grumpy loner this long. How could a high-maintenance, big-city princess possibly make him happy?"

"Do *not* call her that." I know Shiloh's baiting me, and I'm still growling.

She smiles back. "Spoiled socialite?"

"Mom, seriously, the man's hurting enough," Bridget says. "*I'm* hurting. I miss Phoebe. She was really funny when she'd do impressions of all the people back in New York. And sometimes when she didn't realize she was doing impressions of herself too. And sometimes when she'd sit on the muffins I'd sneak onto her seat just to watch her eyes twitch when she thought about how she didn't trust the dry cleaner in Deer Drop but had blueberry crumbs all over her butt now."

"Bridget."

"Kidding. I mean, mostly. I only did it once, and only right after she got here. She's not *gone* gone, is she?" She swings her attention back to me. "You're going to apologize and get her back, aren't you?"

I swallow hard.

Pretty sure it won't be that simple.

I told her I didn't trust her.

I told her I'd protect other people before I'd protect her.

I more or less told her we were *nothing*, when the truth is, she's so much *something* that I'm terrified I'll fuck it up, and this time, when a relationship that matters ends, it won't come with learning to be friends and coparent a really awesome kid who grows into a really awesome teenager while I get to keep the parts of me that I'm most ashamed of hidden.

This time, if I want to have a real relationship with someone who understands me in ways I wish no one ever needed to understand me, I have to trust that who she's becoming is bigger than who she's been.

I have to trust that she won't hurt me if I let her see all of me, and that she won't use my weaknesses against me the way she was raised to do.

Of everyone in the world who could hurt me, Phoebe Lightly knows better than anyone which buttons she'd need to push.

"Dad." Bridget nudges my foot with hers. "Dad, you have to apologize and get her back. She's—she's the best of all of them. Even better than Tavi. I like her here. *You* like her here. And I like that you like her here. She makes you happy. So go find her. Tell her you're sorry. And bring her back."

Shiloh stands up. "Let him go, Bridge. This is one he has to do on his own."

"But—"

"Nope. No buts. C'mon. Your room needs to be cleaned, and I have five dollars for anyone who pulls all the weeds from the tomato plants today."

"But what about meeting Dad's brother?"

"Maybe tomorrow."

"Or today, if he comes into the café," Ridhi says. "Anya told me there was another rich stranger in town. Said he was *so handsome.* I'm *positive* Tickled Pink will be rolling out its best welcome mat."

As they should. My little brother seems like a truly decent guy.

Better than me, truth be told.

"Teague?" Shiloh's watching me from the doorway. "Always darkest before the dawn. This will all work out however it's meant to. Even if it's not exactly what you wanted. But what in life is?"

She's right.

I know she's right.

But life doesn't just happen to you.

Sometimes, you have to happen to life.

I want to happen to life. Question is, *How?*

Chapter 38

Phoebe

The Chos' annual garden party is awful.

Not because the food is bad (it's not) or because the decorations are gaudy (they're quite lovely) and also not because everyone's whispering about me as I make my way through the gardens. Not because I'm confirming with each passing second that I truly have zero friends here and that I don't belong here. Not because Fletcher Barrington is here somewhere, and I have to offer him a bribe to shut the ever-loving fuck up and not go after my old driver to get his grandfather's watch back, but because every last bit of tonight feels so damn fake.

The smiles.

The alliances.

The invitations to brunch that are nothing more than an excuse to try to squeeze out gossip.

I hate it.

I want to be back in Tickled Pink, even if I'm alone. I want to sit out under the night sky, sniffing Tavi's secret chocolate confections that she's making in the basement of a closed-up church and watching for shooting stars while my kitten purrs on my lap. I want to have a beer with Jane and ask for more stories about what Tickled Pink was when she was a kid. I want to convince Ridhi and Anya that they should move the café into that old church that Tavi's squatting in, because repurposed buildings are fascinating.

And I want things that I don't think I can have.

Like living in a tiny little tree house with an oversize lumberjack who's only grumpy because he's afraid of losing the life he's found for himself.

But if I'm going to be as happy as I can make myself, I need to close all the massive, gaping holes that will haunt me if I walk away without doing what my conscience tells me I need to do, even if what my conscience is telling me to do flies in the face of everything I ever learned about how you behave in Upper East Side society.

I finally spot Fletcher on the veranda shortly after dusk.

"Shall I handle this for you, darling?" Mom asks. She's been my shadow for the past three days as we've moved from the spa upstate back to the city for me to do what I need to do here.

I shake my head. "No. Last thing. And then—"

And then, I don't know what.

I visited Antoinette yesterday and thanked her for all her hard work, wrote her a glowing recommendation for a promotion, blackmailed my former boss into writing one of his own—my conscience is just fine on that front—paid off her student loans and prepaid her rent for a year, and then gave her a ridiculously large gift certificate to her *actual* favorite spa, and it still didn't feel like enough. I'll probably anonymously send her gifts for several more years.

I sent flowers and chocolates to the staff who worked for me at my town house, which I'll be selling shortly, along with writing them each bonus checks for two years' worth of pay, and also did the same for the staff at Gigi's brownstone.

I saw my cousins for the first time in years, apologized for not checking in on them sooner, and gave them my phone number if there's ever anything I can do to help their side of the family.

Within the bounds of what my newfound conscience will allow, of course. They *are* still Lightlys, and I don't know them well enough to know if they've overcome their genes after being cut off.

So tonight is the last step.

Giving Fletcher what he wants, or as close to what he wants as I can give him. It truly was not my place to dispose of his family history, and it's his business if he wants to be a despicable human being.

I'll forever know I made amends, and that's weirdly more fulfilling.

A murmur goes through the crowd as I make my way toward Fletcher.

The fallout of our breakup has been circulating through gossip channels nonstop while I've been gone. He's made sure of it.

My name has been dragged so deeply through the dirt that it's a wonder I don't see streaks of mud float through the air when people say it out loud. I suppose people still fear my grandmother enough that they won't outright snub me, despite it being public knowledge that we're not related by blood.

Everyone seeing Fletcher and me together?

This will be all over everywhere before midnight.

I stride through gardens on my way to the edge of the veranda like I still belong here, as though the looks and the whispers roll off my back, as if tomorrow, I'll sit down at brunch at the Bergamot Club with a brand-new sparkly purse that I'll let my best friends touch if they're nice to me, like we're in second grade again, and I don't stop until I'm at Fletcher's side.

How I ever found him attractive enough to settle for is beyond me.

He's arrogant and condescending, and he never smiles.

Only sneers.

The rest of the world is beneath him.

"I don't have your grandfather's watch," I start, and then I choke on my words.

Fletcher isn't alone.

And he doesn't look well.

"He's aware," Teague says softly.

Teague.

He's here.

In New York.

In a suit.

And not just *any* suit but a custom bespoke suit that fits him like he was born in it. His beard is trimmed short.

His hair too.

No sunglasses.

No fishing hat.

No hiding.

And I have completely lost all use of my tongue.

He's fancy and polished and fits in *perfectly* here, which isn't Teague at all. He's not supposed to be posh and suave and superficial.

He's supposed to be rough and grumpy and soft.

I truly did not know him at all.

The pain sweeps through my body all over again, and it's only old socialite habits resurfacing that keep me upright and somewhat in control.

"Seems my new friend Fletcher here owes you an apology," Teague continues.

I almost lift my chin and stare him down, but acting like an imperious ass won't make me feel better.

The very sight of Fletcher is making me rethink my plan to offer him a substitute Rolex.

Is it truly being the bigger person if you let a bully win?

It isn't, is it?

I have *so much* to learn still. I'm lost without a compass.

And that's before the whispers start rising around me. *"Richard Beauregard. Edward Richard Montgomery Beauregard the Fourth, to be exact. Estelle Lightly found him and saved him from amnesia. He's moving back to Texas and taking over Greenright Oil. Most eligible bachelor of the year. And honey, yes, I do believe that is all muscle."*

I know the whispers are wrong. There's no way in hell the man standing before me would leave his family.

But I also would've sworn up and down there was no way the man would even temporarily set foot in New York, yet here he is, looking as polished and composed as though he's been in this world every day for the past twenty years.

Fletcher, meanwhile, looks like he just tried to swallow a sewer rat.

"That apology?" Teague prompts.

Why does his voice still have the power to set my nerve endings on fire?

"What are you doing here?" I manage to ask while I fight the sting suddenly overheating my eyes and the lumberjack-size lump stuck in my throat.

His dragon-egg eyes scan me like he's peering through my own layers of armor—both the clothing and the emotional layers—to discern which Phoebe Lightly he'd find if he could inspect my heart. And I don't know if he's looking because he wants to know if I'm worthy of him or if he's worthy of me, or if he came all the way to New York just to torture both of us a little more. "Looking for you."

My pulse slowly restarts itself. "Why?" I whisper.

"Because being part of a family means you don't have to do the hard stuff alone."

Oh my Oprah.

Is he—is he calling *me* his family?

My tear ducts are threatening to show off for the whole of Upper East Side society. "Your hard stuff, or my hard stuff?"

"You won't last two days around here, you fake little Texas—*erp*." Fletcher's voice cuts off, and I hear my mom murmuring something to him—undoubtedly blackmail material that Gigi's been sitting on, and *I don't care.*

I don't.

I hate this life. I hate these people. I hate how they make me feel and what I do when I'm around them.

Some people here are truly good.

I was never one of them.

The Upper East Side and I have a dysfunctional relationship, and we need to break up.

Teague's hand twitches like he wants to reach for me, but he doesn't know if I'd let him. Indecision flashes over his features, and that temporary break in his composure, that crack in his exterior, makes me crack a little too.

He offers me his arm like we're at a debutante ball. "A minute of your time, Ms. Lightly?"

"A minute? Is that all you want?"

He shakes his head.

More whispers explode around us again.

"Okay," I mouth as I slip my hand into his elbow.

His breath leaves him in a shudder, and he covers my hand with his, that simple touch saying so much as he whisks me deep into the gardens.

"You were right," he says quietly while the sounds of voices fade. "I wasn't protecting Bridget and the town as much as I was protecting myself."

And this is the hard part.

The Phoebe Lightly who was bred to look for advantageous relationships and to climb ladders and to win at any cost would be high-fiving herself for landing an heir in hiding.

The mystery.

The intrigue.

The gossip.

It's a socialite's wet dream.

But this Phoebe Lightly?

The me I am today?

"Would you have ever told me?" My voice cracks, and I let it, because that question is the only thing I care about.

"No," he says quietly.

One little syllable, and it shatters me. "I see."

"And that's why I didn't deserve you."

"Of course." He came all this way to put the nail in the coffin. *Who does that?* "If you'll excuse me—"

He grips my hand tighter. "Do you know how many times I've listened to you talk about doing the hard things in the past several weeks, about facing who you were head-on so that you can learn to be who you want to be, even when you didn't know who that was? And how many times I sat there thinking, *Thank God I'm done with that shit?* And how very, very fucking clear it is now that I was lying to myself?"

My breath catches.

"I was seventeen when I walked away. Old enough to have the balls to do it, but not old enough to know how much of what I grew up with that I'd have to live with still for the rest of my life. The broken parts of me. The ugly parts of me. The unlovable parts of me. I know what you're going through. I was there. I've done it. But you—you've done so much fucking more in under two months than I've done in twenty years, because you're doing it out in the open, with your heart on your sleeve, taking all of the shit that everyone throws at you because you think you deserve it, because you think you have to, and fuck, Phoebe . . . I don't deserve you. That's the honest-to-God truth. I don't deserve you."

I stop behind a hedge. My legs are shaky, and I don't know if he's here just to tell me he doesn't deserve me or if he's here because he wants me to tell him he does. "I would have never hurt your family."

"I know." His voice is getting huskier. "I know, Phoebe. I'm sorry."

"You didn't say that growing up either, did you?"

"No. Never. And we didn't say *I can't*, and we didn't say *it hurts*, and we didn't say *it's okay to fail*."

"Or *I forgive you*," I whisper.

"Never that one."

"Teague—"

"I didn't take all of my trust fund. Just enough to get somewhere to start over. Used some for good. Tried to undo the stuff my family fucked up. And it wasn't just the spill. It was—it was how they didn't even *care*. It was 'inconvenient' that fish live in the ocean. It was 'all the whiners' about how that beach was ruined. It was 'just find another beach.' They were . . ."

"Awful," I finish for him.

He can't stand still. Keeps shifting his weight from foot to foot. "For years, I thought they'd track me down, even after the hoops I jumped through to change my name as secretly as I could. I used to pay cash for prepaid credit cards so I could log on at internet cafés and use private browsers to search my family and see if they were looking for me. Took a while before I realized the paranoia was making me crazy, and then I met Shiloh, and she got pregnant, and I didn't tell her my whole story either. I didn't want them to go after her or Bridget. And I didn't—I didn't want her to know I was broken. I didn't want anyone to know I was broken."

I can't take this anymore.

My Teague isn't *broken*.

He's beautiful and strong and brave and kind and bullheaded, and I couldn't stop myself from wrapping my arms around him if my life depended on it. "You're not broken."

His arms come around me, too, holding me like I'm *his* lifeline. "I am without you."

I suck in a wobbly breath.

"You thought you came to Tickled Pink because someone was forcing you to meet some invisible standard for your soul. But it was more,

Phoebe. You make *my* soul better. You make *me* want to step out of the shadows. You're what's missing in my life, and the thought of losing you forever is scarier than the thought of my past catching up with me. I don't want to live with the fear anymore. I want to live with the light. And you, Phoebe Lightly, are my light. Please come back. Come home. Let me show you I can be better too."

"I'm coming home," I tell him. "Oh God, Teague, I miss home. I miss you. I miss me. I miss *us*."

"You left, and I was so scared I'd never see you again."

I shake my head against his suit jacket. "I was always going to come home. I didn't know if you'd want me, but I know—I know now where I belong. And I finally know who I want to be."

"And who's that?"

"I want to be the woman who loves you."

He buries his nose in my hair while his arms tighten harder around me. "I thought I had everything I wanted in life. But then there was you. And now I can't imagine another day without you in it. I love you, Phoebe Lightly. I love all of you."

I'm crying and laughing as he swoops me up in his arms and kisses me, a complete disaster of a socialite but a total badass in all other ways.

"I'm going to love you so hard you won't know what hit you," I whisper between kisses.

He smiles, and that simple joy in his expression brings me to tears all over again.

"Do your worst, Ms. Lightly," he murmurs against my lips. "It'll still never top how much I'm going to love you."

Epilogue

Teague

Catching fish isn't as easy as it used to be considering I now have someone yammering my ear off in my boat, but turns out it's a lot more fun.

"I don't get it," Phoebe says as she holds up the present I was hiding in the cooler.

I cast out and stifle a grin. "Made me think of you."

"It's a stuffed pink penguin. *Why* does that make you think of me?"

"Dunno. Must've been something I dreamed."

"Reminds me of you too, Phoebe," Willie Wayne calls from his boat. "From that time you tried to waddle into Dylan's boat in that tight pink getup that first day you came to Tickled Pink."

Phoebe lowers her sunglasses and looks at me, lips pursed. "So if I got you a stuffed porcupine making a face like he had indigestion because it reminded me of you . . ."

"He'd cut it up and wear it as a hat," Bridget calls from the pontoon boat where she's floating with Shiloh, Ridhi, Anya, and Jonah.

The whole town came out to celebrate Phoebe and me getting back from New York, and everyone and their brother's out on the lake. Including my brother, who's staying at the motel while he decides how long he wants to stick around Tickled Pink.

If Bridget gets her way, he'll be here until we're all old and gray.

Pretty sure I'd be okay with that.

"You comfortable now?" I ask Phoebe.

She's perched in my recliner, while I'm sitting in the beanbag chair she made me put in the boat and swore she'd sit in, then couldn't get comfortable in once we got out here.

She shifts. "I don't know. There seems to be a spring poking me wrong. I might have to just sit in your lap."

"You do that, we're both going in this lake."

That smile playing at the corners of her lips is making me need to shift too. "Do you know," she says, "in all the weeks that I've been in Tickled Pink, I have yet to see *you* fall in the lake?"

"Tried it once. Lake spit me back out."

She laughs.

"You two are so gross," Bridget calls.

"We do it to annoy you," Phoebe calls back. "It would be annoying to us if you *didn't* think we were gross."

Bridge stares at her.

Phoebe licks her finger, puts it on her own ass, and makes a sizzling noise. "That's right. I'm on *fire* today."

I do almost fall out of the boat then.

I'm both turned on and amused as hell.

"What's that noise?" Jane calls.

"That's just Teague laughing," Shiloh calls back.

"I didn't know he knew how to do that."

"It'll be okay. If it keeps happening, I know a doctor who makes house calls."

"Quit picking on my boyfriend, or I won't take your suggestions for taffy flavors when I open my candy store," Phoebe says to the lake at large.

"Does she know that's not actually a threat?" Willie Wayne asks Jane.

"Probably not," Jane replies.

"I won't let you ride the Ferris wheel when it's done, either, and for the record, I checked this morning, and we do have enough money to start construction." Phoebe settles deeper into her chair and smiles at me. "I really love this town."

We float around the lake while she alternates between reading a book on her phone and telling me her plans to not just stop at building a new Ferris wheel next to our ivy-covered half wheel but also to add a carousel to the park, reinstall the Fountain of Everlasting Eternity, and search every closed-up building in town until she finds the old gates to heaven. I keep fishing, everyone around us talking and laughing. Her family's not out with us today, but it's all good.

We can hear Carter trying to play music inside the school. He's got his amp turned up again.

Estelle and her boyfriend—who she still calls her butler—are at the community center. Phoebe tells me Niles is a painter, and Estelle's set him up with a room with really good lighting and great views. Cranky old lady can't tell anyone her *real* plans. Phoebe says we need to give her just a little more time to get there.

No idea where Tavi is. Michael either. Phoebe says she doesn't know if she'll ever be tight with him, and she's okay with that. Sometimes, coexisting is the best you can hope for.

But she and Tavi have been whispering since we got back, and she won't tell me what for.

I'll figure it out eventually.

In the meantime, it'll be sexual favors and withholding coffee until she caves. Rewards and punishments. I'm still learning which one works.

Fun, usually.

I'm good with fun.

More than good with fun.

"Holy shit," Willie Wayne suddenly says reverently. "No way. *No. Way.*"

"Get a live one?" Jane calls.

He's fumbling with things in the bottom of his boat, and he eventually comes up with his binoculars. "Oooohhhhh, Teague, you're not gonna like this," he says as he trains his attention on the shore.

I glance over, and there's Estelle, walking down the path behind the square, a dark-haired woman beside her.

"Oh no, she didn't." Phoebe straightens, drops her phone, and shades her eyes as she, too, looks to shore.

"Holy shit holy shit holy shit," Willie Wayne's whispering.

"No, she *didn't*," Phoebe repeats. She flaps her hands. "Teague. Shore. *Now.*"

"Fastest way might be to swim," I muse.

"Dad." Bridget suddenly makes a noise I know all too well, too, and my curiosity turns to dread. "Dad, *that's Lola Minelli.*"

"Shut your mouth!" Phoebe shrieks. "It is not! It *cannot* be. I refuse to believe this."

"Akiko isn't going to like this," Willie Wayne groans. "That *she's on my freebie list* thing is a joke, but Akiko is *not* going to like this."

Lola Minelli.

Lola—oh, fuck me.

"Tell me your grandmother didn't bring *a reality TV star* to my town," I say to Phoebe.

My eye is twitching.

My eyeball is freaking twitching.

"I'm sure she's just visiting," Phoebe says, not sounding sure at all. "Gigi was only joking about moving someone new into my room. And my room hardly qualifies as a tiny house, so Lola wouldn't be . . ."

She trails off while everyone in the surrounding boats slowly turns to look at me.

Technically speaking, *I* live in a tiny house.

I live in *the coolest* tiny house.

"No," I say.

Willie Wayne chuckles. Nervously, but he chuckles.

Jane outright cackles with glee.

"Who's Lola Minelli?" Jonah calls to me. "She one of your ex-girlfriends?"

Shiloh cracks up so hard she almost falls off the pontoon.

"She wishes," Phoebe calls back.

"Teague," Estelle hollers from the shore. "Teague, you need to come here. Now. We have something to discuss."

I eyeball Phoebe.

Then her grandmother.

Then the bodysuit-clad woman twirling her long dark hair next to the queen of hell, who will most likely be my grandmother-in-law someday in the not-so-distant future, if one of us doesn't kill the other first.

I settle back into the beanbag chair in my boat. "Welp, Phoebe, hope you don't mind living on the lake," I say, "because I'm pretty sure I'm never going to shore again."

She laughs, and then she does the most Phoebe thing ever.

She tries to crawl across the bottom of the boat, probably to kiss me and promise me it won't be so bad, but the boat rocks, and she freezes so fast that I don't care about Estelle or the reality TV star or anything anymore.

I just care that Phoebe's okay.

"You know if you go in this lake, I'm coming in after you, right?" I murmur.

"My penguin too?"

"Penguin too."

"And my cat?"

"Anything for my love."

She inches forward, slow and careful, until I can reach down and pull her into my lap. She snuggles in, then lifts her face and smiles at me. "You know what?"

"What?"

"I think I could live on this lake. But only if I'm with you, and only if we occasionally sneak to shore to ride the Ferris wheel in the middle of the night once it's done."

That's my Phoebe.

She's nothing like what I expected.

And still everything I need.

AUTHOR'S NOTE

Dear reader,

Writing this book brought me so much joy during a time when joy was in short supply. I hope you enjoyed Teague, Phoebe, and their friends and families and that you'll always consider Tickled Pink a safe place to return to whenever you need the reminder that you're utterly perfect, exactly as you are.

If you're looking for more snort-funny romantic comedies that'll also hit you in the feels, I hope you'll check out my website for a full list of books, and if you're really ready to dive in, sign up for my newsletter for weekly visits with various characters from the Pippaverse, behind-the-scenes peeks, book recommendations of my favorite reads, and more fun.

Keep reading, and stay awesome.

Pippa

ACKNOWLEDGMENTS

Before all else, I'd like to thank *you* for spending time with Phoebe, Teague, the Lightlys, and the residents of Tickled Pink, Wisconsin. Books are nothing without readers devouring their pages. You're a superstar! Make sure you treat yourself like one.

A massive thank-you to Maria Gomez at Montlake for believing in me and making this project possible, and to Lindsey Faber for pushing me to make it even better.

To Jodi, Beth, and Jess, who keep me organized, looking good, and always sending Pipster Reports on time—I would be a puddle of helplessness without you. Please don't ever leave me.

To Jenn, Jenny, Tammy, and Joyce—thank you for keeping the Pipsquad running seamlessly! You are the best. Squishy hugs all around!

And last but never least, a massive thank-you to my hubby and our kids for believing in me, supporting me, and asking strangers to buy my books.

EXCERPT FROM *THE GRUMPY PLAYER NEXT DOOR*

Tillie Jean Rock, aka a Woman Who Should Probably Get Her Eyes Checked

There's a fine art to revenge, and today, I am arting the hell out of it. I'm talking cackles of glee, evil cartoon overlord–style, rubbing my hands together while bouncing on my toes. Reminding myself to *shut up* because my brother will be home from his morning workout any minute now, and I don't want to tip my hand when he doesn't know I'm waiting for him here in his house up on the mountainside.

You would think he would've learned to engage his security system more often by now.

But he hasn't, which means I'm here, armed and dangerous and ready, and I'm cackling with glee all over again.

I know, I know. *Is this really how you want to pay him back for all of his pranks, Tillie Jean?*

Yes, actually.

Yes, it is.

It's payback time.

Also?

I have zero doubt Cooper will have mad respect that I'm doing this.

I cackle again.

And then I slap my hand over my mouth.

He's home.

There's his dark head, bent toward the knob, beyond the tempered glass panel beside his front door. He's dressed in Fireballs red, which is more orange than it is red, and he's probably worn out from lifting at the gym this morning.

I squat into position at the top of the stairs, as hidden as I can be while still seeing my target, Nerf blaster locked and loaded, waiting while he fumbles with his keys.

For the record?

It's not easy to hide at the top of a curved staircase. I'm on my belly now, half-angled behind the wall of the hallway to his guest bedrooms, peering between the slats of the banister, hoping all my target practice pays off.

Steady, TJ. This is what you trained for.

The lock clicks.

I flatten myself lower and take aim.

The door swings open.

Dark hair in the foyer. *Go go go.*

I squeeze the trigger, sending a rapid blast of modified foam darts at the six balloons floating in the space above the door.

The needle sticking out barely an eighth of an inch in the tip of the first dart connects. One helium balloon pops. Then two more, followed by the fourth and fifth. The sixth shifts after getting hit, like it's a tough guy balloon. It's the ninja of balloons, and it doesn't want to participate in my dastardly plans today, but that's okay. The other balloons are bursting in a sparkly, shiny, beautiful pink glitter spray that's splattering on the walls, exploding from its nylon shell and raining down like a spring shower, coating the walls, making the air sparkle, and dusting all that dark hair as Cooper's lifting his head. "What the—"

And in the span of a heartbeat, before he can finish that sentence, I realize my mistake.

My terrible, horrible, very bad miscalculation.

If I were a superhero, I'd be sucking all that glitter into my lungs and redirecting it into my brother's bedroom, which is likely what I should've done in the first place—hindsight, right?—but I didn't. This was so much more dramatic and didn't risk me having to find out which local he's screwing around with in his spare time, as she'd be coated in glitter too after rolling around in his sheets, except my prank has failed.

It has failed *spectacularly.*

"*Oh my god,*" I gasp.

That's not Cooper.

That is *so* not Cooper.

Yeah, Cooper has dark hair. But he also has an easy smile, blue eyes, a quick sense of humor, appreciation for a well-executed revenge plot, and a tall, lanky body.

The man staring at me is tall. And dark-haired.

But he's also thickly muscled. Growling without making a noise. Aiming dark eyes at me. And I have no idea if he has any respect for pranks.

Harmless pranks.

The ones where no one gets hurt.

Even if it means he's gonna look like a pink vampire in the daylight for the next three weeks.

Or, you know, *forever.* Because it's *glitter.*

I swallow hard while those brown eyes silently bore into me from a face that's as chiseled and manly as they come, and which also looks like it was decorated at a birthday slumber party for a fourteen-year-old.

What's he even doing here? He's not supposed to be here.

This isn't where he's staying this winter.

But he *is* here, and this isn't good.

This isn't good at all.

"Hi, Max." I lift a hand and wave, realize I'm still holding the Nerf blaster, and toss it down the hallway.

It hits the corner of the wall instead and clatters to the wood floor.

Stupid thing doesn't even have the decency to land quietly on the hall runner.

Max Cole, right-handed starting pitcher for the Copper Valley Fireballs, is six feet, four inches, and two hundred twenty-five pounds of steely baseball perfection, and he's never willing to do anything beyond glare, twitch, and ignore me when I'm around him.

Possibly spending four years incessantly flirting with him to annoy Cooper—and Max, if I'm being honest—wasn't the best build-up to this moment.

I'm not shrinking into myself.

I'm not quivering in my belly.

And also possibly my lady bits.

Okay, *fine*.

I'm borderline terrified of what this prank-gone-wrong might've just incited, and I am *not* immune to that many feet of muscled baseball perfection, despite the number of times he's rolled his eyes or grimaced at me when I've flirted with him the past four years, and despite exactly how furious I was with him over what he did the day we met.

And who's furious now?

Max.

Max is currently furious.

He's a massive, glittering, growly bear of *if this crap isn't the kind that comes off easily, you better not be planning on sleeping again for the next three months, Matilda Jean Rock.*

Excerpt from The Grumpy Player Next Door, *copyright © 2021 by Pippa Grant*

AUTHOR BIO

Photo © 2021 Briana Snyder, Knack Video + Photo

Pippa Grant is a *USA Today* bestselling author who writes romantic comedies that will make tears run down your leg. When she's not reading, writing, or sleeping, she's being crowned employee of the month as a stay-at-home mom and housewife trying to prepare her adorable demon spawn to be productive members of society, all the while fantasizing about long walks on the beach with hot chocolate chip cookies.